The

Only

Constant

Book Two of
The SON

A Novel

By

Doug Dahlgren

*RH
Publishing*

ISBN: 0983376700
EAN-13: 978-0-9833767-0-5

Printed in the United States of America

Ridge House Publishing

Decatur, Georgia

Cover Concept and Design by :   Linda Stephens Dahlgren
Memory Magic
memorymagic@mindspring.com

Dedication

This title could only be dedicated to one person.

The constant in my life…

My wife Donna

Acknowledgements ...

My proof reading crew: brother Alan, Susan and Don of Pea Ridge, Ruth in Snellville, Bill Griffioen, David the teacher, Wig Nelson and Patty Duke.

And of course, Linda and Donna.

Thanks as well everyone who offered a kind word, a suggestion or better yet, told a friend about the stories.

I thank you all....................

The

Only

Constant

Book Two
of

The SON

The Prologue

The utility pole stood exactly twenty feet, four inches tall and sat eighty-three feet, nine inches from the road. These seemingly unimportant facts would be verified and become a part of the evidence. But that would be later. For now, they waited. Through the dark, the girl and the pole waited to be found. Waited with the patience of death.

How many had driven by that night? Never knowing. Unaware of the obscenity daylight would expose. Other evidence left behind became buried in the light snowfall. Peace and serenity became objects of deception and proof was all but lost in the dark.

"What is it, Hon?" The driver asked.

His wife, startled from her near sleep, abruptly sat up in the passenger seat as the family car cruised north. Staring back into the woods behind them, she said not a word.

"Honey!" The driver demanded this time. "What's wrong?"

A fleeting image had grabbed her attention, but it made no sense to her. Moonlight filtering through the trees touched or perhaps created shapes and mingled with the shadows. Flickering traces that danced past the car's window. And then were gone.

"Nothing I guess," she answered slowly, rubbing her blurred eyes. Then, resting her head back on a mini pillow laying against the car's door she added, "Just thought I saw something out there."

She quickly drifted off, putting it out of her mind. Even the news of the following day would take time to soak in.

The crime was the worst anyone could recall in the history of Pendleton County. Northern Kentucky was not naïve about crime, even murder, but this was different. The slow paced, rural area had maintained a Currier and Ives atmosphere, especially in the winter. Buildings were sparse and the land was rolling, but mostly flat. From one family's rooftop you could barely view another home, even on the clearest day. Winter's haze cut the visibility and the snow added a glare. It had been a mild season thus far, but the nights were cold and the powder did fall. Temperatures down into the teens were average and the thermometer's fall started right at dusk.

The snow was abnormally light for this time of year, but it dusted everything and its look added to the serenity, the normal serenity. The only disruptions to the peace were the ribbons of asphalt and vehicles that roared in both directions. Interstate highway I-75 cut north and south through this horse country. Two black channels of pavement, cleared of snow by the traffic and divided by grass and a concrete median wall as you approached Cincinnati.

It was along the northern bound side of this highway that the body was found. No one saw her until daylight. From the condition of the body, she had hung there for several hours. The pole was some thirty-five miles south of the city, eighty feet from the highway and in an area of quiet isolation.

Crime was infrequent around here. Murder or anything near it was very rare. As unfamiliar with it as the locals were, there was no doubt that this was murder.

Murder can be vindictive or passionate. It could be accidental or well planned and thought out. This was way beyond any of that. This was more than the murder of an individual. This was a message to a community.

The victim was still only a child. A sixteen-year-old girl from a well thought of family. She loved horses and softball. There was a boyfriend, but nothing too serious. The family went to church twice on Sundays and again in the middle of the week. They were known throughout the community and highly regarded.

2

They lived in Locust Grove on a small farm some fifty miles south of Cincinnati. Her father was a patrolman for the state police. Trooper Wallace Ford was assigned to Post 6 and the troopers from that post were tasked with monitoring traffic along Interstate 75 through their ten county area. The interstate was a main drug corridor to Cincinnati and points north.

The troopers of Post 6 in northern Kentucky had learned how to profile vehicles carrying drugs. Most of their stops were small time, but now and then they would hit on a large haul. The success record for Post 6 was in the eighty-five percent range for "good stops." They were good at their jobs and proud of their professionalism.

Around five months earlier, Trooper Ford and his partner, Harvey Wingate, were involved in one of the biggest drug stops in the area. On a tip from Georgia State Patrol officials in the Dalton, Georgia, area, they stopped a white van loaded with black lacquer tables. The tables were made of nearly pure cocaine powder, ninety percent product with only enough resin to hold the table shape. The manufacturer's label on the table boxes was that of an import company known only as Argus. The logo on that label was a round smiling face, a sun god with a joker's smile, like what you would find on an Inca temple.

That stop along I-75 in northern Kentucky was part of an east coast dragnet that shut down the Argus operation, or so the authorities believed. Their main distribution hub had been discovered and closed down. Last minute deliveries to locations around the eastern region were stopped. For all intents and purposes, the drug cartel appeared mortally wounded.

A short-lived attempt to revise the distribution network had been preempted in Charlotte, North Carolina. That event went mostly unnoticed by the national law enforcement community. The fact that Argus was even there had never been established. The new location had not yet begun distribution, yet it was terminated by the quiet efforts of one man, a man who was out to save his friend. A friend placed in danger by the then leader of this cartel. Argus didn't know who this man was or how to get to him, but his efforts were responsible for their reorganization plans becoming further delayed and much more expensive.

Trooper Wingate was no longer Ford's partner. Wingate had been killed three months after the drug bust in a traffic accident while on his way home. While the circumstances were never clear it had been considered just that, a tragic accident, until now.

The body was found on a Sunday morning. Hanging upside down, some twenty feet up a power pole. The discovery of Debbie Ford's body changed the perception of Trooper Wingate's death. Her throat had been cut. Her body was scarred. Burned with some implement or poker that left the mark of a smiling sun god, Argus' logo, on her abdomen. Cut into her forehead was the date of the drug bust last fall. Those who found her prayed that death had happened first.

The killers obviously knew who Debbie was. This killing was an acknowledgement of her father's involvement in that drug bust. The message was clear. They could have killed Trooper Ford outright, but they chose to kill the will of the entire community and the State Patrol with their message. The message was "stay out of our business."

1

There is danger from all men. The only maxim of a free government ought to be to trust no man living with power to endanger the public liberty.

John Adams

From the Mercury sedan parked just off the road on Hwy 71, a man stared at the house that was now more a mansion. It thrust out from the side of the mountain proud and strong. Three stories tall with yet three other unseen sub-levels. Anyone would be proud to call this their home, yet he sat in his car, just looking at it. His mind was active, but vacant. The man could not grasp or understand what he was feeling. It was as though he was somehow lost.

The car had brought him home from a trip to Maryland. The journey had been much less than fulfilling. He'd sought answers, but found only more questions. This too was new to him. Like the house he stared at without feeling he was "at home."

Calm and patience were among his strongest virtues. But he had never before been aware of them, and the fact that they were being tested.

It will settle down and all work out, he told himself as he looked back up at the house. The five-year-old elm tree made him smile. It was newly transplanted and now dormant from the winter. It stood proud on the special patch of ground built just for it in front of the ledge.

My Liberty Tree. He beamed as he thought of it.

That ledge beyond its perch was the top of a driveway. Delivery trucks now filled that ledge. Trucks that contained "must have items" recommended by people who now took it upon themselves to make decisions for him. Items he did not even know existed until these people became part of his world.

Again, he smiled as he thought of those new people. Each one whom he cared for in ways he never believed possible. It was his house, built of necessity more than desire. Necessity brought on by changes; so many changes. Much of that change was about these people now in his life. Some of "them" waited for him inside. People whom, just a year ago were mere acquaintances at best.

~

Sitting in his small office in the old ice warehouse in Doraville, Georgia, Juan Castrono held his face in his hand as he rested an elbow on the desk. Since returning from Washington, D.C. where his former employer had died unexpectedly, Juan had become even more anxious about this job he was stuck in. He wanted out.

"The truck will be here in about half an hour, boss." The assistant announced through his door.

"Si," he responded and waved the man away. Juan Castrono did his job, but against his will. He would have gotten out if he could have, back when his first boss died in an explosion at the main Argus warehouse in Dalton, Georgia. But Juan learned that this was not a job you gracefully retired from, much less quit. He had since been called from his obscurity to replace an assistant to the big man, "The Bird" they called him.

Charles Harley died in Washington, D.C., the prior fall. His medical history, lifestyle and personal habits all pointed to a stroke. His passing was inconsequential other than the position he held. He was a sitting U.S. House Representative from Iowa. Those who investigated his death agreed with all the signs and concluded it had indeed, been a stroke. They so ruled despite the rumors of a "congressional killer," which had spread through the country at about that same time.

Very little time had passed after Charles Harley's death when Juan was told to contact his new boss. That may not be so unusual, but the recklessness of the reorganization since certainly had been. Things were moving too fast. The heat was not off yet. No formal charges or even insinuations about Harley's connection to the cartel had been made public, except for one story by the reporter from Pittsburgh and that remained unsubstantiated. That story tried to claim Harley was part of a kidnapping plot, but it offered no real proof. It was enough to cause the cartel to take pause. But to Juan, that pause was not nearly enough.

Juan had cleaned out a safe in Harley's office before leaving Washington that day, one that only he and Harley knew about. A small brown athletic bag holding money now rested in a different safe, the one next to Juan's desk in the ice plant. He was fearful to spend any of it.

Not yet, he told himself. *It was for later, after the paychecks stopped and he could get away.* If that day ever came.

The old ice plant had been vacant for several years before they came. The building sat near a perimeter expressway, which connected to a major north / south interstate within two miles.

Much work was needed to prepare this space for its new use. Juan suggested hidden doors like the ones they'd used before. There was labor available in the Doraville area to do this. Good, undocumented labor that would keep its mouth shut. But Juan was not given approval to add the secret doors.

Currently, equipment was being brought in through the main dock doors and that brought with it attention. Attention to the location was not a good thing. All this bothered Juan. And then there was Dario. He had not heard from Dario.

Juan Castrono did not particularly care for Dario although the man was his number two. His second in command that he had neither say in or control over. The new man in charge had assigned Dario's position to him. Dewey Hanson did not consult Juan beforehand.

Juan was a thinker, the planner for the southeast territory. He was not though, an operator. An operator could handle problems in a violent way. That was Dario's job. The cartel was reestablishing itself and certain situations needed to be dealt with. Some with finesse, some more directly.

Juan had not met his new boss, Dewey Hanson prior to Charles Harley's death. In fact, he had not really heard of him. Only that he was a replacement U.S. Representative from Pennsylvania. Juan had known nothing of Hanson's prior connections to the cartel until he was told to meet with him.

When Harley died, Juan went back to Atlanta to await instructions. Instructions he hoped would never materialize. But they did. The new orders came quickly and within a week he was back in the Virginia area meeting with his new boss. Dario showed up two weeks after that. No introduction before. No advanced notice, he just showed up.

"You Castrono?" The cocky younger man has asked. "I'm Dario. I'm a fixer."

"Fixer of what?" Juan countered.

"Whatever gets in the way, man." Dario laughed.

Juan looked the man over and found only trouble in his eyes.

"Your office is down there." He told him, pointing to a hallway.

"I won't be in no office, man." Dario snapped. "Thanks anyway."

That was the same day Juan got the message about the Doraville warehouse. He had hoped the location was only temporary. But that was not the case.

This old, formerly abandoned ice plant and storage facility would be transformed into the new Argus distribution warehouse for the entire east coast. While Juan stayed busy with that, Dario would be clearing the way for that distribution to begin again.

Juan knew that Dario had gone to Kentucky.

"I'm going to send a message to the folks around there." He proclaimed.

This was one of the scenarios that the leadership felt could be contained by terror. Scared people tend to look the other way. That's what was required in that part of the country. Folks needed to look the other way.

News of the murder was local at first and it stayed in the Kentucky and Ohio region. Then word of the logo carved on the girl's stomach became widely known and the story went national. Juan had watched the report on a cable news station. He understood the need to strike fear into the community. But for him, what he heard about was over the top. He expected a call or word of some kind from Pennsylvania, where Hanson worked his main job as U.S. Congressman from the 12th district. So far there was nothing. Dario had not returned and the act was now three days old. Juan was concerned.

2

The death of Charles Harley from Iowa had been the fifth "removal" and the killer's last to date. The first four took only weeks, not quite three months in total to investigate, confirm and carry out.

Many people believed his death was caused by a mythical killer, nicknamed "The Son" by journalists. There was no proof of that. Any evidence pointing to this percieved assassin would include the congressman's connection to a drug cartel. The cartel did not care for publicity of any kind. They made sure such "rumors" were never disclosed.

By the time Harley was dispatched to his reward, the headcount of people who now knew his killer included a North Georgia DA, his Assistant and her son; a police officer in Dalton, a police Lt. in another city, a reporter from a northern newspaper and his wife. Three others knew of him through the reporter, though they did not know his name.

To say the very least, things had changed dramatically.

A neighbor's son, who had simply mowed his yard while he was away, was now his trusted aid and assistant. Others helped as they could, but one was determined to set up a team effort to use Jon's "talents" for other needs.

The reporter, who started on nothing more than "gut feelings," had tracked this killer as well as he had tracked his victims. By the time the reporter realized who the true villains were, he had become a near victim himself. The man he sought to expose had saved not only his life, but also that of his wife in a matter of weeks. Things like that can alter your loyalty and redirect your priorities. The others, who now knew him personally, were connected directly to each other and brought to this man by vapors of the same evil he sought.

These were the few that had learned to believe in him. Against all they thought they ever held holy, especially about murder, this man had caused these select few to set aside their judgment and consider the acts through his eyes.

That paradox was not simple for any involved, particularly the man himself. He did not ask to be understood. He never wanted to be known, much less become a friend to those who now protected his secret as their own. The past year had unraveled his life and his mission statement. What was done was done.

He had begun his trek as a secretive and solitary soldier. In less than a year, all that had changed, forever.

~

News of the murder in northern Kentucky had also reached the offices of the Pittsburgh Post-Gazette. The Argus logo involvement landed the story on the desk of Daniel Seay. His heart and breathing seemed to stop a second before both became labored as he stared at the words. It was difficult to concentrate with, *no, no, no* running through his mind.

The drug cartel known as Argus had been a huge story for Daniel Seay. He had stumbled into it while on the trail of a killer, a killer who had become his friend.

The cartel's men had captured Daniel last year. He had been beaten and they were about to kill him when the man he had stalked stepped in. Daniel had recovered physically from his ordeal with Argus. But the word of this group being active again sent a chill through his bones. He knew his wife, Lori, would hear about it soon and he reached for his phone to call her. It rang before he got to it.

"Have you seen the news?" Her voice was elevated and nearly shrill.

11

"I just saw the story. Try to stay calm, will you? We don't know enough to worry about it yet."

Daniel wasn't convincing, not even to himself. He had written about his ordeal. He had told the world almost all there was about it, including Argus.

Drugs Flowing Through Us was Daniel's four part series on his experiences while on the trail of "The Son." The series was carried nationally and even discussed on cable news stations. He wrote of tracing the steps of a killer only to find an even larger story, one in which he had been caught up and nearly killed. He told of his kidnapping and the trip to Charlotte, N.C. He told of Charles Harley's presence and the congressman threatening him. This circumstance was quite odd. Daniel could not verify his claim of Harley's participation, so no further legal action was ever taken to look into it. But no one from Harley's family objected or so much as threatened to sue over the claim either. The story was simply allowed to just hang there unproven, but unchallenged.

"Stay calm?" Lori all but screamed into the phone. "Are you kidding? What if they come after you again? Have you called Jon?"

Lori was firing questions in rapid succession. Daniel drew a deep breath while looking for words that sounded reasonable and reassuring. Few knew of Jon's involvement in the rescue, but Lori did. She knew everything.

The congressional killer, a man named "The Son" by the media, had rescued Daniel. This man had put himself and his mission at risk to do so, but he did it.

Daniel now knew this man. He knew who he was, why he did what he did and, even to Daniel's own amazement, he agreed to keep this new friend's secrets.

Daniel's rescue was described in his story, but more loosely than the other parts of it. There was no mention of the man who had saved him. Jon wanted it that way and Daniel agreed. A younger, stricter editor might have asked for more proof before allowing a story like this one to print. But Daniel and Bill White had discussed the events in detail, including Lori's trip to Washington, D.C.

His boss knew what had happened and fully accepted Daniel's portrayal of events. Bill White did not yet understand "The Son" or his motives. But his years of experience in collecting news stories made the editor aware that something larger than life was in play. Daniel's knowledge of "the Son" and what he does would not be taken well by the public, not yet. Some secrets are worth keeping.

"No, I haven't called Jon. When I know more, perhaps I will. We don't know that those in charge of Argus even know about me." He tried to suggest.

"What?" Lori was almost screaming, "Of course they know about you. The story you wrote told everything. We thought they were done, finished. What do we do, Daniel? What do we do?"

Daniel sat back in his chair. He didn't want to tell her, but she was right. Daniel's profiling of the story brought him to Argus' attention and nearly got him killed in Charlotte, North Carolina.

"I'll talk with Bill right away." He told her. "Go to Susie's and I'll call you there later." Bill White was not only Daniel's boss at the paper he was his mentor. Susie was a dear friend and neighbor. Lori didn't need to be alone right now. In fact, she didn't need to be in their house.

"Ok." She replied softly. "But we need to figure out what we're going to do. We can't just wait for them to come at us."

"Go to Susie's and stay calm, please. We'll figure it out." Daniel finished the call and stood to go to his editor's office.

His door opened and there was Bill White, editor in chief of the Post-Gazette.

"Boss, I was just coming to see you." Daniel stated.

"Pack what you need from here and get to your wife." The boss said sternly. He understood the threat and would not allow Daniel to take any chance.

"Boss, don't overreact." Daniel tried to say.

"Look son, do what I'm telling you. You're on assignment as of now. I don't care where you two go, let me know when you're there. Just go, soon. This will blow over and we'll all be fine."

He handed Daniel a cell phone and a credit card in the name of a Stuart Wilson. "Here's a number you can use they won't know about and a company card they can't trace."

Daniel grabbed his personal stuff and the notes from his Argus file. He looked at his boss and thanked him.

"Will this ever end?" Daniel asked figuratively.

"Sure it will son, we just have to clean out the nest. That's all."

"What if they come here looking for me?" Daniel asked. "Who protects you?"

"Do you actually believe I've never been threatened before, son?" His boss responded. "Now, get out of here and call me when you get settled."

"Ok, Bill." Daniel looked around the office and nodded his head.

White put his hand on the younger man's shoulder, "Take care of Lori." He told him.

As Daniel headed out the door, the editor offered one more word of advice.

"Transfer all the numbers you will need out of your phone and leave it at your house. Remember they could trace that thing just by it being turned on."

"Right." Daniel acknowledged. "Thanks again. I'll be in touch."

3

Jon Crane sat in his car across from the big house he built into the mountain. It was a far cry from the little house in the subdivision where he had lived for over nine years. A time spent mostly to himself.

All this to replace a ranch house with a partial basement, he thought half out loud.

The new house itself was imposing. Though it fit into the mountain nicely, it still stood proud and tall against the rock and earth. Some thirty feet from the road level at its base the structure towered three stories above that. The depth was concealed by setting the house into the mountain, which made it appear even larger than it was.

The first floor exterior was covered in reddish brick with dark gray mortar.

"It looks warm and welcoming," Marsha had commented.

Lt. Marsha Hurst, of the Charlotte, N.C. metro-police had become a fixture in Jon's life since they met following Daniel's rescue.

The dangerous congressman mistook the reporter as the man stalking him. Daniel's kidnapping spurred Jon to actions that put his own life and anonymity into jeopardy.

With the suggestion from the Whitfield County D.A., George Vincent, Lt. Marsha Hurst reluctantly helped with Jon's cover. Her aversion to him was soon overtaken by other emotions.

"You need to come with me," she had told him when they met at the hospital. He was slightly wrong in his remembrance, but close enough. Those words in his head would always make him smile. And how prophetic they were. In a very short time he had gone from not knowing who she was, to not imagining life without her. But it was still very new and strange to him.

He was uneasy about the change and in some ways not quite sure if he cared for it. Yet he was certain he cared for her. He had, until not long ago, always been a loner. How quickly that and his lifestyle had all changed.

He used to live in a very small house and was very happy there. As he watched yet another delivery truck drive up to the new home, Jon thought about the small house and his first attempt at a "safe room."

All the dirt I dug and hauled away, he laughed as he remembered.

He kept his equipment in that small space. The computers and gear he had collected to help with his missions. Those things were his business and his alone. What he did had been a complete secret to his closest neighbors, even from Ben for a while.

Ben Shaw was the neighbor kid. He cut Jon's grass in the summers for several years. Shaking his head, Jon laughed again, "It's all Ben's fault." But even in jest those words didn't sound right. Ben was the first person Jon felt comfortable trusting with his secrets.

He figured me out on his own, Jon recalled. The next-door neighbor kid, who had cut his grass while he was away, was now a trusted friend and partner.

The initial attack on Ben, school thugs beating him up, was what set everything into motion last year. Those young hoodlums worked directly for Argus.

It was also through Ben that Jon began to meet others. He learned he was capable of caring about someone other than himself. Caring enough to risk everything if need be. That had snowballed on him last fall and almost went out of control.

Twisting in the Mercury's large front seat, Jon thought again of the small house.

"It was near perfect," he heard come from his lips. And it had been. But that too, had changed. The old small house in the subdivision was no longer safe, neither was Ben's and his mother's home next door. Ben's mother, Doris, was the first to be abducted and nearly killed by the drug cartel.

Besides being Ben's mom, she was also the fiancée of George Vincent, the Whitfield County District Attorney. Doris had worked in the D.A.'s office for years and had compiled substantial evidence of Argus' activities in the Dalton area.

The cartel had sought to learn the extent of her knowledge of them. Argus had grabbed Doris and held her for more than a day. Their tactics were harsh and brutal. The one thing they did not count on was Jon's involvement. They didn't even know who he was.

"You found her in less than an hour," Ben had told him. "When the cops couldn't do it in a full day."

Jon used his talents, unrestricted by law, to locate and rescue Doris. Her injuries, from the ordeal, took months to heal and during that time Jon and Ben had bonded nearly as father and son.

Ben was now a partner and a trusted ally. It was less than a year ago that Ben had calmly declared, "I know who you are Jon, it has to be you." And he honored the confidentiality that was required.

The second level of the house was coated in large rocks that actually protruded out beyond the bricks below.

"That looks tough," Ben had said when the contractor brought the stones to the site. The tan and gray colors of the rock went well with the brick and where they faded into the mountain made the house seem to jut from the mountain itself.

The contractor was terrific for this job. He asked few questions and did everything that was requested of him.

"Long as it's legal," was his motto. It was he, with Jon that picked out the exterior for the top level. It was covered in wood shakes.

They were large twelve-inch square, wood shakes that were half-inch thick at their base. They hid the three-quarter inch steel skin, which shielded that level from most any projectile.

Huge metal-framed windows, three each on either side of the recessed entrance cove, held FS-3, three-quarter inch thick glass from Armortex. The density of the glass could withstand 50 caliber rounds fired from close range.

"Bad ass!" was all Ben said about them. Jon remembered smiling at the description. There were no shutters on the first level. The apprearance was crisp and clean, but solid.

Slightly smaller banks of windows sat above those on the first level with a tall, crown topped, fixed glass window in the center. The glass was again, from the armored glass company. Behind that glass was the large den.

"A man needs a big den to relax in." Marsha had declared. Jon had intended it as an office, but gave in without much discussion. Her tastes were quite different than Jon's, but then he had never considered anything other than comfort in any furnishings.

"This will look so good in that corner," she proclaimed while pouring over decorating books. With the help of Doris, Marsha had invested in items Jon never knew he needed and had lived quite well without before now.

He smiled to himself as he thought of some of them. They did look good, he admitted. Even though his favorite paintings and other wall hangings were no longer "acceptable." The new "window treatments," as they were called, did look very nice.

The windows at the top level were armored as well and this level did have shutters. Heavy wood shutters mounted for appearance only. The shakes were painted a putty gray color and the shutters were black. All together, it was a very handsome and rugged looking building.

Those looks were not deceiving. This house incorporated the latest in defensive materials. The contractor offered a few questioning looks as products were delivered, but Jon's explanation, "I just don't want any damage from falling rocks," was accepted with a smile.

Jon's mind again thought about his attempt to build a "safe room" in the small house.

"Lucky it didn't cave in and kill me," he said to himself.

The new third level basement was still incomplete, but held great promise. It would be the revised version of the "safe room" concept. This time there would be access for both secret entry and escape. A tunnel through the sidewall led to an old abandoned service station down the road.

Jon planned to obscure that entrance by using holographic projections over the tunnel opening. The third level basement was also heavily ventilated. That would allow safe parking of the specialized vehicles Jon kept on hand. The sidewall of the basement had been cut through to the escape drive, but all was not finished. The cameras and holographs still needed to be installed. For now, steel doors would suffice.

The front driveway of the main house approached from the right side and the drive itself climbed to the garage in a horseshoe shaped curve landing at the pad with two double and one single garage door sets. They were armored, but much lighter than the rest of the house. An intruder may get inside the garage, but that would be it. Walls connected to the house, even the ceiling of the garage, were lined in the same steel skin as the third floor.

Standing proudly in its special space, carved out in front of the garage area and just off the drive path, was the Elm tree. The tree added to the grace of the elevation and more than that, it represented the spirit of the men Jon revered so. The tree was homage to the Liberty Tree of Boston and the patriots who met beneath her branches, including Silas Downer.

Overall, the appearance was not unlike many other large mansions in this area of carpet making millionaires. But there was a big difference. This house was a fortress. Anyone who got in was there because Jon wanted them there. If he could have chosen, he never would have moved, but life and circumstances had other ideas.

4

It was now nearly four months since Washington, DC, and Harley's death. The start of the move into the new house was only one of a number of things that had occurred since then. Marsha had been to Dalton, three times now. Her addition to his life was undoubtedly the biggest change for him. Marsha was an old family friend of George's. Her trust and help through the time of Daniel's rescue was more than he could have asked for. He knew he liked her right away, but as the events in his last removal became complicated he realized she had become a source of strength and renewal for him. No one had ever affected his life in that way before. Marsha was good, to him and for him. Yet her being in his life was still a struggle to get used to.

Other changes were nearly as dramatic. At Daniel's persistence, he had met with several other men in mid-December. He traveled to Ohio for that meeting, protecting his anonymity the best he could by staying behind a one-way glass for the get-together. The others, two newspapermen, one from Louisiana and one from Iowa, and a police captain from Louisiana wanted to form a league to put Jon's talents to "better use." He turned them down at that meeting.

"I work alone." He declared through a voice modulator.

Other than Ben, he wanted to keep it that way. Every extra person involved made the venture more risky. It was already risky enough. The others didn't argue with him, not even Daniel. They would give him time. Time to think and perhaps see it their way. Time and situations were changing.

The car was starting to get cold so he reached for the key to start the engine and heater. A phone rang. It was his private cell phone. Only Marsha, Ben and George Vincent had the number. The caller ID said only "DA." It was George.

21

"Yeah, George," he answered. "What's going on?"

"There's a disturbing report on the wires from Kentucky." George sounded serious.

"A young girl has been found dead with an 'Argus' logo burned into her belly."

The phone line was quiet for a minute. Finally Jon spoke.

"Anything more?" He asked. "A note or a threat of any kind?"

"No," George stated flatly. "That's all I know. I just figured you would want to hear. Have you heard from Daniel Seay?"

"No, not yet." Jon pushed back against the car seat as he considered what this news would mean to Daniel. The cartel did not know who Jon was, but they knew about Daniel Seay.

"They'll need to go underground for awhile, Daniel and Lori." Jon told George. "I'll see if I can reach him."

"Ok," George responded. "I'll stay in touch."

Jon sat the cell phone down on the seat and reached to start the car. The phone rang again. This time it was Ben from inside the house.

"Jon, Daniel Seay is on the phone. He needs to talk to you, quick."

"Get his number and I'll be there in a minute, I'm right outside." Jon threw down the phone and pulled the car across the highway and up the drive.

"Man," he mumbled to himself. "Everything happens at once."

Jon had been away from Dalton the week before. He needed to verify a candidate was worthy to be his sixth removal.

This candidate came to him through one of his Internet associates in Maryland. He was yet another congressional incumbent with a lust for power and a mean streak that fed his ego.

This man had a grown family. Adult children are great for campaigns, but they need to be kept in line. This guy did so through terror and abuse. So bad, it reportedly led to the death of his son last year.

Now there were reports of a daughter in trouble and a boyfriend being threatened. The story seemed incredible at first. But Jon soon understood how this demon supposedly operated. He had dinner several times in a local pub frequented by two of the congressman's household staff. On the last night there, he bought the assistant cook a drink and chatted with her.

The story was the daughter had gotten pregnant and wanted to get married. She was nineteen years old.

This high-ranking, public official could not tolerate such news, especially during an election year. He demanded she go abroad and get an abortion that could be kept quiet. Both the mother and daughter had protested, but he would not hear otherwise. In one screaming match, the cook heard him threaten the boyfriend if he wouldn't disappear on his own. He then reminded them of the departed son and how he had come to meet his end.

He was known to strike his family if provoked and the cook thought he was about to when several other staff members gathered and the scene was calmed.

Jon had checked into the son's death and found it to be a closed case of accidental death by drowning. The boy's body was washed nearly to the Atlantic down the Chesapeake Bay in January two years ago. It got caught in a fishing boat's net or might never have been found.

A quick check of weather records and navigational charts raised some questions in Jon's mind. To get to the currents, the boy would have had to swim out 300 yards from the shore in 15-degree temperatures. It didn't make sense yet the local police closed the case within two weeks.

Jon could not determine what the kid's offense had been, though he was known to gamble heavily. Could that be another possible source of embarrassment to the congressman who would tolerate none of it? Perhaps, but there were also the possibilities of a hit by unpaid gamblers or even suicide.

There was room for serious suspicion, but little actual proof. Jon's requirement for action on his part was proof, clear undisputable proof.

Jon left Maryland unconvinced, but with this congressman still high on his list. He was, in fact, at the top of Jon's list until these phone calls about the Argus murder. Now that spot was overtaken. No one other than Ben knew about Congressman Stubblefield from Maryland. If at all possible, it would stay that way.

Jon made the hard left turn up the driveway and squeezed in between two delivery trucks. He jumped from his car and ran through the main garage into the house. Ben was waiting for him with a phone in his hand.

"He held." Ben told Jon as he tossed the phone to him. "It's pretty important."

5

Dewey Hanson learned of the violent message left in northern Kentucky when an assistant brought him the word in his sauna. He leaned back, sweat pouring from his brow and smiled.

"The kid does good work," he said out loud.

Dewey liked the rough stuff, the rougher the better. He had been a staffer to Congressman Perry several years ago. Hanson's connection to the cartel became known and he was asked to step aside. When Perry died on his yacht last year the Governor of Pennsylvania appointed Hanson to the open congressional seat. The appointment was controversial, but the urging of some influential friends won out.

Hanson knew and understood rough, though he mostly hired it done. He was a slight built man to be such a thug. Nearly comical, he stood only five foot five and one-half inches tall.

"I'm five-seven." He claimed, but only in certain shoes.

He weighed in at around 185 lbs., which shaped him much like a bowling pin. His stature, or lack thereof, didn't stop him from being aggressive. Dewey always had several heavies around him to do his bidding and he hardly ever showed any mercy. He was particularly enjoying the power his new position afforded him.

This new job he had inherited came with baggage as well as perks. The newer yet responsiblities of Argus overrode even his congressional duties.

Deep inside, a fear was building up. One he was desperate to hide. It was a new feeling to him and he didn't like it. This new job would make him a target of the congressional killer. He covered his fear with bluster, parties and women.

The freshman representative thought of himself as a ladies' man, although most who entertained him did so out of fear more

25

than anything. Dewey loved big parties, big, extravagant parties where he could dress in his tuxedo and strut for the ladies. If he could, Dewey would wear that tux everyday. It made him feel important. He never seemed to notice the smiles behind his back or hear the comments relating to a flightless bird. If he had, there would have been hell to pay.

Re-establishing Argus' routes would take some doing. The type of doing Dario was good at. Dewey Hanson liked Dario. He liked the way the man worked. It was messy and it made people notice. That's what he wanted in this case.

~

Juan Castrono nearly jumped out of his skin when the phone rang.

"You want I should get that, boss?" A warehouse worker asked him.

"No, no, I'll take it. Just get out for a few minutes, will ya?"

He just knew something had gone wrong or the boss was going to be upset over the Kentucky mess and hold him responsible. Juan did not know Dewey Hanson at all.

The phone rang twice and quit. Not long enough for him to answer, but long enough to leave caller ID info. The number shown on the screen was not a phone number. It looked like one, but Argus had devised a system of codes and message processing that was hard to pick up. The number on the caller ID was 438-651-0345.

Juan pulled a card from his wallet and read the simple code. The first numbers, 438 meant GFT or get fax today. The second set of numbers, 651 was on Juan's card, it designated Comfort Inn and Conference Center in Doraville and the last set, 0345 was the time he should be in the business center of that motel. It was imperative that he be there on time. The fax message would not mean anything to anyone else and it would only be sent once. Juan checked his watch. It was two o'clock. He had plenty of time.

~

Stepping into the new mountain house, it did not take Jon long to find his young assistant.

Ben Shaw was waiting for him with phone in hand; the caller was still on the line.

Jon Crane took the phone from Ben and spoke very firmly.

"Daniel, are you two alright?"

"Yes, Jon," Came the response. "We're fine. Have you heard?"

"Yeah, I heard. You two need to take a trip...now."

"That seems to be the consensus of opinion. We're packing as we speak."

"Is this a secure phone?" Jon asked.

"Its not traceable to me, yet." Daniel told him.

"Ok, can you get to the airport tonight?" Jon asked him.

"I'll need to make reservations and see." Daniel was caught off guard by the question.

"No, no," Jon corrected him. "Can you get to the Pittsburgh Airport tonight?"

"Yeah sure, but I still would need to be sure we can get a flight."

"I'll send a plane for you." Jon stated. "Either Ben or I will call with the details, you and Lori get there tonight with what you need to bring, OK?"

"Then what?" Daniel still didn't understand the total plan Jon was forming.

"I'll have you picked up at the gate." Jon told him. "You're staying here."

"Jon thanks. But we can't put you out like that."

27

"I have room," Jon smirked. "More than you can imagine. We'll call you back within the hour with the information and who to see at your airport." Jon paused for a second and continued. "The man picking you up here will be Gil, Gil Gartner. He's a cop, but he works with me some now. He'll have a sign with my name on it. Got that?"

"Yeah, are you sure about this Jon?"

"Won't have it any other way, man. See you guys tonight."

With that, Jon Crane hung up and looked at Ben. "Call the Pittsburgh Airport and charter a flight to Dalton in my name, two passengers, tonight. Then call Daniel back with who to see about the flight and when, got it?"

"Sure," Ben's voice was pensive but he could tell Jon was not in the mood for twenty questions. "I'll get right on it."

"Thanks, man. Remember, in my name only. Don't use Daniel's name at all."

"I understand," Ben answered. "And call Daniel back on the number he used?"

"Exactly." Jon was looking around like he'd lost something. Then he pointed at Ben and added, "Can you bounce that number he called from off a couple of satellites so it can't be traced to here? He'll need to use it a time or two when they first arrive."

"I know someone who can." Ben nodded his head with the response. "And I'll order a case of disposable phones to be here by tomorrow."

"Good," Jon was moving toward the door already, "have some men move my personal things out of my room to the second floor, will ya?"

"Sure." Ben followed and finally called out to ask, "What's going on?"

Jon looked over his shoulder and said, "Argus."

~

As he drove into town, Jon could feel his blood warming. He never got rattled or excited. Staying calm was a natural asset to what he did. But the thought of this group stirred something within him.

Was this what they call adrenaline? He wondered.

Jon pulled the car into the Dalton Police parking area and an officer waved him through. He parked in a spot marked "DA" because George was not using it at the moment.

Jon was a minor hero to the local police after his help to them last year. Only Gil Gartner knew just how much help he had been.

At the hospital where Doris was recovering, Argus had staged an attack with fifteen armed men. They were determined to silence Doris at all costs. The private guards at the hospital had little police help because of a huge explosion south of the city. Most uniformed officers responded to the carpet plant that blew up, leaving the hospital vulnerable. Gil and two other officers were all that was there. Jon organized a defense and took out several of the attackers using Gil Gartner's gun.

When it was over, he asked Gil to take the credit, which he reluctantly did. The two men remained friends and Gil had helped to handle security for Jon and George. He knew Jon Crane was a very talented man, but he didn't know everything about him. Gil was loyal and could be counted on when needed. Right now, Jon needed him.

Gartner looked up from his desk and saw his friend approaching. He smiled and stood, reaching out his hand to the man.

"Jon, what brings you here?"

"I need your help with something tonight," Jon told him. "Do you have some time?"

"Of course," Gil responded. He cocked his head as he asked the obvious question. "What's going on?"

"I need you to pick up some friends at the Dalton airport and get them to my new house."

Gil wasn't a chauffeur and Jon would never treat him as such, so Gil's face became stern as he asked the next question. "Is this to do with that report about the Argus organization?"

Jon nodded his head in the affirmative and Gil understood.

"How many men should I take with me?" He asked his friend.

"Don't make a big show, just enough to get them here quietly."

Gil grabbed his notebook, "How will I recognize them and who are they?'"

"They'll find you. Hold a sign at the gate with my name on it. Ben will call you with the flight information and time as soon as we know. It's Daniel Seay and his wife."

"The reporter?" Gil seemed surprised.

"Yeah, keep that to yourself. They could be in danger with all this, again."

"You got it, Jon." Gil told him. "I'll take Albie and Walt. They can blend into any crowd for security and," he paused a second, "keep their mouths shut."

"Thanks man." Jon said. "I'll need some security at the new house for awhile. Can you arrange that? Same rules."

"I'll work it out," the officer told him. "What are you doing?"

"I have some things I need to look into." Jon told him as he shook the officer's hand and laid a cell phone on his desk. "Use this for communications, OK?" It was a prepaid unit listed in an assumed name. Jon turned to walk away saying as he left, "Thanks, Gil." He walked back to his car before making his next call. It was to the Dalton airport.

"Hey, this is Jon Crane. Could you see if Gordon can arrange a private flight to Cincinnati for me, tonight?"

6

It was exactly 3:45PM and Juan Castrono stood alone in the business center of the Comfort Inn and Conference Center off Interstate 285 in Doraville, Georgia.

"Can I help you?" The desk clerk asked from across the lobby.

"No, please." Juan waved him off. "I'm fine."

Two fax machines sounded off at the same time, they were at opposite ends of the table. Juan waited for the paper to drop from each machine and walked to his left first.

"It's two bucks a page for incoming." The clerk yelled again.

Juan looked toward the desk and nodded as he picked up the message. It was addressed to an M. Martin in Room 327 and had to do with pricing for a tool bid. Juan laid the paper down on the table and moved to the machine at the right end of the room.

The message there appeared to be a mistake. It was in fact, a code. "Virgins Hope for Fairness, time is lost, count two" was all it said. The header for the sending Fax machine showed the number 1-888-555-5555, which was nothing.

The message was not traceable and meant little to anyone other than the intended recipient. "Virgins" was Virginia, "Hope" stood for Hopewell, a small town south of Richmond, "Fairness" was the Fairfield Inn. "Time is lost" was simply the room number 424 by the numbers of letters and "count two" meant in two days. The codes were not elaborate, but very effective. It was from his boss, Dewey Hanson.

Hanson had called a meeting in Virginia. How Juan got there was up to him. He had a budget that allowed for travel any way he felt he needed, car, plane or whatever.

Returning to his office at the ice warehouse, he noticed the big trailer was gone and only a few laborers were still there working on the racks. Things were much quieter than before, less attention getting.

That was good, he thought. He had travel plans to make.

As he stepped into his office the cell phone rang. Not just any cell phone, "the" cell phone. The one Dario used to call him, when he chose to call.

"Hopewell, huh?" the voice on the phone said. "You going too?"

Juan was disappointed that Dario would be there with them, but not surprised. "Yeah," he said. "Where are you now?"

"Around, not far. Got a tip we need to follow up on and then we're off. Got another delivery to make." Dario stated bluntly. "Same message, different location."

"What tip?" Juan asked him.

"Just a little surveillance I need to see about before I go to my next stop."

Juan didn't like that comment, not even a little bit. He had warned Hanson about a possible connection between that reporter the Bird tried to kill and the north Georgia area. His short time working with Harley had exposed him to the suspicions "the Bird" had about Daniel Seay.

He figured that if anything ever spooked the reporter he would head down around here to hide. Hanson didn't give Juan any go-ahead to look into it or even make a comment about it. Juan had taken action to plant "watch teams" as soon as he heard about Dario's plans. Now it appeared that Dario had been told to watch for Daniel's movements. Not only was it a slight toward Juan, but they were possibly duplicating efforts, another side effect of not working together.

Juan fought off the urge to ask directly and quickly thought of something else to ask.

"You going to be on time for the meeting?" Juan asked rhetorically, he knew the answer.

"Hell, yes, man." Dario was almost laughing. "You don't keep that man waiting."

The phone went dead. That was it. Dario just wanted to know if Juan was coming. What was with that? Did he think Juan had lost favor with the boss already? Given charge of Juan's idea probably made him feel cocky. At least Juan found out what the killer was up to. That, and another message was being sent, he just didn't say where.

Juan tossed the cell phone across the desk and watched it bounce off the glass window.

"Whose child will die now for the sake of this mess?" He wondered out loud.

~

Ben Shaw was signing for a delivery when the phone rang at the mansion. It was Daniel, checking on the flight information for him and Lori. Ben gave him the details and told Daniel about Gil and how to find him at the Dalton Airport. Daniel offered some news that Ben wrote down and then ended the call with, "See you soon."

Ben pushed a button on his phone to call Gil and let him know the flight info. He and his men would have about three hours to be in place at the airport. That was plenty of time.

Ben walked back to the package that had just arrived. It was a large box and it contained items Ben had been anxious to work with. He thought about opening the box, but that was all. He would wait for Jon. The movers reported they were done and Ben thanked them. Then he called Jon.

"Hey, you got those cameras we've been waiting for."

"What?" The statement caught Jon off guard and annoyed him a bit. He had things on his mind.

"The cameras." Ben said again. "For the Station."

"Oh," Jon paused to let that soak in. "Good, I mean we'll have to look at them later. I need you to pack me a surveillance bag with the usual. I'll be gone a couple of days."

"When are you leaving?" Ben asked next.

"Two hours." Jon responded and then was quiet for a good while. "Can you handle getting the Seays set up?" He continued, "I need to look into what's caused all this."

"Sure, the room is already changed out. They'll be fine." Ben assured him.

"Count Gil in for dinner for a few days. He's going to be around, him and maybe a couple others. Oh, let George know what's happening, Ok? I don't have time to call him. If he knows anyone in northern Kentucky I could use some influence."

"Yeah, you got it, Jon."

"I'll be by for the bag in thirty minutes, see you then." Jon said as he hung up.

Stopping by one of his downtown warehouses, Jon picked out a few lipstick cameras and several audio devices to take with him. Ben's mention of the cameras that were delivered made him think about these.

The new cameras Ben was telling him about were the holographic projectors. If they worked right, the tunnel could be active in a week or two. Couldn't worry about that now, he must concentrate on the matters at hand.

Calling the Cincinnati airport, Jon reserved a car for his trip down I-75 from there. The airport was actually in northern Kentucky so the trip to the crime scene wouldn't take long. It would be dark by the time he got there, but that was good. The body had been hung in the dark. Jon wanted to see the area as the killers had and if there was any chance someone passing by could have noticed anything.

He knew they were Argus, or paid by Argus to do their dirty work. He hoped to find out where they were from and maybe even who they were. If they were locals from that area somebody would be talking. His instincts told him they were more than likely from somewhere else. But it was worth looking into.

Jon understood what they were up to and realized it wouldn't stop with northern Kentucky. But where else would they hit...and when?

Ben had the bag packed and waiting. A surveillance kit included many things. The black Kevlar suit, Jon's hydraulic arm, night vision goggles and the Glock 23 with six magazines. I.D.'s and credit cards in varying names, and cash, plenty of cash. Ben had printed out detailed maps of the area Jon would be investigating and a listing of local eateries and motels. A separate bag held a few changes of clothes.

Ben had been working on the arm for several weeks. He was intrigued by it and felt the functions could be expanded. Besides being an organizational nut, Ben had always excelled in the sciences at school. Math, physics and mechanical functions had been his strong suits. Ben was finishing his senior year of high school as a "home school" student. Another of the changes forced on those close to Jon because of the Argus mess. Ben didn't really mind, it offered him time to apply his studies to more practical areas.

His ideas for the hydraulic arm were to extend the strength offered by the system down through Jon's legs. Adding support for what the arm could do while making Jon even faster than he was already.

He would not change the original arm, itself. Jon wouldn't like that. Ben was designing a completely new system using the new Kevlar reactive cloth they had found and newer, stronger tubing to supply the fluid. It wasn't ready to show Jon, not just yet. There were always interruptions, but that was the job and Ben liked the job.

Jon drove up, as he had said, to collect his bags for the trip.

"George didn't know anyone in Kentucky." He told Jon. "But Daniel thought of a contact when he called in."

A friend of his in Burlington, Iowa, had called. Daniel said the guy's name was Earl Johnstone of the local newspaper there. Johnstone called Daniel about the northern Kentucky mess and said a Lt. Draper of the Burlington police had a brother-in-law with the State Police in Kentucky.

"Daniel thought that info might be of help somehow." Ben told Jon.

"Daniel comes through again. Did you get the guy's name?" Jon smiled.

"Yeah," Ben was looking through his notes. "Sawyer, Col. Hugh Sawyer."

Jon took the note and his smile became pensive. The names of Johnstone and Draper rang a bell with him. He was surprised Draper would offer help, but then Lt. Draper did not yet understand the connection of Daniel to what had happened to his friend, Thomas Ames, the former editor of the Burlington Hawk Eye. Ames had been responsible for the name the nation knew Jon by, "The Son."

He and Lt. Draper had formed a plot to capture him in Burlington last year. Ames released a story about his success a couple of hours before the plan fell apart. The failed plot and premature story cost Ames his job. Now, here's the police Lt. unknowingly offering help to the man he was after back then.

"Small world," Jon quipped as he waved good-bye, "and it's getting smaller."

7

Daniel and Lori Seay lifted off in the private charter from Pittsburgh at nearly the same time Jon was leaving Dalton on the way to Cincinnati. The only plane available for Jon was a corporate Gulfstream 5. Owned by one of the area's carpet companies, it was pricey to rent and operate, but it was fast. He would be on the ground in northern Kentucky in an hour and a half. Well before the Seays would reach the approach at Dalton airport.

Jon left the car rental lot at 8:50PM and was on his way to the crime scene some sixty miles away. He reported in to Ben and then called the number for the Kentucky State police to ask for a connection to Col. Sawyer. At the mention of Lt. Draper's name, the Colonel became very cooperative and told Jon the name of the chief investigator on site and offered to call ahead to clear the way for him. He didn't even ask what Jon's business was.

Draper must be well respected, Jon thought.

The road was dark and not heavily traveled, in either direction, at this time of night. Mostly tractor-trailers with loads of produce or other goods, very few passenger vehicles.

At forty minutes from the airport, Jon could see a glow in the distance. The view was eerie, like one from a science fiction movie. The light appeared to be a large mushroom of white just off the road and on his left as he drove south. He was at that point, still six miles away. That shape dissipated as he neared it and he could see it was from many lights, set at all heights and in several directions to illuminate the area. There were two large tents erected deep into the field and more than a dozen vehicles along the roadside. The only vehicle that was actually in the field appeared to be a large generator truck.

The median was not crossable at that section of expressway so he had to travel several miles further south to exit and turn around. Getting closer he became aware that the site looked more like a carnival scene than one of a major crime. Driving past the cars lining the freeway, Jon found a spot that had been vacated by another vehicle. As soon as he parked a trooper approached him.

"Can I help you, sir?" The officer challenged. "This is a closed crime scene."

Jon showed his ID, his real ID since that was the name he was using right now and asked to speak with Captain Swanson. The trooper checked his cards and nodded his head.

"Yes, sir," the trooper responded. "She's in the second tent, back this way."

Jon followed the trooper, stepping over large cords leading from the generator truck to the various lights and to the tents. The walkway was clearly roped off to keep traffic away from the path the murderers had used. As they walked, the trooper looked back at Jon and added, "she's expecting you."

Jon noticed a pole just beyond the larger tent. It was covered, but not touched by tarps, to try to protect it from the elements. That was "the" pole. They walked straight into the tent and there, at her desk, sat a rather large, yet pleasant woman who looked to be in her late forties. She was reading some papers on her desk. The set up was quite good for a field operation. There was a floor to the tent, her desk and several other chairs for meetings.

A main light hung from the center of the tent and three other smaller fixtures and lamps offered a comfortable level of lighting.

Jon stepped to within four feet of the desk and waited for her to acknowledge him.

"Mr. Crane," she spoke, glancing over the frames of her reading glasses. "You seem to come highly regarded by my superiors."

"Captain, I thank you for seeing me." Jon responded sincerely.

Sharon Swanson pulled the glasses from her face and folded them, slowly and deliberately. She laid them down before finally raising her head to look at him.

"You must be some famous son of somebody or other." She watched him closely for his reaction. "Civilians are not normally allowed at crime scenes."

Jon's expression did not change. He actually expected some resentment for the special treatment he was accorded. The "son" reference was sharp though, he could tell this was someone he would like.

"Captain Swanson, I'm somebody's son for sure. But they weren't famous and you wouldn't know them." Jon paused and looked her directly in the eyes, then he continued, "I'll tell you this, if you did you would respect them." He stayed calm, polite and respectful.

The Captain smiled just a little. "I'm sure I would, sir. You do appear to have friends in high places. Now, how can I help you?"

" I have friends with severe interest in this case, Captain. It could well be a matter of life and death to them." He remained polite, but firm. The Captain pointed at a chair for Jon. As he sat he continued, "We suspect a drug cartel's involvement and possibly more incidents like this in other areas."

The officer was impressed with his directness. She leaned back, a bit more relaxed with his presence yet still skeptical of who he was.

"I agree with both assessments, unfortunately," she answered. "So far, it appears to be someone who knew what they wanted to do and who they were after, even though they were not from around here. We'll probably never find them, not here anyway."

"Are you sure of that?" Jon asked.

"Sure as I can be," Captain Swanson was direct in return. "But of course, that won't be the official finding. The public wouldn't stand for it. Not for a while anyway."

"This is a rather large, elaborate investigation scene for having no evidence." The visitor challenged her back.

"I agree," her smile grew more at his observation. "It's necessary for the locals. They have to believe we are doing something, even when there's little to do."

"Have you found anything, anything at all?"

"Some, but that's the problem, not enough." She stood at that point and grabbed her overcoat. Heading for the tent's opening she waved at Jon, "come with me."

They walked to the pole, stepping over more cords along the way. The cold was sharp and painful. Those few minutes in the tent had made the outside feel worse. When they got to the pole where the body had been hung, it looked like a shrine. Lit up from every possible angle and with blue print dust from top to bottom. The pole was cordoned off in a circle some twenty feet in diameter. Swanson pointed at the ground. "Do you see that?"

Jon looked at the area and noticed the snow was flattened and the grass was all bent down, but there were no footprints. He nodded his head as the Captain continued.

"They brought in plywood we figure, so as not to leave footprints of any kind. Locals don't think about things like that. This was professional and we don't have those kind of professionals around here."

"How far does this extend?" Jon asked her.

"All the way back to the road." She pointed a flashlight at the pole itself, "no prints there either. Footprints and tire tracks were raked over. No prints on the pole at all. Gloves, I suppose. Somebody climbed that pole and strung the rope over the top wire stud. He or they, we think it was at least three of them, then pulled the body up like a flag." She moved around the pole pointing the flashlight at the ground. "The truck they used didn't stay the whole time. Someone drove it around and came back. That way a parked truck didn't get noticed."

"What else is missing?" She asked him.

"Blood... I don't see any blood." Jon responded.

"No blood anywhere," she continued. "May have been some on the plywood, but they took that with them." The captain liked that he noticed that.

"You sure it was plywood and not something else?"

"Yeah, there were small pieces left in several areas." Captain Swanson then directed Jon back towards her tent. " The lab already reported back. Thin veneer, pine plywood."

Carefully stepping back over a large cord, Swanson looked back at Jon and suggested, "Let's get in out of this cold."

It was mind numbing. Jon wondered if it was this cold the night they left the girl here. If so, surely they made some sort of mistake. Left something to identify themselves.

"Did you see the body?" Jon asked.

"No, the coroner had her back at the county morgue before I got here." Swanson said as she pulled the flap back on the tent and stepped into the warmth ahead of Jon. It had to be in the 50's in there. And it felt very good after those long minutes outside.

"Has the coroner issued his report yet?" Jon asked as a shiver made him tense up his shoulders. Swanson saw that and smiled again as she pulled her overcoat off.

"You don't get used to the cold, not ever." She stepped to her desk and sat before answering his question. Whoever this guy was, he was competent as an investigator. Jon was earning her respect, slowly.

She picked up a stack of papers and fingered through till she found what she wanted.

"Here it is," she said. "COD was exsanguination from a laceration to the throat."

"Anything about markings on the body?"

"Yeah," Swanson held out a picture of the disfiguring for Jon to see, "post mortem for sure. Doesn't indicate how long after, but certainly after."

Jon's face strained as he looked at the picture of the Argus logo carved on the girl's body.

"You've got history with these creeps, these Argus people, don't you?" She asked.

"My friends do." Jon laid the photo on her desk and looked up at her. "Serious history."

He thought again about the plywood lead. There had to be more about it that she hadn't told him.

"I know you've already checked with the building supply stores in the area." Jon said as a compliment.

With each exchange, the captain liked this stranger more.

"Yep, they bought it at a Lowe's back near Sadieville the night before the body was found." She told him.

"They?" Jon lit up.

"Two Hispanic males, late thirties early forties. Paid cash."

"Any surveillance photos from the store?" He asked the captain.

"Oh yeah, problem is we do have lots of Hispanic workers in the area. There were several groups who bought plywood that afternoon. Got pictures of all of them."

"No leads then?"

"Captain Swanson then smiled wide as she laid down another picture on her desk. She tapped it firmly with her finger and asked Jon, "Notice anything?"

He looked hard at the shot, no faces were shown, and the clothes were not special. Then he saw it. What the captain had noticed.

"They're wearing cowboy boots," he said. "Fancy cowboy boots."

"Nice catch," Swanson congratulated him. "Those are not working boots, folks wear working boots around here. Those are fancy dancing boots. Those two guys weren't from around here."

"That fits the Argus profile to a tee." Jon confirmed. "Hispanic, but OTM."

"If they were "other than Mexican" where are they from?" The captain asked him.

"Argus is a Colombian operation. I bet on them being from there."

"All we have to do now is find the SOBs," the captain lamented.

Jon started to stand up, but paused. He sat back down and asked her another question. "You know they bought the plywood, how about the rake?"

Captain Swanson was impressed. She stared at Jon for several seconds before commenting. "You caught that, huh? I wasn't sure how good you were. But you've done this type of investigation before, haven't you?"

"I have some experience in looking into facts and determining what happened, yes."

Swanson stood and walked over to the small heater near her desk. With her hands stretched out over the heater and her back to Jon, she spoke at a level he was sure to hear.

"I don't know who you are mister, and my gut tells me I don't want to pry too far into it." The captain's instincts were to be cautious, but she somehow liked this unknown, private citizen who her superiors had inexplicably asked her to cooperate with. She decided to share the last detail she had. "The rake was stolen from a small farm near Florence," she told him.

"Stolen?" Jon gave her a puzzled look. "How are you sure? Why not just buy one?"

"The report was made the night before the body was found. The farmer heard the commotion and chased after him. It was a single Hispanic male driving a rental car. He took a rake, some work gloves and duct tape. As to the "why" I can only guess. He got lazy maybe, opportunity that turned on him. I doubt he meant to get caught by a farmer."

Jon didn't think that made much sense, "the farmer made a report over that?"

"That, and the perpetrator killed his dog getting into the shed. The farmer fired a blast from his shotgun at the car. He thinks he took out a tail light."

"That should be easy enough to locate." Jon stated.

"Depends." The Captain said while turning back to face him. "All depends on where he turned the car in. We haven't found it yet."

"Where is Florence?"

"Up around the airport area, near Cincinnati." She answered.

"The Lowe's is down state near Lexington, right?"

"Yeah," the Captain answered. She could tell Jon was getting the whole picture now. "They came in separate, best we can figure. Two flew or drove into Lexington and the other one likely flew into Cincinnati because of the rental car." Captain Swanson turned back to the heater again and continued. "Where they met up we don't know for sure, but they got a truck somewhere and came here."

Jon rubbed his forehead and considered what he had just learned.

"You're exactly right, Captain. They had to get their hands on a truck to haul the plywood."

"I don't have any information about the truck. That's where I'm stumped." She said.

"How much longer are you going to stay out here?" Jon asked.

"We'll start clearing out in the morning. The official statement will be that we found fiber evidence that could lead to an arrest. I don't believe that, but it's not a lie." With that Captain Sharon Swanson leaned back in her chair. "We've done all we could here," she said.

Jon nodded in agreement.

"I think I have what I need." Jon said as he stood and reached out his hand. As he was thanking the Captain his cell phone rang.

It was Marsha.

"Excuse me, Captain Swanson, I need to take this."

"Certainly," she told him while getting up. "Make yourself at home. I'm going for a coffee from the other tent." She slipped into her overcoat again and from her tent's entrance called back to him, "care for a cup?"

"Please, that would be great." Jon flipped the phone open and put it to his ear.

"Jon?" Marsha started. "I called the house, where are you?"

Normally, that question would have been out of bounds. Their relationship was good, but not that good. It didn't upset Jon though. He checked his watch. It was 11:15PM. Lt. Marsha Hurst was the Watch Commander of the night shift at her precinct in Charlotte, N.C. Marsha had gotten to work and found the report about the girl in Kentucky. Jon was expecting her call.

"Do you know about Kentucky?" She continued.

"Yes, I know." Jon answered.

Marsha was quiet for a minute, and then she asked him. "You're there, aren't you?"

"Yeah," he admitted. "I'm here. Just got here."

"I should have known." Marsha seemed to be relieved. "What about Daniel? Have you heard from him?"

"That's all under control. They should be at the new house by now, he and Lori."

"Good, and you have security set up?"

"Yes, dear," he teased. "Gil and a couple of guys will be there with them."

There was quiet on both sides of the call for a couple of minutes, but Jon could hear her breathing. Finally she asked, "What can I do?"

"I'm sure there's no activity in Charlotte, but you can check out that warehouse one more time."

"Already have a team on the way over there." She responded. "Anything else?"

"Just keep me informed of anything you hear about from anywhere that might be connected."

"OK," she answered sounding a little professional. "You be careful."

"Always." He said flatly. "Talk to you later."

8

As Gil Gartner turned off Hwy 71 and started up the driveway he could hear Daniel mumble in the back seat, "Are you kidding me?"

"Nope, this is it." Gil smiled. "Those investments really paid off. Some folks are just blessed, huh?"

"I'll say."

They got to the garage doors and Ben was waiting for them. He shook Daniel's hand and introduced himself with, "very good to finally meet you."

"Same here, Ben." Daniel managed a smile and introduced Lori. "My wife, Lori Seay."

"Pleasure is all mine, Mrs. Seay."

Gil was helping get the bags when another car pulled up. "It's okay, they are with me." He assured the others.

He walked back to the other car and the driver rolled down his window. "You had a tail coming out here." The driver informed him.

"You sure?" Gil questioned. "Where did they go?"

"Straight down the highway when you pulled into the drive."

Gil rubbed his chin. "Did they see you guys, too?"

"Naw, they were intent on watching you." The driver told him. "We stayed back and I'm sure they think you didn't see them either."

"Yeah, well I didn't." Gil was upset with himself. "Why would anyone...how would they know it was us?" Gil couldn't figure it out. "Could you tell anything about who they were?"

"Not really," the man told him. "There were three in the car, that was plain. But we couldn't make out anything else."

"Where did you first notice them?" Gil pushed.

"Well, I think they made you at the airport, must have been waiting for you there."

"Alright, change of plan. Put your car in that garage," Gil said pointing at the separate building. "Then come in, set up on the first floor and keep a look out."

The driver nodded and pulled back to maneuver into the garage.

Ben was already showing Daniel and Lori to their room. Lori hardly said a word. Her expressions spoke for her.

The house and the room were overwhelming. Jon's room was just over 24 feet by 26 feet and the bath and closets were offset from that. She sat her overnight bag down on the bed and looked at her husband. Her eyes said, "This can't be real." Daniel just smiled at her and turned back to Ben who was offering details about the room. He took Daniel to the special elevator, as Jon had requested, and showed him how it worked. "2B and 3B are not shown on the list." He told the guest. "Hit 3 twice and then hold 2 to get to the second sub-basement. Hit 3 twice, release it, then 3 again to go to the third sub-basement."

"What are they for?" Daniel asked the young man.

"Safety." Ben told him. "You can relax here, it's safe here. But should you need to get away, those sub-basements are secret. Understand?"

Daniel nodded his head. Gil went about helping his men set up in the living room.

"How are we fixed on hardware?" One of them asked.

"We're good, believe me." Gil assured him. "There's an armory downstairs if we need it."

Ben walked in on the conversation and asked, "what's wrong?"

"It's all good, Ben." Gil tapped him on the shoulder. "We're good."

Ben looked at Gil as the others walked away. He reached out and tugged at the officer's arm.

"Have you heard of the T-Rex?" He asked with a slight smirk on his face.

"T-Rex?" Gil thought a second. "What are we talking about?"

"I heard you mention the armory we have," Ben was now smiling, "I added a new unit to the weapons list, it just got here yesterday. I haven't even unpacked it yet."

"I still don't follow." Gil shook his head.

"It's a Hannibal 577 Tyrannosaur." Ben proclaimed. "Jon ordered a Barrett M-107 last month. This is stronger."

"The Barrett I know of, this other one...no."

The Barrett M-107 sniper rifle is a 50-caliber weapon with a long range and high velocity. The joke among military snipers is "you are dead before you hear the round discharged." Its primary use was in the Middle East wars. It could take out a truck, an armored personnel carrier even a light tank with one round from over a mile away.

Gil cracked a smile as he considered what he just heard, "You got one of each?"

"Yep, no ammo for the T-Rex yet. It takes a special .577, 750 grain solid round. They are hard to come by."

"Who the hell could fire a thing like that and stand up?" Gil asked. The recoil has to be like a whale's tail."

"The film I saw of guys trying is great. Only one man stood through it. It is a bear."

Gil face became serious as he looked at his men and then the floor.

"What's wrong, Gil?" Ben didn't understand the turn in his friend's attitude.

Gil looked up at the young man, "It's neat to have weapons like that. But you know what? These are some bad people we're up against. I sure hope we don't need 'em."

A chill ran down Ben's back. He quickly recovered, nodded in agreement at Gil and walked over to the other men.

"You guys hungry?" He asked.

"Are you kidding? We're always hungry." One of the men said.

"There's Chinese on the way, plenty for everybody. Should be here in about 10 minutes."

As Ben went towards the kitchen area, Gil pointed out the added strength details in the walls, glass and roofing that made the house a fortress for its occupants. The men were quite impressed.

~

Jon had left the crime scene in Kentucky and drove south to just outside the Lexington area and found a motel. He would start his own investigation in the morning, but right now he needed sleep.

9

Bobby Ray Phillips had the world by the tail. Looking forward to his senior year at Green Oaks High, just north of Shreveport, La, the star quarterback could do no wrong. Or, at least he couldn't be held accountable for it. Girls fawned at his glance and he, and his best pal Aleksei Torbof, had no problem finding female attention anytime they wished. The only thing they liked more than girls was partying. They were two golden boys who enjoyed doing what they pleased when they pleased and believed they could walk through any valley and feared no evil.

The attack on them, that Tuesday evening, rocked the area with its severity and its outcome. The boys had been out drinking, as they were prone to do. They walked out of the party, being held in an abandoned house near their school, sometime after 11:30PM. The van screeched in front of them and three men jumped out with handguns.

It was determined later that Bobby Ray was the target. His father was Major Randolph Phillips of the Louisiana State Police and Bobby Ray was intended to be another "message." Aleksei's presence is what caused the disruption of that plan.

After their Afghanistan war, the Russians were left with an appreciation of the country's southern poppy fields. The heroin derived from the poppy's opium was a quick cash product with a worldwide customer base. Rivaling cocaine, heroin was experiencing resurgence in the U.S. when Argus began to have its problems with distribution.

Enter the CCCY cartel based Rostov near the Black Sea. Product entering the U.S. through New Orleans was received and distributed by the CCCY. "Three Cs" were known to be "over the top" violent. They hardly ever sought confrontation, but when it occurred they would complete it and harshly. Members were rotated in and out because of immigration status, but the local leader was a naturalized citizen who lived in Shreveport with his family. Vasily Torbof was general counsel to the Russian Federation for the southern district and had chosen Louisiana as his home because of its climate, so the story goes. His larger job was head of the vast Opium and Heroin Empire operating in the region. His eldest son, Aleksei, lived the life of an average American teenager and was quite unaware that his every move was monitored for his safety.

~

Jon didn't know exactly what he was looking for. Some form of confirmation of who had been to Kentucky and where they were from. He had kept the small piece of plywood he'd found at the crime scene. Walking through the two big box home improvement stores he compared the piece with 4x8 sheets in the racks.

At the Lowe's near Sadieville, he found the closest match. The color of the glue was a muddy shade of gray and it stuck out from the other selections. The sheets, which had this odd color glue, were 11/16" exterior rated, smooth on one side. There were cheaper grades available, but they all had a more tan colored glue.

Why this stuff? He wondered, but he had confirmed for himself what Captain Swanson told him. This was the store. *Now where did they get the truck?*

The Lowe's offered rental trucks, which seemed the easiest answer, but Jon had a feeling there was some other way these guys had come up with their vehicle. Walking to the end of the building where the loading docks were, he noticed a man with a young daughter asking about a truck rental. The store had trucks to rent, by the hour, for customers to carry do it yourself projects home.

The man first baulked at the price, so the man behind the counter leaned over towards him. Jon eased closer to hear.

"There's a guy who will rent you his truck for $5.00 an hour plus gas. It's over on Whitmore near 3rd St."

The customer didn't appear to like the idea of the location. He looked down at his daughter and then agreed to take the company's deal on one of their trucks.

Jon walked inside and asked about a local street map, they had one on the wall. He found Whitmore and 3rd. The map indicated that was about two miles from the store.

"Worth a look see." He told himself as he got back into the rental car.

At the corner of the intersection he was looking for stood three working girls in attire fitting their occupation. He could understand why the customer wasn't interested in bringing his young daughter to this part of town.

Turning up Whitmore for about half a block he noticed a dirty building with signs claiming it had once been an auto repair shop. He slowed to take a closer look at the property. Old cars up on blocks and stacks of tires littered the yard. There was activity inside the building, but he couldn't tell what kind. As he passed to the far side of the one story block structure he saw it, a 24 foot panel truck, all white with no markings of any kind parked just barely in view.

Pulling his car to the curb, Jon looked around and carefully approached the vehicle. He saw it right away and almost couldn't believe what it was. All down the step bumper and some on the sliding door, it looked like blood.

He went back to the rental car and got his bag from the trunk. A small bottle of spray luminal was all he pulled from the bag. The spray proved what he found was indeed blood. Opening the sliding door, he found a much larger stain inside.

This is not only the vehicle used, it's likely the murder scene as well, he thought almost out loud. Then there was a voice from behind him that sounded old and graveled.

"Can I help you, sonny?" It said rather sarcastically.

Coolly, Jon turned and responded in his most official voice, "Yeah, tell me about this truck. Where has it been lately?"

Identifying himself as an ICE agent from Cincinnati, Jon asked to see the records when the old man said it was a rental unit. They walked inside and Jon could see the remnants of a poker game he had interrupted. Three other men stood around an old open top coke machine staring, but not saying a word.

The proprietor went behind his counter and pulled up a dusty record book and laid it on the counter.

"It's all in here." He told Jon and backed away to give him access to it.

The hand written notes in the logbook were right there, the last renter used a driver's license from Florida. The date matched the girl's death.

The name was Saul DeMarcos.

Must have been the only one with a valid driver's license. He told himself and then chuckled at the idea such was required in a place like this.

That name was very clear to Jon. Dalton DA George Vincent had explained who that was when the young cartel boss had fled the country last fall. When everyone thought Argus was through.

The log showed the truck out that night for just over five hours and 178 miles were driven. He figured it was seventy-five miles back up to the crime scene so everything fit.

Jon closed the book and thanked the old man. He left the building as the other three men began talking to each other about what was happening.

He started to call Captain Swanson with this new information, but thought better of it for now. His knowledge of certain facts might be tough to clarify. He was satisfied, it was Argus and Saul was back and involved.

So, the family was making a come back and they wanted young Saul to get some needed experience on the rougher side of the business. His mind conjured the former cartel family representative as now part of a wrecking crew.

Interesting. He thought as he smiled to himself. *But where are they off to now?*

10

Juan Castrono arrived at the Fairfield Inn in Hopewell, Virginia at the appointed time. *This is odd,* he thought. He did not notice any other vehicles he recognized, particularly Dario's Charger. "Dario is usually early," came out loud from his thoughts this time.

In fact, the parking lot was oddly vacant even for this time of the morning. He sat in his rental car for several minutes, watching for anyone else he might recognize. For a brief moment he allowed his mind to play with the idea that they weren't coming, that this was all over with and he could go about his life without Argus and all the grief. As the moment of fantasy passed, Juan took a deep breath and was thankful that at least his job was cerebral and not one that applied muscle.

Opening the car door, he stood and looked around one more time before heading inside. It was strangely quiet. A doubt flashed through him, *was this the wrong day*? Quickly, he cast that aside. He had the right information. *This was the when and where,* he assured himself, but something didn't feel right.

Juan hated these meetings and certainly did not want to be the first one there. Walking to the lobby, he got a cup of coffee and looked around some more. Two men in suits sat watching cartoons on the lobby's big screen TV. He walked by and could tell they were part of Hanson's guard detail. Rather than bringing relief of being in the right place at the right time, seeing them made him aware that he was sweating. His shirt collar was now uncomfortable and he could feel his armpits getting damp. He checked his watch; it was time to go upstairs.

The door of room 424 was held open by the top latch so he pushed without knocking and was met by two more guards. The plainness of the room struck him. Hanson liked to show-off, this was not his normal style. This meeting was being held under deep cover, there were seriously big plans in the making.

One of the men at the door knew Juan by sight, "they're all out back," he said and waved Juan through to the balcony. The others there were speaking loudly and with great animation. Something was wrong.

~

An uneventful night was followed by a quiet morning at the mountain mansion in Dalton, Georgia. A light rain had become a mist and fog by daybreak. The window glass was highly protective, but like most glass it fogged up in weather, making viewing difficult at best. It added tension to a situation that needed no enhancement.

Gil Gartner and his men had been outside twice, walking the grounds and driveway, looking all around for any sign of intruders. Whoever had followed them last evening, whoever they were and whatever their purpose, they were gone.

"One of two possibilities as I see it," Gil proclaimed to Daniel and Ben. "They saw this place and thought better of it, or just locating the house was all they were after this time."

Daniel nodded almost unnoticeably and his eyes went from a stare at Gil to a blank gaze at the floor. He clearly showed the effects of a long, sleepless night.

Neither he nor Ben offered any disagreement with what Jon's trusted friend had said. There was nothing to base any argument on. Gil knew his business and they felt he was right about that. But what he had not said was also true. It wasn't over.

The other men remained quiet until Daniel finally spoke.

"This whole thing is unreal."

He walked back to the kitchen and poured another cup of coffee, Ben was right behind him.

"It's going to be ok, seriously," Ben tried to sound confident. "Jon's after them right now. He'll clear this up and it'll all be over."

Daniel leaned against the counter and smiled at Ben the best he could muster. He was impressed with this young man. Ben reflected the courage and confidence Daniel wished he had. But even with Jon involved, this was looking like they were in over their collective heads.

"We all thought it was over before, remember?" he told Ben. "They just keep coming."

Ben did not reply this time. He sat down at the table and hugged his cup with both hands in silence. *Jon will handle this*, he thought to himself.

Gil and his men stood in the doorway of the kitchen without saying anything. He, his men, Ben and Daniel had each witnessed Argus' wrath and tenacity. Gartner quietly glanced at the other officers and motioned with his head for them to go. Before they had taken a step, Lori stormed into the kitchen wrapped in her bathrobe, with Daniel's cell phone outstretched in her hand. She interrupted the guy's pity party. The phone was ringing.

Something in the look on her face made Gil stop and hold up his hand. He and the other officers would wait to see what this was all about.

~

As Juan stepped onto the balcony of the motel room in Hopewell, Virginia he could tell one thing right away. He was being ignored. He recognized Hanson and Tomas Vaga was with him. *What was he doing here?* Juan thought.

Vaga was Sergio DeMarcos' right hand man. The others with Hanson were not Argus associates. Most were distributors, customers of the cartel. But the discussion was not about moving merchandise. *Whatever was wrong was really bad,* Juan feared.

Pleasantries were not in order so he walked to the closest corner and listened to the conversation. The original agenda for this meeting had been cancelled. That was obvious. Then he heard someone mention the cause of the concern.

Dario was missing. No word from him, at all, in over a day. He was to have checked in last night and of course, be here today. That was not good. He dared not say it out loud, but caught himself thinking, *Dario loved the attention he had been getting lately and would not have missed this for anything, but why all this concern over Dario?*

Then he heard the words that sent a chill through him.

"The family hasn't heard from Saul either and they are getting really anxious."

Saul? Juan thought, *Not Saul Demarco, what would he be doing back here?* Suddenly, Juan understood why Tomas was here.

The youngest son of the drug cartel's leader had been the in-country family representative until the Dalton mess. When the main distribution warehouse blew sky high and the raids on the delivery vans cornered nearly their entire product supply, the family shut down operations and called Saul home to Colombia. Now his name is being used along with Dario's. Had Saul been sent back to learn killing from Dario?

And now they were both missing.

This was bad, he thought. *Muy mala.* He moved in closer to hear and the discussions were all the same. Argus had another problem and this was bigger than Dalton. Juan's concern about what was happening finally overrode his fear and he stepped into the conversation.

"Qué pasa?qué está pasando?" He asked. "What's going on?"

59

~

"It's your private line, Danny." Lori said as she handed the phone to Daniel. It had not been a good night, she was not fully awake and she was worried. Daniel could tell her mood was a cross between apprehension and anger. Her eyes were bug-wide and her jaw set firm and she would vent her anxiety on him in a heartbeat. He really didn't care to deal with that just now so he took the phone without a word.

Flipping the unit open, he saw the name on the caller ID screen, "Matt."

Daniel's eyes showed that he was not comforted by the potential of this call and his chest suddenly felt very heavy.

Man, what could this be about? he thought. Still, he tried his best to be upbeat.

"Hey, guy," he said, sounding as cheerful as he could, "how's Louisiana doing?"

"Not so good right now, Daniel." Turlock's voice was stern and almost quivering.

"Phil asked me to get in touch and see if you can find your friend who knows about Argus."

Phil was Captain Phillip Stone of the Shreveport Police. He and Daniel had met last year through Matt. Daniel had been on the trail of the congressional killer at the time.

"What's going on, Matt?" Daniel asked and he could tell that all eyes in the room were on him. He tried to sit straight and firm, but could tell his shoulders were slouching.

"We're not sure." Matt continued. "Least I'm not, and I don't think Phil is either, but he won't say. I've never known him to be like this and it gives me the creeps. He just wants to talk with your guy, you know, the Son."

Daniel knew Captain Stone's reputation. Stone was a cop's cop. The man had worked homicide cases for over twenty years. It would take a lot to shake him.

"I can reach him pretty quick, actually." Daniel didn't let on that he was in the man's house. "You want him to contact you? I don't know if he'll do that, he's kinda finicky about talking to people." He didn't press any more than that. Letting Matt have time to think.

"We've had a shoot out down here, a big one. From what we can tell, and we're not sure of the numbers yet, it looks like there's five or more dead and two wounded, badly." Turlock told him.

Daniel listened without interruption as his friend paused and then continued.

"Two tattoos on some body parts indicate they were Argus members."

"Parts?" Daniel wasn't sure if he had heard correctly.

"Yeah, parts. Looks like four Latinos were cut into pieces and left in a ditch. It's blood and crap like you can't imagine."

"Who did...who would do that?"

"Phil is saying it was a Russian gang. They run heroin in down here, he called them the CCCY."

"Never heard of them. Why... do you have any idea why they would do that?" Daniel pressed.

"The gang's leader's son was one of the dead. He hung around with a kid who's a jock and real popular with everybody. That kid is the son of a state police major. Looks like the Latinos tried to grab the boys and things got out of hand."

Daniel lost the color from his face and sat down as he listened.

Lori had heard enough from one side of this conversation and leaned over the table, asking loudly, "Danny, what is it?"

He waved her off and replied to Matt Turlock. "I'll call my guy right away, he will want to know about this. I'll call you back, Matt, sit tight, ok?"

"Yeah." And Matt's phone went silent.

Daniel scrolled down on his speed dial to Jon's number. He looked at his wife and the others in the room and proclaimed, "It's happened in Louisiana too, but worse. I've got to tell Jon."

~

Jon Crane was on his phone. He had called Marsha Hurst before she went to bed for the day. Lt. Hurst worked the overnight shift; she was watch commander for her precinct and normally slept from around noon till 8 or 9PM.

They were talking about what Jon had learned and how he needed to find out where these guys were going, and fast. Marsha had suggested he come to Charlotte and they would search the abandoned warehouse together. Surely there must be some clue about other locations or something, anything. Just as they were about to agree on a date, Jon's phone beeped.

"Hang on a sec', very few people have this number," he told her as he looked at the screen. "Daniel" it said. "Hey, Marsha, let me call you later or in the morning, ok? It's Daniel, something must be up."

"Let me know what's going on, Jon. I won't be able to sleep if you don't."

"Alright, talk to you in a few."

He hit the accept button and Daniel was now on the line. He told Jon about Matt's call and all the details he had.

"It was another kid, Jon. They are still intimidating people by killing kids."

"Who is this CCCY bunch, again?" Jon asked.

Daniel explained and reiterated that the son of their boss was killed in the attack.

"Call Matt back right away," Jon was breathing hard and talking fast. "Get him to tell Stone to gear up for a shit storm and that I'm on my way there."

"A what?" Daniel asked. "Why do you say that?"

"One of that Hispanic crew that the Russians killed may well be Saul DeMarcos. I've got reason to believe he was with them."

"Oh, man." Daniel looked at Lori with fear in his eyes. She didn't challenge him, but she knew he was not being normal. Sitting down at the table she could barely hear Jon's voice as he continued.

"Really, that town is going to have a gang war on their hands in a major way. Call them back, quick. Tell him I'm coming and will call him when I get there, ok?"

"Yeah, right now. Be careful, Jon." But the line had gone dead.

Jon was calling Marsha back to share the bad news. This thing was escalating and more people could be dead very soon.

"Hold those plans about the warehouse till another time, I've got to get to Louisiana now."

"Watch your backside, Jon. You've got your gear with you?"

"Whole bag full, baby. You get some rest and I'll call you tonight."

As they completed their call, three town cars pulled into the lot of a bombed out warehouse near Dalton, Georgia. Five men got out and looked around in surprise. One took a phone from his pocket and pushed a button.

"Boss, there's nothing or no one here. This place is destroyed already."

From his roof top suite in Shreveport, Vasily Torbof pounded his fist on a table.

"What?" he demanded. "What do you mean destroyed?"

"It's been blown up, boss. Crime scene tape everywhere and it looks like this happened some time ago. I don't know what else to tell you."

"You have another address from that notebook you found on them, no?"

"Yeah, boss. It's in North Carolina."

"Get up there and level the place. Nothing lives do you hear me? Nothing."

"Got it. We'll grab something to eat and head that way."

They drove several miles before finding a place to eat and then things got more complicated. Not being familiar with the area, when they got to Atlanta, they continued south all the way through the city. The group completely missed the interchange to Interstate 85 north and Charlotte.

All in all, with downtown traffic and getting lost a couple more times, it took them over ten hours to get to the North Carolina city. Another hour was spent finding the warehouse listed on the note. It was 12:45AM as they pulled up to the building. There were eleven tired, but still violently motivated, men who got out of their cars, checked their weapons and looked for the entrances to the warehouse building.

11

Jon arrived in Shreveport on a chartered plane at 4:20PM. The plane had been dispatched from Dalton to Georgetown, Kentucky to pick him up. His travel gear could not fly commercial.

Louisiana was sticky, even for late winter. He could feel the pores in his skin rubbing against his clothes. It wasn't a comfortable feeling and it hit like a brickbat the moment he stepped off the plane.

Get a grip, he said to himself. This situation had him on edge in more than one aspect. Meeting with yet more people. Folks who would now know who he was, and all in order to go against the Argus bunch again. *This just keeps getting better and better*, he smirked.

The rental car was waiting. All had gone well thus far, but it was still a very long day. As he walked toward the car counter the path took him through the flow of a crowd that had just left the baggage claim area. In that crowd was a Hispanic man.

Jon did not flinch or miss a step as they passed each other. But the Hispanic man was not as subtle.

Juan Castrono passed him going in the opposite direction. When Jon's face registered with him he stopped dead in his tracks and stared straight ahead. The color drained from his own face as he turned, blocking the fast moving human traffic that bumped into him and then twisted around him. He strained to get another look but the crowd was just too large. Juan eyes searched for the man he thought he saw, but the image had melted into the throng.

A prayer ran through Juan's mind. Then he thought, *was what he saw really a man or just an apparition? Was that face real or just an omen of bad things to come?*

He had seen that face in Atlanta before the first warehouse blew up, then in Washington before Harley died and now here.

Standing in the flow of other passengers finally caused him to turn and continue on with them. Juan's stomach was twisted up and his knees were weak.

This was not going to be good. He thought. *No good at all.*

Jon found the lot and his rental car. He was feeling tired as he sat down in the car so he leaned back, closed his eyes and took a deep breath. It wasn't there yet, but that good old "second wind" was close.

Reaching for one of his cell phones, he called Daniel to check in.

"I'm here. What's a number I can reach your friend on?" He asked.

Daniel gave him Matt's cell phone and office numbers.

"Can I trust these men, Daniel? This mess is causing me to do things I normally wouldn't consider." He paused momentarily, "I'm taking a huge risk here."

"Matt gave me his word, back last fall, when they wanted to meet you. This situation just adds to it." Daniel told his friend. "You have my word on that."

"All right then," was all Jon said in reply.

Reaching into his bag, Jon found one of the disposable cell phones Ben had packed for him. He punched in Matt's number. No voice changer this time. He planned to meet with them anyway.

"Hello? This is Matt Turlock," the voice answered.

"I'm a friend of Daniel Seay. He tells me you want to talk."

"Yes sir," Turlock stood from his desk chair. "I sure do. And Captain Stone, you've heard of him?"

"Daniel mentioned him, yes."

"Well, we both need your help with a situation here."

"Where can we meet? No offense, but somewhere in the open."

Matt thought for a few moments and then answered.

"Can you find Betty Virginia Park? It's off I-49." He told the man.

"I'll get a map. How long till you'll be there?"

"One hour ok with you?"

"See you there."

~

Oxford, Mississippi, had been overcast that afternoon. Representative Steven Wilcox, of the 12th District of Mississippi, was hosting a guest in Oxford. The guest was a nationally known senator from the state of New York.

Rep. Wilcox had recently made some statements, which ran against the grain of the people of his district. He needed some high profile help.

Immigration was again a hot topic in the country and the south in particular. The amnesty of 2011 had long since run out and a new group now demanded the same actions allowed to their predecessors. With unemployment creeping towards 13% from the standard 10.4%, opinion was running hard and fast against any further blanket amnesty.

In front of a friendly audience at the University of Mississippi, Wilcox had suggested he might support the senator's call for "acceptance" of these much-needed workers. Within a week, the calls to the representative's office and polls were highly opposed to his stance. The senator, his ego swelled by the stature the national press accorded him, had come down to lend his standing and prominence to try and shore up what little support the local representative had left.

As the two walked from the host's offices towards a rally being held on campus, a lone figure lay prone on a large magnolia limb, some 8 feet above the ground and 375 yards away.

The first round from the Winchester 308 struck the representative on the right shoulder, near his neck. Impacting the man's collarbone it then glanced slightly upward as a ricochet. That angle carried it directly into the senator's head behind his left ear.

Both men fell instantly as the second round missed and struck a mortar joint in the building behind them.

The man in the tree lay still as the initial panic and chaos subsided. Leaving the weapon in the tree with a note, he slid quietly away through the heavy brush around the tree.

There were no prints on the weapon and the identifying numbers had been filed away. The note simply read, "The Son has spoken."

Within the hour, news of the event was on all media.

~

Juan Castrono would not hear of the assassination until he got to his hotel room in Shreveport. This news added to his confusion because the mention of "The Son" meant the face in the crowd at the airport could not have been the assassin. He rubbed his face and thought out loud, *Spirits, bad spirits haunt this job.*

The meeting in Hopewell had been cut short by a phone call Dewey Hanson received. The "family" had learned of the massacre near Shreveport and believed their youngest was indeed one of the victims. Hanson made note of the orders he was being given as the others stood in shocked silence. His slight stature became lost in the group that surrounded him. Juan heard Hanson repeat the name "CCCY" as he wrote it down. One older man there grimaced, the rest had not yet heard of the Russian gang.

Juan's orders were the first to be issued by Hanson.

"Get down to Shreveport and arrange for 50 men coming in from all directions."

These men would not be drug mules. They would be warriors. The family was about to wage a war.

Juan was to find a suitable building to house everyone for a few days, then relay the locations through the channels and wait for the arrivals. The men would know what to do. Juan didn't need to worry about that, just find them a place to get organized, eat and sleep till the "go" signal was sent.

Where do I start? He thought. *I've never done anything like this, or this fast.*

~

It was raining harder in Dalton, Georgia. Daniel had talked with Lori, alone, and had gotten her to go upstairs where she finally gave into exhaustion and took a nap. The night before had not been kind to any of them. Fatigue added to the gloomy weather that was working on everyone.

Gil sat with Daniel by the front windows on the main floor and looked out at the rain and the clouds. It was quiet, both outside through the thick glass and where they sat. They had nothing much to say.

Ben was downstairs in the computer room. Without fanfare, he had called George Vincent to bring him up to date. George and Ben's mother, Doris, were engaged. Besides that, they worked together, he the local D.A and she as an assistant. It was Doris' investigation into Argus that had brought the Dalton connection into clarity. That clarity included Charles Harley.

George understood the potential danger this reemergence of Argus meant to all of them. His home was well protected so he opted that he and Doris would stay there, for the time being. Ben trusted George's judgment and said he was sure Jon would as well.

Ben dug into planning and going through printouts of weapons, looking for items he wanted to buy. There was added urgency on his latest project and the need for it to be perfect.

The total uniform was nearly done. He lacked only two pieces.

12

The front edge of the weather system effecting Dalton was just reaching Charlotte, North Carolina. It could have been the humidity pushing in or maybe just too much to think about. Either way, it had been a restless sleep period for Marsha Hurst. She rolled her head on the pillow and looked at her clock, it read 5:35PM. Her shift didn't start till 11:00PM and she didn't get up until 9:00PM.

Sitting up and stretching she noticed light coming from under the door. It was always there, but not normally an issue. Sleeping through the afternoons could mess with your body's clock. Her schedule was like anything else you have to deal with, you get used to it and go on. This was the first time, in a while, that she had trouble sleeping.

She couldn't get that warehouse out of her mind. Jon wanted to be there when it was searched, but now with this Shreveport escalation in the violence any info found could be vital and timely. *Who knew how long Jon would need to stay in Louisiana?* Other people could die by then and waiting wasn't an option. She made a decision.

If the shift starts out slow enough, I'll take a detail and go through it myself.

Her mind seemed to ease after that. Laying back down she rolled to her side and slept easy for the first time that afternoon.

Heck... I'm a cop. She smiled. *I can do this.*

~

The route to Betty Virginia Park was not as easy as it sounded. Still Jon arrived as he had hoped, early. The main parking lot led to a small concrete bridge as access to the park. Silas didn't care for that as either an entrance or hurried exit.

The side area had a little more promise. He parked near a ball field and slowly walked around, looking for a place to blend in and see who all showed up.

Blending in would be another issue here. There were picnic tables across from a kid's playground and larger, covered areas with more concrete tables off to the side. Everything was out in the open. One of the tables was off to itself, sort of private. It was not being used at the moment and looked like a good meeting spot. He figured that was where they would come.

The kid's playground was small and fenced in. There were five children playing and two adults standing outside the fence watching the kids. An empty bench sat just inside the play area near the gate. He would have a good view of the whole park and the table from there so he stepped into the playground and sat to wait. Before he even considered how foolish that idea was, it became obvious that one of the parents had noticed him. The man stared sternly; a loner sitting inside a kid's playground didn't look good, so that idea was abandoned.

Pretending to answer a cell call, Jon rose, nodded at the man and walked past the picnic table and across a small park road. This little park was becoming a frustrating place to hide and do what he needed to do. The man at the playground was still keeping an eye on him. *Don't really blame you, man,* Jon thought to himself.

The ball field now looked like the best place to wait, he shook his head and took a step in that direction. The grey sedan pulled into the park and eased to a stop on the small paved road. Two men got out. One was in uniform.

Well, they've got me if that's what they want. Jon thought. He froze but held his ground as the man in the suit slowly looked in his direction and took a step his way.

"I'm Matt Turlock," he said nearly shouting. "Are you here to meet me?"

Jon raised his right hand and meekly nodded his head. Turlock stepped across the road and reached out his hand to shake.

"Pleased to meet you, sir," he said. "Can we sit over here and talk?" pointing to the smaller picnic table. Matt continued talking, but Jon's attention was drawn to the other man, the man in the uniform. He had turned away from them and walked to the small picnic table as though there on his own. Positioning himself at one end, he never looked back at them as they approached. They met up with the uniformed officer at the table and sat down with him.

Jon couldn't help but glance around. There was no other activity, other than the kids on the playground.

"Daniel told you what we had here, right?" Turlock's voice registered with Jon at that point.

"He did," Jon responded.

The police officer sat directly across from Jon and stared down at the table, his hands out in front of him and the fingers of the right one silently drumming on the tabletop.

The voice sounds like him, the officer thought. *That man hiding behind the mirror back in Ohio.* Stone was not impressed by the secrecy then. Though he did try his best to understand it.

Jon thought he noticed the man glance up at him once, but barely. His attitude was indifference, almost not even paying attention.

I thought he wanted to meet me? Jon said to himself in silence. While shifting his position he noticed movement to his right and cut his eyes in that direction. It was two of the children leaving with their father, who still glared intently at Jon as they walked away.

Matt Turlock picked up on Jon's distraction and leaned back to look for himself. With a puzzled expression, he sat back forward and asked a question that was in line with the problem at hand.

"What makes you think there's more trouble coming?" Matt asked him.

"Like I told Daniel," Jon looked directly at Matt for the first time. "I have reason to believe Saul DeMarcos may be one of your unidentified victims."

That name DeMarcos struck a cord with the Captain and he looked up and spoke sharply.

"How can you be so sure of that?" he challenged.

Pausing for just a moment, Stone then leaned toward Jon and continued, "you haven't even seen the bodies and we haven't identified them yet."

Jon could see the officer's eyes, finally. They were squinted and intense. The face reflected distrust that Jon could understand and relate to. He liked that.

He gave Stone's question a few seconds to settle and then answered deliberately.

"That's all well and true, officer," Jon answered almost sarcastically. "But I came here straight from Kentucky." He knew that would give credibility to what he had to say next. "I found evidence that puts DeMarcos with the crew there and I figure there's a good chance it's the same group that came down here."

Stone looked hard at him for a moment and then the atmosphere seemed to clear up. He stuck his hand out toward Jon.

"Call me Phil, will ya? 'Officer' makes me uneasy. That's what the bad guys call me."

"Ok...Phil," Jon smiled a small smile as he took the man's hand. "Thank you."

"And what do I call you?" Captain Stone inquired.

Jon didn't show it, but he was stumped by the question at first. He had never been asked that before and had not considered a proper response. He wasn't about to divulge his identity just yet.

His mind ran a full circle and then he heard himself say,

"Call me Silas."

"Ok, Silas. What can you tell me about Argus and how they operate?"

Matt Turlock realized he had become a mere witness to the exchange as his long time friend and this new stranger discussed the violent situations that had already happened and the potential for more.

"Have you heard of the CCCY?" Stone asked.

"Not really, I understand they're Russians." Jon was ready to learn.

"The leaders are. The guy in charge is a diplomat; immunity and the whole nine yards." Stone leaned back a bit; his dislike of what he had just said was obvious. "The worker bees are from all over Eastern Europe. Mostly thugs with little to lose and very short tempers."

"From what I've heard, their 'work' is rather brutal." Jon stated, looking for confirmation.

"Fortunately we haven't had many examples, but yeah... real brutal. They keep their business so low-keyed and smooth there's not much need for muscle. We know they are here, we know what they do, but there's little sign of it so we have nothing to go after them on. Their reputation precedes them."

"Well, if I'm right, and I'm afraid I am, they're going to be drawn out and forced to fight." Jon said flatly. "The DeMarcos clan won't take lightly to one of their own getting cut up like you described."

There was an audible buzzing sound that came from one of Capt. Stone's pockets. He reached for a phone and glared at the text style message that appeared. Matt looked quizzically at Silas whose expression did not change. The officer twisted his wrist, checking his watch before he raised his eyes and looked directly at Silas. He shook his head before speaking.

"There's been a shooting in Mississippi. Some senator from New York is dead."

Matt pulled his own phone from his coat, "When?" he demanded.

"About an hour ago," he was still staring at the man, Silas. "A note was left at the scene claiming it was done by The Son."

Half through dialing his office, Matt put his phone down and stuttered,

"You don't think... that's not possible, Phil...he's right here."

"Relax, both of you." The cop barked.

"I'm fine," Jon said rather calmly. "I was afraid something like this would happen sooner or later."

Stone nodded his head and agreed. "Copy cats," he declared. "Once you let on with any facts they come out of the woodwork."

Matt was relieved. "So, you don't believe..."

"Of course not," turning his head to Matt, the senior cop was almost smiling. "Hell it ain't possible. Besides, this wasn't our friend's M.O. at all."

Jon remained silent, letting his two new acquaintances hash things over.

"Doesn't mean you won't catch blame and have heat on you." Stone cautioned as he looked back at Silas.

Jon slowly nodded. *Things were getting completely out of hand, but there was nothing to do except fight and work your way out of it.* He thought quietly.

"Can you tell me," Phil asked suddenly, "how did you do Harley?"

Jon, again, did not respond with any change of expression. He flatly looked back at the officer and stated, "I can tell you this. That man had a young reporter killed in Iowa. His gang nearly killed my neighbor and her son over their drug business and then he tried to murder our mutual friend, Daniel Seay." Jon changed his stare to Matt and then back to Phil. "He needed to be removed and he was."

"Ok, look...I'm sorry I asked," Phil Stone sounded sincere. "He's one I wish I had done myself, that's all. There should be a reward and a parade if you ask me."

"I don't talk about that stuff, not to anybody." Jon was firm.

"Understood. It's also understood you didn't have anything to do with this deal in Mississippi, but only by us." He paused. "That means you're gonna get pressure from it."

"Yeah, I know." Jon responded

Matt Turlock suddenly realized they were in a paradox. "We can't help him, can we? We can't be an alibi for him or anything. What do we do?"

"I think our friend here can deal with this himself, am I right?" Phil looked at Silas and waited for a response. Jon nodded his head before he spoke.

"I don't have much choice. Can't have this going on, it's bad for business."

"Any help you need," Capt. Stone dug out his wallet and pulled a card from inside, "you call me. I can help you from inside the department, nationwide. You understand?"

"I appreciate that Captain, I mean, Phil." Jon smiled. "I have resources of my own. But backup would be nice."

"I do hope you'll treat this local situation as the priority." Phil said as he altered his cheeks on the hard concrete bench.

"Absolutely, you could have a war on the way here. I can find this copy cat whenever."

Matt Turlock pulled a card from his pocket and added it to Phil's for Silas' collection. Jon nodded and stuck them both in a pocket of his jacket.

For the next half hour, the men traded info on Argus and the CCCY clans. It struck Jon that Daniel's perceived crime fighting group was coming together after all.

Jon didn't even realize how much he had learned about Argus until he was asked to share it. But with all that, he cautioned that this was different. They would be coming in, guns blazing, as they say.

"Normal procedures did not apply," he cautioned.

The CCCY reaction was fairly normal, as Capt Phil Stone explained it. For an event involving one of their own, quick, harsh and messy for all to see, was a trademark.

Jon would try to track down the Argus people and Stone would focus on the Russians, for now. Jon gave Phil a phone number to a special cell phone. That was about all they could do right then. Both needed to start looking around.

Matt made sure his office was on the Mississippi assassination story, but stayed with Phil and Silas till nearly dark.

"Anybody hungry?" he asked. "I'm buying, actually it's on the paper."

Jon Crane stood and put his hand up, out in front of him, "Next time, I've got a bunch to prepare for tonight and people to call."

"When do you think Argus will get here?" Captain Stone asked him.

"Oh, they're here," Jon answered. "At least one is and I bet more are not far behind. I'm thinking twenty, maybe more."

"I'll have patrols watch for gatherings and try to keep the kids off the streets. Any other ideas?" Stone asked.

Jon asked where the CCCY's Headquarters were. Phil told him and added his troops couldn't go in there because of the diplomatic status. The offices the Russian used were atop the building housing the consulate. His penthouse living quarters were one level below the seventeen story high, roof top area he used as his "office." Some of the space up there was enclosed, but most was open to the air. Torbof loved the outside air.

"I'm not tied down by your rules, Phil." Jon smiled wide. "I have that advantage. At some point, I may take a peek around there as well."

Stone smiled and shook his new friend's hand. "Long as I don't know about it," he laughed. "Just be careful, huh?"

"Always."

13

Ben sat in his workshop in the second sub-basement level and tested the strength of the new suit he had put together. Things like that kept his mind clear.

The suit was totally black and made from the same fabric as the first "seal team" unit. This one had a major difference. Firmly attached to the outside, yet nearly invisible, were flat tubes running down both legs and across the back in a web shape. They connected to the right arm mechanism, which was identical to the solo unit Jon had used before. Storage for the additional hydraulic fluid was held across the shoulders and down the back. A small pump, powered by flat batteries would increase the activation speed.

Extremely lightweight and flexible, this suit was, for all practical purposes, impenetrable. It offered added strength to the legs, not necessarily any running speed, but about 8 times the normal strength. Jon's natural quickness would not be hampered in any way and his agility would be heightened.

As Ben was completing the tests his private phone rang. It was Jon.

"Hey man, you doing alright?" Ben answered.

"Ben," Jon got right to his point as he usually did. "Did you tell me the hologram transmitters got there?"

"Yes, sir. They are here. Still in the boxes."

"The steel doors are up, and working, right?"

"I had that done last week while you were away."

The steel doors operated on heavy spring like hinges that caused the doors to spring open in an instant when needed. The exterior of the ones in the old garage were painted to look like stone.

That illusion did not hold up to close scrutiny, but the holograms would.

"Would you call Samuel and see if he can hook them up, like... yesterday? I'll pay whatever he asks."

"Ok, right away." Ben responded.

"And the visual cameras, to view the doors from the tunnel, get those in and connect the interface to our vehicles' touch screens."

"I guess you've talked to Gil, huh?" Ben suggested.

"Gil, no, why?" Jon didn't understand that question at all.

"You sound like you know about them being followed here last night."

"No," Jon's voice sounded hollow all of a sudden. "I didn't know that, though I'm not all that surprised. Everything ok?"

"Oh, yeah. They can handle this end fine. There's been no further sign of whoever it was. Gil and the guys are sharp, heck, you know that."

"Well, there's more than that going on. I thought it was what you were going to say."

"More what?" Ben asked him. "I've been down in my shop all afternoon."

"There's been an incident in Mississippi this afternoon and a claim it was me."

"Haven't been paying any attention to the news at all," Ben pushed against the table where he was sitting and propelled himself across the room to the TV sets. His rolling office chair spun as he grabbed a remote and hit the "on" button.

The assassination was being covered 24/7 by this point. He watched a couple minutes and got what Jon had been telling him.

"Crap, that ain't good."

"Not at all," Jon agreed. "That's why you need to get those cameras working. I don't know what all is going to happen... or when.

80

It's getting out of hand, Ben." Jon asked Ben to set up a program to collect all the stories about the Mississippi assassination.

"I don't know how you do it, but I'll want a listing of the unique aspects of the story and a timeline. I've got to play this mess out first, but I can't forget somebody claiming to be me out there." Jon's words were beginning to run together.

"I'm on it. How did your meeting go?"

"They were as Daniel described them," Jon meant that as a compliment, "about the best I could ask for."

"Anything else happen there yet?"

"Yeah, it's shaping up. I've seen signs of Argus moving in. In fact, I need you to do something else."

Jon asked Ben to tap into the airlines' passenger manifests for flights coming into Shreveport that day.

"Anything from the south or the east. You're looking for groups of Latinos, maybe four or more to a group."

"All flights?" Ben verified the request.

"Everything today, and I'll need what you can find in about 40 minutes."

Ben was already programming a system to do what Jon needed.

"I'm on it." He proclaimed again.

Jon gave Ben some words of encouragement before hanging up.

It sounded like things at the house were ok; everybody there was safe for the moment. That was one less thing to worry about. Now it was back to the airport for starters.

Ben set up Jon's request and then got in touch with their electronics techno geek. Samuel said he was on his way. Now he needed to tell Gil and the guys to expect Samuel without letting on why. That would be the hard part. Those doors were a secret, to everybody who didn't need to know.

Everyone in the house had, by now, heard of the killing in Mississippi. Only Lori so much as even appeared that she thought it might be Jon. Daniel quickly corrected her and she accepted it. That was not Jon's style and the senator from New York had never been on Jon's hot list.

Ben ordered in some burgers from a fast food place. That was about all anyone wanted. Food just didn't seem the priority, but they needed to eat.

Downstairs, the printers were spitting out lists and highlighting the groups Ben programmed for. Jon said he needed the info in 40 minutes.

Ben checked his watch, "Gil, I need to go back to my workshop for a while. Would you just let Samuel in when he gets here? He knows what to do."

~

Matt Turlock and Phil Stone split up about three blocks from the park. Capt. Stone had a pair of detectives pick him up and he got busy issuing orders for surveillance at flophouses, their club and other locations the Russians might congregate. He basically issued an All Points Bulletin on any unusual gathering that might be of a suspicious nature. It was hard to define, but his people knew what to look for.

Matt went back to the paper's offices to check on the work being done to cover the assassination story. As much as he wanted to soft pedal "The Son's" connection to it, he had to let the reporter's run with the story as they had it.

Nationally, that part of the story was hot. It had been several months since Washington and even though there was no evidence of foul play, the suggestion of it was discussed on TV and in the papers.

Time having run out on that story, the media were eager to pick up this new "confirmed" lead and run wild with it.

By morning local law enforcement, in all parts of the country, would be charged with searching for "The Son."

"This timing sucks." Matt thought. They needed Jon to be able to do his thing for them. A major drug war was on the horizon and now this.

~

A Greyhound Bus left Oxford, Mississippi at 7:42PM that evening. It was late leaving, as was most all transportation in the area that night, due to extensive screening of all passengers and cargo. A huge net had fallen around Oxford as authorities were seeking a killer trying to leave their town.

The bus was scheduled for Baton Rouge by way of Jackson, Mississippi. Initially traveling on two lane highways, the route would pick up Interstate 55 just north of Grenada, Miss. At the small town of Coffeeville, Miss. the driver noticed a soldier standing along side the road with his duffle bag. The man was waving for the bus to stop.

He told of his old car breaking down a few miles back and his need to get to New Orleans. The driver quoted the price for a ticket to Baton Rouge, as close as the bus would get to New Orleans. The soldier paid cash and went straight to the rear of the bus.

The driver had a strange feeling about his new passenger and radioed in to the rest stop in Jackson, Miss. for authorities to check the guy out when they arrived. He attempted to keep an eye on the man, but darkness and the location the soldier chose to sit made that impossible.

As the bus pulled into Jackson's terminal, the passengers got off in an orderly fashion through the watchful eye of several officers and Mississippi Bureau of Investigations Agents. No soldier got off the bus. The authorities climbed aboard and searched for stragglers.

They found the duffle bag, with the uniform inside it, but no one was on the bus.

An immediate lock down of the bus station proved too late. All the passengers in the terminal were ticketed from the Oxford station; the additional rider was nowhere to be found.

Two blocks away, an elderly woman, with a limp, transformed into a young male by removing her wig, glasses and tearing away the long dress to revel jeans and a tee-shirt. He unlocked the late model Chevy Malibu he had left there a day earlier and slowly drove south to Interstate 20 and then headed west.

14

The Shreveport Airport was a teaming mass of noise, lights and people. It was nearly 8:45PM as Jon Crane parked and headed inside the terminal building looking for a business center. A counter agent pointed the way and he found a fairly quiet room with a monitor and two fax machines.

Dialing Ben's number, he sat down and made a note of the fax number he was nearest.

"Have you got what I asked for?" he quizzed Ben.

"That and more." Ben was being cocky.

He gave Ben the fax machine's number and sat back to wait. Within minutes it started spitting out pages with flight numbers, times and passenger lists. Two flights were from Miami with three Hispanics each on board. Another from Orlando listed six Latino males and one from New York showed four aboard. A flight due in at midnight listed six more and one for 3AM would bring in four additional.

"Twenty-four by my count," Jon said into the phone.

"Yeah, but look at this one." Ben then sent a listing from the bus depot for a bus that came in from New Orleans. Twenty-two males with Hispanic surnames made up most of the passenger list. That bus had arrived in Shreveport just before dark.

"Nice thinking, Ben." Jon commented. "If these guys are all together, they're bringing in an army for sure."

"Oh, and Sam's here." Ben injected. "He went down to the station end to start there."

"Good," Jon was pleased. "Thanks for handling that, too. I'll talk to you later."

Jon pulled his ID indicating he was with the ICE, Immigration and Customs Enforcement, and took two of the printouts to the car rental line. He inquired about Hispanic males renting vans at times shortly after the arrival time of the flights Ben had found. At his second stop he hit pay dirt.

There were four vans rented to Hispanic males that afternoon. Two for the times he had on paper and one that matched up with a flight earlier. The last one listed the renter as a Juan Castrono from Atlanta, Georgia. His arrival was around the time Jon's flight had gotten in.

So... Juan, Jon smiled to himself. *We have a name.*

Leaning very officially over the counter, Jon asked the rental agent if the vehicles had Global Positioning Satellite, GPS systems in them.

"Yes, sir." The agent declared proudly. "All our cars do."

"I'll need the VIN numbers of these vans. Right away, ok?"

Vehicle Identification Numbers are unique to the vehicle it is assigned to.

The agent went into a back office and sat at his computer. Jon looked around and checked his watch again. It was 9:20PM. Marsha would be up getting ready for her shift. He would have to call her later, *too much going on right now,* he told himself.

The rental agent came back with four VIN numbers and Jon thanked him, for the department of course, and headed back toward the business center room. He pulled Phil Stone's card from his pocket and dialed the number.

"You've got Stone...go." The voice said.

"Phil?" Jon asked.

"Yeah, is this Silas?" Capt. Stone was curious to hear from him this quick. "What is it, man?"

"Can you locate a vehicle through its GPS unit in this area?"

"Sure can," the Captain replied. "I'll need a tag or better yet, a VIN number."

"Have you got something to write on?" Jon asked him.

Stone pulled a pad from his pocket and answered, "Go."

The man he knew as Silas gave him four Vehicle Identification Numbers and then became quiet.

"Ok, what have we got here?" The officer asked him.

"I have reason to believe," Jon told him. "Those might well be our DeMarcos "army" vehicles, so I'd be careful and not approach them just now if you find them."

"Nice work," Phil was impressed. "I'm not even going to ask how you got this info."

"Thanks. You wouldn't want to know. Call me if you find 'em, please."

"Oh, yeah. I'll get my people right on this."

The reply he heard was Silas hanging up.

Interesting guy, Stone thought as he looked at his notes.

~

Samuel Atterson had helped Jon with his computers and cameras for a year or more. He was intrigued by the holographic cameras, but had learned not to ask questions. With his own high definition, digital camera, he took several pictures of the rock walls inside the rear of the old gas station.

Mounting the projectors at the correct angles he then loaded the images from his camera into the projector unit and turned it on. The heavy steel doors that sealed the tunnel were now obscured by the image of real rocks. Sam adjusted the edges until he was happy with the bland from real to hologram. The image did not give off its own light, but rather reflected what light was present, much like the actual stone would.

He connected the power to the long life back-up generator purchased for this job. It would work and store electricity and should power fail, would operate the image and the doors for over a full day on its own power.

Standing back, Sam was proud of his work. Now he was off to set up the visual cameras that would be seen from Jon's vehicles as he approached the doors.

~

Capt. Phillip Stone arrived at his office to be met by an obviously excited young officer.

"Sir, those VIN numbers you wanted scanned, we found all four."

Stone wasn't really too surprised, given the source of the information and the reputation that came with him. The veteran officer stepped around his desk and looked at the man with the note in his hand.

"Ok, where are they?" He asked.

"All in the same place, the same hotel downtown."

The trace had found the four vans at the Eldorado Casino. An exclusive hotel and casino complex located downtown and right on the river.

"Besides those you asked about, we sent an unmarked car to look around. They listed three other rental vans also there. That's seven, nine passenger vans."

"How many rooms are rented to this group?"

"Boss, they are not even trying to hide. One guy paid for all the rooms, the whole top two floors really, for three days."

"Did you get a name?" Stone asked.

"Juan Castrono out of Atlanta." The young man replied.

"Ok, get surveillance on the whole place. I want to know the minute they move, that's a mass move, not just two or three. Understand?"

"Yes Sir. Right away, Captain."

Phil Stone sat down, brought a program up on his computer and checked some numbers he had filed away. Then he pulled his cell phone from his pocket and dialed.

"Yeah." Jon answered as Silas.

"Well, you were right. I suppose you knew that." Stone said smugly.

"You found the vans?"

"Oh you bet, those and a few more. They've got the entire top two floors of our most exclusive hotel booked for the next few days."

"Do you have a headcount of how many are here?" Jon asked.

"No, not really. There's 35 total rooms on those floors so it could be that many or more if they doubled up...could be a bunch."

"Three days, huh?"

"Yeah, and there's something else you need to be aware of." Stone advised him. The Russians operate their own nightclub here; it's called Igor's Manor. It's four blocks from the Eldorado and both buildings are on the river."

The Red River swings through the city heading south towards the gulf. The highest priced property in the city was along the river.

Jon asked another question, "You think they are going to hit them at that club?"

"Where else?" Stone offered. "It would be a matter of timing. I'm sure they want to catch as many in there as they can. If it was me, I'd watch the place for a day or two...make that a night or two."

"What's your plan?"

"We've got the hotel bottled up. When they move in mass, we step in and shut them down. Until they do something, we really can't touch 'em."

"When they do move, they'll be armed to the teeth." Jon added.

"That's what I figure. Probable cause, my friend, that's what we call probable cause."

"Do you think I have time to get some sleep? My day started in Kentucky and that seems like last week right now."

"I'm betting they won't move till tomorrow night at best, you get some rest."

"Talk to you in the morning." Jon hung up with that and looked at the time. It was 10:15PM and he had not talked to Marsha yet.

~

Lt. Marsha Hurst was just about to leave her home for work when the phone rang.

"Well, I thought you weren't going to call tonight." She faked being upset.

"Busy evening. What can I say?"

"I guess so, since you've added being in two places at once."

"You've heard, huh?"

The Mississippi Assassination was "the" story on all the stations, especially with the Son label attached to it.

"What do you plan to do about that? You can't let that stand, can you?" Her voice let on that she was more upset by the allegation than she first thought.

"No, you're right, I can't let it stand, but there are more important issues down here to deal with. Big issues, I'm afraid."

"Did you meet with Daniel's friends?"

"Yeah, I think I can work with them. It's just, the numbers keep getting bigger and bigger. How many people need to know about me and who I am?" He was quiet for a second, but then added, "I like things as they were. I don't like change."

"It will all settle down, Jon. You know the only constant is change. Remember me? I was a change in your life. You just have to decide where you are really needed and invest yourself there. You have to face the change."

Jon had no comeback for all that. He knew he was just whining, so he let it go. She was right after all, he never whined at all...not to anyone, till she came into his life. Things were pretty much the same, fundamentally. It was just a few basics of that, which were different.

Marsha thought about telling him her plan to go ahead and check the abandoned warehouse, but decided he would only worry. If they found anything of value, then she would tell him. If not, he need never know.

"Well, you get some sleep, you sound beat. I've got to get to the precinct." She tried to be official.

"Yeah, ok. I'm checked into my room here. I think I will crash for a while." There was an exchange of sweet nothings and then Jon said "good night."

She muttered something into the phone that made Jon blush and then she hung up. He looked down at the phone in his hand and smiled. He thought he was too tired to smile, but she had made him do so. His plan was to get a shower, order something to eat and go to bed. He sat down on the edge of the bed with the phone still in his hand. Without thinking he laid back and was "out" before realizing it.

He would stay that way until the phone rang again.

15

By 12:20AM that night, Samuel had all the cameras set up and ready to test. He sought Ben who was still in his workshop.

"Can we do a run tonight or do you want to wait till Jon gets back?" Sam asked Ben.

Ben smiled a wide grin and walked over to Jon's desk in the work area. He opened a bottom drawer and pulled a set of keys. Holding them up at Sam, he declared,

"Let's go."

They went to the elevator and rode to the lowest level, the third sub basement. The lights came on as they stepped onto the floor. Ben pointed to the Jeep parked in one of the stalls. The floor around the sidewalls had been "cleaned up," but some rock dust was still apparent. The steel doors were closed and Ben went over to sweep up some more as Sam connected the monitor in the Jeep.

As Ben climbed into the Jeep, Sam pointed to the main switch for the new unit. The screen lit up with a view of the opposite side of the doors and the tunnel, all was clear. Ben pushed the green light on the screen and the doors opened.

He looked at Sam who was quiet, though his grin was loud. Ben cranked the Jeep and pulled into the tunnel. He took it slow this first trip. Ten yards into the tunnel the view screen changed to a view outside the old gas station.

The road was clear, both ways and the interior of the station was empty. As they got closer to the station end, two more green lights came on and sensors on the front bumper activated. If anything came into view on the cameras, the view screen lights would become red and the vehicle would automatically brake to a halt. With nothing in view, the Jeep moved forward and tripped a switch in the steel doors with its sensors.

The door snapped open in a second and the Jeep emerged through the holographic image of solid rock. Ben turned hard right onto the highway and they drove down toward the house. Behind them the steel doors closed, but the image was of a rock wall.

They turned around in the driveway and went back toward the station. As the Jeep got to within a hundred yards of the station, the view screen in the vehicle lit up with a view of the station and the back wall. The two green lights again came on and would do so from this side provided there were no obstructions picked up.

This part took a bit of faith. Through the windshield, that back wall looked like rock. With the green lights both on, Sam said to go through. Ben aimed the Jeep straight thru the station's service bay and right at the back wall. They emerged in the tunnel with fifty yards of space to angle to the left toward the sub basement entrance.

Back in the basement with the doors closed solidly behind them, Sam looked at Ben.

"Well, what do you think?" He asked.

"Man, that's the coolest thing I've ever done. Jon is gonna love it. It's exactly what he described." Ben looked at the stalls for all the vehicles and added, "you've got the screens in all these, right?"

"Yep, those and two extras. Jon wanted two spares I guess. They are on the work bench."

They parked the Jeep and slapped each other on the back, laughing as they went back upstairs. In the kitchen they ran into Gil who asked what they had been up to.

"Just testing some new equipment." Ben quipped as he walked Sam to the door and thanked him. He wished he could tell Gil or better yet, show him. But Jon would not approve of that. That would be up to him.

Gil handed him a cell phone he had found in the kitchen.

"This thing rang for you a few minutes ago. I couldn't find you and they wouldn't say what it was about."

The phone was one of the many private numbers he and Jon had set aside for special contacts. He looked at the phone and asked Gil, "Who called?"

"They said they were from the Charlotte PD. That's all they would tell me."

~

The Shreveport Police Department had set up surveillance totally surrounding the Eldorado. Patrol boats even expanded their numbers and routes along the river.

Phil Stone made a personal trip to the area before he went home for the night. Everything looked normal, with the exception of all the white vans parked in mass in the parking lot.

They might as well put out a sign. Stone thought. *Amateurish for a group like this.*

~

Roll call for the overnight shift at Charlotte's 9th Precinct went smoothly and the desk sergeant reported to the Lieutenant, his watch commander, that the patrols were dispatched and all was good.

"Thank you, sergeant." Lt. Hurst responded and then asked him if there were two or three detectives available for a special project. He checked his book and answered that there were.

"Have them meet me in the motor pool in ten minutes." She ordered.

The drive to the warehouse district took 20 minutes and the two unmarked cars of the Charlotte Police Department pulled in and weaved their way back to building number 425. The power was off to that set of buildings so the big flashlights were in order.

Marsha cut the yellow tape across the door and unlocked it. The echo within was very apparent and that indicated the building was basically empty.

"I'm looking for a note, a piece of paper, anything that might tell us where they've been or where they might have gone." She told the others. They spread out and slowly walked every inch of the warehouse.

They found a torn lottery ticket and a crumbled, empty pack of cigarettes with a Georgia State Tax stamp on it. The lottery ticket would later prove to be from Georgia as well. No big revelations in either.

They had spent nearly an hour searching when Marsha and one other officer stepped out to check the loading dock area. She noticed it was 12:46AM.

What at first sounded like firecrackers became evident it was much more. Gunfire and lots of it, sounded off in the distance. Some small caliber and others sounded quite large. It continued and got more frequent.

The Lt. grabbed her radio and called for back up as the other detectives emerged from the building and opened the trunks to retrieve what heavy weapons they had with them. Jumping back in the cars they drove in the direction of the noise.

Near the front of the industrial complex, three town cars sat with their lights directed on a building. One man at the vehicles opened fire on them as they approached. He held an AK47 and it raked the front of the lead Crown Victoria and broke through the windshield. The officers inside the car had ducked as they slid to a stop and popped the doors of their cruiser open. As the intruder with the machine gun fired at the passenger side door, the Crown Vic's driver stood and fired three rounds from his 9mm. Two found their target.

Next was almost a turkey shoot. The Russians came from the building one at a time, firing indiscriminately as they ran. The officers kept sights on that door and dropped them as they came out. Marsha counted five down when they heard the dock door slide open at their side.

Three rolled from under the partially open door and began firing. Now three others came out the main door together, also shooting wildly, as the explosion went off.

The concrete block walls bulged and two sections actually blew out leaving large holes. The steel roof rafters were shaken loose and several fell inward collapsing the roof. The men from the loading dock had been pushed by the force of the blast and fallen five feet into a truck well. The officer who had been with Marsha got up from behind his car's door and ran to the well with a shotgun and held the nearly unconscious mobsters where they were.

The officers from the second car had opened fire on the men who tried to run from the other door. The metal doorframe they had just run through had flown out in the blast and almost decapitated one of the bad guys. His partners, who had come out with him, both died of gunshots and effects of the blast.

As the backup units screamed into the area and surrounded the shattered building, the detectives looked for each other. It was then they first noticed that their leader was down.

16

From his room at the Eldorado in Shreveport, Juan Castrono was on the phone to Colombia. Tomas Vaga was on the other end and he was chewing hard on Juan's ear. Vaga was Sergio DeMarcos' personal secretary and the call from American Express had come in to him. He was not so upset about the $22,000 charge for the three days, but he did not like the extravagant appearance.

Juan explained that it was the best he could do on short notice for that many rooms. As they talked, Tomas calmed and realized the showy nature of the flashy casino was, in fact, in line with the statement the Cartel was trying to make. Loud and proud and do not get in our way.

He instructed Juan to use a different card for the food and other needs and that a delivery would be arriving for them at the bus depot on a 1:20AM bus from New Orleans. Juan understood what that would be, the weapons for the attack. He didn't know how the family got things through customs like they did, but he didn't care about the details. He really did not want to know.

After the phone call, Juan checked his in-room city directory to locate the bus station. He called four of the thugs to his room and gave them instructions and the keys to a van. It was already 12:45AM, Louisiana time, so he told them to leave.

The surveillance team watched the men get in to the van and pull away.

"Should we stop them?" Crackled a radio to the sergeant in charge of the stake out.

"Negative. Unit three...give 'em a two block cushion and follow, confirm?"

"Roger, one. Will do," came the response.

~

Ben hit redial on the cell phone and a man answered right away, "Charlotte PD."

"Sir, this is Ben Shaw in Dalton, Georgia. There was a call from there for me."

"Hold, please." Came back at him and the line became silent for a minute.

"Chief Pennington, who is this?" Resounded as the line opened back up.

"Sir, I'm Ben Shaw, I work with Jon Crane in Dalton, Georgia."

"Yeah, I need to speak with Mr. Crane, right away." The Chief commanded.

"Chief, Sir...he's not available right this minute... can I take a message?"

"Mr. Crane is on the notification list I have, you're not, son. Sorry."

Ben could feel his color draining as he pleaded for more information. "Is this about Marsha?"

"I can't say...wait...hold a minute, will you please?" The Chief asked.

Ben put his hand over the phone and looked at Gil. "Something's going on with Marsha. But he won't tell me." Now Gil's color began to change and he rubbed his chin.

The cell phone spoke again and Ben pulled it to his ear, "Yes, Sir?"

"Who did you say you were, son?"

"I'm Ben Shaw."

"Do you know George Vincent?"

"Sir, do I know him? Yes, yes Sir. I sure do."

"Contact him, right away. You need to get what he tells you to Jon Crane."

"Thank you, Sir." Ben responded. But the man had hung up.

The phone rang again as soon as it was cleared. It was George.

"George, what's going on?" Ben pleaded.

"Ben, you need to get a message to Jon right now, can you do that?" George sounded very serious.

"Yes, Sir." Now he was almost afraid to ask what the message was, but he did.

"Ben, tell Jon Marsha has been hurt. We don't know how badly. There was some sort of shoot-out at the warehouses there."

"Oh, no. She is alive?"

"Yes, but it's serious from what I was told. She's at the main Carolinas Medical Center. He needs to get there." George added another statement. "Ben, if you want I'll call him. Just give me the number he has now."

"George, I'll do it. I can do it. How is Mom?"

"She's upset about this, but she's fine. Just call Jon, Ok?"

"Yes, Sir."

~

The Chevy Malibu from Mississippi rolled into Texas around 4:25AM. It stayed on I-20 for another hour and then turned north toward Lindale. The trip had taken the copycat killer through Shreveport without anyone being aware of the coincidence.

Four miles off the interstate, he pulled the car off the road and into the dried field to his right. A van flashed its lights from about a hundred yards away. The Malibu driver returned the signal and turned the motor of his car off. As the van pulled along side, three other men jumped out and the group celebrated their success with high fives and some whooping and hollering.

"Damn man, it went perfect," one said to the driver.

"Didn't get him, but I got that other sanctimonious bastard."

The group gathered by a cooler in the van and each had a cold beer, then it was time to go to work. They pulled four concrete blocks from the van and a toolbox. Then several bales of dried hay were pulled and stacked to one side.

The Malibu was jacked up and placed on the blocks. The tires and wheels were removed and placed in the van. Most of the interior of the car was unbolted and taken out, as was the steering column and dashboard.

The hay bales were stuffed into the cavity of the Malibu and soaked with gasoline from the tank. As they cleaned up the area and swept the dirt, leaving no footprints or van tire tracks, they tied the brush piles behind the van and weighted them to stay in line with the vehicle's tires.

A wooded match was tossed as they drove away and the fire was quick and enormous. The van reached the paved road where they stopped to remove the brush piles and tossed them to either side of the roadway. The group then continued on through Greenville, Texas to their hometown of Whitewright.

The clubhouse, as they called it, looked to be an old storefront at the end of a long closed strip mall on the outskirts of the community. No markings decorated the exterior. But inside, the expressions of their inspirations were clear. Swastikas and an odd looking, homemade flag hung on the walls. Statements about Jews, blacks and Mexicans were written on the parts of the walls not covered by other garbage.

It was nearly daylight and the town would be up and about very soon. Not needing to draw attention to themselves, they left the van parked against the rear of the building and drove away in their own separate vehicles.

~

The patrol car following the truck in Shreveport radioed into the control headquarters only 20 minutes into the accompaniment.

"Sir, these guys pulled over and are putting signs on the van."

"Yeah? What kind of signs?" Came the reply.

"They say Newhouse Funeral Home in Homer, Louisiana."

"Interesting," the watch leader answered. "Stay back and let this play out."

"Oh, sir?" the officer continued.

"Yeah?"

"My wife is from Homer. There ain't no such funeral home there."

"Didn't expect there was, but thanks for the confirmation. Just keep an eye on them."

"Roger that."

The Hispanics looked around and climbed back into the van. They drove north to Fannin Street and turned into the bus station there. The patrol car cut its lights and rolled into a vacant lot across the street. The officers watched as the men from the van were approached by two more Latinos who were each carrying two large bags. Those were loaded into the car while yet a third new member of the group came from within the terminal accompanied by a bus line agent.

A transport truck with the bus line's name on it was opened and helpers pulled two coffins from within. The van moved closer and the coffins were loaded, paperwork signed and all six Latinos jumped into the van and headed back to the Eldorado.

"Lieutenant," the radio proclaimed," they are coming back your way, Sir."

"What's going on, what happened?" the leader asked.

The patrolman explained what he and his partner had just witnessed and the watch commander replied with but one word. "Weapons."

17

Ben stood with Daniel and Gil and all three looked at the cell phone in Ben's hand. He had not yet called Jon. It had only been a few minutes, maybe 20 or so, but he had been trying to get more information before he contacted his friend.

He called the hospital in Charlotte, but they would only tell him she was "critical" and would not go into any details about what the injuries were or anything else. Ben scrolled down the phones listed numbers to Jon and was about to push the button when a car horn sounded just outside the garage.

Gil pulled his service issued 9mm and opened the door. It was George Vincent.

He had Doris with him and handed Ben her small suitcase and started issuing orders.

"You've talked to Jon?" he asked.

"I've been trying to get something to tell him, George. I haven't been able to and was just about to make the call."

"I understand," George put a hand on Ben's shoulder. "Tell him I'm on the way with the G5. I called and have it waiting for me right now. Figured he'd want to get over there right away."

Ben nodded in agreement and asked George to wait one minute, "I've got a bag he may need, let me grab it."

Within two minutes Ben was back from his shop with the bag. George didn't ask what it was. He simply took it, smiled at Ben and turned to go.

Ben flipped his cell phone open as George walked out and backed his car down the drive. As the headlights disappeared, he hit the button to dial.

The phone rang nearly a dozen times before a not quite awake Jon Crane answered, "this better be good." He wasn't kidding.

"Jon... Jon are you awake? Can you understand me?" Ben pleaded.

"What?" Jon could tell from the tone things were not all right.

"Jon, Marsha's been hurt. We don't have details, but she's in the hospital in Charlotte."

"Hurt? What happened?" Jon demanded and sat straight up.

"I don't know, something about a shootout there."

"Call my plane..."

"Jon, its on the way, George is handling that and he's already enroute."

There was silence on both ends as the two tried to compose themselves and think what to do next. Jon could feel his brain slamming against the inside of his skull and his stomach crawled up into his throat. *Is this fear?* He thought to himself. He had been concerned for others before, obviously. But this was worse. This was way beyond anything.

"Ok, Ben..." he finally spoke.

"Yes, Sir?" Ben snapped back quickly.

"I need to make some arrangements here. How long till George gets here?"

Ben looked at Gil who mouthed, "about two hours at most."

"We're thinking they should be there in two hours." Ben relayed.

"Call him and tell him I'll be at the private terminal, ready to go, and give him this number."

"Are you ok?" Ben asked.

"I'll be better when I find out how she is."

The phone went dead and Ben looked at his friends there.

"We need to consider what happened to Marsha as another potential threat to us."

Gil nodded and walked toward his two men, "this just keeps getting better and better." He was being sadly sarcastic.

~

In his dark motel room, Jon tried to clear his head. He took a hot shower and made a pot of motel room coffee. When the cobwebs were gone he checked the time. It was after 3:30AM in Shreveport, George and the plane would be at least another hour and a half. He hated to bother anyone at this hour, but someone needed to know he was leaving.

Dialing the number for Capt. Stone, Jon sat on the edge of his bed and sipped on the brown liquid in his cup.

Phillip Stone was awake. He had been apprised of the goings on with the Hispanic visitors only moments before. The call from Silas was not a surprise. In fact, he had considered calling him.

"Hello, this is Stone," he answered.

"Phil, Silas here. Sorry to bother you at this hour, I really am."

"Small world, I was just going to call you, but... you go first."

Jon started to ask what the officer meant by that, but his mouth clicked into gear with its prepared statement, "I've got to leave town for a bit. A dear friend has been hurt."

Stone seemed genuinely concerned, "I'm sorry. Must be serious for you to pull away from this."

"My friend is a police Lieutenant in Charlotte, North Carolina. I don't know what's happened, but she's hurt pretty bad. They said something about a shootout."

"She, huh?" his comment indicated he understood. "Is this connected... to our stuff here?"

"I really don't know, Phil. Hell, it could be...I just don't know yet." Jon stood and walked across the room, one hand on his

104

phone and the other rubbing his forehead like it ached. "What's going on that you were going to call me about?" he asked the officer.

Stone told Jon about the report he had received. The two coffins and the large bags with the three additional men at the bus station.

"Their armory is here," said Jon.

"You got it."

"What are you going to do?"

"Well, the weapons weren't unloaded from the van when they got back to the hotel. I don't think I can afford to let them do that. We're going to move in right before dawn and take them down, the van first of course. If we're wrong about the contents we look pretty foolish."

"Good, I agree and you really don't need me for that."

"How can I help you, Silas?" Phil asked him.

"I don't know if you can, but thanks."

"We work together, you know, the different departments. I can ask for some professional courtesy for you on my behalf."

Jon was quiet for several seconds. That offer might be useful, especially with Marsha out of commission. George would be there, but an active homicide Captain probably carried a bunch of weight. This type of clearance was very helpful in Kentucky and he would need it now more than ever. This could be an escalation of the war, who knew?

It would mean Stone having his real name. The cops in Charlotte all knew Jon Crane was Lt. Hurst's friend, some remembered he was connected to that reporter's rescue. Beyond that, the name meant nothing else. For Stone to help he would also need to know Silas' real name. Could Jon risk that? As he ran through all the questions in his mind, Stone spoke up.

"Look, Silas. I understand that's just a name you use, I mean, seriously, I do this for a living. If you need my help that's all you'll get.

No interference or problem about anything else. You have my word on it, and believe me…I don't understand why, but I mean that sincerely."

There was quiet while the cop tried to find the words to explain himself and then Stone spoke again, "I made my mind up about you and what you did some time ago. There are rough edges out there we all want cleaned up, but the law gets in our way. I don't see you as the stories describe; to me, you're just cleaning up the edges and some of those edges pass as human."

The sincerity in Capt. Phillip Stone's voice came through. Jon made a decision to move forward, adding one more soul to his list of the reliable. The decision sent a sense of calm through him. The issues had been piling up and becoming a huge weight, but there was also a growing number of those willing to help.

He had known the comfort of solitude and kept his faith in it, but solitude had its limitations. Those gaps were becoming more and more obvious.

In the nanoseconds that were this thought process, he remembered his studies of the revolutionary heroes. Exposure of their identity could and did mean death, yet they learned to trust others to insure their mutual success.

Daniel's ideas were closer to being right than he had realized. But he would take it slow and respond only when he was reasonably sure.

"Thanks Phil, I have to trust you, too. You're too straight not to be honorable." He paused again and then added, "You can tell them Jonathan Crane of Dalton, Georgia is coming." He explained that they know the name, but only as Marsha's good friend.

"I would appreciate any courtesy you could convince them to extend. Marsha Hurst, Lt. Marsha Hurst is very special to me… and I will find out what happened to her."

"I'll clear the way best I can." Stone assured him.

"You guys be damned careful here, too." Jon warned, remembering what he was leaving unfinished, "they'll have more than what's in those coffins on them."

"That's what we figure. We're taking steps to make this go really smooth." Then the cop added one more thought before hanging up, "God's speed... Jonathan Crane." He said deliberately. "I hope your Lieutenant is alright."

18

Room 314 at the Eldorado was one of four single rooms in the block that Juan had rented. He was there, quite alone, when the phone rang at 5:05AM. It was the room phone, not one of his cell phones...the room phone. After several rings, Juan answered.

"DH, 147332, C 3, now," in a woman's voice, repeated three times.

It registered with Juan what was going on with the last repeat and he wrote down the numbers. They were serial numbers for one of the cell phones Dewey had given him to take to Louisiana.

He found that numbered unit and pushed auto dial number three. Dewey Hanson answered on the first ring.

"Juan, I need you back in Georgia," he proclaimed loudly.

"Georgia?" Juan was confused. "What's going on?"

"Look, everything down there is going fine. Carlos checked in earlier. They have the cargo, they found the location and the job will be done tonight," he told Juan. "I told him I needed you back in Georgia because of something else I've been watching."

Juan Castrono asked again, "What is it?"

"Since the hit, and I know it was a hit on Harley and then the Colombians made me the boss here, I've been keeping an eye on that reporter from Pittsburgh. He ain't the guy that's killin' guys like me. But he's connected with who is. I can feel it."

Juan still didn't understand.

"Look," Hanson continued. "I've had a tail on that reporter since last fall. When the Colombians sent Dario to Kentucky and that news got out, that reporter and his wife were out of Pittsburgh like a covey of quail. They flew in a private jet to Dalton, Georgia. Do you know where that is, Juan?"

"Si', uh yes Sir. I know where Dalton is."

"Anyway, I had another crew follow him to some big house just outside of town there. They went in and haven't come out."

"Ok? So what's happening now?"

"An hour ago, the local DA drove up to that house, dropped off some lady and picked up a bag. He drove to that local airport and jumped on a waiting Gulfstream Jet. A friggin' G5, my guys think. DA's from Georgia don't travel in G5's, Juan. I can tell you that."

"Alright. Now what?" Juan pressed.

"I ain't waiting around for that killer to come get me. That DA is in on this too. I think he's going to pick up this guy, whoever, and that great big house must be his.

The name on the papers for the house say something about a Liberty Tree Company, but I had my guy dig deeper and the name Jonathan Crane came up."

"Jonathan Crane?"

"Yeah, that's the killer. It has to be. I've got a specialist coming to Georgia to deal with him."

"A specialist?" Juan repeated.

"Yeah, I'm hittin' this guy before he hits me, ya got it? You're going to make sure this specialist has what he needs. You pick him up at the Atlanta Airport in four hours."

"Four hours? Boss, how...?"

"There's a cab on the way for you now," Hanson checked his watch, "you've got 10 minutes to be down in the lobby and your flight to Atlanta is booked. Don't say anything to Carlos or anybody, you hear? This is my deal and it's off the grid."

"Si, ...huh, yes, Sir." Juan muttered as he grabbed for his clothes.

"Get my boy to Dalton, Georgia. He'll do the rest."

Juan barely made it to the lobby as the cab pulled in. The stake out squad did notice the Hispanic man leaving and radioed in for instructions.

They were told to let him go. The raid was scheduled for 6:10AM. The rest would be taken down then and it was too close to time to bother with one guy getting away.

~

The Gulfstream G5 touched down and taxied to the service facility to refill. George pushed the door open as Jon was walking up.

"You didn't have to come, man." Jon greeted his friend.

"Right, I'm sure you're surprised to see me. Her dad was a dear friend for many years, she's important to me too." George let Jon climb aboard and find a place for his bag before he continued, "how are you doing?"

"I don't like this, George. I don't like people I care about getting hurt." Jon looked directly at George. "It sounds so stupid, like I think other people have a hold on stuff like this, but I don't know how to act."

"I understand, Jon. Believe me."

"Do you have any more details on how she is?" Jon asked.

"No, they won't say over the phone. We should be there in a few hours, you look like you should try to sleep."

Jon grimaced at George, but agreed with him. He stretched out on the sofa that was almost long enough. The feel of the leather made up for what it lacked in length.

The ground crew had the jet checked and refueled and the pilot had filed his flight plan. As they buckled in for take off, George pointed to the bag Ben had sent.

"He thinks you might need that stuff, I didn't even look."

"If Ben sent it," Jon shook his head, "it will come in handy."

As they screamed down the runway, the little jet caught the eye of another early traveler. Juan Castrono tried to trot toward Gate Twelve and his flight to Atlanta. The airport was nearly full, "even at this ridiculous hour," he muttered aloud. The small Gulfstream lifted and soared away from sight.

That's the way to travel, he thought. *First class all the way.*

~

The large task force assembled two blocks over from the Eldorado in Shreveport at 5:40AM. Team leaders gathered around Capt. Phillip Stone for instructions. Dressed all in black with vests and headgear they appeared to be a SWAT unit, but only a few of the officers were actually SWAT team members. They gathered in and around the used cars on the lot they now occupied getting as close to their leader as possible.

From his vantage point, standing in the bed of a used pick-up truck, Stone's attention was drawn to an unmarked car pulling up and a high-ranking officer easing out from it and walking intently towards him. It was Chief of Police Bill Henderson.

"What have you got going on here, Phil? Starting a little war?" the Chief asked sarcastically.

"Taking down some bad guys, Bill. This is my call, ok?"

"You need the whole department to take down some bad guys? Christ, Phil what's the deal here?"

"I've got a hunch, boss. That's all I can tell you." Stone retorted, "and it ain't the whole department, it's ninety three, not counting me."

"Ninety three! Jesus H... Phil, you know the budget hassles I'm already having. You need this much manpower to take down some gangsters?"

"Bill, I told you, I've got a hunch." With that Stone leaned down and looked right in his longtime friend's eyes, "if I'm wrong you can put the heat on me, but you owe me this hunch and more."

The Chief and his Captain stared at each for nearly half a minute. Bill Henderson turned suddenly and headed back to his car. Over his shoulder he fired one last shot, "you bet I will. Be careful out here...all of ya."

As the head of the department left the scene, Captain Stone pointed to one of his Lieutenants.

"Give me a four man team to check out that van," Stone ordered. The van in question was the one with the coffins from the bus station. The squad moved down the street in complete quiet. Reaching the van, they verified its contents visually and then used heavy bars to open the rear doors. It only took two minutes for them to signal they had weapons and the raid was a go.

Stone stepped up on the wheel well cover so that everyone could see him.

"Check your own weapon and pull your badge and ID out where it can be seen." He looked at the three Lieutenants awaiting his command and could not help but think about the injured friend of Jon's in Charlotte. A silent and quick prayer ran through this tough veteran's mind, *Lord, protect these good people tonight,* before he leaned down to speak directly to them.

"Everyone knows what they are to do here?" he asked. "Especially if one of them comes out of their room early?"

Nodding their heads vigorously, each answered, "Yes, Sir."

Stone checked his watch and after a few seconds ordered, "Move out."

An officer motioned with his index finger and they all moved in unison. As they reached the hotel's grounds they separated into specific units. One group surrounded the building quietly and took aim at the staircases on both ends and in the middle. Some climbed to the second floor exterior landing and set up in position.

Seventy-seven officers entered the lobby and signaled for the attendants to stay quiet and calm. Stone grabbed a handful of pass key cards and handed them out to the officers.

All elevators were brought to the main floor and locked open there. The interior stairs were spotted at each floor and two men per room walked down each hall. They walked as though they were on eggshells, making no sound at all. On the fourth floor one early riser opened his door to retrieve the newspaper left for him. Before he could look up and tell what was happening, an officer grabbed him around the neck with one hand and sealed off his mouth with the other. The chokehold quickly rendered the man unconscious and the teams lined up outside each door.

At 6:10AM exactly, the strike team entered each room on the top two floors of the Eldorado at virtually the same moment. Of the forty-five men in those rooms, only nine pulled any weapon as their doors were unlocked and if needed, kicked open. Six of those fired at the officers and were all shot. Four were dead instantly and one died later at the hospital.

Stone walked the hallways and surveyed the work his troops had handled. He reached to his shoulder and keyed a radio.

"I need eight wagons and six ambulances, now," he barked. Not one of his people had been hurt in the least.

Good Job, he muttered to himself at first and then pulled the mask from his face and shouted out loud, "Great job, people. Great job."

A voice barked from his radio's receiver, "Captain, this is Lt. Broussard. You need to see what we've found here, sir."

"Where are you Broussard?" the Captain answered.

"Room 317, repeat, room 317."

Stone walked down the stairs and found 317 to be mid-way down the hall. His Lieutenant and four officers stood around a small closet. Beyond them lay the body of Carlos Morales.

A quick look at the scene did not make sense initially. Morales had been sleeping on the right side of the king size bed near the exterior glass doors, yet when disturbed by the officers he tried to jump to his left toward the closet. A Desert Eagle .50 caliber handgun was on the floor; his fingers still lay over the grip.

"He never fired the 'Dezzy'," the Lieutenant declared. "He was more interested in getting to this closet," he continued as he reached out with his arm, pointing to a bag on the closet floor.

Stone motioned for them to step back and he leaned into the closet. The flap on the backpack style bag had been pulled over, exposing a stack of C-4 blocks within. The way they were stacked it could have been eight or more blocks of the volatile explosive.

Something Silas had told him about these guys rang in his head.

Don't give them notice when you corner them, he had cautioned. *They like to blow themselves and any evidence sky high if they have the opportunity.*

"That bag could have taken this whole hotel out," the Lieutenant stated.

The Captain looked at him and smiled. Stone's worries about repercussions from his military style raid were now completely gone. *Jon was right about these crazy SOBs.* But no one could know about Jon. He could only say he had inside information that they might try something like this, but there wouldn't be much discussion. Not now.

"Get the bomb squad to clear this thing out of here. We'll need to evacuate the building till that's done." Stone ordered.

There were just four guests on the second floor who had heard any disturbance at all. They had called the front desk and were told all was ok. Now, the evacuation was on and police were knocking at each door, asking them to leave their rooms for a while.

The removal of the bomb was accomplished in an hour and breakfast for the hotel's legitimate guests was on the city of Shreveport.

In all, the raid itself only lasted thirty-two seconds. The threat was over, just like that. Captain Phillip Stone had another feather for his cap and though he could not give credit for his "hunch," he knew full well, the value of the information Jon had offered.

CSI was called in and task force dismissed. The clean up would take most of the day.

19

Murray Bilstock had moved to Caddo Mills, Texas, in the fall of last year. The town fit Murray's mood and the land prices suited his pocketbook. He could afford room for a few horses now and in time the cattle. The ranch house was livable, but it was just him most of the time and Murray didn't seek company that often.

His father, Senator Warren Bilstock, had been found dead on the family's huge ranch in Southwest Texas several months before. Some said Sen. Bilstock had been a victim of "The Son." Others, including Murray, clearly stated that any possible murderer simply beat them to it.

Daniel Seay had come to the Brownwood ranch early last fall. He was a real Johnny-come-lately investigative reporter, but with a twist in his search. Daniel was seeking a serial killer he believed to be targeting government officials. His frankness had led the Bilstock clan to share a dark secret about their father, one they had not verbalized before or since. Yet rumors can be powerful. Daniel had left Texas with compassion for the Bilstock family and a strange new angle on his killer theory.

Gossip about their father had driven their mother to leave the area they loved. She sold the massive ranch and split the profits among her son, her daughter, some to a close nephew and most to herself.

Murray's share enabled him to buy the medium sized ranch that needed all the work. He had negotiated with his mother to keep the Bell 407 helicopter the family had used on the big ranch. Murray was the licensed pilot in the family and he wanted it. The copter came in handy, hauling supplies to the new ranch and flying back to Dallas to check on his mother and sister when need be. Besides that, he liked it.

116

The town of Caddo Mills was effectively closed and deserted. Development wasn't happening here. It was a bit of deep southwestern Texas stuck out in the northeast corner just thirty-five miles from Dallas. The area resembled Brownwood, the town they had left and that appealed to Murray, but few others.

The cousin Stephen, known to family as Slick, came out to help now and then. But was mostly busy spending his share of the inheritance on girls and liquor.

Late the week prior, Slick had been to Caddo Mills to assist with a new fence line and while there shared some news he had picked up at a bar in Garland.

"Some boys were talking about a group they met up near Greenville the week before." Slick told Murray. "They were bragging about a job they were going to do and throwing the name "The Son" around. Wasn't that the guy that reporter was looking into last year?"

Murray became curious at the mention of "The Son." "Just who were these boys?" he asked.

"Just transient cowboy types," Slick explained. "I didn't talk to them myself, I just overheard the conversation, that's all."

"You know about Mississippi, don't you?" Murray challenged him.

"Naw, what about it?"

"Never mind," Murray couldn't see the use in an explanation. "I'll check it out."

He made a mental note of Greenville and later that afternoon put a call into Daniel's office in Pittsburgh. The call was immediately transferred to Bill White, editor of the Pittsburgh Post Gazette.

Murray didn't want to talk with anyone except Daniel, so White took a number and promised he would have the reporter call him. Bill White reached Daniel within ten minutes.

"Thanks, Bill. We can't say anything, I know, but this Mississippi deal is a copy cat."

"I kinda figured as much," White responded, "but I see your predicament."

"This Texas angle could be a lead on the copy cat. I'll get it to the right guy...when he has time. Things are a bit busy right now."

"Can I help?" his boss offered.

"Thanks again, but I don't even know what I can do."

"I understand. Stay safe and tell Lori I said 'hi'."

20

General Counsel Vasily Torbof was awakened early and it did not please him. The prior day had been spent planning his son's services and transportation back to Russia for burial. Sleep had not come easily for him or his wife that evening. To be disturbed at 6:45AM was maddening.

"Tell me they found them. The North Carolina people, nothing short of that will be acceptable," the counsel screamed into the phone.

"Sir, there's no word from them yet, but this may be bigger," the voice trembled.

"Go on," Torbof scoffed. "What is bigger?"

"There has been a big bust this morning at the Eldorado Casino. Many Latinos arrested and rumors of guns and bombs with them."

Torbof sat up on the edge of his bed, "Many? What is many?" he demanded.

"Over forty men in all, boss."

"Shit! I didn't think that cartel had that much juice left." He tried to hide his concern. *That's a small Army*...He thought, *what were they up to?*

Torbof told his caller to get as much in details as he could and report back later. His wife, awakened by the commotion, asked what was going on?

"Nothing, sweetheart," Vasily assured her. "Go back to sleep."

He rose, grabbed a robe and went up to his roof top offices. The sun was just coming up across the river and it was cool. If you weren't a Russian, it was cold.

Argus, he thought as he dug into his memory. *DeMarcos family out of Colombia.* He looked at a file box he took from a safe. *Cocaine, ah. Yes.*

The CCCY did not normally fool with coke. They preferred "H," heroin or even black tar if that was all they could get. They only began distributing cocaine when they believed Argus was wrapped up last fall. Somebody had to fill the hole left, *it might as well be us,* he had told himself.

Now his son, his pride and joy, was gone and this dead cartel had sent forty some-odd men to his town. He did not need a full-blown war right now.

"Why was this happening?" He now thought out loud.

Maybe he could reach out and stop this. He looked to see who he had listed as a contact for Argus. The notes showed Charles Harley's name scratched out and over it was written Dewey Hanson of Pennsylvania. There was no phone number, but that was easy enough to find.

He opened a cell phone and dialed his top aid.

"Leonid, I need you to find a phone number for me." Torbof barked into the phone. "A Dewey Hanson from Pennsylvania. Contact for Argus Imports."

The aid answered with a firm, "yes." The counsel folded his phone and walked to his favorite chair, a folding aluminum lawn chair, which he kept backed into one corner of the rooftop. He liked it, and he liked it there. The top of the chair barely reached the top of the slender brick parapet wall that surrounded the rooftop. It was a single course of brick above the floor line with a flat, angled cap serving as a ledge. A wall like that was not code, not by any measure. It was more decorative than functional and if the building wasn't its age, over eighty-five years, it would not be allowed. Yet Vasily liked his wall and his corner. His desire to sit in that corner was a "Wild Bill Hickok" tick in his personality. From there he could see and not worry about being snuck up on from behind. It was his spot.

The temps this early were in the low forties, but he bundled his robe around him and sat down to think. *How quickly these things get out of hand*, he lamented.

The sun started to flood the rooftop with warmth at that point, and it felt good. His head leaned to the back and left, and he fell asleep despite his thoughts.

~

The sensation of speed that transfers to the human body within a flying object that touches down is, for lack of a better word, jarring. George Vincent had fallen asleep sitting in one of the leather passenger seats on the G-5. The pilot greased it in, but suddenly there was landscape whizzing by the window and the sound of air rushing. His eyes flew open and it took him a moment to realize where he was and why.

George looked over to the sofa across the aisle from him; Jon was fast asleep and had been for most of the flight. Blinking furiously and rubbing his face to wake up, George let his friend sleep until they were near the private aircraft hanger and rolling to a stop.

"Hey...hey we're here," he reached and shook the sofa. Jon bounded to a sitting position and went through similar attempts to regain consciousness.

"What time is it?" he asked.

"9:50AM. We lost an hour coming east."

Jon's thought immediately went to Marsha, "Have you heard anything?"

"No." George reminded him there would be no real update over the phone. They needed to get to the hospital.

Jon signed the paperwork for the pilot who asked if he should wait in Charlotte for him.

"Thanks, but I don't think so. In fact I may need some more stuff brought up here, depending on what happens next," he replied.

The town car George had ordered was there so they loaded up the trunk, checked the GPS for directions and headed out.

Police vehicles were everywhere at the hospital.

"This must be the place." George quipped, but in a serious tone.

Marsha was in ICU on the fifth floor. Outside the room they met the doctor and Chief Pennington.

"She is awake," the doctor told them. "But she is confused right now." He pushed the door open and he, Jon and George walked in.

Marsha recognized George quickly and asked in very muffled speech, "Mr. Vincent, what are you doing here? Is Daddy ok?" Her eyes displayed her concern.

George looked to the doctor who motioned for him to play along right now. They knew the retired Capt. Hurst had died five years before, but what she did not need was confrontation.

"He's fine sweetie," George smiled at her. "How are you feeling?"

"My head hurts...a lot," she said. Her eyes turned toward Jon who was standing there quietly. Not knowing what to do.

"Are you a doctor?" she asked him.

Sheepishly he nodded in agreement and very slowly reached out to touch her hand. The doctor stepped in before Jon got to her and looked firmly at him. "Let's go outside," he spoke evenly and softly. "She needs to rest some more."

Once in the hallway the doctor directed Jon and George to a private office where they could talk.

"I know how difficult this is right now," he spoke directly to Jon. "But we feel it should pass in a few days."

122

"What happened to her?" Jon asked.

"She got hit in the head by a flying piece of concrete block. Luckily, it really just grazed her. The damned thing could easily have killed her right there."

Jon's face was completely pale when they sat, but the thought of someone doing that to her made his blood boil. The doctor noticed and returned to his explanation of her condition.

"She has a severe concussion and a form of retrograde amnesia." The doctor paused to allow any questions the men might have. Neither said anything, they clearly needed more information.

"Your visit has helped us put a timeline on her memory loss. It definitely carries back over five years," then as if he realized how that sounded he lifted one hand and emphasized, "but that's not unusual nor is it a great cause for added concern."

Pulling a chart from his papers he spoke in words the two men could comprehend. "Normally this type of memory loss is very temporary and involves only the few hours prior to when the injury took place."

Pointing to the chart, which graded injuries on a graph, he told them Marsha's was much more serious. "Her damage boarders on what we call Acute Traumatic Retrograde Memory loss. That is caused by intense pressure on the brain. It's that intracranial pressure that is blocking her brain's access to certain areas where her memories are stored."

Jon sat and listened quietly. George spoke up and asked how long this condition would continue?

"There's no surgery needed, the brain is simply swollen in those areas. That swelling should reduce in a matter of days." The doctor was direct and candid.

Jon and George seemed relieved at that news.

"The one other thing you need to understand," the doctor cautioned then. "Her memories may well return in random order. She won't be able to put them back as they belong until she is completely healed from this." He looked at both men sternly and finished with, "no matter what, you cannot interfere with her progress. She will be totally confused for several days, but it is very important you do not correct her or challenge what she might say."

George Vincent's brow wrinkled and he looked at the floor for a moment.

"Who will be with her through this time?" he asked.

"Myself, the nurses and you two can be in for small spaces of time."

"She'll be ok, then?" Jon was stoic.

"I have every reason to believe she will get there." The doctor said.

21

Delta Flight 937, non-stop from Shreveport landed in Atlanta on schedule. Juan Castrono walked out onto the concourse and checked his cell phone reception. He was supposed to have a message from Dewey Hanson by now, but nothing showed on the phone. The train to the main terminal building took several minutes in the heavy crowds.

This was a busy place, even this early in the morning, he thought, but then checked his watch to realize it was already 10:00AM.

There were benches lining the wall outside the baggage claim area, so Juan grabbed a seat to wait. He needed to know who this guy was, what he looked like, *what flight he was coming in on would be nice*, it was hard to understand why he hadn't heard from Hanson yet. Then his phone finally rang. It was Tomas Vaga from Colombia, and he was screaming into the phone.

"Where the hell are you, man?" he demanded of Juan.

"Why?" Juan was not supposed to let on; this was a secret mission for Hanson only so he didn't know quite what to say. "What is wrong?"

"What is wrong? What is wrong, you asked me? The whole crew has been taken by the cops. Carlos is dead, we don't know how this happened and Hanson says you left with no reason."

"He said what?" Juan was beginning to understand his new boss's true nature.

"You're not there, are you?" Tomas' voice was being sarcastic. "Why did you leave, what did you know about this?"

"About what?" Juan panicked, "I don't know about anything."

"You leave twenty minutes before the bust and you want us to think you know nothing?" the voice from Colombia was now screaming again. "You have much to answer for, friend. Much."

Juan understood from those comments that his explanations would have no bearing on his future. He was a dead man.

Rather than say anything else, he hung up and sat back on the bench to try to figure his next move. Then it hit him like a ton of bricks, *that's why he hadn't heard from Hanson.* Colombia had called Hanson first and he threw Juan under the bus. Hanson didn't want them to know he had gone rogue with this "hit man" he had hired, the hit man who was somewhere in this airport looking for him.

Oh, God...he is looking for me. his mind yelled at him. *What do I do?*

Juan's eyes slowly searched the area. There were people everywhere. *What does a hit man look like?* He wondered and then, there he was. It had to be him.

A large, beefy man was standing near the entrance to the baggage claim holding a brief case and a long leather coat over his arm. His eyes panned the crowd.

Juan found a newspaper on the bench beside him and quickly held it open in front of his face. Peeking over the paper, he watched as the man reached for a cell phone and answered it. On a strange thought, Juan took out his phone and again called Dewey Hanson's number. After four rings, Hanson answered.

"Yeah, who's this?" he asked. Caller ID doesn't work on some call waiting calls.

Juan didn't answer, but watched the man with the long coat. He had pulled his phone down, but did not hang up. *He's been put on hold!* Juan realized, *it is him!* Juan hung up and continued to watch. The large man put his phone back to his ear within seconds of Juan's disconnect with Hanson.

126

His instincts were to run, but his good sense told him not to. Juan sat still and kept the newspaper in front of him. The large man completed his call and continued to look around. Then he began to move right towards Juan.

Frozen in fear and too late to run now, Juan held his ground. The end of the bench was at an opening into the main terminal area. The hit man walked right past Juan and into the crowd.

After giving him several minutes to be far away, Juan rose and left in another direction. Walking the long way around to his car, Juan drove away as quickly as he could without drawing attention.

But now what? he thought. He was clearly a marked man. There was some money he had hidden at the old icehouse in Doraville. *Do I dare go there?* There really wasn't much choice; he had to have that money.

The drive to Doraville took almost an hour. Half way into it another thought crossed his mind. This guy couldn't kill him if the congressional killer knew about him and got to him first. Juan reached for his cell phone and punched 411.

It's all I can do, he told himself and he asked information to look up the number of the newspaper in Pittsburgh. They placed the call for him and when the receptionist answered, Juan asked to speak with the reporter named Seay.

~

By mid-morning Shreveport was the center of the 24/7 news universe. ICE had been notified out of necessity. The nationalities of the men held required that agency be involved. Then word of the weapons and the bomb brought the attention of Homeland Security.

The numbers of those arrested; the guns, the bomb and the positive outcome were just what the embattled Secretary of HS needed. By the six o'clock news programs, Homeland Security announced they had been investigating the group for weeks and

127

with some assistance from the local Shreveport police, had been able to derail a major terrorist attack.

Just what terrorists wished to attack in Shreveport was never explained and though many of Phil Stone's people were more than a little upset by the transition of facts, the Captain managed to keep a perspective on the whole thing.

"You guys know what you did," he told his senior officers. "That's enough for me and you can tell your troops the same."

Among the services sent to do their due diligence was an agent of the Naval Criminal Investigative Services out of New Orleans. One of the visitors in the Eldorado was a Naval Commander on leave with his wife. His presence there required the NCIS to make their report, along with all the others, and Special Agent Timothy Spiegel was on the job. Spiegel was a tall, rugged looking man with a square jaw and a stern stare. He didn't say much until asked, but if the subject interested him he would speak freely and he would speak volumes. His interview with the Commander was brief and conclusive. Though his job was really done, Spiegel was intrigued by what he was hearing about the case and opted to hang around.

After a full day of having their offices overrun by strangers the Shreveport Police Headquarters began to settle down. A few of the agents were stuck overnight so Phil Stone asked who was buying dinner?

"I'm happy to play host guys, but somebody else is buying." he laughed.

The group quickly voted for Homeland Security and Agent Wilson checked his wallet for the agency credit card and asked, "Where we going?"

Stone recommended his favorite spot Cub's, and called to set aside a table. Taking a headcount, he came up with four and told the others he was including a friend, "if they didn't mind." Smiling, he told them, "he's a newspaper guy," and the others groaned and threw papers in the air. "Wait, wait now," Stone insisted, "He a good guy. You can trust this one."

Stone, Wilson, Agent Spiegel and FBI Agent Wilfred all headed out and met up with Matt Turlock at the restaurant. They were an eclectic group in their appearance. Stone, still in his black SWAT attire, Wilfred in a black suit and tie, Spiegel had on khakis and a jacket over his shirt, Wilson had his Homeland Security tee shirt and jacket on and Matt Turlock was in his wool blazer and an open collar shirt.

Other customers openly turned to stare and could be seen asking the servers what was going on. The group couldn't care less. It was the end of a long day.

All enjoyed the food and the conversation, which ended up on stories of each man's background. All were ex-military including Matt, but the stories told by Agent Spiegel captured everyone's attention.

Spiegel was a former Navy Seal and had one macho adventure after the next to share. But his greatest adventure, in his mind, had been the joint operation his unit had with another six-man seal team in Afghanistan several years back.

Everyone listened intently as he told of the teams dropping from over 40,000 feet to a mountaintop to rescue an Army Ranger Company that had gotten itself surrounded and cut off. No one else spoke or even looked away as he told of how they found only one young Ranger alive on that mountain.

It was a story that bordered on incredibility, but a man like this wouldn't lie. He shared about the Ranger having fought off the insurgents alone, for two or three nights and how they had fought their way down that mountain, finally needing to carry the wounded Ranger to safety.

Phil and Matt were impressed with the story, as they assumed the others were. Special Agent Spiegel left Shreveport the next morning, but they were glad to have met such a man.

22

"This is all wrong," Jon exclaimed. Several officers of the Charlotte PD had offered to take him to the warehouse, the site of Marsha's injury. He and George had determined it would be best if Jon not see her until her memories of him cleared up. George stayed at the hospital and Jon couldn't just sit around.

"This isn't the right building," he repeated himself. But patrolman Snyder assured him it was the scene of the blast.

The building was racked and partially collapsed. Sections of concrete block were missing, debris was scattered everywhere and the side door to the office area was blown away. There was no identifying marks or number on the structure. With a puzzled looked, the visitor walked back toward the officer nearest him.

"What number building is this anyway?" Jon asked him.

"1425." Snyder replied. "The number had been right next to that doorway."

That was way off. *How could they hit the wrong building*, Jon thought and he asked to see the small notebook the cops had found on one of the attacking men.

Flipping through, it was not easy to understand the notations inside. Some were in Spanish, some English and the order wasn't clear.

They took this off one of the guys killed in Shreveport. He quickly realized.

Jon found a reference to Dalton and from that was able to follow the path to "Chrlnc." "*Charlotte, N.C.*" he muttered as he turned the pages. Then there was a note that said "Maflrmag park #1425," written in blue pen.

Ok, Mayflower Managed Warehouse Park, that's right, but 1425 isn't. He reached up with one hand and brushed the page. A

131

small piece of blue thread or lint left the paper and corrected the number showing to # 425.

Holy, crap. The lint took them to the wrong building.

Jon showed the officer what he figured out and he asked to go to the correct unit. They drove around to #425 and found it still standing open. This was the building Jon remembered. The other officers who had been with Marsha had not thought about that building again, not after the attack they fought off at # 1425.

It hasn't even been twelve hours. Jon thought.

They could tell the Charlotte PD team had been in this building searching.

She went to see what she could find. he realized. "The bad guys got lost and hit the wrong building," he said aloud. Then he looked back at the notebook. "Had it not been for that piece of lint the Russians would have been all over them here. Marsha and her officers would be dead."

The officer's eyes got wide and he shook his head in agreement. "This could have been much worse," he said sullenly. "We've really got to stop these jerks. When did these people start thinking they could just kill anybody, anytime they want?"

Jon went to his car and got several lipstick cameras out. He looked around and found the spots he wanted to survey.

"They may not come back here, but if they do, I want to know about it," he told the young cop.

~

It was the middle of the afternoon when Bill White at the Pittsburgh Post Gazette had received the two messages for Daniel. He dialed the cell phone number to his reporter in seclusion. Daniel answered and his boss started right in.

"This mess is coming to a boil or something." White told him.

"Now what?" Daniel had about all he could handle already.

"I've got not one, but two messages for you to call back, today."

"Two?"

"One from Atlanta this morning and one from Texas just a bit ago," the editor advised. "What is happening down there?"

"We don't know, boss," Daniel explained about Marsha and how upset they all were over that. Then the news from Shreveport didn't make any sense at all, but had to be something.

"Yeah, that Shreveport deal is a smoke job." White told Daniel. "I've got some guys looking into that one. Terrorists in Shreveport? Come on." The editor paused for a moment then added, "I hadn't heard about Charlotte, didn't make national news."

"No, I guess not. But it's pretty big to us."

Bill White gave him the numbers he was to call and ended the conversation with "anything I can do?"

"Boss, you're doing more than I could expect already."

"You're welcome," White quipped and hung up.

~

Vasily Torbof woke from his nap hearing his name called from downstairs. He nearly lost his balance in the rickety aluminum chair trying to jump up. It was only 9:30AM and he was dressed in a nightshirt and robe. The Louisiana rooftop was cool. That earlier bath of warmth had lost itself as the sun climbed and then he heard his name called out again.

"What?" he demanded in a broken Russian dialect. "What is it?"

"Leonid is here," Torbof's wife hollered. The aid had come to the residence rather than call with the outcome of his task, to get the phone number of Dewey Hanson.

Vasily rubbed his face with both hands and adjusted his robe. Walking to the stairs he looked across the Red River where the sun had climbed to 45 degrees in the sky. He realized his neck hurt from the nap and he massaged it roughly while going down the stairs.

"What do you have for me, Leonid?"

The aid walked up close to his boss, not wanting to shout or even speak loudly. He leaned into the disheveled looking man, "Boss, he didn't want to talk to you till I explained just who you are. This Hanson must be an amateur, he doesn't sound too organized."

"So?" the boss looked the man straight in the eyes. "Do you have his number?"

Handing Torbof a small piece of paper Leonid replied, "Yes, this is the man you wanted to talk to, he just tried to deny it at first."

"212?" Vasily read from the paper, "this is a Washington D.C. number. Is this one a congressperson too?"

His assistant nodded in the affirmative and Vasily waved him away with one hand. *Another damned congressman,* he thought walking to the phone. *They really like to use congressmen.*

He dialed the complete number and went through two assistants there until a voice finally stated, "Dewey Hanson here, who's this?"

"Mr. Hanson, we seriously need to have a discussion about what has happened down here." Torbof paused as he tried to think of how to describe just what had happened. "Numbers of those present here make this a very bad situation. We must work to ease this tension."

Dewey Hanson didn't quite know what to make of this. *He knew everything of course, but how did this guy know? Just what did he know?* Hanson spoke in almost broken, near trembling English, "I have... my own troubles, mister. You say... what situation are you talking about anyway?"

Torbof understood what Leonid meant, "Your people came down here to massacre my people. Over 40 strong they came," he raised his voice in anger.

"Look, friend," Hanson's tone had completely changed, "if you're going to talk specifics on a God damned open phone, this call is over."

"Specifics?" Torbof screamed, "you want specifics? You bastards killed my son."

Hanson started to hang up, but paused, "Your son?"

"Yes, damn you all. My only son."

"Do you realize the family's youngest was killed by your butchers and left in a ditch?"

Torbof froze, that was the answer to "why" the DeMarcos family reacted as he, himself had. Vengeance, fast and sure, it was how they lived and now could be how they all died. He needed to stay on the offensive and tried to think of what to say. All that would come to him was, "They were the ones who killed my son."

Dewey Hanson muttered several profanities as he walked around his office. He finally spoke again into the phone, "this is a real cluster...." he caught himself, took a deep breath and continued. "Both sides lost very important people, unintentionally it seems. I really have problems of my own to deal with. I answer to people who like to blow stuff up if it gets in the way. I may be in the way right now."

"If you can't help with this who do I need to talk to?" Torbof was nearly pleading. He didn't need a huge bloodbath war, not now not ever. "I'm not sure how this attack was stopped. But it was. If I know anything about the DeMarcos... it ain't over, but... it has to be."

"I can't help you, man." Dewey tried to be sincere. "I wish I could, but this is over my head."

"You know I won't sit here and wait to be killed." Torbof challenged him.

"I understand that sentiment more than you know." Hanson laughed. "Good luck with that." And he hung up.

Vasily Torbof held his phone and glared at it. It rang almost as soon as he had ended the call to Hanson. The caller ID showed that it was Serge, one of the crew he had sent to find the Argus nest. It would be news from North Carolina.

Good, it's about time. he thought.

The news from Charlotte was not what he expected. Serge did not know or understand how things went the way they had. He could only report that it, too, was a mess.

Vasily's mind was still spinning from the talk with the congressman and his men were in custody in Charlotte, those who had survived anyway. Serge was told to sit tight and stay quiet; he would send help for them.

Vasily Torbof stood leaning on a small table for several minutes. This was the last straw; the ideas of a peaceful compromise were gone. He was left with no other choice than to prepare for war.

Standing suddenly straight and filling his chest with a deep breath, Torbof focused on what he must do. He swapped his robe for a heavy coat and wool sock cap. Back on the rooftop he went through his files and found numbers for his counterparts in New York and Missouri.

In calls to both the message was the same, "send your best fighters." From New York he added a special request to have Ivan call him as soon as possible. Between those two territories he would muster over 100 men. *If the Colombians wanted war, they shall have it*, he thought, "they shall have it," the repeat came out loud.

23

Jon Crane had spent two hours going through the warehouse that had been Argus' spot last fall. He found nothing, but made a note to check with the guys who had been with Marsha. He set up two cameras to watch the area. The next hour and a half was at the #1425 building that had been partially blown down.

The car Marsha had ridden in was still there wrapped in yellow tape. There were two bloody spots outside the passenger door, one rather small, the other much more significant.

"Is this where she fell?" he asked.

The young officer with him answered with a somber nod.

The chunk of concrete that had hit her still lay very near the larger bloodstain.

"She got hit by something in the foot or ankle as she got out the car and that took her down. She was lying on her back when the concrete came over the car and hit her." Jon declared and the officer agreed. There was no satisfaction in the conclusion. Those facts didn't help her now and he wasn't finding anything to do with the bad guys, either group. *This was a waste of time,* but he set up cameras there as well.

He walked toward the other patrol car as his private phone rang. It was Daniel.

"Yeah, what?" he answered and then tried to smooth it over a bit. "I'm not in the best mood so cut me some slack, will ya?"

"Jon, I hate to even bother you. But I've had two calls you need to know about."

"Ok, good news, I hope."

Daniel didn't even favor that remark. He could not find humor in any of this.

"The first was from a cowboy I met out in Texas last year. He's not a bad fella and he says he was told some information about a group of punks bragging in a bar about being with The Son."

"Really?" Jon was sure something would break on that deal, just not so soon. "I'll have to talk with him. What else you got?"

Daniel took a moment before he continued and Jon picked up on it.

"What's the matter, Daniel? What's wrong, now?"

"The second call was from someone I don't know. He knows of me."

Jon stayed quiet while Daniel constructed his thoughts and then said,

"He is a Hispanic guy and he sounded really nervous, scared even. He claims there is a hit man out looking for you."

"Me?" Jon laughed. "How would he know me?"

"He used your name, Jon. 'Jonathan Crane.' He said his boss, Dewey Hanson had hired some guy to kill Jonathan Crane."

What Daniel was saying could not be possible, how could Hanson or this Hispanic guy know who he was? He sought a remark to a discussion that didn't make sense, none at all.

"Lucky guess, maybe?" He asked Daniel.

"He also knows I'm at your house. Jon, we were followed here the first night when we flew in. They know I'm here and they know this is your house."

Now it made sense. Jon leaned back against the patrol car and asked in jest,

"Don't suppose he left his name, did he?"

"Juan Castrono." Daniel told him. "Juan Castrono.

Sitting upright, Jon heard himself mutter, *Shit.* He thought for a moment and then told Daniel, "It's ok, at least we know.

Look…Daniel, you guys stay in the house and let me speak to Gil right quick, will ya?"

Juan Castrono…he must be the guy who worked with Harley. He just traded bosses! Jon thought as he waited for Gil Gartner. *Juan was in Shreveport though*, Jon had heard from Stone that the raid was a success. *How did he get out of there?*

The phone barked a voice and Jon held it back to his ear.

"Gil?"

"Yeah, Jon. Sorry about this."

"Not anybody's fault, my friend. Look…you've heard they know about the house. Nobody exposes even a finger outside, you hear me?"

"Got it." Gil responded.

"This guy will be a sniper among other things and they know where you are. Get Ben to open the armory and you guys pull what ever you need. There are firing slots from the main attic, front and sides."

"Ben has mentioned that."

"Good, just hold on and keep everybody in. It could get rough." Jon remembered something else and grabbed a paper from his pocket.

"Gil, have you got a pen?" he asked.

Mumbling around for second, Gil answered he did.

"Take these serial numbers down. They are cameras I need Ben to monitor and tape activity. He knows what to do."

"You be careful up there, yourself. Say, how is Marsha doing?"

"She's awake, but it's day to day according to the docs."

"Tell her we're all praying for her."

Jon smiled; he needn't tell them she did not know him right now. "Thanks."

~

Dewey Hanson was in a near panic. He was playing both sides against the middle and he knew it. Not that he was working for the Russians, but just offering what he had was enough. Then bringing in his own button man to take out someone who he thought was a personal risk, it was all too complicated and extremely risky.

Now the Russians would surely build their strength and the coming apocalypse would be monumental. As the Russian had told, "this thing was spinning out of control."

Where was Juan? he thought. Wasting Juan was not in the original plan, but he had to be sacrificed since there was no good explanation for the absence from Shreveport. Hanson had told his killer about the Doraville site and that if things went wrong at the airport, to look for Juan there. He figured correctly that Juan would try to collect his things before bugging out.

He was right on that score.

~

Castrono arrived in Doraville and parked across the street from the plant. Things appeared normal, not much was going on.

He slipped in a side door and carefully worked his way up to the offices. No one was there. *Good,* he thought in Spanish and pulled the door open. Then he saw the man, sleeping in a chair. He had not noticed him through the glass, but there he was. Juan picked up a large catalog and took it in both hands. He hit the sleeping man in the side of the head, knocking him from the chair. The man hit the floor and did not move.

Quickly he opened the safe and got all the funds he had kept there and stuffed them into a paper bag, it was close to $575,000.00. There was also a gun and two magazines. Juan did not like guns, he was not that familiar with them, but these were hard times. He stuck the weapon in his belt and put the clips in his pockets.

140

As he approached the office door to leave he could hear the main building doors opening. Juan crouched down and low crawled to the stairs and down to the lower level and out the side door he had come in. He never saw who it was and really didn't care, as long as they did not see him.

He drove north on Peachtree Industrial to the freeway where he had to make a choice. Right was toward I-85 and Carolina, left was to I-75 and Dalton. He opted to go straight north and swung over to the Dahlonega Highway, Ga.400 about five miles up, then into the north Georgia Mountains. He would hide there.

~

Murray Bilstock had enjoyed talking to Daniel again. That struck him as strange, given the circumstances surrounding their first meeting. Daniel had been trailing what he thought was a congressional killer and he believed this killer had done in Murray's dad. Those facts were never proven, never pushed for that matter because hardly anyone cared. The rumors of what Sen. Bilstock had been up to were strong, but he was just stronger and too scary for anyone to go up against. His demise was accepted as a transition back to normal for the folk who lived near Brownwood, Texas.

The big losers were Murray, Charlene and Slick. They had grown up on that ranch and they each loved it. Mrs. Bilstock, though, couldn't wait to get away from there and she held all the cards, being the widow and new owner of the property.

The memories were not good, but still Murray had liked Daniel once he got to know him. He realized that more after they had talked this time.

It was funny, he thought, *Daniel didn't even mention if he'd ever caught this guy. But he did seem very interested in the lead.*

It had been a long week and he needed some relaxation himself. The information he had shared with Daniel had all been third hand through Slick. He figured he would take a ride up north, to Greenville and see if he could find that bar Slick spoke of himself. If these boys did know anything about "The Son," he'd like to see them first hand.

24

Phillip Stone and his people spent the day after the raid going through the personal effects of the Hispanic gang they had busted. They had traveled light, one change of clothes per man and little in anything else.

"Didn't plan to be here long, did they?" a junior officer asked out loud. His answer came mostly in grunts as the others felt his statement too silly to address.

"These men are gladiators," Stone remarked. "They came here to do one thing, kill." He stood and looked around for smirks, but found none. They seemed to realize how serious the attack could have been. "Any IDs?" he asked. There were none. They didn't even bring their plane or bus ticket stubs with them, nothing.

"Alright," the Captain finally ordered. "That's it, bag this stuff and go home. Good work, people." He walked around after they were gone and pretended to look a bit further. It was just frustration. He had stopped one major attack in his city, but he knew that wasn't the end of it. Not with these guys.

He had men watching the Russians headquarters the past two days, little activity there either. One man had come in early yesterday morning, about two hours after the raid, but that was it. Torbof had not left the building. He wasn't sure if that was odd or not.

Could be to do with the mourning period or something, he thought. *Hell, who knows?*

A call came into his cell phone, it was Matt Turlock from the newspaper.

"Evening, Matt, what's going on?"

Turlock had talked with Daniel and so he wanted to bring Phil up to speed. He was told about the hit man, but little in details. He told of the group in Texas and the cowboy Daniel had met there.

"Is Silas still in Charlotte?" Stone asked him.

"Yeah, I believe he is. The girl is awake, but something's not right. Daniel seemed worried, but didn't know what it was."

"Dinner, old friend?" Matt asked him.

"I'm just gonna grab a burger and go home, Matt. I'm beat."

"Next time, then." Turlock replied and hung up.

That's what Phil liked about his newspaper friend. That call had just been to check on him and fill him in with some news, not to pump the policeman for a story. Matt knew if there was a story, Phil would share what he could.

The Captain pulled on his overcoat and headed out for the night, his mind swirling with concern over when and where the next attempt would be.

This ain't over by a long shot, he told himself.

~

Northeast Texas was dark on the roads after dusk. Murray took his older pick-up so as to blend with the working folks. He was working class, but he had a chopper, not a bike chopper, a real fling-wing helicopter. That could have had him in Greenville in twenty minutes, but the attention it would bring he did not need.

He drove through the town and saw several bars. None like Slick had described. Slick admitted to be more than a little drunk that night, "but the neon sign looked kinda like a reared-up horse with wings," he had recalled.

Passing through Greenville completely with no luck, Murray started to turn around when some lights on the horizon caught his attention. Straight out the road, another three miles was the Flying

Deuce. It's proud glowing sign was of a numeral two with wings on its back.

"This is it," Murray assured himself.

The lot was sparsely filled with trucks, plenty of motorcycles and a few regular cars. The entrance was up five wooden steps to a wide porch that held a row of high top round tables and stools. There was another row of rocking chairs against the front wall. But none of either were being used at the moment. Old fashioned swinging saloon doors opened into a huge room that looked to be from a John Wayne movie.

It was bright enough inside. Large chandeliers hung from the center of the room. But the predominant lighting was from neon beer advertising on every formerly exposed wall surface.

The bar itself, extended down the entire left side and wrapped halfway around the back wall. Large mirrors, protected by heavy screen wire, lined the wall behind the bar and the ceiling dropped just over the area. Two men in cowboy boots sat at the bar, one talking up a female companion the best he could.

Murray could see a game room at the back and a mechanical bull in the far corner. Most of the "crowd" sat at tables near the empty performer's stage or were standing around the dart pit.

The crowd did not match the parking lot in his mind, but Murray shrugged it off and took a seat at the bar. He didn't have to yell to get the barkeep's attention and that's when it struck him how quiet it was.

A bar in west Texas was like a NASCAR race, he remembered. *Couldn't hear yourself think.*

He asked the barkeep about that and was told this was a slow night.

"Folks tend to stay away on Fridays anymore." He relented as he scrubbed the bar surface like it had a stain you couldn't see. "You're new around here, huh?" he added.

"Yeah, drove up from Garland this afternoon." Murray offered.

"Passing through?"

"Just stopped for a beer, man."

The host's eyes had darted around as they spoke. The man was clearly nervous and as he picked up his rag to walk away he muttered, "Be quick, ok?"

Murray leaned back and spun his stool around. The other occupants had not moved, or so it seemed. Several were now staring at him.

What the hell is this place? Went through Murray's mind as he noticed a large bald headed man emerge from the game room area. Several other bald faces appeared in the doorway as the tattoos on the approaching man became more evident.

Murray sat still and stared directly into the man's eyes. Murray didn't scare easily.

"You couldn't find a beer elsewhere, pal?" the man more demanded than asked.

After glancing around the room, the cowboy pushed his hat brim up with the beer bottle then looked directly at the bald man. The aggressor curled his hands into fists.

"Maybe," Murray smiled at him. "But I like this one."

"Smart-ass." Was the next comment from the bald headed man as he swung a round house right at Murray's head.

Sliding from the bar stool, Murray grabbed the neck of his beer bottle with his left hand. As the punch breezed past him, he stepped back toward the charging man and landed a solid blow with the bottle on the back of the baldhead.

146

The attacker's face hit the bar surface with a thud and bounced. The man's knees buckled and his body collapsed in a pile. Murray turned to his left to see four others rushing at him. Jumping up on the bar, Murray spun and dropped behind the unit. He searched frantically until he found what he knew had to be there.

He popped up behind the bar, a few feet down from where he had dropped holding the barkeeper's scattergun, a sawed off double barrel. The others stopped, but one reached into his belt.

"Now don't be selfish," Murray warned him. "You do that and I'll use a full barrel on you alone, my friend." The man slowly raised his arms.

Now all four held their arms in the air and Murray could see yet more faces in the game room doorway. They were just standing there. Not a hair on any of them.

Ugly bunch, Murray thought as he moved to the entrance end of the bar.

"I'm through with my beer, so I'll be leaving if you fellas don't mind."

There was some movement at the game room door, but then a voice rang out,

"Let him go."

The owner of the voice was not visible. But his command was obeyed.

Murray glanced left to the barkeeper, raising the barrel end of the shotgun he told the man, "I need to borrow this for a little bit."

The other man nodded and Murray stepped out, checking the porch area first and then backing down the stairs. He calmly started the truck and backed out to the highway.

Driving with one hand on the shotgun, he checked his mirror several times as he drove back home that night. No one followed.

That was a weird reception for just being a stranger, he told himself. This was Texas after all and things could get wild at times, yet that was beyond anything. His presence struck a nerve for some reason. *I just bet those boys Slick heard bragging are part of this bunch.*

As he neared the ranch house, Murray dialed Slick on the cell phone. He could hear bar noises in the background.

"Hey, cuz," Slick answered.

"That bar you were telling me about, the one up near Greenville?" Murray said.

"Yeah, what about it?"

"Was that a Friday night you were there?"

"Friday?...Naw, it was more the middle of the week. I was up there looking for work and found the place. It looked cool, but there wasn't much going on."

"You run into any trouble there?"

Slick didn't understand the question, "What? I got shit faced, but that's about all."

"Ok, talk to you later." He closed his phone and sat still in his truck, thinking.

Murray remembered the bartender's comment about Friday nights.

Club meeting night. He smiled. *It's got to be them.*

25

Saturday morning and the house in Dalton, Georgia, smelled of coffee. It was good. Ben, Gil and the other two officers had been up late setting up defensive positions and checking the weapons.

"If we had this stuff in the department no bad guys would ever mess with us," one of the officers joked. His buddy smiled and Gil shook his head in the affirmative, but said nothing.

"I'm sure Jon could work something out," Ben quipped.

"Getting permission to use it would be the bigger issue," Gil finally spoke up.

There had been no sign of anything odd, but Jon felt the hit man wouldn't be so particular as to who he shot, so they stayed inside and low. Drawing fire would not penetrate the walls or the windows, but it would give the guy knowledge of what he was up against. Who knows, he might be able to adjust his attack from there.

"What do we do about food?" Daniel asked looking up from the computer Ben had set up for him. He was wirelessly connected with the office in Pennsylvania and could keep up with stories and even add to them. "Corn flakes and Pringles will get old pretty quick."

Ben looked at Gil. "I know what Jon said, but I can get out and back without anyone knowing."

Gil didn't like the idea, but he listened. Ben would wait until dusk, he didn't tell them about the third level basement, only that there was a way he could leave and return unseen. Ben would lie and Gil was aware there were secrets. He agreed to try.

"Can you live on Corn flakes till tonight, Daniel?" Ben teased.

"We'll see," he replied, more concerned with the article on his screen.

As their conversation continued a rental car from the Atlanta airport slowly rode down the road outside the house. It didn't stop. The driver looked for a place to turn around. He found one about a mile down the road at an abandoned gas station.

He turned into the station and looked both directions for any on coming vehicles. The station stood open and was empty, only the rocks of the back wall were visible from the outside. He backed out onto the highway and drove again up toward the house he had been told to watch.

A side path led up the mountain on the far side of the road. Following it, the driver found a spot about a third of a mile away on a ridge overlooking the road and the house. He parked his car behind some trees and brush and pulled a large bag from his trunk. He had made a few purchases along the way from Atlanta. There was a sleeping bag, three thermos bottles, long-range binoculars and a Kimber 8400 rifle and shooter's ridge mounting bracket.

After setting all that up he returned to the car for two blankets he had bought, just in case. He was glad he did. Cushioning the hard ground with one, he kept the other nearby for later as he began his watch, a sniper's watch. It could take an hour, it could take days. It was all the same.

Traffic was light on that stretch of road, but there was some. Nothing went up to the house or came from it so he gave them no mind, not even the pick-up truck that rumbled by towards town just after dark.

~

Just before noon on that same Saturday, Ben had "hits" from his camera surveillance of the warehouses in Charlotte. The same guy appears at both locations. The pictures are clear; it's the same guy for sure.

Messaging them to Jon's phone was no problem and Jon stood with George, looking at the image, wondering who this guy was.

Had Juan's hit man found Jon here in Charlotte? They wondered.

"Is my bag still in the car?" Jon asked George.

"I haven't bothered anything out there, " he replied.

"I'm gonna check this guy out if I can find him there." Jon stated. "From Ben's message this is a big dude. He estimates him at 6'5" and about 245lbs."

Jon smiled as he headed out to the car, "I may need my arm."

"Hey," George hollered after him. "Would you bring me my other pair of shoes? My feet are killing me." Jon waved and got into the elevator.

Walking out to the parking area Jon tried to think of where to look for this guy. He would most likely be gone from the warehouse area by now. But he may have dropped something or left a clue as to where he's staying, something, anything.

Have to start somewhere, he told himself.

The car was parked with the trunk against some bushes so he punched the power release button on the key chain and had to reach in from the side to get his bag.

He slipped into the hydraulic mechanical arm and gave it a quick test. Then he put his jacket on over it and got the small Glock from the bag. He planned to leave the car for George and take a cab, so he might as well get everything he might need.

George's shoes were in the back seat area, so he grabbed those, locked the car and headed back up to the room. The hall was quiet. They had Marsha on a secluded end of the third floor for security that seemed silly since her story had been on TV and in all the papers. It would be hard to find someone in Charlotte who didn't know where she was.

Jon pushed the room door open gently. Marsha was asleep and George stood by the window. She slept most of the time they'd been there, but that was no problem. She still didn't know who Jon was anyway. No point in wanting to talk to her right now, it just wasn't possible. She had no idea who he was though some memories were returning slowly. At least her being asleep made it possible to look at her without freaking her out.

George turned, saw his shoes Jon had brought up and grabbed them.

"Oh, man, thanks," he said as he sat in the chair and pulled at the laces on the oxfords he wore so he could relax in his loafers. "These dogs are killing me."

Jon leaned over Marsha and kissed her forehead without waking her. He dragged his left hand along the edge of her bed as he walked toward the door and then waved again at George who didn't notice. Still adjusting his socks before sliding into the loafers, the DA was smiling in relief in the corner chair. As Jon stepped into the hall he heard the elevator open and a very large man stepped out. He was the type of person that would get your attention anyway, an intimidating figure that altered the light coming down the hallway.

The man checked both directions for numbers and finally turned toward Marsha's room. Jon saw the face and immediately knew. From the pictures Ben had sent there was no doubt. He might be some larger than Ben's estimates of size, but this was the man from the warehouses.

Without flinching, Jon continued forward. Walking steadily down the middle to left of the hall pretending to pay more mind to the floor than where he was going, Jon looked up at the last second. Attempting to change course and pass the man on the right side, he bumped into him, but kept going. The large brut grunted and stopped for a moment, looking at Jon before resuming his path.

"Excuse me, friend." Jon exclaimed as he continued to walk, but he had confirmed his concerns. Touching his belt, he powered the arm and after a few steps drew his Glock from the leg pouch. He had been able to tell through the bump that the large man had a gun under his coat on the left side.

Jon turned back toward the still walking man, extended his arm aiming the Glock high on the back of the man's head and announced firmly,

"Say there... excuse me again would you?"

The big man paused and slowly turned to him, glaring. He found himself looking at Jon's Glock.

"What is dis?" he asked in broken English with his hands out at his sides.

Jon took three steps forward, closing the distance between them and then ordered,

"First, I'd like you to pull that weapon out from under your coat and do it with your left hand, ok?" Jon's voice was loud enough to be heard yet not draw attention.

The large man turned red with anger, but did as he was told. Reaching under the coat he glided the weapon gently with his fingers from its holster. Jon moved closer to him, neither man blinked or spoke until the smaller man had taken the weapon and tucked it into his own belt.

Standing toe to toe, the large man had to look down at Jon. With a wrinkled upper lip, he asked, "Who the hell are you?"

"I'm the guy you're gonna tell just who sent you here." Jon looked up and smiled at him.

"Like hell," the bruiser bellowed. "What do you plan to do, kill me?"

Jon put his Glock back in its pocket and looked back up at the now confused man, "No, that's where we differ. I'll make you wish you were dead."

Realizing there was no longer a gun pointed at him, the large man drew back his right fist and launched it at Jon's head. Jon's right hand sprung forward and caught it in mid-flight. The impact broke both wrist bones in the large man's arm. Jon held the fist where he caught it, squeezing tightly.

The large man grimaced and his knees bent. First looking surprised then shocked, his eyes rolled back in their sockets as facial color drained away. The pressure being applied to the fist caused his body to sway uncontrollably. The pain went beyond anything imaginable, yet he was powerless to retaliate.

"Who sent you?" Jon repeated calmly.

The man's jaw trembled and he spit as he spoke in defiance, "Go to hell."

Holding the fist next to his own face, Jon squeezed even harder. The pressure being applied to the hand now crushed bone. The sounds of the knuckles breaking were audible down the hall. The tips of the man's fingers dug deeply into the fleshy lower palm and finally there was a scream. He was trembling all over now, but still refused to talk.

"Kill... me... if you... want." He stammered and tried to look Jon in the eyes.

Jon suddenly released the now useless hand. Before the man could fall he grabbed his belt and spun him around, face to the wall saying, "I told you...I don't do that."

As he spoke, the index finger of Jon's right hand pushed into the large man's back. He put pressure low on his back, just beside the spine and above the tailbone.

"What are you doing?" The man cried out in fear.

154

"One more try, friend. Just one." Jon leaned into the man's left ear. "Tell me who sent you or I'm going to stick this finger into your back, wrap it around your spine and rip it out from your tailbone."

He pushed harder and could feel the edge of the man's backbone. Changing to the man's other ear, Jon taunted him, "I think it could hurt really bad... what do you think?"

The pressure was convincing. The large man began shaking uncontrollably and turned his head toward Jon.

"Torbof, Torbof...Vasily Torbof sent me." He screamed out loud. "God no, no more."

The large man was a complete pile of nerves and meat. Jon stepped back, releasing him and he collapsed onto the floor in a wad.

Jon turned and looked toward Marsha's room to see George standing there, staring at him. George's expression was between shock and disgust.

Jon reached his hand out to George as if to plead with him.

"He came here to kill Marsha and the other injured Russians, you know that?"

"Yes, Jon." George replied. "I know." George grabbed Jon's elbow and walked him away from Marsha's door, "Who is Torbof, do you know him?"

"I know of him, yes. This isn't what we thought George, but it could be worse in the long run."

George shook his head, orderlies were on their way down the hall and the police would be soon.

"I'll deal with this," he told Jon. " Now get out of here while I figure out how to explain what happened to the cops."

Jon did not argue, he went to the elevator and the doors opened. George called to him as he stepped inside, "I'll call you when it's cleared up."

As the doors closed George had a thought. He kneeled down next to the large man and pulled his face towards his own. George waited for eye contact and then started.

"Listen to me, your hand got caught in that elevator, you understand?" he said.

With a face combining fear and pain the large man exclaimed, "Nyet, no way."

George leaned in, "Do you want him to come back?" He asked the man, staring right in his eyes. "I can make him come back."

The Russian giant didn't take long to answer; he bowed his head and said, "Caught in the elevator, now please... get me help."

"Its on the way," George told him while standing back up. "Its on the way."

As Jon made his way outside the hospital, he grabbed his cell phone and punched in Phillip Stone's number.

"Yeah, you've got Stone," came the standard answer.

"Capt. Stone. Seems I'm going to have to look at this Vasily guy a little closer and a lot quicker than I thought."

"Me first, my friend." Stone declared. "I hadn't bothered you about it, but your info turned out to be golden."

"I don't understand," Jon countered.

The police Captain brought Jon up to speed on the events of Friday morning, the bust and the bomb that didn't go off because of Jon's tip on how to proceed with these guys.

"I can't thank you enough. There's no telling how many dead we'd have if it had not been for what you told me."

Jon's mind swirled as he tried to keep up with everything going on right now,

"I'm glad it worked out, Phil I really am. But I need your help now."

"Name it."

156

"Two things, I need more about Vasily Torbof and his building. Anything and everything you can give me. The jerk sent a hit man over here to clean up what was left. That would have included Marsha, my friend."

"I take it the threat has been eliminated?" Stone asked.

"That's the other favor. Can you get a hold of anybody that might be in charge of security cameras at the hospital here in Charlotte?"

Stone thought for a moment, "Jon, that's a tall order. Those are usually private security people and don't answer to the police without a warrant. When did this happen?"

"Ten,…fifteen minutes ago, I guess."

"Those tapes are already pulled if there was an incident. I'm assuming you had a starring role in this?"

"Possibly, I'm not sure. The cameras are at the elevators so it may just be my back. But I can't be sure."

"Is your friend alright, Jon?"

"Oh, yeah, sorry. She's doing better and this guy didn't get in the room. We were lucky this time."

Stone finished by telling him he would collect all he could on Torbof and keep an eye on the building for movement.

"You coming back this way soon?" he asked.

"Probably, not much I can do here and I might need to lay low anyways."

26

Murray Bilstock had placed another call to Daniel Seay. It was Saturday, but the newspaper's operator said she could relay the message to the right person. Using the paper's intranet, she sent Daniel a message that appeared on his computer in Dalton.

The more Murray thought about it, those guys at the bar were either the real deal or some wanna-be group using the Son's name for notoriety. His bet was on the latter. Either way, the trip to Greenville had put a big asterisk on the situation and Daniel was the only one he could think of that should know.

He was out in the larger barn on his new property, the one he had cleaned out to house the Bell helicopter when the return call from Daniel came back.

"Thanks for returning my call again," Murray started. "I don't mean to be a pest, but you never did say if you caught up with that fella?"

"Is there something more that's happened?" Daniel asked without answering the other question. He realized he was being rude, but couldn't help himself at the moment.

Murray explained his trip to the bar and his conclusions. Daniel didn't speak, but he now understood Murray's desire to share what he had learned.

"I think you need to come look into this," the cowboy told Daniel.

"I'm not the one to do that," Daniel said and then without thinking added, "let me have the right person call you about it."

"Well I'll be damned," the cowboy half muttered.

"Excuse me?"

"You have found him, haven't you?" Murray was blunt.

"Found who?" Daniel tried to be sincere.

"Aw, come on, you know who this guy is. He is real, huh?"

"I didn't say that at all, Murray..."

"You didn't have to," Murray interrupted him. "You know, I actually feel better about getting involved." There was quiet on both ends and Murray finally commented.

"Have him call me, any time."

Daniel didn't know what to say to that, so continued obfuscation was in order.

"I'll have someone be in touch, soon," he told the cowboy.

"Yeah, someone. You do that." Murray laughed. Then became serious again. "He didn't do the Mississippi thing, did he? These clowns over here did."

"Murray, just talk to him when he calls, will you?"

"Absolutely." The tone in Murray's voice was justification. "I'll be waiting."

Daniel knew Murray's comments were not a threat, yet still another person knowing who Jon was...Jon wouldn't like that.

He walked up to the attic to check on Gil at the shooter's slot.

"Anything?" Daniel asked him as he looked around at the heavy metal supports carrying the weight of the roof down and through the still stronger walls. It was dark up there, yet you could see clearly enough to move around. Any artificial lighting would shine through the slots and be seen for miles away, so illumination was kept to a minimum. Walkways were marked with luminous tape and low voltage mini bulbs lined the backs of several beams. The effects were eerie yet effective.

"Naw, not sure yet. I thought I caught a glimpse of a reflection up on that ridge across the way. Just can't be sure." The look on Daniel's face compelled Gil to lean back in the mounted chair and swivel in his direction. "What's up with you?" he asked him.

Daniel shared the message in the conversation with Murray. Gil was quiet at first, nothing to say at all. What to do wasn't his decision and Gil was not here to interfere. Then as Daniel was stepping down the staircase he spoke out anyway, "Jon needs to go see about that deal, those skinheads. If these guys did that once, they'll try again."

Daniel looked back at Gil and nodded, "Yeah, I know. I just hate piling more on. There's so much going on right now. But you're right... There's nobody else to do it."

~

Jon had gone to the IHOP near Marsha's precinct to wait. He figured he would have to stay out of sight for a while, but needed to hear from George so he would know what he was dealing with. The waitress had just brought another small pot of coffee when George finally called.

"Well, I took a shot," the DA explained meekly.

"How's that?"

"I convinced the big guy to tell them he caught his hand in the elevator."

Jon couldn't help but laugh, "And they didn't buy that?" he quipped.

"Now I thought it was reasonable, what's so funny?"

"Cameras for one thing," Jon stated. "And the fact there isn't any blood or tissue on the elevator probably didn't help. He actually told them that?" he laughed again.

"Yeah, but that didn't get too much attention."

"So," Jon calculated, "they're looking for me, now."

"Yep, Mr. Hero. They sure are. Everybody wants an interview."

What George had said didn't make any sense at all. He ran it through his head one more time and still couldn't understand. Before he asked, George spoke again.

160

"Our boy is an international criminal, a terrorist in some countries. His name is Ivan Shotsky and his picture lit up every watch list in the country."

Jon sat in stunned silence until George continued. "The cops are so pleased to have this guy, they haven't said much about what you did to him, or how." George paused to let Jon absorb what he was saying, then added. "They only want to know how you knew who he was."

He could hear Jon breathing into the phone, so he waited.

Jon finally spoke on the matter, "I don't need this either."

"Yeah, I figured," George was ready for him. "The plane is on the way, should be here in about an hour." Then he announced, "I'm staying here. I'll let you know how she is and you know we'll get security set up, big time."

Jon thought for a minute. "Thanks, man. I will need to come back by the hospital and get the bag out of the car."

"No, don't do that right now," George cautioned. "I'll bring it to you. Where are you?"

"That pancake place I told you about." Jon said.

"In plain sight, huh? I'm not surprised. See you in a few. I'm already in the car."

~

Lori Seay and Doris Shaw had spent much of their time together since Doris' late night arrival. Lori had heard the story of Doris and her abduction and the cane she still occasionally used brought those stories to life.

Early on they discussed Marsha. Lori had only heard of her and was very interested in hearing about her more from another woman's perspective. Having worked with Marsha on the decorating plans for the house, Doris felt she knew her well and what she knew she liked, very much.

161

"Jon is somewhat of an odd bird. He still has that reserved look about him, but when he's with her, he seems to open up a little," she told Lori.

Lori got her first complete tour of the big house including a secret Doris and Marsha had discovered and really didn't know what it was. The small round elevator in the corner of Jon's closet would go further down than the four levels of the house they knew about.

"Marsha had traveled down, quite by accident, to a mysterious level that had no lights." Doris shared with enthusiasm. "She asked Jon about it, but he was evasive."

Lori listened intently as she looked all around the elevator unit, not touching anything.

"Ben claims it must have been a maintenance position for the elevator and wouldn't say much else."

"You believe that?" Lori asked her.

"Knowing Jon... no." Doris grinned. "Not really I don't. There's got to be more to it than that. But I'm not worried about it. It's just interesting, one of the boy's secrets."

They talked about the house, the furnishings that Jon didn't understand he needed and almost anything else except the obvious dangers that had brought them all here. These things were not beyond either of their scope, not by a long shot. They simply chose to defer to the guys right now. They were both very strong willed and capable in their own right and if need be could deal with bad situations. They just hoped that wouldn't be necessary.

Looking into the den, Doris pointed out Jon's books, his treasured books.

"So, he's into history?" Lori asked as she let her fingers glide over the volumes.

"Very much so," Doris responded. "The American Revolution was a fascinating time, Jon reveres the men of that period."

"I remember Daniel saying something about that...messages Jon would leave, that sort of thing."

They walked on and both felt they got to know the other. They liked what they learned about each other. Finally, they came up on a meeting of the men who were discussing the plans for the evening.

As time came for Ben to make his mysterious run for groceries, it was Doris who asked if the famous pick-up truck was back. She had never really seen the heavily armored vehicle that played a great role in her rescue, having been unconscious at the time, but had heard about it and of course, she saw the hospital security pictures.

"That thing would be a good one to go in," she told the group. "If whoever is out there does take a shot at you...." She didn't finish her comment.

Everyone looked at each other and immediately agreed.

"I think I know where the keys are." Ben responded. "Thanks, Mom. Good idea."

Lori and Doris compiled a list of items for Ben to look for, things men just don't think about till they need them, things other than food. Ben disappeared back to his workshop and the other guys continued their watch. The hours passed slowly, but they did so without incident.

~

The residents of Lexington Park, Maryland, had awakened to some disturbing news that morning. It had not gone national, but was of great concern to the locals. The wife of the U.S. Congressman from that area, her daughter and fiancé were missing. They had not been heard from in over a day and the family and friends in Lexington Park were making calls and searching as they could. Police would not create a case file until forty-eight hours after the report. The neighborhood had hosted a social gathering the evening before and when none of the three showed up that in itself was unusual. Small towns knew even if they seldom spoke of unsavory things, especially if those things involved a high-ranking politician. Staying quiet was one thing, ignoring possible harm was something else altogether. Small town folks protected their own and this situation had history. Unproven history to be sure, but history nonetheless.

The congressman himself was in Washington, DC. But that was a mere fifty miles away. He had not made any statement concerning his family; others were sounding the alarm. The family yacht was gone from its mooring at Zahniser's Center in Solomon. It would be found that afternoon, run aground near Windmill Point at the southern tip of Virginia. It had hit the rocks hard and wedged itself tightly against the waves and chunks of ice in the bay. The boat would be found empty with slight traces of blood on a chair, the floor and the rug in the main cabin.

The story would go national by Sunday morning, but a version of it already sat on one of Jon's printers in the workshop area. The congressman was one from Jon's watch list and the computer had selected the local story as significant.

27

George Vincent parked in front of the precinct building and walked to the IHOP. He carried the bag with the remains of Jon's special items by the strap. It wasn't that heavy and he commented on that fact to Jon.

"That's one of the great things about what Ben has been able to do for me," Jon responded, "He reworks everything and makes it lighter, but stronger."

They sat in the booth and George looked around and smiled, "So this is the place she took you?"

"Yeah, reinforcements close by," Jon laughed for a second and then became quite serious. "She still asleep?"

George nodded and poured some coffee into a cup in front of him.

"The doctor says we just have to be patient, but the MRI looks good, she is healing and so...it's a matter of time."

Jon twisted in his seat, uncomfortable with what was on his mind more than his sitting position. Patience was his main asset. *Why was this so damned hard?* He asked himself.

"I really hate leaving right now," he told George. "It's not like I don't have things to do. I'm thinking I should go back to Dalton, but I might need to wait till the jerk Hanson sent for me shows his face."

George was about to answer when Jon's phone rang. It was Daniel. Jon held up his hand asking George to wait and answered. "Yeah, Daniel. More good news?" He asked sarcastically.

Daniel was not pleased with the greeting. "You know, I appreciate everything you're doing for us Jon, but this is no fun on our side either."

"Man, I'll explain later." Jon apologized. "I'm sorry about that, it's just been a bad day."

"I've heard from Murray Bilstock again," Daniel restarted. "He has found the bar and feels it's where the copy cats get together."

"So, he's a real 'cowboy,' huh?"

"More than you know," Daniel was blunt. "This guy is a straight shooter, problem is when he said I should come look into it, I screwed up."

"Screwed up?"

"I said I knew someone else who should do that. He figured out I know you."

Shaking his head, Jon chuckled to himself and then said; "I guess I need Ben to set up a data base with everybody who knows, so I can keep up."

"I don't think he's a problem, Jon. I really don't. I just hate being the one that slipped up."

"Has he got a number I can call him on?"

"Yeah," and Daniel gave him the cell phone number for Murray Bilstock. "Oh, there is one more thing," he added. "Ben said this local news report spit out because you were watching this guy."

"What guy?" Jon asked.

"Congressman Jason Stubblefield of Maryland." Daniel reported to him.

The name jarred Jon. It had only been a couple of weeks since he had been to Maryland to investigate this man. He didn't qualify then, not by what Jon could prove to himself.

"What's happened?" he asked Daniel.

Jon listened intently as Daniel read the story. He added, "this is just from the local folks, there's not even an official missing persons report yet."

"Have Ben stay on top of that, will ya?"

166

He asked if everybody was doing all right at the house and Daniel reported all he knew except about the plan for Ben to slip out to get supplies.

Jon had thought about coming home, but the news led him to think more about heading out west. He needed to talk to Murray first, but it may require a trip to meet this Texas cowboy. Daniel's judgment of people was usually pretty good, this bar in Greenville and the bad guys there might be important.

"I think I may go by Shreveport and check on some things," he told Daniel. "I'll call Mr. Bilstock from there and see if we can get together to talk somewhere."

They had not discussed the latest Charlotte incident, though reports of it would be on cable news stations within the hour. Ben was tickled by the headline that finally ran across the Charlotte Observer that afternoon, "<u>Superman Foils Terrorist</u>." Jon would not be.

~

The Russian troops Torbof had requested began to enter Louisiana that Saturday evening. They came individually and by much more varying means than did the Hispanics. They stayed in the homes of other gang members and smaller motels. A few came by the consulate to report in, but most then left. All the activity appeared normal so the observation teams of the Shreveport Police Department were left unaware.

The Russian gang leader received word about Ivan Shotsky's capture, but was not concerned with any fears of exposure. Shotsky did as Torbof knew he would. The now finished hit man could not tear open the collar of his shirt as planned, but he could chew on the fabric, breaking the plastic wrapping and releasing enough of the arsenic to handle the job. He died in the back of the emergency room lobby, sitting upright on a gurney, waiting for a doctor to look at his hand.

The other problems this offered were monumental. He would never know how his number one assassin got caught; the job was not done and now that effort would be much more complicated. Vasily went to his rooftop office and after an initial internal temper fit, reason took over and he decided to abandon that mission and concentrate on the Colombians. He immediately scheduled meetings with small groups of the troops who were arriving. The plan would not be one major assault, but rather a series of tactical hits throughout the southeast and if necessary, elsewhere.

The void in the cocaine distribution system clearly mapped out the Argus territories they would target. A force large enough to defend his headquarters would remain here and teams of fifteen to twenty would look for Argus operatives in cities and towns along the routes he knew. Their strikes would be more than a message; they would be a total destruction of the cartel's ability to function. Argus was weakened by events of the past year, some thought they were gone; these hits would finish the job for good.

Walking back and forth in the cool air on the roof cleared his head. Considerations of his Argus counterpart and what to do about him flashed color to his face and caused his fist to ball up unconsciously.

Vasily Torbof spun on his heels as if called by some unheard voice. He walked toward the short wall overlooking the river and stood quietly. The fist loosened as his mind again calmed down and seized on a plan. He would find and eliminate Dewey Hanson if need be, but with no soldiers left Hanson would no longer be a threat.

Why kill him, then? he puzzled.

He was momentarily proud of himself for even thinking in such humanitarian terms. As he looked out at the Red River his mind changed, as did his facial expression. This time he was sure. The decision was as firm as a marble landing in a slot on the roulette wheel, and just as certain.

Nyet, we kill them all, the thought pulled an evil smile from within.

28

Juan Castrono drove north to the town of Dahlonega, Georgia. Just off the town square was an old inn with a family style dinner advertised. Not lacking in cash at the moment, Juan attempted to check into a room. The establishment asked for a credit card as security, even though he wanted to pay cash. The cards Juan had were all backed and in fact, owned by Argus Imports. He didn't need them getting a trace on him through one of those. He would use a card in an emergency, but only that and then if the thing still worked. He wasn't sure if Hanson had said anything to the family or not. That really didn't matter right now. He declined to check into a room. Yet while he had stood there the smells from the dining room had captured him.

Walking outside to where he had parked took him past the stone steps leading down to the source of the aromas. His years in this country had brought an appreciation for American cooking, especially Southern style. The place, this Smith House, served meals like Juan had not seen before. They sat him with a group of people he didn't know at a very large table. Then brought out every known vegetable Juan could think of, four types of main course meat dishes, fried chicken, spaghetti, salads and rolls the size of dinner plates. Food was being passed around and everyone took what they wanted. If one bowl was emptied, more was brought out.

It had been two days since Juan had eaten a serious meal; he ate as though it had been a week. After dessert he left the table with rolls wrapped in napkins and stuffed into his pockets, a trick he learned watching a teen-age boy from across the table. The bill for this feast was steep, but he paid happily. The people he had sat with all spoke and said good-byes as if some family reunion was breaking up. It was a odd gathering of strangers, but Juan nodded and shook

170

hands with the rest of them. Now he needed to find a place to stay for the night.

The town had other lodging available, some that didn't ask for a credit card, so he checked into a Motel 6 just out of town and settled in. A full stomach can make a person sleepy, but there were things to consider and plans to make. He would need a new cell phone and soon. Afraid of being found by keeping his old one, Juan had thrown it out of the car near a city called Cumming. A large truck behind him scored a direct hit on the phone so there was no longer a fear of it betraying him.

Though he felt safe for the moment, Juan knew this could only be short term. Trying to concentrate on the future and what to do next was simply not working. He decided to get some sleep and figure out his plans in the morning. As he lay down and closed his eyes he rubbed his bulging stomach and wondered *if the Smith House served breakfast?*

~

Dewey Hanson missed two roll call votes that day. Saturday sessions were not the norm and missing a vote in a special session was highly frowned upon. Rep. Hanson couldn't care less at the moment. His life hung in a very peculiar balance.

Colombia had called twice that afternoon, wanting to know where Juan was and Hanson truly didn't know. Then there was what happened in Shreveport. Rumor was most of those arrested there would be shipped back to the country of their origin. That was mostly in South America. The materials were lost in the confiscation and getting more weapons of that magnitude into the US was not as easy as it used to be.

Dewey had little in the way of answers and he could tell their patience was wearing thin. Add that to his private hit man having thus far failed to get Juan and not even seeing a soul at the big house in Dalton, Georgia, and Dewey was at his wits end.

He had spent last night in his office in the Eisenhower Building, sending out for meals and thinking no one could get to him there. The flamboyant little man found his bravado falling apart and paranoia setting in. His superiors were losing faith in his abilities and so was he. All he wanted right now was to survive. With the Russians after his operation, the assassin called the Son after him, and his support collapsing, the total value of his congressional job, at this point, was a secure place to sleep.

He thought about Torbof's call, *we're really in the same shape,* he told himself. *The Russian jerk just doesn't get it yet.*

Hanson slipped out of his suit and hung it in the corner. Making himself a pillow out of a loose chair cushion, he stretched out on the couch in his office and closed his eyes.

I didn't really want this damned job, "damn it!" The last part came out loud.

~

The G5 came in easy at the private freight terminal in Charlotte. Jon had dressed in an appropriate uniform, should there be any surveillance cameras watching, and helped unload mostly empty boxes with five other hired helpers. Jon wasn't in trouble with the law, but George did not know that when he set this up. Carrying a box containing his gear, Jon climbed aboard and lay down on the sofa. He was beginning to like that sofa.

The plane taxied over to the refueling station and got a once over before being cleared to take off. The press who may have been watching for Jon, had no clue. Once in the air, the pilot asked, "Where to, boss?" almost as a joke.

"Let's go back to Shreveport. Tell me when I can use my phone will ya?"

"Shreveport it is, and I'll turn out the seat belt lights when it's okay to use your phone."

Jon pulled the number for Murray Bilstock from his shirt pocket and looked at it. *I've had people find out who I am, but never a removal's relative. This could get interesting.* He leaned against the back of the sofa and looked out the window across from him. Bright lights were replaced by stars and a few moonlit clouds. They were chasing the sun, but it had dipped below the horizon ahead of them. He thought of Marsha, and then those held up at his home. *So many loose ends,* kept repeating in his mind, *and all at the same time.* He wasn't sure what kind of test this was, but it was a doozey.

At 24,000 feet the seat belt sign went out and Jon reached for his phone.

~

In Dalton, Georgia, as darkness settled in that Saturday night, an older model pick-up truck entered the highway unnoticed and headed toward town. Ben's trip for groceries had gone without a hitch. The New York assassin was in place as was the one looking for him.

Gil watched the suspect spot on the ridge for any movement as Ben's pick-up truck passed the house. There was none. No glare or reflection, nothing.

The assassin, who was there, had watched the truck go by. But seeing no connection between it and the massive house built into the mountain, he did not react and did not give himself away. Not even later that night, when the truck went back down the mountain road and out of sight before reaching the old gas station.

For that evening, both he and Ben would go unnoticed. The chess match continued.

29

The voice answered the phone abruptly, "Yeah, who's callin'?"

Jon blinked and leaned back a bit on the sofa, *a man of few words*, he thought. *I like him already.*

"Is this Murray Bilstock?" Jon asked.

"You got him," the man responded, "what's up?"

"I'm a friend of Daniel Seay's," Jon spoke very distinctly. "He said you might have some information for me."

It was Murray's turn to react in silence; unconsciously he turned as if to face the voice from the phone. A slight smile came across his face as he settled down.

"What good it is... will be up to you," pausing, Murray took a deep breath. "I think I've found some sickos claiming to be something they ain't."

"Daniel tells me you are a straight up guy. I want to hear what you have."

"You got a name, friend?" Murray asked pointedly.

"Call me Silas."

Murray tilted his head and looked skyward. His smile had disappeared. "Ok," the disgust was apparent in his pause. "Call me Captain Kirk, then."

The quickness of that retort hit Jon and he smiled. He really did like this guy.

"No offense," he begged of the cowboy. "I'd just like to meet you face to face before I give out too much about myself."

Murray walked into his house and the sound of the boots across the porch carried through the phone. Jon waited as Murray then stared at the floor of his home and considered the other man's position. He realized he would likely do the same.

"All right, Silas," he took a breath. "When can we get together... face to face?"

"I'm coming into Shreveport, Louisiana, tonight and I'll be there tomorrow. Where are you located?"

"Shreveport? Heck," Jon could hear the man spirits light up. "I can be over there in about forty minutes." Again, the cowboy paused, "should I come in the morning?"

Jon was taken back by the suggestion, but it really sounded fine.

"How will you be coming in?" he asked.

"Fling-wing, I've got a chopper," Murray now sounded braggadocios. "Not no two wheels and high handle bars, neither," he switched the phone to his other ear. "I'll need a place to set down."

"A helicopter?"

"Yep, a Bell 407." Murray could then be heard opening a door and moving back outside. "Can you find me a spot to set down?"

Jon thought about the police heli-pad. He would need to clear it with Stone, but didn't see that as an issue.

"Yeah," he answered. "I think I can. Let me call you in the morning after I verify that, ok?"

"Look forward to it, Silas. Kirk out." and Murray flipped his phone closed.

Me, too, Jon thought as he smiled internally.

The Gulfstream Jet banked slightly left as it headed to the south. Gliding over Dahlonega and just north of Dalton. Jon checked his watch, 7:30 PM on the east coast. Captain Stone was probably having dinner about now. He decided to wait a little while before calling him. Sliding the phone into his pocket didn't prevent it from ringing. It was Ben.

"Jon, I'm afraid you made the paper here." Ben's voice was concerned and serious.

"How bad?"

"One of the cameras got a profile shot of you, it's pretty clear it's you."

"Crap, George said they were concentrating on the bad guy." Jon lamented.

"They are really," Ben stated. "But it's the headline with the pictures you're really gonna love."

Jon stayed quiet, but Ben could hear him grunt in displeasure.

"You want me to tell you, or not?" Ben asked him.

"Go ahead."

"Superman Foils Terrorist. Cute, huh?"

"You're kidding... please?"

"No sir, there's a second picture of you holding his fist. The look on his face tells the story. It's David and Goliath all over again."

"Did they use my name?"

"No," Ben assured him. "The police are keeping that buttoned up, so far. I think George had some influence there. You're an 'unnamed hero' at this point."

"Well, that's something, anything else?" Jon was being sarcastic again.

"Might as well tell you now..." Ben started...

But Jon jumped in, cynically interrupting him." What?"

"The station entrance works great."

"You went out?" Jon's voice went up an octave. "I told you guys to stay put."

"Jon, we needed supplies, man. I took the pick-up and the hologram and the doors, aw... they worked like a charm. It was great."

"Who all knows about the way out?"

"Nobody, I mean they know I got out and back, but they haven't asked 'how' other than 'where did I have the truck hidden?'"

"Damn it, be careful will ya? This is not a joke, ok?" Jon pleaded.

"We know, Jon. We all know. But if you need to come in, I know I can come out and get you without anyone knowing."

Pride in his young assistant started to set in and Jon realized that last statement might be very important and soon.

"Just be careful," he repeated in a much friendlier tone.

"You got it, boss." Ben quipped as he heard the connection break.

Jon did get the phone into that pocket this time. He leaned against the sofa back and swung his legs around to stretch out. *Pictures?* he thought. *Oh, man.*

Looking around at the vehicle he was riding in, Jon realized there was another change he needed to consider seriously. Those pictures in the news and the impending fact that he would be ID'd and very soon, created a new scenario. He may well need to stay on the move.

Calling to the cabin, Jon keyed his microphone and asked the pilot if he could come up and talk to him.

"Sure, we're just cruising right now. Come on up."

The cabin door opened and the view was quite different from the side windows. Jon sat in the right seat and looked at all the controls and gauges. There were digital readouts of everything. *Overwhelming,* came to his mind.

He looked over at his pilot who returned the stare, as if to say, *this is your party, what's on your mind?*

"Can I ask you how much you make in a year doing this?"

"Flying for Gordon? I make about $145,000.00"

"Are you married or have any ties to home?"

"Definitely not married," he laughed. "No ties that can't be broken and mended. Why, what you got in mind?"

Jon looked straight ahead at everything rushing by in the night sky.

"I may need to see if Gordon will sell me this plane or get another like it. I'll need a pilot who can follow me around and be there when I'm ready to go."

"I'm listening." The pilot said.

"You know what I do, right?"

"Not really," he said dismissively. "But I know Mr. Vincent respects you and that's good enough for me."

"Could you work exclusively for me for say, $200,000.00 per year?"

The man in the left seat smiled a broad smile and answered, "Starting when, like yesterday?"

"I'm getting a bit ahead of myself. But this may be what I need to do, and soon." Jon reached out and shook the pilots hand, "Let me work out the details. Oh, yesterday is doable far as I'm concerned. Thanks."

"Seriously," the pilot added. "If this is for real I would need to help the commissioner find another will-call pilot. He's been very good to me thus far and I wouldn't leave him in a lurch."

Standing up to go back to the passenger area, Jon nodded in total agreement.

"That's settles it for me, if I do this you're my man. Loyalty is critical with me. You're a good man." He then turned and asked, "say, what does one of these things cost, anyway?"

"New... about fifty-five million."

"Excuse me?" Jon had nearly gotten to a point where money, or the cost of things, didn't impress him much. That one did.

"Maybe thirty five to forty used." The pilot restated, "But fifty five million new."

"Really? That much, huh?"

178

"That's with everything, of course," the pilot grinned.

"Spare tire, floor mats and all, huh?"

"You wouldn't begin to believe what all comes with it. The G550 is the top of the line."

"I should hope so." Jon laughed. *I wonder if I can get one with vinyl seats?* he thought to himself.

30

George Vincent had gone downstairs for some fresh coffee. He also checked in with the business office. He was getting daily updates from his office back home and papers he needed to sign were being faxed to him at the hospital.

Life goes on and so does work, but George had great people back in Dalton and the job got done. Riding alone in the elevator he allowed himself to think with pride of his staff. His head nodded unconsciously until the unit stopped and the doors opened. As he stepped from the elevator a nurse ran towards him, it scared him.

"What? What is it?" he demanded as coffee spilled on his shaking hand.

"Sir, she's awake and she's fine. It's just that she saw the newspaper and she's screaming she knows the guy in the picture."

George sat his cup down on a ledge and followed the nurse into the room. Marsha was almost sitting upright, which was a new thing. Her expression was one of concern; almost fear. She reached out with both arms as George approached the bed.

"George, George I know that man. I know him," and then her voice went into a whisper. "He killed that congressman."

George quickly looked around the room to see who all was there to hear that. He took Marsha by her shoulders and then hugged her close.

"Baby, it just looks like someone you've seen on TV, that's all."

"No, no George. I know that man, I know I do." She was adamant about it.

George Vincent stood and put his best stern face on. He turned to the staff in the room and asked for a few minutes alone with Marsha.

"She's upset and I need to try to calm her down."

The doctors there leaned into each other and conferred for a minute, then nodding with their heads at the three nurses to follow, they left the room.

George sat down on the side of the bed and picked up the newspaper. He looked very hard at Jon's picture there and then turned to Marsha.

"Do you trust me?" he asked her.

"Trust you?" She looked more confused. "Why of course, I do." She blurted out.

"Your memories are coming back to you, but in a strange order." He started. Marsha looked at him, now totally lost. He took her hand and cupped it in his own and looked into her eyes. "Marsha, you know this man, yes. But not as you are remembering it right now."

"I don't understand."

"That's why you have to trust me." He said squeezing her hand gently. "It will all clear up and soon. I assure you, when you fully recover you will not want people to believe what you said a few minutes ago."

"But I do know him?" She asked, nearly pleading.

"Yes, sweetie, you do and he cares a great deal for you. You will remember that, too."

"But, I know he killed someone, Why is that, George?"

"Your mind is not remembering in the right order. It will be clear to you when that happens, I promise you. You'll understand everything, ok?"

"He's not going to hurt me," then she looked hard at George, "or you?"

"Not in a million years." George reached out and wiped her forehead. Then he held up the paper and asked her, "did you identify which of these men you were talking about to any of them here?"

She tried to remember and then said firmly, "No, not really."

"Good." George pointed to the other man in the picture. "This one...this one was a very bad man." He shifted even more in her direction. "I know it's not true, but it's important you let the others think he's the one you were talking about. Can you do that?"

Marsha stared at the pictures again. She looked at George and nodded.

He leaned in and gave her a big hug. "You're looking so much better. Does your head still hurt?"

"Not as bad. Thanks, George." She paused and then added, "I know papa's gone, isn't he?"

"Yes dear, he's been gone a few years now. He loved you very much."

"I'm glad you're here, George. I'm so glad you're here."

The sun peeked in through the blinds. It was harsh, but filled the room with a warm glow. George sat with Marsha for an hour that morning. She was starting to remember and she needed him there. The grey-blue walls perked up as they brought in her breakfast. A nurse adjusted the blinds, though the sun continued to get in. It was Sunday morning and it was a new day.

~

Jon woke up that morning in new surroundings. It was the guest room at Phillip Stone's house. The smell of bacon cooking made his stomach rumble and his mouth water. He sat up on the edge of the bed and remembered how he got here. He had called the police Captain as the G5 landed last evening and Stone insisted he come to their home. Jon resisted, but Stone would have none of that.

There was coffee and bananas foster when he arrived. He was treated like a long lost friend. It seemed weird, but it was nice. They briefly discussed the use of the heli-pad for Murray Bilstock and the incident with the big man in Charlotte, but most of the evening

182

was lighter. Stone's wife and daughter were there so talk was of things other than murder and mayhem.

Jon got a quick shower, shaved and dressed that morning. As he entered the kitchen area he could see his new friend on the phone making arrangements for use of the helicopter facilities.

"Yeah," he was saying to someone, "I don't know how long, we've got three pads don't we?"

The conversation was mostly one sided with Stone explaining what would happen. He finally hung up and turned to see Jon standing there.

"Hey... coffee?" he offered as he pointed to the table.

"Please."

"You can tell your guy he can come in on these vectors," he handed Jon a piece of paper, "and use pad number three. It'll be marked, he can see it from the air easy."

The numbers on the paper meant little to Jon, but Phil assured him they would mean more to a pilot.

Stone's wife, Sara walked over with the coffee pot and asked how Jon would like his eggs.

"However you're fixing 'em, Sara. Thank you."

"Scrambled it is," she announced and turned back to the stove. "Hot sauce?"

"Uh, no please." Jon was a bit concerned at that thought.

Mrs. Stone smiled, "I thought not, it's a Louisiana thing."

The three had breakfast without the daughter, "She sleeps till noon on the weekends." her dad explained. Then he handed Jon a newspaper. "You've got quite a profile for a superhero," he joked.

Jon finally saw the pictures he had heard about last night.

"Matt called this morning," Stone said. "He had no idea you were here. He just wanted me to know he had no choice but to run the pictures and the story."

Jon nodded in acceptance and laid the paper down on the table without saying a word. Phil picked it up and looked again.

"Damn, how did you do that hand thing?" he tilted his head at Jon and smiled.

Jon mumbled something to himself and Stone didn't press it.

"Don't sweat it, Jon," the Captain was being sincere. "This will die down in a few days."

"Argus won't let it die down." Jon took a sip of his coffee and continued, "that big jerk in those pictures was sent by your man Torbof to silence Marsha and any other witnesses, of which I am now one."

"Do you even know who that was you went up against?" the police officer asked.

"Some goon, Torbof sent."

"Yeah...some goon alright. He was wanted internationally. Ivan was a stone cold killer. You took a real deal off the market."

"Just don't need the damned pictures." Jon mumbled.

"Call your man in Texas, we'll work these things out one at a time. There's an answer here, we'll find it." Stone asserted as he glared at Jon quite fatherly over his cup. Jon got up and went to get his cell phone. He stopped at the door for a second and looked back. "One at a time. You're right."

"Damn straight, I'm right." Captain Stone smiled and raised his cup in a salute.

Jon reached Murray and asked if the coordinates meant anything to him.

"Sure," Murray was confident. "I can be there in an hour and a half."

"You said forty minutes last night," Jon teased.

"Hell, man. I got to get her out of the barn first. See ya in a bit."

184

31

It was 10:30 AM when Phil Stone pulled his unmarked cruiser to the side door of his home to wait for Jon.

"I'll drive." Jon hollered as he pointed toward his rental.

"You can't get in where we're going in a private vehicle. Jump in."

The drive would only take a few minutes and Stone had several questions he did not ask around his family. Jon sat quiet, looking out his window as the Shreveport suburb of Brunswick Place streamed by. Turning out the large gates onto the main road, Stone opened up.

"I've shaken hands with you. You're in good shape, but seriously..."

"It's a hydraulic enhancement," Jon interrupted. He looked over at his friend and repeated himself. "A fabric framed hydraulic enhancement."

"I'll be damned...so that thing works?" Stone sounded surprised.

"You've heard of it?"

"Oh, hell yeah." Phil smiled like a cat. "Couple of years ago, maybe longer, the defense department sent out a memo to be on the lookout for folks trying to use the thing. They claimed it wasn't reliable."

Jon just smiled and Phil Stone said again, "I'll be damned."

They turned into the air vehicle post of the Shreveport Police Department and Phil parked near a flat concrete pad.

"This friend of yours, from Texas?" he asked.

"It's a friend of Daniel's. Name is Murray Bilstock."

"Bilstock? Ain't that the name of a senator that got dead out there last year?"

185

"The same."

"Does he know?"

Jon's look became somewhat perturbed with that. He opened the car door and climbed out. Phil leaned over and shouted out the door.

"You'll really rather be in here when he sets down, believe me." He offered.

Jon got back into the car and gestured with both hands, "I'm not sure what all he knows." he said in frustration. "The man claims to have info on a group of bad guys that might have had something to do with the shooting in Mississippi."

"He knows these people?"

"No, no...no. Not like that." Jon tried to organize the little he did know about it. "A cousin of his stumbled over them at a bar. Then he went to check it out for himself and seems to think it could be them."

"Do I need to caution you?"

"I have a good feeling about this guy, I think he's good people. I just don't know if he's put two and two together yet, that's all."

The wind began to pick up severely and Jon understood what Phil had meant. The Bell 407 eased down as though from nowhere and gently bumped down on the concrete. The police car rocked in the force of the wind.

"Sit tight till he's killed the engine," Stone warned.

The props had a bit of a forward lean to them, and as they slowed Jon could see how lethal they could be. Heavy metal blades spinning at great speed, a virtual open air blender if they came into contact with something.

The left side door opened and a cowboy climbed down, holding his hat in place with his hand. Jon climbed from the car and approached him, "Murray Bilstock?" he asked with his hand extended.

"That's me." The cowboy looked him right in the eyes, "you must be Silas."

"How was your flight, Captain Kirk?" Jon teased him.

"Just fine, Silas." Murray smiled and tipped his big hat, "just fine."

"That's a nice machine, a real nice machine." Jon looked past him at the copter.

"Lucy," the cowboy said. "Yeah, Lucy's cool."

Activity picked up around the area as Captain Stone emerged from his car and several police mechanics came from the surrounding buildings. Some tied down the copter and others began looking her over. Murray looked as though he was concerned about all the attention when Jon spoke again.

"You call her Lucy?" He grinned and stepped toward the machine.

Murray squinted his eyes, "she look like a Shirley to you?"

Jon laughed and turned back toward the cowboy. "Not at all. Can I check her out?"

The general walk around inspection continued.

"Sure, everybody else is." Murray pulled on the door panel and slid it open.

As he leaned in, Jon could see Captain Stone's reflection as the officer approached. Stepping back, he pointed toward Stone and announced,

"Murray, this is Captain Phil Stone of the Shreveport police."

"Pleasure, sir." doffing his hat. "Thanks for the hospitality."

The men shook hands and Stone asked him, "what kind of fuel does she take?"

"JP-4," Murray replied out of reflex, then added. "Why's that?"

Stone looked to one of his mechanics who nodded affirmatively and then Phil turned back to Murray.

"We'll service her and fill her up for you while you guys talk." he told him. "They're good. They'll take real good care of your bird."

"That's mighty nice of you, sir." Murray tipped his hat again. "Thanks much."

"Welcome to Louisiana, son."

He then directed Jon and the Texas cowboy to a conference room in a nearby hanger. As he excused himself he told them to make themselves at home,

"It's pretty private in here, stay long as you need to."

"Thanks, Phil." Jon shook his hand as the captain left.

~

Whitewright, Texas, was quiet that Sunday. Three men met in a small building at the end of an abandoned strip mall. The beer was only half cold, but they didn't mind. They were making plans to add to the changes they had already caused.

One big, paunchy member of the group, with hair everywhere except on his head, rose from the barber chair he used as a recliner and walked over to a small table.

Picking up a photo, he turned back to the others, "This guy is next." He proclaimed. "Smart-ass, big talking scumbag," he took the photo and handed it to one of the others.

"Who's this?" was asked in a near drunken stupor.

"Who's this? Ya dumb shit, that's Red Yardley." The first man barked.

The last one of those there spoke up, "Gov. Yardley of Arkansas, moron." Then he looked at the large, standing man. "What'd he do?"

"He appoints these jerks after the other ones gets killed. We get him outta the way first and then take out Hollings."

They knew Rep. Markus Hollings was on their list, but news reports showed a close connection of Hollings' brother-in-law to

188

the governor, so the brain trust in the room had decided to eliminate that replacement possibility first.

"How we gonna get him?" the second one asked.

"Blow his ass up." the first one smiled.

"With what?" the last one asked meekly.

"Damn, fool. Where you been?" the leader was getting upset with his troops. "C-4, we got C-4 blocks from the army depot. They thought we was stealing gasoline. We did some," he laughed. "But we got 6 blocks of C-4 and two caps."

"Hot damn, gimme another beer," said the second one.

"We got to pick who we send. This needs to done by end of next week." The leader told them. The others looked at each other. Handling explosives was not what either wanted to do. They thought and listed off the members in their heads. After a couple of minutes, two came up with the same answer.

"Willie." They said in near unison

The big guy sat down and took a swig of his beer, "Willie," he repeated. "Yeah."

"You know how and where this is gonna happen?" was asked.

The big man stood back up. He walked across the room to a desk piled high with papers. Scattering the surface documents about, he found the instructions from their sponsors. He didn't know just who they were, but the sponsors were powerful men with money. And it took money to do what they wanted done. The money had been nice, lots of beer, big parties in Greenville and several new bikes for the club. But now, they wanted jobs in return. The Mississippi job was the first. The sponsors supplied all the materials and the ideas. The gang supplied the manpower.

The big hairy man found what he sought. Holding it up, he proclaimed, "There's an event the Governor will be at in Hope, a week from Thursday."

Hope, Arkansas, was not that far away, just across the state line and up I-30 a bit.

"When he leaves, the caravan will travel up '30' to Little Rock. They will go by car cause the mighty Governor has a girl friend in Arkadelphia he wants to see."

"Those politician types get all the good..." the second man started, but was interrupted by his boss.

"We blow the overpass at Delight Highway as they go through Prescott, Ark."

"The whole overpass?" the question came from across the room.

"Yeah," the whole damn thing, with him on it." The leader answered.

"How does Willie get away from there?" the second man asked.

The leader turned and looked hard at the questioner. He said nothing for several moments then asked another question in return, "Willie shot his mouth off at the bar a couple weeks back, didn't he?"

No one responded, they all knew he had.

"Then that bad ass cowboy comes snooping around last week. He knows something. I'm having his tag traced to find out just who he is."

"What ya gonna do with him, Tommy?" the second man implored.

"Damn it, don't use my name while we're here, fool." The big man stormed over and stood threateningly above the other. The smaller man tried to make amends.

"Sorry, Tommy. I mean, shit... sorry, ugh... Turnip."

Tommy Tyler climbed back into his barber chair and leaned back. "We're not taking any chances with that cowboy. When I find out who he is, he's done."

Still having trouble keeping up with the conversation, the second man asked again, "and Willie?"

"Willie don't come back from Arkansas. You got a problem with that?"

The second man shook his head "no" and kept quiet that time.

"Alright, that's it then. Council's done. See everybody Friday night at the Deuce."

32

The hanger was nice, but the conference room was nicer. A large table, nearly five feet wide sat in the middle with high back leather chairs all around it. The sidewalls were covered in cabinets and there was a sink near one end.

Jon started looking through the room, "There must be a little mini fridge in here," he suggested.

Murray went down the opposite side, opening doors and commenting; "You'd think they'd have whiskey and doughnuts in here somewhere."

Jon chuckled as he found the doors hiding the mini fridge. "Here we go, you want a ginger ale or a diet coke?"

Murray looked across at him and wrinkled his nose, "That's it?"

Jon pulled one of each and held them up as displays.

"Give me a diet coke," Murray tried to sound disappointed.

They found chairs across from each other and settled in. Jon looked out the window and saw the ground crew checking the helicopter.

"They're putting air in the tires for ya, now," he smiled at Murray.

"Your friend seems like a good one to have." The cowboy proclaimed as he tipped the small bottle up.

"Stone? Oh my, yes. He's a good man." Jon thought a minute then added, "if I'd known there were friends like him out there, I'd have started getting to know people a lot quicker."

Murray nodded and then pulled his hat off. He ran his fingers through to straighten his "hat" hair and sat the Stetson on the table.

"How long have you known Daniel?" The cowboy asked bluntly.

Jon figured that question was loaded, but couldn't think of how to avoid it.

"Met him last fall," he answered and then continued with, "but I've really known him since a few weeks after that."

Murray didn't speak. He just waited for the follow up.

"He got his butt in a crack and I was able to help him out." Jon finished.

"Hear tell, you saved his life."

"That may have happened... yeah."

"I like Daniel," Murray laid out there. "Not sure why," he smiled. "But I do."

It was Jon's turn to stay quiet and simply agree. Murray leaned forward and put both forearms on the table. He looked hard at Jon before he started with his story.

"My cousin Slick, found 'em first." He took another hit on the diet coke. "It was by accident, he was bar hopping and just happened to be there."

Jon didn't interrupt. He let Murray take all the time he wanted.

"I didn't think too much of it at first, 'cept the part about using your handle." He took a deep breath and let it out slowly. "Decided I'd go up there and check 'em out myself."

Letting the reference to "Jon's handle" pass without comment, Jon studied the man across from him. He was clear and calculating. He wasn't fearful or concerned by what he was telling.

"Unfriendly bunch." Murray went on. "I had to leave there the best I could that night." He chuckled a bit and added, "Still owe a nice man a shotgun."

That in itself described the circumstances to Jon. Those men in the bar had not scared the cowboy, not one bit.

"I learned they get together there on Friday nights." Murray looked up at Jon. "If they was claiming to be me, I'd want to know." He pushed back against the leather chair until it tilted a few degrees and concluded, "That's why I'm here."

Jon leaned back himself. His left hand compulsively rubbed his chin as he looked blankly at the tabletop. It was time to ask the question. Murray had referred to who Jon was twice now.

"Murray, do you believe you know who I am?"

The cowboy was ready for him. He responded with a question of his own. "You gonna bring my Daddy into this right away?"

The frankness made Jon lean back for a second. This man knew no fear. "So, you do know?" He answered with yet another challenge. His tone was stern.

Murray twisted sideways and looked back across the table. "You know," he rubbed his forehead and then continued. "I never really was...sure," Murray glanced outside and then back at Jon. "That you or anyone had any part in it. Until now." There was another lengthy pause till he went on. "All I knew was... he was done...no more of his bullshit. And that's all that mattered."

He didn't know if Murray was carrying anything or not, but Jon's right hand lay at his side in the chair. He pulled the flap loose over his Glock.

Murray seemed to sense Jon's concerns. He bent back over the table and stretched both hands forward.

"I had tried to find a way to do something myself." He confessed. "But I didn't want to go to jail or get killed trying." He looked Jon right in the eye again, "You knew about the kids... and what he did, didn't ya?"

Jon nodded, slowly.

"I found out through my sister," Murray tilted his head back. "She still ain't over it, even with him gone."

Jon's tension eased as he listened, but the grip of the Glock was now free of the pocket. Daniel had shared what he knew about this story some time back. But this was first person, from one of the "removeds" family members. The sincerity could not be denied.

"You stopped a bad thing, Silas." Murray squinted hard trying to hold back emotions. He covered his face with his hands and rubbed his eyes. Then pushing his chair back from the table, Murray's chest heaved with a deep breath of composure. He looked straight across the table at a man obviously waiting to hear what came next.

"You have my word, I hold no harm against you," Murray professed, "none at all." He then looked Jon square in the eyes. "If I did... we wouldn't be sitting here like this." The cowboy then leaned back and finished with, "you can believe that."

Jon slid the weapon back into the pocket and slowly put his hands on the table as well. He was aware of himself breathing deeply; it was not a usual thing for him. He sought the right words to respond.

"Murray, my name is Jonathan Crane," is what came out. "I'd be proud if you'd call me Jon."

It was Murray's turn to simply nod.

A knock on the door barely preceded the entrance of Phil Stone.

"Can I come in for a second?" he asked. Looking back and forth at the two men he could tell the discussion had been fairly serious. *Guess they cleared that up,* he thought as he stepped forward.

"You wanted information on the Fairmont Building, here's what I got." He handed Jon a folder about an inch thick and sat down at the table.

There were floor plans and architectural drawings of the buildings construction. The former apartment building had been purchased by the Russian government twelve years earlier and converted into office space. The plans showed both before and after the physical alterations were made.

Another section had records of inspections and registration forms for the Consulate Offices. Something in the inspections caught Jon's eye. As he looked up to explain what that was to Stone, Jon noticed Murray's expression. He was watching them go through the papers in total quiet, but his face asked, *what does this have to do with anything?*

A fast consult with the Captain, who agreed and Jon began to bring Murray up to speed on why he was in Shreveport to start with. In the briefest of terms, they told of the Russians and the Hispanics, their budding war, the attack in Charlotte and Jon's girlfriend getting hurt.

The cowboy's face grimaced with the weight of what he was hearing and when Jon told of the big Russian hit man sent to silence Marsha, Murray raised his hands and spoke.

"You guys got a bit of shit going on," he started. "My little tale fits in here somewhere?"

"Not in a direct way, no." Jon responded. He tried to think how everything tied together so he could explain it. There was no real connection, other than him.

"This other stuff is what has had my attention, over the killing in Mississippi." Murray appeared to understand that without commenting so Jon continued, "I need to deal with your biker friends and you stepping up has saved a ton in time. There's just," he gestured at the papers on the table, "a bunch more going on."

"I see that," Murray reached for his hat. "I'd be glad to help, but if I'm in the way I can head out," and he stood as though to leave.

"You got time?" Jon asked. "We could use some help."

"For stuff like this?" the cowboy laughed. "Hell, yeah. I might could pitch in. I don't like drugs and I don't like murderers...usually." He winked at the officer.

Phil Stone was getting the same impression of Murray Bilstock that Jon had. He pushed his chair back in jest and faked complaining.

"Shoot, with you two on this, you probably don't need me."

It was a silly thing to say, but it let Murray know he was welcome, by both of the men. They asked the cowboy what he knew about building. He had worked construction in younger years, some on high rises in Dallas. Jon passed him the plans and then completed the point of what he had noticed in the inspection papers.

"The roof has never been inspected for fire as an occupied space," he noted.

Phil reached over and took the papers from him. He studied the documents for several minutes and concluded, "Damn, you're right."

"I need to get up there and look around." Jon added. But then he remembered something. "My dang picture is in all the papers, I've screwed my chances of going unnoticed." He tossed the folder on the table in disgust and shook his head.

"I can do it," the voice announced. It was Murray. "They don't know me, I can play your role and get what you need."

Jon and Phil stared at each other, then at Murray.

"How long can you stay? We'd need to do this on a weekday." Jon asked.

"Yeah, I can stay." But then the cowboy had a thought. "Can I leave Lucy here?"

"I'll fix it so you can." Phil said confidently, "and we'll need to get you some credentials that look real in the meantime."

"Speaking of Lucy," Jon thought out loud. "How about a ride to check out that rooftop from the air?"

Murray Bilstock smiled in approval and pointed his thumb at Capt. Stone. "It's his gas," the cowboy cracked.

33

It had been a quiet morning in Dalton. A cold front brought frost and that offered reflections. The grass across the highway sparkled in the sun and Albie Kurtz, one of Gil's men, was on duty at the gun slot. He too had noticed the spot at the top of the ridge, where what could be the front end of a rifle scope would fire the light of the sun in their direction from time to time.

The cold made the hit man fidgety. He was a pro. But not all things can be blocked from a person's mind. Cold in his case, was one of them.

"Have Gil come here." Albie called to Daniel. "There's definitely something up there that's moving around."

Gil checked the view through the scope of their rifle and agreed.

"I want to talk to Jon." He announced. Daniel threw his hands up and reached for his phone.

"I don't know if we should bug him," he said as he scrolled through to the number.

"We're tired of sitting here like captives." Gil took the phone and hit the button to dial. It was ringing on the other end as Ben walked up to the attic.

He listened to the conversation from one side and figured what Jon must be saying. "Be completely sure and don't risk anybody to do that, otherwise...take him out."

When Gil had hung up, Ben stepped up, "I may know how you can flush him out."

"Ok," the senior cop replied. "What have you got?"

Ben told him of the T-Rex, the .577 caliber rifle he had ordered.

"A box of shells came in last night," he told them.

"Last night? We didn't get any deliveries last night," the officer challenged.

"Not here, from the warehouse in town. I ran by while I was out. You should see the things, they are almost five inches long."

"You want I should shoot a man with an elephant gun?" Gil handed the seat back to Albie.

"No, just uproot the ground under him and see what he does." Ben's eyes widened as he spoke.

"Show me," the cop said and they went downstairs. Gil waited in the living room while Ben pulled the weapon and a box of twenty cartridges from his workshop. He also brought the extra "arm" unit with him. When Gil asked what that was for Ben waved with a finger to follow him into the kitchen. On a Dell system simply for the house use, Ben pulled up a U-Tube video of men trying to fire the T-Rex, and remain standing. Most let the rifle fly out of their arms; some fell on their backsides.

"This will help?" Gil asked as he held up the hydraulic arm webbing.

"I don't know," Ben laughed. "Guess we'll find out."

Back in the attic, they got Gil hooked up in the arm unit and activated the power. The cop said he couldn't feel any difference except in his shoulder.

"That should come in handy, don't ya think?" Albie was looking at the box of cartridges. "750 grains of powder... damn."

Ben quoted from the manual, "That round will travel at 2750 feet per second."

"He's about 700 yards out," Albie spoke up.

"He won't hear it till after it hits." Gil smiled.

Daniel stepped back and went down to warn the women about the impending noise.

"You guys are nuts," was his parting shot at them.

The barrel of the weapon barely fit through the slot in the roof.

"Can you see through the scope?" Ben asked him.

After fiddling with it a minute, the reply was affirmative. Gil braced himself and pulled the rifle tight against his shoulder. The hydraulic arm held it firmly.

"You might want to aim low," Ben suggested. "I haven't calibrated the sights yet."

Gil twisted his head and gave Ben a stare, then settled back into firing position. Albie opened a slot some twenty feet down from where Gil was and stuck his .308 through the opening. When he was ready he hollered to Gil, "I'm set."

"Fire in the hole." Gil muttered as he squeezed the trigger on the T-Rex.

The sound bounced around in the attic as if a jet plane had just blasted its engine in there. Gil rocked back and slid off the stool, but kept his feet. He didn't see where the round went, but Albie did.

The ground under the unknown man swelled as though a bomb had exploded under him. The edge of the hill then collapsed, dropping him nearly two feet at a forty-five degree angle. The rifle he held was dislodged from his grip as he flailed wildly for something to hang on to. "Oh, man." He yelled. "That's him alright."

"What happened?" Gil was trying to get back where he could see through the scope.

"You hit just below him in the dirt and rock. It looked like a C4 stick went off in there, man." Albie looked at them a second and continued. "He's still alive, but he needs new drawers! The whole damned surface under him collapsed into a big, deep hole." He twisted his head to look back at them again, "He about went over the side. His rifle did."

A rumble of footsteps charged up from below as the third and youngest of the cops there, Walt Reinhart burst into the attic with his 9mm in hand.

"What the hell?" Came out before the scene in front of him required that he shut up and listen. Reinhart holstered his weapon, but remained befuddled with what was happening. Daniel and Ben were rubbing their ears while his cohorts shouted at each other.

"Where is he now?" Gil demanded, straightening his chair and trying to sight the area again.

"He bugged out, man." Albie was still laughing, "Gone looking for those new drawers I reckon."

They picked up the dust of a vehicle leaving that area and Albie sighted in on the road coming down the hill. He placed two .308 rounds into the road just in front of the car causing it to swerve and nearly wreck.

"Fulton County tag," Gil called out, as he was able to zero in on the car turning up the highway. "Rental, I'll bet. From the airport in Atlanta."

The men had their obligatory victory dance with high fives and knuckle bumps all around. Then Gil regained control of the moment.

"Let's get up there and see if he left anything beside that rifle."

~

The friends and neighbors of the Stubblefield family spent the morning trying to organize a search of Lexington Park, Maryland. There wasn't much they could do, especially about the boat found on the bay. A search there would take more than they could muster. State police and Coast Guard would have to do that.

The congressman was still absent from his hometown and still had not called or sent word of any kind. The close friends knew in their hearts what had happened. They had feared this for a long time, but could do nothing about it. The gathering was to organize a search, but it became more a commiseration. The sharing of grief they all knew would soon become very real.

~

It was several minutes before 2:00PM in Charlotte. The remainder of the morning and lunchtime had gone quietly. George Vincent sat with Marsha most of the time, but she said little more. She was beginning to come around and he knew she would ask questions if need be. He could tell Marsha was calmer now. The pictures in the paper and her foggy memories of Jon were not the problem they had been. Jon's name was still lost to her, but she didn't appear stressed over it at all. She was less concerned and that pleased George.

The quiet was so intense that he could clearly hear the elevator doors opening again. George leaned over from his chair to look down the hallway.

Two men in dark grey suits emerged and immediately were directed toward Marsha's room. One of the nurses who had been in the room that morning was doing the directing and stepped lively with a self important, near smile hanging from her face.

A doctor met them just short of the room itself and George could tell he was not approving of their visit yet they convinced him of their need. There was a slight knock and the door pushed open.

"Lt. Hurst?" One of the men asked.

The doctor quickly corrected him, "It's Miss Hurst right now, we haven't progressed to that stage."

The man in the dark suit nodded his understanding and stepped closer to Marsha's bedside.

"Miss Hurst, I'm Special Agent Wilbanks and this is Special Agent Kurtz, we're with the FBI." He paused as though that information needed time to be absorbed and then continued. "We understand you recognized one of the men in this morning's newspaper. Is that true?"

Marsha glanced momentarily at George, his eyebrows were drawn down and his lips were pressed together tightly. "Oh, yes sir, you bet." She smiled at Wilbanks. "My daddy arrested that big one."

The nurse jumped forward and grabbed Wilbanks' arm, "That's not what she said at all, not this morning."

The FBI agent removed her hand from his arm and gave her a stern look. The doctor took a step and leaned into Agent Wilbanks' ear and said something. The Agent's expression barely changed though his eyes widened just a bit. He then moved closer still to Marsha and held a copy of the paper for her to see.

"This is the paper you saw this morning?" Wilbanks asked.

"That's it," Marsha smiled a broad smile and looked past the visitors to George, his face had eased and he was nodding very slightly. "That big guy," she touched the paper with her finger, "shot a congressman right here in Charlotte and daddy caught him, you can talk to him about it." She looked around as though seeking someone, then turned to George and asked directly. "Is he coming in today, Uncle George?"

The nurse was shaking her head and mumbled, "Aw... come on."

George quietly stood and answered Marsha's question.

"Not today, baby. Not today."

With that, the nurse could no longer control herself, bursting with another complaint, "She lying. I don't know what's going on, but she's lying. I know what she said this morning."

The two men in dark grey suits looked to the doctor, who said nothing, but was clearly displeased, then at each other. Agent Kurtz motioned with his head for them to leave. The nurse glared at Marsha and then noticed the doctor staring at her.

"Can I see you outside for a moment?" The doctor asked her and they stepped into the hallway.

George said nothing. He simply walked over to Marsha and squeezed her hand gently.

"You're sure about this" She asked him.

He again lightly squeezed and smiled at Marsha.

The nurse was not seen on that floor again.

34

Murray showed Jon how to use the helmet as a communication device and got him strapped into the right seat in Lucy. As the rotations increased so did the noise and the vibrations. Jon said something, but did not have his microphone in the right position so Murray had to gesture for him to fix it.

"Damn, this thing is loud," he finally managed to express.

Murray smiled and said, "Hang on," and the helicopter lifted off from the pad.

Jon's hands instinctively grabbed the bottom of the seat, but he did fabricate a small smile. Lucy rose quickly and banked left all in one smooth motion as Murray headed them toward the river. From there he banked left again and slowly reduced altitude as they approached the Fairmont Building. He slowed to nearly dead stop as Lucy made her first pass.

Jon had a camera he borrowed from the police department and was clicking fast as he could. The rooftop was not occupied at the moment, but the structures were there and the aluminum lawn chair sat in the corner.

Murray pulled up and Lucy roared ahead till they were out of sight from the building and then he swung her around. This time he passed at almost the same height as the rooftop with the building at Jon's right. The camera clicked again as he tried to capture every angle of view.

As Murray leaned Lucy forward and again sped away, he could see a figure coming out through a door on the roof. The copter was getting a hard look over by whoever it was. Murray swung around and made another pass, this time at a different building some eight blocks away. It was close enough for the inquisitor on the roof to witness and he soon left as he had entered.

"That's all for this time," Murray told Jon. "They're about on to us. But they don't know why."

"That's fine," Jon replied. "In fact, that was great. If these pictures come out we've got what we need."

"I'm impressed." The cowboy stated.

"Impressed," Jon was puzzled. "At what?"

"You didn't barf." Murray laughed.

That was closer to being a fact than Murray realized. It had been years since Jon's training and riding in Apaches, the Army's AH-64 attack helicopter.

The mind remembers, but the stomach forgets. He thought quietly.

"That roof wall doesn't look right to me." Murray commented. "I'm no engineer or architect, but I've never seen a parapet that weak. It should be at least two brick thick."

Jon simply looked at his pilot and nodded. He made a mental note of the observation as he settled back against the seat.

They crossed the river and went out a few miles before turning back to the police flight field. Phil was waiting for them as they set down.

"We're going to dinner with Matt," the officer announced.

Jon looked over at Murray, nodded once and said, "You'll like him."

~

The woman's voice pierced the other noise within the small house. It was harsh, shrill and loud, "Tommy, phone." She screeched.

The voice belonged to Liz Tyler. Her husband, Thomas Tyler, AKA Tommy, AKA Turnip was who she hollered for. Their home in

Savoy, Texas, was only seven miles, as the crow flies, from Whitewright, more like twelve by highway.

Yelling was a normal thing in the Tyler home and sometimes went unnoticed, but Tommy heard her this time. He lowered the volume on his TV and twisted his head toward her voice.

"I got it, damn it," he fired back as he pulled himself from the broken recliner and walked to the wall phone in their kitchen. "Yeah, what is it?" He demanded of the caller.

"Turnip, Gincy here. I got a message from the sponsors on that cowboy."

"What?" Tyler was surprised. "So soon?"

"Yeah, the call came in from Connecticut, just now."

Turnip Tyler rubbed his baldhead and looked around to see who might be listening.

"The clubhouse, thirty minutes." He ordered and hung up the phone.

Turnip and Gincy met at the clubhouse where the group's leader was informed of the message. The sponsors wanted this cowboy out of the picture.

"His tag had traced back to a Murray W. Bilstock of Brownwood, he had just moved to Caddo Mills to set up a ranch there." Gincy told him.

"Bilstock?" Turnip thought out loud. "One of them Bilstocks?"

"Looks like it." Gincy looked very concerned. "What would he want with us?"

Tommy Tyler felt a weak spot in his gut start to move on its own.

"Shit, they had us use that 'Son' label. Folks say he's what killed that senator and that senator was a Bilstock."

Gincy's eye's lit up, "You think he heard Willie shooting his mouth off and now he's after us."

"Is or ain't, can't take the chance." Tommy declared. "Too damn close for me, we got to take him out. Where is this ranch?"

Gincy showed his boss a map of the area and they planned to get a crew together for a ride.

"Call the boys, we go in the morning. Gas can saddle bags on the hogs," Turnip ordered.

Gincy left the building and Tommy Tyler went over and sat in his barber chair to think. *Why the hell did they want us to leave that friggin' note about that 'Son' guy?*

The sponsors had been supplying money, guns, beer and liquor to the club for months. They requested a few small robberies and break-ins, one at the National Guard Armory in Garland, Texas. But it was mostly small time stuff.

They never identified themselves or said what they wanted; just that they might need some muscle for a few big favors in the future.

Well, the future is here, murder is 'big time'. Tommy realized he had gotten his boys neck deep in shit. *Nothing to do, but 'do' the thing.*

He spun the chair around and smiled, *hell...we take out this cowboy and we're golden. The threat's gone, ain't no more like him around anyways, this will be it.*

Tommy laid the note Gincy had brought on his desk and slapped the light switch off. Locking up, he looked down the street of Whitewright; there wasn't a soul anywhere. As he drove home he considered the other problem he now had, what to tell Liz about not going to work tomorrow.

Shit, she'll git over it. He convinced himself.

~

Dewey Hanson was not having a good Sunday. The couch in his congressional office was not nearly as comfortable as he

209

remembered from those afternoon naps and the pizza he ordered for lunch got there cold.

The newspaper stories of the situation in Charlotte didn't help. He had almost convinced himself that the paranoia he felt was overdone. *Apparently not,* was now his thought on the subject.

The stories from Charlotte did not use the title "The Son," yet he looked at the pictures and knew that was the man he should fear.

Hanson almost missed the phone call. His cell for communications with his "hired man" hung in a coat pocket across the room, he barely heard it ring.

"Yeah?" he answered cautiously.

"This deal is done, man," the excited voice proclaimed. "I'm outta this."

"What are you talking about?" Hanson demanded.

"Sons a bitches shot a cannon at me, that's what." The sounds of him driving, and fast at that, could be heard through the phone. "No movement, no sign of anybody and then that. Hell, how did they know I was there, man? I never moved."

"I paid you, Bertalli..." Hanson tried.

"Screw that, man." the caller interrupted him "The plane ride and the rental car are on you, the rest I'm sending back. If you don't like it, you come get me." The man was breathing deeply and trying to regain his voice. "You don't scare me...they do."

Hanson attempted to respond, but the line went dead. He threw the phone against the back wall of the fireplace where it shattered into pieces and then burned.

That was the only muscle for hire he knew he could call on without alerting Argus, *hell, Argus is over*, he thought. *It's the cartel now.*

~

Albie was familiar with the view of the area through a shooting slot so he stayed in the attic to cover the others as they searched the sniper's former position. Walt was sent to collect the weapon, which had fallen nearly to the highway level. The blue steel shone brightly against the gray rock dust. Walt was impressed.

"I've got a Kimber 8400 down here," he radioed up to Gil.

"Nice... This guy was serious." Gil knew that weapon well. The Kimber 8400 is a sniper rifle using .308 rounds. It was extremely accurate and for that reason, pricey. "That'll make a nice addition to Jon's collection."

Daniel was on the hilltop with Gil. They looked for anything left behind by the hit man. Blankets and thick paper cups were all they found. The man must have had a bag he grabbed and took with him, but he still had spent a spartan existence while there.

The cups were placed in plastic bags to check later for DNA or fingerprints. As with the rifle, no prints were found. He had worn gloves. The cups had been sprayed with a bathroom cleaner, something containing bleach. No DNA, no prints, no identification.

Ben sent several small, remote microphones with them. Gil and Daniel set them up in various spots around the hilltop. Any future visitors there would be monitored.

~

A copy of the "Dahlonega Nugget" had lain in the hall outside Juan Castrono's motel room since early that morning. Juan slept in, skipped breakfast and missed his chance to look at the paper. The cleaning crew picked it up while making their rounds.

The story of the terrorist in Charlotte was on page four and the picture was small, but it was clear. That didn't matter. Juan did not see it. He went out, for only a short while, around 4:30 to 5:00 PM to pick up a burger at a drive through. The huge meal from last night was good, but not something you did two days in a row.

211

Juan ignored the news, hardly had the TV on in his room, and just chose to sleep most of the time away. He was not a drinker and it was too late to start, so sleep was his escape from reality. Staring at a small crack of light that crept into the room through the blinds, Juan slowly drifted out.

It would be Monday morning when he next awoke.

35

The car was followed by two stretch vans as it made its way north on Peachtree Industrial Blvd. in North Atlanta, Georgia. An arm suddenly pointed out the passenger side window and the car turned right into an industrial park. Several additional turns later the arm again pointed and the car stopped. An old, worn-out sign on the building said "Doraville Ice Company."

In all there were 16 men who emerged from the three vehicles, all were heavily armed and none stopped to ask any questions. The attack was fast and violent and within minutes anyone in or near the ice plant was dead.

Most inside were employees of Argus, but not soldiers. They were first thought to be warehousemen and drivers for the delivery company helping to set up. They had come in that morning to try to find out what was going on. No orders had been given and nothing appeared to be happening. The boss of the facility was missing and there had been a small incident a couple of days before.

There was a meeting of some type in an upstairs office, but no information was filtering down to them. Yet they stayed. Work was hard to come by and the men needed to find out what was going on. Eight were inside and six around the exterior of the old building. Four others were in the meeting.

The car and two vans were gone in ten minutes. It would be twenty minutes before any emergency vehicles arrived. The perpetrators split into three separate directions for their escape and would not meet up again for four hours.

A cell phone rang in Shreveport atop the Fairmont Building, Vasily Torbof answered.

"It's done," the voice from the other end, stated. "Ice house is done."

Torbof turned his back on the men there with him and softly said into the phone, "Tonight, call after 7:00PM my time."

The massacre was on the noon news throughout Atlanta and the southeast. National cable picked it up and the story was now wall to wall.

"Eighteen dead at Doraville warehouse. No motive or reason yet established." The local newsreader recited the words as she would any other story, with wide eyes and an inappropriate smile.

The word hit Bogotá within two hours. The translation was roughly the same text, but the pictures there were more graphic. Sergio DeMarcos had heard all he could stand, literally. First his son is killed, then the raid in Shreveport and now this.

Those around him were also intent on the television and did not notice the color drain from him. He fell back into a chair dropping his drink and staring straight ahead. The glass did not break, but it got the other's attention. When his aid got to him he was still breathing. But that was about all.

~

Phillip Stone was in his office arranging credentials for Murray's pretense as a fire inspector. News of the Atlanta shooting came across the wire service police jurisdictions used to communicate. It meant little to him till the descriptions of the victims began. "Mostly Hispanic and only a few carried any identification," the report read.

Stone grabbed his desk phone and called home.

"Sara, is Jon up yet?" he asked without even saying hello to his wife.

"Yeah," Sara responded. She'd heard this tone before and knew not to ask anything. "They're sitting out back with coffee."

The Stones had more than one spare room and Murray had also been convinced to stay the night. He and Jon were up, enjoying the sunroom while Sara made breakfast for her guests.

She handed Jon the cordless phone and he listened without speaking. His expression changed abruptly just before he spoke, "I need to call a couple of places and we'll be right in," he told the captain.

"Jon, there's nothing we can do from here. Sit tight, I'll be home in an hour."

Pushing the off button on the phone, Jon brought Murray up to speed on what had happened. Looking to the doorway, he saw Sara standing there, looking concerned.

"I knew something big was going on, boys." She took a deep breath and slightly trembled as she continued, "take care of my Phillip, please. He's not as young as he once was."

The two men gave her a solemn stare and Jon nodded just a bit. Sara went back to finish her cooking and never said another word.

A cop's wife is a tough job. Jon told himself. His thoughts immediately went to Marsha as his mind took a full circle in those silent comments. He pulled his cell phone and called Charlotte.

"How is she this morning?" he asked George.

"Cloudy, but better." George explained. He didn't tell Jon about the excitement with the FBI, Marsha had handled that with flying colors. "There's still some pieces that don't fit for her, but she is much less nervous and not as worried about everything."

"Can you move her, yet?" Jon asked bluntly.

"I know," the DA walked away from Marsha's bedside and spoke softer. "I saw it. What was in that ice house, anyway?"

"Heck, I don't know. I looked in the notebook the Russians found in Shreveport, nothing about Doraville or even Atlanta for that

215

matter. I just don't know how it plays in or how they found that ice house either."

"I've called for the doctor to talk with him." George turned back to check on Marsha, she was napping. "I know they are not going to like it, but we can't stay here."

"And...." Jon interrupted, "make it known you're gone. If they think she's still there they'll hit the hospital anyway. These guys are vicious."

"You're right," George told him. "I'm on it and I'll keep you informed, ok? Say... what are you up to?"

"Working on a way to take these Russian bastard's motive away from 'em."

"That would be nice. This deal has really mushroomed, huh? We need to slow it down."

"Working on it, George. I appreciate you, man."

"Talk to you later." George closed his phone as he noticed the doctor walking toward Marsha's room.

~

Phil Stone pulled into his driveway and jumped from the car. His pace was reminiscent of years past, when he was much younger. The situation was dire and the consequences were potentially traumatic, yet he loved it.

He kissed Sara without a word, grabbed a cup of coffee and stepped onto his patio with the guys.

"Ok, first...Murray can you stay a bit longer?" he started. "The inspections are done on Tuesdays and Thursdays. It would look way out of place to try it today." With that, he tossed a badge and ID showing Murray to be a Lt. Dan Spare of the SFD. The picture was clearly Murray.

"Spare?" He asked with a grin.

Capt. Stone shrugged, "Short notice...best I could do."

216

The cowboy smiled and then had to think about the delay, "I suppose tomorrow could work." He looked up at Phil and then over to Jon. "I should go home, check on some stuff and pick up a few things. I could run over there this afternoon."

Jon went right into business, as though Murray's words had gone clean through him. "How did they know to hit Doraville, Georgia?" He asked Phil.

"I thought about that, right away," Stone answered. Again he was impressed with how quick Jon was on such details. "I had my people go through everything and there's one mention of Doraville on the room registration at the Eldorado."

Jon stayed quiet, but his look asked for more information.

"The guy who signed them all in, a Juan Castrono, listed his address as 41253 Duffy Road, Doraville, Georgia."

"Duffy Road? That's the ice house address." Jon confirmed quizzically. "But how did the Russians find that out?"

"I may have a leak." Phil said in his most solemn tone. "I hate to think about it, but it's happened before." He shook his head as he sat, "likely will again, too."

"What else could be out there we need to know about?" Murray interjected.

"The IDs of those killed in the raid, the numbers we caught...hell, everything."

They were all quiet for several minutes when Jon looked up at Phil.

"We need to flush this guy out, and quick. Could he know about Murray?"

"Naw, I've only talked with one contact over at the Fire Department. Made sure not to say too much."

"But they know someone new is here, word has to be out about him flying in."

217

"Yeah," Stone agreed. "That's possible."

"I can make the trip home look like I'm gone for good." Murray offered.

Jon thought a second, he was hoping to ride with him, but this was a good idea.

"Could you pick me up outside of town, somewhere? I'd like to go with you today."

Murray hadn't considered it, but it was okay with him. His expression made Jon aware of that, but also that Murray didn't see the need. So, Jon explained.

"I'd like to see the area, get a feel for the terrain before we go back and do what we need to do."

Murray nodded his acceptance of that and even smiled a bit. *Not a bad idea,* he thought.

"They need a good wild goose chase." Captain Stone blurted out. He had leaned back in his wicker chair to think. "I can feed them some bad info and see who bites."

Jon immediately thought of Captain Sharon Swanson of the Kentucky State Police. "I may know someone who could help." He said as he pulled her card from his wallet. Punching in the numbers he tried to think of how he would approach his request. "We might even get two birds as they say," he quipped as he raised the phone to his ear. The voice answering on the other end was sharp and to the point.

"Swanson." It said.

"Captain, this is Jon Crane."

"Yes... Mr. Crane. What can the Kentucky State Police do for you today?"

Her tone bothered Jon; he thought they had left on good terms. Perhaps not, he now considered. Best to follow through and see.

After a brief back-story of the situation, including the possibility of an internal informant, Capt. Swanson spoke up. "What can I do? I hate departmental snitches."

Jon asked if they could use her as bait. He asked for an address in her district that she could then monitor and hopefully catch these Russian butchers. The trace of the information would help Capt. Stone find his traitor.

"Hold on one," she said firmly. After a brief consult with a few associates, she returned to the phone. "A few miles up from where we met, at the crime scene, there's a small place called Dry Ridge. There's an abandoned horse farm about three miles east. It's on US25 toward Sherman, the address is 1400 Route 25, Dry Ridge." She paused for a second to let Jon write that down. "There's a fairly new stable, a nice one that the owners couldn't pay for. That's why it's abandoned right now; anyways... we'll make that stable look like a meeting place for the next several days. See if they come to visit."

"These guys are barbarians, they kill like the Argus crew." Jon warned.

"Understood," she answered calmly. "No kid gloves."

"We're not talking about kid gloves, Captain. They use high explosives and they don't accept being caught. They'll try to take you with them if they can."

Swanson was quiet as she let that sink in. When she did speak again, she was still defiant. "I'll remember that... but I don't back down."

Jon looked at Phil who was in total agreement with the plan. "Thanks Capt. Swanson." He said into the phone, "we appreciate your help."

"Russians, huh?" she still sounded serious. "Always wanted to throw down with some of them," and Jon could hear her chuckle as she disconnected the call.

36

The hallway to the House Chamber was busy that morning. Dewey Hanson was on his way to an important vote on something or other, he couldn't remember and didn't really care. His suit was wrinkled and he hated that. It had been another rough night in his office and he had fallen back to sleep on the sofa after getting dressed that morning.

His cell phone nearly caused him to jump straight up. It was "the" cell phone, the one with global coverage. This call was from Colombia.

Stepping into a deep side entranceway, he answered with a harsh tone, "I'm going in for a vote, don't call me here."

The voice on the other end didn't care. "Where the hell is Castrono?" it demanded. "You know more about this than you say, don't you?"

Hanson became visibly concerned. *Who was this?* he thought. It wasn't his normal contact; this was a very well spoken English voice. "Who is this?" He asked.

"Hanson, I'm not going to ID myself on your stupid phone. But you'd better think before you speak again. Where is Castrono?"

Oh my God, Hanson panicked. *It's Santonio Lendono*. Saul's uncle and leader of the Cartel in Colombia. Lendono had been imprisoned in Colombia for years, but his upbringing had been in London. His accent was more cockney than Colombian. The cocaine wars of thirty years before had the family move him to safer ground. The Escobar-controlled cartel was finally taken over by the police, who ran it for themselves. The DeMarcos family was still seen as a threat so Lendono was jailed. From his cell he managed a large, quieter drug smuggling ring that was quite profitable until recently. Movement of his product had stopped and he wanted to know why and how to fix it. His question to Hanson about Castrono's whereabouts was not rhetorical in the least, and Hanson knew it.

"I swear, I don't know where he is, Sir." The "sir," just popped out instinctively.

"Why did he leave Louisiana?" the voice demanded.

"That zealot is after me, that... "Son" guy. I was trying to protect myself."

"Imbecile," the voice raised a full octave. "You don't know where he is?"

"No," Hanson admitted. "He thinks I'm trying to kill him."

"Are you?"

There was a deep hesitation in the congressman's voice, "I had to."

"Well?"

"He got away. I don't know where he went."

"Find him," the voice declared and the phone went silent.

Dewey Hanson stood in the doorway and stared at his phone. He wanted to run, but where to? Then a hand touched his shoulder and another voice spoke.

"Dewey, you're gonna be late again, man. Let's go." It was a junior congressman from Wisconsin, Fred...somebody, he didn't really remember. Hanson waved and assured the man, "I'm coming." He went into the House Chambers and voted. Then returning to his office he set his mind to the new task, even more important than hiding from "the Son." He must do as Lendono ordered. There would be no hiding from him.

~

After two nights in Dahlonega, Georgia, Juan knew he would need to move on. He spent the afternoon walking around the town square, checking out the quaint shops and playing tourist. The

Gold Mine coffee shop had a television on against the back wall. Several men were gathered around it like there was something important.

The news was about the massacre in Doraville and Juan recognized his building immediately. He stepped back in near shock, mesmerized by the story.

A man sat next to where he stood in a high backed wooden chair. A newspaper, opened to the main story from the day before, lay in his lap. Juan glanced down at the pictures and there was that face, the one that always appeared when trouble was near.

"Diablo," Juan heard himself speak out as he turned to leave the shop. The others there said nothing, but they did notice him.

He packed his belongings quickly and checked out of the motel. Driving to the parkway he turned south towards Gainesville, but that scared him. He needed to stay away from big towns. A small exit pointed to a town called Dawsonville and he drove through the quiet of the north Georgia Mountains. Through Tate, then Fairmount and Sonoraville the road then went under a major interstate. He followed the road he was on and the signs said "Rome - 23 miles."

Rome, he thought. *That sounds like a nice place to hide for a while.*

Juan pulled into the college town late that Monday afternoon and found a small, non-chain motel sitting just under an overpass. He was but a mile from one of the major colleges and a small shopping center just beyond that. A well lit diner sat in front of the shopping center, right on the highway. The large neon sign said "Landmark." *An odd name*, Juan thought as he went inside, but the meal was good. Many of those inside were young people and many of them had shirts that proclaimed, "Berry" in one area or another. It was a warm place and he made note of it to come again. On the way back to his motel, the stately campus to his right caught his eye. The sign at the road also said "Berry" and without thinking he turned into the long driveway and was waved in by a friendly guard at the gates. The traffic circle ahead confused him, but he took the right "off road" and found himself in jolly old England. The buildings appeared to be Oxford itself and looked nearly as old yet well maintained at the same time. The large grassy areas were especially beautiful to him and the small deer were everywhere. He stopped and parked in front of a pair of buildings joined by an open archway. Looking away from the buildings, at the open field, gave him a sense a peace. For a short while Juan forgot where he was and why and simply enjoyed the view.

This is good, he thought. *I'll be safe here for a while.*

As darkness took over the view, he drove back out the gates and down the highway to his motel. Once there, he returned to his room and settled in for the evening.

~

Murray made a big deal about leaving that afternoon, shaking hands with the ground crew who had taken care of Lucy and then the send off from Phil and Jon. He flew some 10 miles out of town and sat down off the highway to wait.

Phil drove Jon to the spot where Lucy idled. He then joined the cowboy for a ride over to Texas. Once airborne, Jon dug into a small bag he had brought with him.

"I didn't want to involve Phil in this, cause he shouldn't allow it." He held out his hand. Cradled in it were three small remote microphones, all fitting neatly into his palm. "These and a couple of these," he put the mikes back and pulled out equally miniature cameras, "should help us know what they are up to."

"You want those left on the roof top, I suppose."

"It is an international crime, so I'll understand..."

"Sure," Murray grinned. "International crime is my specialty."

223

Within half an hour they were nearing the Caddo Mills area. Jon saw it, but did not recognize what it meant. A trail of smoke ascended skyward on the horizon. Black, ugly smoke.

Murray didn't comment. But suddenly Lucy lurched forward, nose low and tail up as they propelled at maximum speed toward the smoke. Jon looked over at Murray, his eyes were intense and he appeared more than a little concerned.

"Is that something bad?" Jon asked.

"It sure could be." The cowboy replied.

What seemed like forever, was actually only a few minutes and the chopper was close enough to see the blaze. It was a house, Murray's house, and it was fully engulfed in flames. Tracks circled the house in the dirt and then led out to the highway, tire tracks. Murray started to set down when Jon grabbed his arm and pointed with his other hand, "Look, out there." He said.

Small, fast moving dots were up nearing the highway and heading north. Murray realized there was little to do about the house, Lucy roared as he spun her right and once again picked up speed. The dots began to take shape; they were motorcycles, maybe twelve to fifteen of them. He approached them low and fast; soon he would overtake the group. Murray didn't say anything, but his intent was clear. He bore down on the riders from behind and would soon be on top of them. Jon had another idea.

"Hey," he yelled into the headset. "Can't you get up high where they don't know we're here?"

Murray didn't respond other than to look hard at his new friend.

"If you stop them now we won't be sure." Jon continued. "We can follow them back to the lair and figure out what we're up against."

Murray's expression did not change. He looked back to the still unaware gang ahead of him. It looked as though he would ignore Jon's request, but within a few seconds he eased up on Lucy's throttle pulled the stick back raising the altitude quickly.

The lurching back and up drew an unconscious reaction from Jon who reached out with both arms for something to grab on to. His stomach climbed into his throat, but he managed to save his breakfast. As they leveled out Jon looked to his left. The pilot was still serious in his glare, but a bit less pressurized. They stayed far enough behind the bikers to be out of their sight.

"Can they see us up here?" Jon wasn't sure.

Murray didn't answer right away. It was as though his current mode did not allow conversation. He looked at Jon and deliberately said, "No... now what?"

"We follow them to where ever they're going." Jon's tone also became more serious. "Then come back on our terms with what we need."

Murray stayed quiet and Jon took that as understanding, at least he hoped it was.

As the riders neared Whitewright, Texas, they slowed and soon surrounded a small strip center. There were other bikes already parked to one side and an older, gray van sat right in front of the end unit with its side doors open. The approaching riders lined up in near military formation around that end of the strip center and stopped.

Murray arched back and swung around, staying in the western sky with the setting sun. Lucy hovered as they watched the men dismount and go into a building. Once they were all inside, Murray eased a bit closer to be sure where they were.

"Does this look like the group you found last week?" Jon asked.

"Oh, yeah, that's them. I recognize several of the bikes." Murray assured him. "And that guy with his nose bandaged up...I know him personal." The man he pointed out was clearly the one Murray had introduced to the bar's surface last Friday night.

"Alright," Jon was thinking and planning while Lucy was bucking and rocking. "You say they always meet in Greenville at that bar on Friday nights?"

"That's what I heard."

"Then that's when we hit 'em. We come back and wait for them here."

That plan didn't take long to agree with. Murray looked at Jon and barely nodded. He spun Lucy around and they launched back toward the house at breakneck speed.

As they again got within sight of the burning house they could see emergency vehicles coming from Dallas up I-30. It would be several minutes before they arrived. Coming in on the northwest side of the house Murray suddenly let out a low moan. A car was parked next to the house, one they had not noticed before.

"That's Slick's Jeep." He said almost mumbling and he almost bounced the Bell 407 as he sat her down hard. "Naw...no, no." He uttered as he ran from the copter.

Looking around frantically, the Jeep was soon not the worst of it. As the men ran to the still burning structure they could see a body laying face down on the front porch. It was burning with the rest of the surroundings; a 30-30 rifle lay near the body. The heat radiated out with intense pressure. The cowboy still tried to get to the porch. Jon had to grab Murray and hold him back till sense kicked in.

"He's gone, man. He's gone." The name Slick rang a bell with Jon. It was from the story Daniel told him about first meeting the family. He wanted to express sympathy, but there was no time. The emergency vehicles could now be heard approaching. Jon turned Murray around and looked him right in the eyes.

"You've got to decide something, right now." Jon shouted.

The anger in Murray's eyes changed to curiosity at Jon's comment.

Jon shook him again and bellowed at the cowboy, "You either tell them," he pointed toward the oncoming vehicles, "that we know where those creeps are...or... you keep that part to us and we deal with them Friday."

~

The doctors at Charlotte Medical understood, but did not totally agree with George's proposal. The media were alerted and told that the wounded police Lieutenant was to be moved to another facility, as were the two injured Russians.

The doctor gave Marsha a sedative to help her relax and they fitted her with what appeared to be a football helmet. The padding inside was extremely soft and would not allow any jarring. Small frames protruded from the ear hole areas to a padded shoulder harness, which in effect, held her head perfectly straight.

They created as much publicity for the move as possible. Reporters arrived to cover the story at 11:00 AM and Marsha was rolled out and down the hall to cameras and reporters watching every move. No questions were allowed, though the media types tried at every step. A few reporters were even permitted on the elevator as they rode to the loading dock. The actual loading area for the ambulance was more private, simply by virtue of its location. The reporters were suddenly restricted and held back.

What George had arranged, was a bit of a surprise for the media. Not one, but three ambulances pulled away from the hospital at the same time, each heading in a different direction. Chase cars had to decide quickly, which way to go. Two had chosen correctly and followed Marsha's ambulance. But they were dismayed when the unit pulled into an abandoned warehouse. The appearance was that this vehicle had been a ruse.

Marsha's crew waited in that warehouse for over forty-five minutes before it and four others emerged, none with her aboard.

She stayed inside the warehouse for another fifteen minutes having been transferred to a limo. Sitting upright as it finally exited, she rode for only a few blocks in the tinted window limousine. That vehicle pulled into the garage area of the rental facility that owned the limo where she was placed back into another proper transport for the ride to the airport. That's what none of them expected, the airport.

~

The cowboy had only seconds to consider Jon's proposal. He stared at the ground between his boots before he responded over the sound of the screaming sirens.

"We kill 'em?" Murray asked with all sincerity.

"I don't see any way around it." Jon told him. "But we've got to learn what they're up to first, so we can stop it."

The first of the fire response vehicles thundered onto the ranch. Murray stiffened his back and adjusted his hat. Looking at the trucks coming in, he spoke without looking at Jon.

"Us," he said. "We do it."

The responders quickly realized there was little they could for the structure, but the body on the scene required coroners to be called and investigations to begin. Murray and Jon were asked hundreds of questions as the investigation went into the night. To Murray the situation was all too familiar.

It was discovered that Stephen, aka Slick had been shot three times and was dead before he burned. Somehow, that was some consolation to Murray, yet he still had to call his mother and sister to tell them. The fire had so consumed the body that positive identification would be left to the autopsy, but there was little doubt.

Charlene wanted him to come home. He told her had a few things he needed to take care of and did not explain. He never did.

"The body is coming to Dallas," he told his sister. "But it will be after they do an autopsy locally." He left out the part about how badly the body was burned, those details wouldn't help right now. "Don't set anything up, far as services go, until Saturday. Saturday afternoon," he continued.

"Murray, what are you up to?" Charlene asked in fear.

"Just don't set anything up before Saturday, I can't be there till then. Ok?"

"I love you," his sister sobbed. She knew him well and was concerned she might not talk to him again.

"I'm going to be fine." He assured her. "I'm in good company, believe me." He looked over at Jon who was explaining one more time how they came in to find the house burning. "Take care of Mom," he finished and hung up.

The two men had been kept separated from the time Slick's body had been found by the authorities. At one point Jon called Phil Stone to let him know what had happened. Captain Stone spoke with the locals, verifying that the two men there were working on a case with him and had simply gone to Texas for Murray to gather a few belongings. He asked for some professional courtesy in allowing them to return to Louisiana. They told him there was still more to look at, but they would consider his request.

When the phone was given back to Jon, Stone shared that he had set the trap they worked up earlier that day. He had broken the possible suspects down into three groups, one potential traitor per group and let out the new info about the meeting in Kentucky. Each group was told a different night, Wednesday through Friday and to keep the information secure. If the attack occurred, the night chosen would expose the guilty party.

Jon was very impressed with the Captain's work and told him so.

"Been doing this stuff for awhile." Phil bragged. "Ya learn things."

Finally allowed to talk with each other again, Jon got to ask what had been bothering him through all this. "What was he doing here?"

"He had a key." Murray stopped and again adjusted his hat. It was a stalling tactic for him to regain his composure. "Slick would drop in when he felt like it. There was no schedule to it, just when he needed something or if I needed help."

"I am sorry, man." Jon said as he too stared at the ground.

"Yeah," was the reply.

Murray's comment seemed strange at first, but Jon realized that Murray had not yet absorbed what had happened. Losses like that take time to process. How well he remembered.

The fire was out, Slick's body had been taken away and the investigation over. Jon stood silently with Murray as the cowboy looked at his home. "It wasn't the house so much," he offered. It's just it was mine." He kicked the dirt and walked up to where the steps had been to the front porch. "They probably thought poor Slick was me," he turned to look at Jon. "The damned fool...he shouldn't be dead. They were after me."

Jon just let him talk. When he appeared to wind down some, he asked the cowboy about insurance for the house.

"I suppose," he waved his arm out. "I got the whole place insured."

"I can help you rebuild, man." Jon offered. "We'll do it up right."

There was a half grin and half grimace on Murray's face. He slapped his leg with his hat and walked toward Lucy. Jon followed and they lifted off. There was no looking back or circling around, he pointed Lucy southeast and headed back to Louisiana. It was past

230

2:00AM when Jon and Murray got back to Shreveport. It would be a busy day on that Tuesday and they needed to be sharp.

Murray tried to sleep, but thoughts of his cousin kept him awake till daybreak. He was allowed to sleep till 9:00AM. That was it.

37

The hour was late in Dalton when the Learjet 36 air ambulance touched down from Charlotte, North Carolina. It had been a long day; each step to that point had taken time. Time for her to rest and be reassured all was ok; time just to be careful they had not been followed. She slept peacefully through the flight and the instruments connected to her indicated she was fine.

The Lear 36 was equipped with all the latest monitoring gear and a qualified neurologist on board. The flight left Charlotte around 10:45PM and they arrived in Dalton after 1:00AM.

Hamilton Medical was ready and she was checked in under an assumed name.

The doctor on the flight ran tests and offered an opinion that Marsha's memories should begin to coalesce within a few days. Her napping was less frequent and she was more alert to her surroundings. The only real fear she had expressed lately was to George about a dream she felt was inappropriate. The dream consisted of her and Jon.

George smiled and convinced her that would all make sense to her soon enough.

He had attempted to reach Jon by phone as the plane took off, but there was no service. He decided he would call him in the morning after they were all settled in.

He did call the house and talked with Doris. She understood he would stay with Marsha, at least through the night. All was under control at the mountain mansion; the guys had even cooked out steaks the night before in celebration of their victory over the hit man. They talked for over an hour. Not having seen each other in several days was new to them and neither really cared much for it.

Doris told of getting to know Lori and how much she liked her. George tried to explain the condition Marsha was in. But that was difficult. She was improving so rapidly there was no time to describe one stage as she was on to the next. George assured Doris that Marsha should be well soon and then Jon could be around her again without causing confusion.

"It was good to at least be back in Dalton," he told her.

Things seemed to be calming down.

They were really just getting warmed up.

~

Congressman Dewey Hanson walked to his parked car and was surprised to find it unmolested. His paranoia was nearly complete. He really expected to find it broken into.

How could he find Juan? he asked himself. He normally hired or ordered that stuff handled. Now most of the hired hands he knew of were loyal to the cartel first and him second, *if even that*, and the one guy he could use on his own had quit.

There was an apartment Juan kept in Washington for when he was needed up here. Hanson thumbed through his day planner for the address. *I'll check that out*, he told himself. *Maybe there's a clue in there about where he might go.*

Driving into Georgetown drew unwanted attention, just by nature of who he was. His diminutive, child like size driving a large Cadillac sedan had heads turning. He focused on the road and where he was going trying not to concentrate on his fear.

The apartment building had no available parking on the street. He remembered his congressional decal, which could be used for emergency parking, and double-parked near the front door. A few horns blew, but most just went around him. Hanson climbed the steps to the third floor and checked under the mat. There was a key.

Juan's Washington home had little in the way of anything. A foldable bed served as both that and a sofa. A small TV sat on what had to be an ottoman. Two lamps were standing, not really arranged in any form and the kitchen was empty.

"Shit," Hanson declared. There were no clothes in the closets, no notes anywhere, nothing. He pulled the door closed behind him and left. Walking past the mailboxes at the door he could see something in the one marked 3D. Hanson looked around, no one was visible so he popped the glass window with his elbow and pulled the contents from the mailbox. A post card from Cuba, signed Maria. *Who the hell is Maria?* he thought. He stuffed the card into a coat pocket and got back in his car. *Girlfriend or maybe a sister?*

If he could find her she could tell him where Juan was.

His first attempt as a sleuth and he had not come away completely empty, a small grin flashed across his face as he turned back toward D.C. He knew some people who could help with this post card. *They could find her,* he assured himself.

~

The courier drove through customs at Nogales, Arizona, that morning, legally. His passport was in the name of Carl Holmes and he was by all appearances a gringo. Though Colombian by birth, he had been raised in Denver, Colorado, until he was nearly fifteen years old. Both parents had strong European features so Carlos, or Carl could pass as the all-American boy.

His mother had died in childbirth and his father moved them to Colorado shortly after. Carl didn't have any idea what his father's business was, other than they had plenty of money, right up until the feds came and took him away.

With his father in federal prison, Carlos was deported to his home country to live with relatives in a culture he knew nothing about.

He learned from the streets of Bogotá and became a runner for a
234

local drug supplier. It was through this man that he met the DeMarcos family and began to work for them. One other young man in this new group of trainees thought Carl looked English and teased him about being "Sherlock Holmes." The nickname caught on and the group referred to Carl as "Holmes."

Carl Holmes was now a top courier, charged with only important delivery jobs for the cartel. His package for this trip was not with him yet. He would pick that up from a ranch near Sierra Vista, right under the nose of the U.S. Army at Fort Huachuca. His next contact would be in Sweetwater, Texas. There he would learn the address for his delivery.

38

The ID badge he held had his picture on it, but the name said Lt. Dan Spare. Murray wanted to smile, but the events of the day before made that difficult. The clothes were not comfortable either, but they fit he guessed. At least Phil said he wouldn't have to wear the dorky hat. The only thing he halfway liked was the short jacket.

Jon walked into the room with a look like he was visiting a terminally ill friend.

"You doing alright?" he asked.

"I'm good," Murray nodded without looking up. He was good, even more than he appeared. This situation wasn't directly tied to Slick's murder, but he had given his word to help and that's what he would do, the best he could.

"You have the remotes?" was the next question. Jon was reminding him of the microphones and cameras they needed to keep just between them.

"Yeah," Murray finally glanced up at him. "I put 'em in my fire department purse." The job came with a small bag for notebooks, reference guides and other items an inspector would need to carry.

Jon was relieved that his friend could joke about something. "That's a good look for you." He teased. Then he asked to see one of the units and pointed out the small switch on its side. "If they're on when you go in, the Russians will pick them up on their equipment scanners." He looked at Murray who was listening intently to the instructions. "Just flip this switch as you decide where to place it. Use as many as you can hide effectively."

Murray nodded and Jon was quite comfortable this man could handle the job. Walking out to the driveway where Phil had the SFD pickup truck for Murray to use, the police captain was sitting in a lawn chair waiting for them. He tossed the keys to Murray and reminded him, "You're an official fire inspector. You can park wherever you need to in front of that building." He looked at Murray and continued, "In fact, make it as conspicuous as you can."

The drive downtown took thirty minutes, the GPS helped. Murray, aka Lt. Spare double-parked right in front of the Fairmont Building. A guard at the entrance challenged him first.

"Fire inspection," Murray told him.

The man called somewhere and asked Murray to wait. Within five minutes Vasily Torbof came walking towards him.

"What is this?" he sharply demanded.

"Fire inspection, sir." Murray repeated. "Our records show the roof was never inspected as an occupied space."

"Diplomatic Immunity." Torbof spouted as he turned to leave.

"There's no immunity to fire."

"Insolent!" Vasliy roared, "Be gone...I will have your job."

"Yeah, you can do that, I suppose." Murray paused as he got out a notebook. "That would be the hard way."

Torbof spun and stepped right up to the impertinent official. "Hard way? What is this?"

"Well," the cowboy flipped through a few pages of his book for effect. "You can stop me now for sure... if you choose. But then they'll condemn this building as a threat to the surroundings and you'll have to evacuate till we check it out... top to bottom." Murray smiled at the General Consul and added, "Your choice."

The glare on Torbof's face intensified, but he stepped back.

"How long will this take?" He asked.

Murray shrugged and tilted his head, "Depends on what all is up there." Then he threw the old man a bone, "maybe, thirty minutes if I'm not bothered or anything."

"Come with me, and please...be quick. I have people coming."

"Yes, sir." Murray followed and rode up the elevator to the penthouse level and from there Vasily pointed to the stairs leading to the roof.

~

Jon had talked with George at the Hamilton Medical Center and also with Daniel and Gil at the house. He planned to go home for the first time in just over a week, a week that felt like two months.

"Have Ben be prepared to go over my suit, he'll know what I mean. Tell him I have a big meeting coming up soon and it needs to be just right."

Daniel leaned over the table he was near and made a note of Jon's request. It was odd, but Daniel was getting quite used to his and Ben's cryptic messages. *Best to just go with it*, he thought quietly. He did have a question for Jon, "How's it going with Murray?"

Jon told Daniel about the trip to Texas and what had happened. The news left Daniel with little to say. "How did the sister take that?" he asked.

"I'm not sure," Jon told him. "I think Murray spoke with her. I'm just not sure. He's focused on what we're doing, that I am sure of. I'm going to try to get him to come with me."

"It would be good to see the cowboy again." Daniel commented out loud.

"He is that, ain't he?" Jon quipped.

~

Marsha woke up and appeared to be more alert that afternoon. She knew she was in different surroundings and asked about that, but not with concern. She was relaxed. At one point, as George came back from getting some coffee, she looked at him and asked, "How's Doris?"

George smiled wide as he heard that. "She's doing great. Can't wait to see you." He told her. The expectation of any follow up was short lived. She seemed confused by what she had asked herself and simply became quiet. George was becoming used to these "stages" of her recovery so he just sat down and drank his coffee.

When George relayed the event to one of the doctors, he was quick to smile and reassure the man. "Her short term memories are coming into focus for her, this is good. She just needs to stay calm because things can get confusing."

"I'm trying, believe me." George pleaded.

"Sir," the doctor reached out and touched his shoulder, "I've watched you since you been here. Nobody could handle this thing any better than you've been doing. She's very lucky to have you right now."

George thanked the man and walked back into the room. She was sleeping. *Would this need for his patience ever end*, he thought. It had only been months since the vigil for Doris over her injuries, *she wasn't completely recovered yet*, and now this. He tried to imagine what Jon was dealing with. How did he keep everything in balance or was he? This had become serious business. Jon going after the bad guys had just seemed to mushroom. It was approaching overwhelming.

He sat still for a few minutes and could feel his control coming back to him. That doctor was being nice, but he had opened a release valve with his kind words. There's both good and bad in that. Letting off some pressure helps, long as it doesn't carry you away with it. George regained his grip on the situation.

Hell, it's really only been about a week, he chided himself.

He looked at Marsha and smiled. *She's a strong woman*, he told himself. *She and Jon make a good pair.* He felt lucky to be able to help them. He leaned his head back against the chair and actually felt like he could nap. Being home will do that for you.

39

Lt. Dan Spare checked the rooftop very closely. When Vasily received a phone call and went downstairs he looked even closer, this time as Murray Bilstock.

Quickly placing microphones in planter boxes and inside an open two-inch pipe he looked for the right spots for the cameras. The pipe opening turned out to be a better place for a camera, as it looked directly towards the folding chair Torbof liked to use. Another was secured to a section of the air conditioner stack, which sat like an old vent box near the doorway. From there, they could monitor who came and went. The last microphone was placed under the lawn chair itself, right in the corner. The location was obscured by a brick lying sideways in that corner and wouldn't be noticed for a while.

Murray paid close attention to the brick wall surrounding the rooftop. He made photos and notes. It was one course of brick thick above the flat roof and from what he knew of construction, was never intended to be used as a safety barrier. It was merely decorative, to partially hide the utilities on that roof.

Must have been an afterthought, he figured as he looked for signs of it being "added on" after the original construction. The parapet wall rested on the outer veneer brick and just barely sat on the edge of the roofing system. He wouldn't want to lean or fall against it, though it appeared to be intact. *Seventeen stories down*, he thought. *Not good.*

He heard Torbof climbing the stairs and pretended to be preparing his report.

"Is everything in order, I hope?" Vasily asked very politely.

"Looks pretty good to me. I don't see anything that should cause us a problem." He smiled and closed his notebook. Vasily stretched his arm out toward the stairs and Murray nodded and started down.

"Do you have a copy for me?" The consul asked as they got to the doorway.

That was one thing Murray hadn't considered.

"Actually," he stalled, trying to think. "A copy should be sent to you within five business days. If you don't get it, call the office, would you?"

Torbof seemed to accept that as typical American red tape and excused himself. Murray drove back to the precinct where Jon and Phil awaited his real report. The Fire Chief was also waiting and motioned for Murray to follow him. Jon and Phil leaned against Phil's car while the Chief got his debriefing and his stuff back.

~

Lori and Doris were watching a special "News Alert" on the cable station. A congressman from Maryland was holding a press conference pleading for help in the search for his wife, daughter and her boy friend. The fact that this meeting with the press corps was happening from Washington, D.C. struck more than a few people as odd behavior. The reasons offered for his absence from the direct search were his loyalty to the folks back home, "who needed his representation of them" here in the nation's capital.

Lori looked at Doris, whose mouth hung open like a set bear trap.

"Come...on," she moaned. "What a piece of work this guy is."

Ben stepped into the room and saw what was on TV. His face changed shades of color as he recognized the name of the congressman. He could not share why he knew of him.

Doris noticed the perplexed look on her son's face and was about to ask him what the problem was, when Walt sounded an alarm from the attic.

"Car," he yelled. "Black sedan, coming up the driveway."

Gil jumped and ran to the garage drawing his Colt as he moved. Through the glass of the garage door he could see two men in suits climb from the car and walk calmly to the front door.

"Feds?" he sounded as he trotted back through the house toward the front door. The doorbell rang and Gil undid the locksets and pulled the door open.

"Mr. Crane?" one of the men asked.

"No, Mr. Crane isn't here right now." Gil told them. He pulled his badge from under his shirt to let it hang fully visible on the chain. "I'm with the Dalton Police Department. Can I help you?"

"Officer...?" The first man started.

"Gartner. Gil Gartner."

"Officer Gartner... could we come in, sir?"

Gil stepped back as the two entered the foyer area and took their identification from their coats.

"I'm Agent Carter and this is Special Agent Weston. Can you tell us where Mr. Crane is?"

"What is this about, sir?" Gil challenged back.

"An incident in Charlotte, N.C. we believe he was involved in."

"Involved?" Gil played dumb.

"Appearances are, he apprehended a very dangerous and highly wanted terrorist single-handed. I say again, apparently. We just want to know what Mr. Crane knows about this man."

"I heard about that deal." Gil looked at Daniel and continued, "you remember?" He then directed his comments at Agent Carter. "That was Jon?"

"Yes, that much we've verified." The agent changed his approach and his attitude. "Are we gonna play games here? I don't have time for that."

Gil didn't respond other than to look confused.

242

"Listen," Carter restarted. "Crane is not in trouble. There's a bunch of us who would love to know how the hell he did what he did, but that's not the question we were sent to answer." He looked back at his partner who nodded approval of this tactic. "The guy he took down was one of a kind, a really bad character. If he said anything to Mr. Crane about who he worked for we need to know." With that Carter shrugged and looked at everyone in the room.

Ben, who had not been in the area when this discussion began, finally broke the quiet of the standoff. He stepped into the foyer wearing the spare hydraulic arm. Gil was stunned, but said nothing. He didn't know what to expect next. Ben activated a button on the belt and powered the arm up.

"If I show you how he did it, will you leave him alone?" Ben asked.

Agent Weston stepped toward Ben and spoke for the first time. "Son, what do you know about this?" As he spoke the agent reached out for Ben's arm. The enhanced arm came across Ben's body and took Agent Weston's wrist. As gently as he could, Ben raised the agent's arm up and held it there.

His look was more of surprise than shock. Carter turned towards them, but did nothing else. When Weston tried to move, Ben asserted a little more pressure to the wrist.

"Ok, that's enough." Weston called out. Ben let him go. The agent rubbed his arm as the demonstration began to sink in. Both agents waited for the boy to explain.

"Jon Crane was defending his girl friend at that hospital," he started. "He and I develop items like this and fortunately he had one with him in Charlotte." Ben's voice was firm and strong. "It probably saved his life...and hers."

They asked if they could look at the unit and Ben allowed it. Then Agent Carter asked another question, "What about the gun Crane had with him? Is he licensed for that?"

"Yes sir, Jon Crane is a pharmaceutical representative and he sometime carries controlled substances. His license is on file with the state and the Federal government."

"Amazing piece of equipment," Weston remarked.

"We'd appreciate it if you would keep knowledge of that to yourselves. When we're done with development we may want to sell it."

The agents looked at each other and agreed. The "how" wasn't their mission anyway, just finding out if Crane knew who had hired the hit man.

"You don't think he told Crane who sent him?" Weston asked once more.

"I've talked with Jon twice since then. If he knew he would have told me."

"Where is Crane?" Agent Carter stepped in.

"Louisiana, on business. I don't know when I expect him back, honestly."

Carter handed Ben a card with a local Atlanta number and added, "We'll need to talk with him personally when he gets back. Just a formality...unless there's anything else we should know about."

"I'll tell him when I hear from him." Ben assured them.

The two agents turned for the door and looked back, Carter said, "Thanks for showing us that machine, kid."

"Yeah," Weston added, "we thought we were hunting Superman or something."

As the black sedan turned and drove down the drive, everyone looked at Ben.

"What?" he demanded.

"You're sure Jon will be okay with what all you told them?" Daniel looked apprehensive.

"It was either that, or have them on his tail." Ben turned to see who was answering on his behalf. "And he doesn't need that right now." The voice was Gil Gartner's. He slapped Ben on the back and gave him a "nice going" along with it.

~

The attack team that had hit Doraville was enroute to Florida when the call came to them.

"Turn around," the voice ordered. "Be in Kentucky Thursday night." The caller gave them the address for the stable in Dry Ridge. "There's a meeting that night, kill them all. That's the order."

The man who received the call rolled down his window and stuck an arm out as he had his driver pull off the interstate. A short meeting with the two vans decided traveling back through Atlanta together would be too risky. They split and set a time to meet up in Chattanooga, Tennessee, in eight hours.

There was plenty of time to make Kentucky by Thursday. One van exited the freeway at McDonough to follow highway 81 north. The other van headed west to seek US Highway 27 while the lead car would use the Atlanta perimeter and wait for the others closer to Tennessee. They should have time to stop just north of there to rest before the final drive and assault.

On his rooftop in Shreveport, Torbof leaned against the back of his lawn chair and asked the man with the phone one question. "Did you reach them?"

"Yes, sir." The man answered. "It's being handled."

Torbof nodded and looked skyward, pausing there for a moment then standing abruptly and declaring, "have the others here tomorrow night."

"Many are here now, sir." Leonid told him. "There was a crowd at Igor's last night and more expected tonight."

"That's not a good idea," Vasily directed him. "Can't we find somewhere else for them to play?"

The aid looked perplexed. That was a tall order indeed. Igor's Manor was "the" place for the Russian mob in town. Vasily Torbof, on the other hand, was not a man to be told "no."

"I will see what I can do, sir." Leonid offered meekly and then backed away, turned and left the rooftop.

40

The road to Sweetwater from Sierra Vista was long, but Carl Holmes was used to long treks. This one would be cut short. Just inside the cell service area for Deming, New Mexico, the cell phone in glove box went off. That phone was for important messages only. Carl pulled the car to the side of the highway and opened the phone.

The message light was on and when he pushed the button it said, "S.L." The big man himself.

Lendono had received word from a lookout in Shreveport that the gatherings were getting big at the club used by the Russians. He did not want to miss the opportunity so he ordered Holmes to El Paso to catch a flight booked in his name to Shreveport.

This was odd, Carl thought. The boss was usually more prudent and careful than hurried as this appeared. "Must be a reason," he figured.

The package he carried could not fly so he was to abandon it and another would be waiting in Louisiana. He took the package from the back seat and walked it into the desert. He had not passed or even seen another vehicle in over an hour; there was no one around to witness his actions. Placing the box in the sand, he turned and headed back.

At about half way to his car, some hundred and fifty yards from the box, he pulled his handgun and fired. The first shot hit dirt short of the box and Carl was disgusted with his aim. He looked at the weapon in anger almost threatening it and again stretched his arm out full.

The second shot released an eruption that caused him to stagger back, even as far as he was from it. The dust cloud settled quickly and the sand showed no ill effects. That evidence was gone for good.

Carl walked on to the car, tossing the gun off to his right along the way. As he got to the car door, Carl bent down and wiped the dust from his boots with a handkerchief. When pleased with their appearance, he climbed in the car and drove to El Paso. His flight awaited him.

~

After a rather informal debriefing, Murray Bilstock handed his fake ID and other fire department paraphernalia over and thanked the Chief for his help. Captain Phil Stone was waiting for him with Jon in the back seat.

"How'd it go?" Jon asked first.

"Not that much up there...I mean, it went good." The new sleuth had much to say, but he didn't have it organized yet. "I got on the roof just fine, he even had a phone call that gave me some alone time up there." He looked around inside the car and added, "Where's my hat?"

Phil glanced over as far as he could without turning his head, "In my office."

Murray was not pleased, but said no more about that.

"The roof is not really built up much." He resumed. "There's a glass room in the middle with a table and chairs, conference room, I figure. The wall is more than weak if you ask me." He twisted and looked back at Jon. "I'm not an expert, but I don't believe it's legal. I mean up to code. It really wouldn't take much to push it over. I don't know why the guy hadn't figured that out."

Jon took a deep breath and nodded. He looked like his mind had just stored something away.

"What's the roof top made of?" He asked.

"Rolled out tar over a slim concrete pad. That's what it looks like." Murray remembered a detail about that, "oh... there was a spot in the corner where the concrete showed through. About six to eight inches almost square."

"Where his chair is?" Phil piped in.

"Naw...a far corner that ain't being used."

"What's the chair like?" Jon asked.

"Ha!" The cowboy wiped his mouth with his opened hand, "It's a real cheapy. I mean aluminum with that web stuff, like you used to get at Wal-Mart."

"That's really strange. They don't even sell those things anymore, do they?" The Captain noted with a tone of superiority in his voice. "He could afford a recliner up there if he wanted one, but he chooses that." Stone paused and shook his head. "Folks can be really weird."

Murray grinned and added, "Besides, there ain't no maintenance on that thing, you just replace it."

"They are comfortable." Phil added seriously.

The other two looked at him for a minute and broke out laughing. While they were doing that, Murray turned to Jon, winked and nodded very slowly. Jon understood clearly. Murray had planted the remotes. The receivers were set to begin recording immediately. There would be info waiting in the equipment bag.

~

George Vincent was napping in the room's most comfortable chair with his feet up on the wall air conditioner. At first he thought he was dreaming, but the voice became louder.

"George...George." It called.

Sitting up, he rubbed his eyes and checked the time. He had been out for more than two hours. Looking over to Marsha he found her sitting up, smiling at his attempts to make sense of the moment.

"Well," he yawned. "You're looking chipper. How do you feel?"

"I want to go outside." She grinned.

"Whoa...I don't know." That caught George off guard. "We need to check with the doctors, don't you think?"

"Do that," she challenged him; holding up both arms for him to see that all the IV tubes were disconnected.

George stood and stepped over to her, arms outstretched, "Well, you could have had them wake me. This is great."

"You snore..." she laughed. "Loudly."

George gave her a long hard look. She appeared normal, like the old Marsha. She could tell he had questions and looked out the window past him. "Is Jon coming today?"

"Oh my God!" George hugged her and told her he was out of town. Then she threw the curve.

"He's supposed to have breakfast with me after my shift."

There was a slight let down, but George held onto her so she couldn't see his face.

"I'll try to call and check on him later, ok?"

"Sure. That'll be fine."

George pulled back and smiled. He thought she was back. She was closer. Much closer, but it was still a process.

"You're making great progress, baby. You really are." he told her.

There was a soft knock on the door and it was pushed open. Doris stood there with a small bag and a young police officer, Gil Gartner.

"She insisted, boss." Gil begged.

George jumped up and almost ran to Doris. "It's still dangerous for you to be out." He scolded as he hugged her.

"You needed some clothes. It's been nearly four days."

250

"Great to see you, honey." Then he softly cautioned her about Marsha's condition.

The patient leaned forward on her bed and asked, "Aren't you going to introduce me?"

"Marsha, this is Doris Shaw, a dear friend of mine." George said carefully. He watched for her reaction.

Marsha looked confused. She looked away, out the window and then back to them.

"I know a Doris," she said meekly. "Is that you?"

After checking with George who nodded approval, Doris stepped up to Marsha's bedside. "Yes, sweetheart. It's me. How are you feeling?"

Now the woman appeared embarrassed, she lay down and turned her head away. "It's still a bit...foggy, I guess." She turned back to Doris standing near. "I know I'm better and I know I'll get better still."

Doris reached for her hand and squeezed it. "Yes you will." Seeming to know what to do, Doris then added. "I have to go now. You watch after George for me and you have him call when you want to see me again, okay?"

Marsha smiled and stared at her like she was trying desperately to remember. Doris noticed and squeezed her hand again, "Relax...it will all come to you soon enough, just relax."

George walked into the hall with them.

"I can see why Jon is better off away." She told George. He shook his head and thanked Gil for bringing her, who quipped,

"The overtime is going to be something on this one."

George laughed. He and Doris hugged again and they left. He watched them all the way to the elevator and Doris blew him a small kiss. *Just a few more days, just a few more,* he promised himself.

41

The red spot under his car was obvious even to him. Juan didn't know cars; he had no idea what this meant. He climbed in and started the engine. It sounded fine to him so he put it in reverse and tried to pull away from the motel.

The noise was a combination of sounds, spinning and grinding noises and then a thump. He pushed the gearshift back into "park" and the engine ran as though he had stepped hard on the accelerator. Juan turned the car off.

Damn, his mind spoke in English at his anger. He slammed the door and stared at the vehicle. *It had been fine, no warning lights or anything.* He had left it at the Atlanta Airport for the trip to Virginia last week.

Last week, his brain repeated the thought in disbelief, *was that only last week?*

He picked it up in a hurry when he thought the hit man was on his tail. He didn't check anything then, he just drove. He wanted to remember some telltale sign that maybe he just ignored, but there was none. *Like that would make a difference.* He sighed.

The car was a Chrysler product, fairly new and still under warranty, he was sure. Walking into the lobby of the motel he asked where the closest dealer was.

"Across town, over near US 27," he clerk responded. "Can you drive it?"

"I don't think so." Juan told him.

"I'll call you a wrecker if you want."

"They take cash, right?" Juan tried to think about the spot he was in. "I want to pay cash."

"Oh, yeah...they kinda demand it." the clerk almost laughed.

An hour later Juan and his Chrysler were at the dealership and he was checking in with the service writer.

"I want to pay cash if there's any charge," Juan nearly pleaded.

"Looks like all warranted stuff from here." The man told him, "It's the transmission I'm pretty sure." He pulled the door open and started writing down numbers. "I've got all I need right here."

Juan began to get nervous, but there wasn't anything he could do.

May not even be a problem if it's covered. He thought.

The service writer pointed to the lounge area and told Juan it would be a while.

"You can call a cab from there, it'll be at least till morning before she's ready," and he held out a clipboard with an "x" where he needed Juan's signature.

He checked his watch; it was already past lunchtime. Juan wondered what they served this time of day at the Landmark. He called a cab and rode back across town to see.

~

Carl's flight into Shreveport was smooth. Foot traffic at the airport was light that time of the afternoon so he had no problem noticing the small man with the sign, "Holmes."

"I'm Holmes," he told the man.

"How's Nogales this time of year?" The small man asked him.

Carl realized that was code to verify who he was. There hadn't been time to set things up clearly, or maybe he didn't get that message. He thought for a minute.

"I lost a package near there and I need another one." he tried.

The man looked puzzled and stepped back from him, holding one finger up to say "wait." He put a cell phone to his ear that apparently had been connected somewhere all along. He shook his head and closed the phone.

"Your car is waiting outside," he told Carl. "Your package and instructions are there." He reached out and handed Carl some keys. "It's blue." he said and walked away.

Carl Holmes walked outside and looked around. There were cars parked across from the drive through pickup area, one was clearly blue.

The key worked and inside was a folded note in the ashtray. "Trunk, Igor's 9PM tonight."

He didn't need to look at the package; he knew what it had to be. That was why he was here. He cranked the vehicle and pulled away. The time said 4:45PM so he had over four hours to find this Igor's and be in place.

Foot traffic had been light in the airport; the roadways were a different story. It was "quitting time" and folks were everywhere headed home for the day.

~

Murray had been taking a much-needed nap when Jon barged into the room and closed the door behind him. Jon had been monitoring his units the cowboy left on the rooftop. They had already paid off.

"Wake up, dude." He urged. "Wake up."

Murray wasn't happy about it, but he swung around and sat up. He said nothing, but looked at Jon with an expression that screamed, "this better be good."

"You did good, man." Jon started. "There's going to be a meeting tonight at some club in town." He paused for a few seconds and then continued, "It sounds like there's a bunch of their muscle in town we didn't know about."

Murray still said nothing, but he took a huge breath and tried to stretch his neck. Jon stepped toward the door and turned back, "I'm gonna be there." He declared. "You want in?"

The cowboy leaned over on one elbow and answered, "Sure."

"This is just us," Jon cautioned. "Can't let Phil know how we know about it or anything, ok?"

"Got it." Murray yawned. "Can I go back to sleep now?"

Jon pulled the door closed and stepped into the hall. Phil was leaning against the wall a few feet away.

"For the record," he smiled. "I don't know anything."

Jon froze and tried to look like he had no idea what the man meant. Phil pulled his back from the wall and walked away saying, "Remember this. I didn't start this job last week... be careful at Igor's."

42

The Vehicle Identification Number entered at the Chrysler dealership authorized the work to proceed. But it also triggered hits in two other places.

Dewey Hanson's cell phone sounded off. The one connected to Colombia that was hardly ever used. This was twice in two days and it was the man again.

"He's in Georgia." The voice shouted.

"Georgia? He's still in Georgia?" Hanson was shocked.

"Someplace called Rome."

"I'm on my way." The congressman promised.

"Take care of this...no screw ups this time." The voice was slow and deliberate. Then the phone went silent again.

Hanson immediately called for a flight to Atlanta. Chattanooga would have been closer, but he didn't know his geography that well. Rome was yet to be determined; he just reacted to the order and knew he needed to get to Georgia.

Another computer spit out info on the car service. This one was in Dalton, Georgia. The VIN number was attached to the name in Ben's search. The service computer at the dealership entered the VIN number into the web. Juan's name was on the lease for that number, which then was found by Ben's search. The system did the rest.

Ben found it within an hour and followed his instructions to the letter. He called Jon.

"I found that Juan Castrono guy." He told him.

"Really? Where?"

"He's right here, just down in Rome with a busted car in the shop."

"Put a tail on him, anybody you can trust. I can't come right now, busy as hell. But I'll call you in the morning."

"Got it. I'll check with George and Gil about a tail. I'm sure they can come up with something."

~

Igor's Manor was a hot spot in Shreveport. Suspected "mob" activity made it special to the younger, drinking age crowd. The Russians liked the rock music and this age group was fond of it as well so the atmosphere appealed to both.

The manager actually reported to Vasily Torbof, but unofficially. Ownership of the club was registered to a Charles "Chick" Venter of New Orleans. Mr. Venter operated a chain of fast food shops that specialized in fried chicken. He was never seen on the premises though his picture hung in the lobby.

The club opened into a large circular lounge with a dance floor at one end and glass surrounding three quarters of the exterior walls. When lit up, it was quite impressive within and from outside. Tables that could accommodate up to twelve were spread out and smaller units spotted the floor. The food was five stars, but not three string beans making a tent over a nickel sized piece of steak. It was really hefty servings of American fare and Louisiana specialties.

The manager was nervous this afternoon. He had called Torbof to complain about the crowd last night. They were obvious and that drew too much attention. The manager was aware of the team from Colombia that had been stopped short of their plan. All these guys hanging out together was like chumming the waters for sharks and he didn't like it.

Torbof agreed and had promised to do something about it. He had so ordered in fact. He wanted to organize another team of twenty men to go to Florida. His first team was diverted to Kentucky to deal with some meeting up there, but he didn't want to let Argus go without punishment.

Leonid had attempted to spread the word about Torbof's request. He should have phrased it as an order. Requests were considered just that and often ignored. The word for certain members to attend a meeting in the morning was interpreted as "orders to the front lines." That didn't help the attendance level at Igor's for that evening. No one wished to be left out.

Many planned to eat elsewhere and show up to party around 8:30PM. That should help and look like they tried to obey the request. The crowd that night would be huge.

~

Murray was awake and cleaned up. It was nearing dinnertime that Tuesday and he found Phil, Sara and Jon on the back porch sipping iced tea.

"What's for dinner?" he started..."My treat."

Jon turned and laughed, "Well, if it ain't sleeping beauty." Then he recalled what Murray had been through and wished he could take it back. The cowboy wasn't offended, but he was hungry.

Phil then looked at Jon and winked, "Sara and I are meeting up with the Turlocks for dinner and a movie. It's a chick flick, but you're welcome to tag along."

"Looks like you and me," the cowboy nodded toward Jon. "You know your way around this town?"

"I can find something to eat."

Phil had set this up to clear the way. Jon knew it, just not before right then. *This guy is something else. He is like me in his thinking,* went through Jon's mind.

The Stones left shortly before 7PM and Jon went out to his car and grabbed his bag. Walking back in past Murray, he waved it at him and asked, "You're about my size, right?"

"I guess," the cowboy was taken back. "Why?"

"I got a shirt and pair of britches for you to try." He opened the bag and pulled two sets of the khaki and tan shirts and pants. "We'll look like twins if we stay too close," he threw a set at Murray. "But that can't be helped right now. We may be glad we had these."

Murray rubbed the fabric and looked surprised. "What is this stuff?"

"Protection against flying objects."

Murray felt the leg pocket and what was inside. Jon had ordered replicas of the small Glock. One of the new ones was in the pants. The cowboy pulled it out and looked it over closely.

"This thing can't take much heat, can it?" He asked.

"Enough to get away if we need to." Jon smiled. "It won't be noticeable to anyone and it doesn't set off metal detectors."

Murray made a face and slid the gun back into the pocket. "You carry one of these a lot?"

"Most of the time."

"Huh." Murray's head rocked up and down. "Not too surprised." He added.

Jon left the room, "I'm gonna clean up and change shirts." He declared and then added, "What do you want for dinner?"

"Steak," Murray blurted. "Steak and fries."

"My man!" Jon laughed. "Just what I was thinking!"

43

Santonio Lendono had been imprisoned in Sabanalarga, Colombia for almost twenty years. The sentence began as a legitimate one, but Lendono quickly learned that his business interests would not be slowed by his location. The right amount of money applied to the right areas kept communications flowing and business humming.

Over the years, he realized that his prison cell was more an asset than anything else. The Colombian drug wars were vicious and murders of opposing cartel leaders had become a way of life. His "office" was one of the more secure places in Colombia and as time went by, it looked more like a CEO's suite than any prison cell anywhere.

While his brother-in-law, Sergio DeMarcos, was the named head of the DeMarcos Cartel, Santonio had called the shots for years. When the series of events this past week reduced Sergio to a vegetable state, he became more visible.

He was really free to move around and go out at his own pleasure. He had a beach getaway near Turbo and would be whisked there by the Colombian army whenever he asked, for a price. Money was the key to everything and that had not been a problem... until recently. The entire empire was cracking at its base and,without money coming in it could not be sustained.

Those who had protected him and the family would turn in a heartbeat and they would no longer exist. Such was the high life of a cartel kingpin.

The last week was a low point and things weren't getting better. Santonio had moved his family, including his stroke stricken brother-in-law to Panama and himself to the beach house, which was also a quick run to that country. His military guards knew nothing and didn't care. They took orders from the government, or factions of it, and those orders depended upon money.

From Turbo he had taken a larger "hands on" role in day-to-day operations, or to be more correct...the lack of them. His U.S. operations were vital to his success and without the revenue from there the cartel would soon collapse. His head of operations and assistant were now at odds with each other, his best collection of warriors were arrested and the deportation orders, which would benefit him, were being held up. He was running out of options. The Juan Castrono situation bothered him the most. Castrono was a thinker, not a troublemaker. He had called him to the beach house several years before to help plan a financial arrangement with a rival cartel. Juan was smart. He liked Juan, but now the circumstances had made him a liability. One that had to be eliminated.

Word had been sent to members of a particular gang that were good drug customers. They would pay, but not always on time. The money was good when they did. The unreliable hoods were from Central and South American countries and ruled cities like Los Angeles, San Antonio, New Orleans and Mobile. Murder was part of their initiation ritual so asking for soldiers was not a problem. Keeping them directed and on target would be the problem. Their asking price for service was steep. Lendono had paid a deposit of $45,000.00 for a small army to be gathered near the Texas – Louisiana border. He now needed the balance, some $155,000.00 available before they would act.

Lendono sat in his beach house and tried to call in markers, favors and debts.

He wasn't having much luck.

~

Superior's Steak House had been recommended by Phil and Matt Turlock. Matt preferred the Club, but that was a bit high hat for Jon's taste. The parking lot was full for a Tuesday evening but, *that's the way things go,* they thought. The wait wasn't bad and the food was great. Half way through the meal, Jon and Murray had both noticed the same thing. Groups of large, European males all sitting together, several groups of them to be exact.

Still more groups of the same make-up were coming in as they left, Murray offered odds on if they would see these guys later.

"No, thanks." Jon laughed. "And I hope it's still funny when we do see them again."

Murray had a jacket with him to wear over the shirt Jon had given him. "Will this prevent the shirt from working?" He asked in all sincerity.

"Naw, but let's not prove that, ok?"

The drive to Igor's Manor took fifteen minutes. They left the car with a valet and walked in. The cover for tonight was $10.00 a person and it was crowded.

Tuesdays really hop in Shreveport. Jon thought. As they walked through the lobby and to the entrance of the main room, Jon suggested they split up and look around.

The large tables were full of big men. A few women sat on men's laps. While not in chairs, they were still part of the group. The music was loud and some twenty-somethings were dancing near their tables.

Jon had scanned the entire room twice before he became aware of the man. He sat alone at a small table near the center of the room. There was a drink in front of him and he had ordered what appeared to be an expensive cigar from the waiter. A dark brown leather brief case sat under the table, but he was dressed in a suit and it fit with him. He took his time lighting the cigar, playing with it as he watched the clock on the wall.

Jon began to concentrate on this man. His presence and actions were not out of line. But it bothered Jon nonetheless.

At five minutes till 9PM, the man finally lit his cigar. He took a few strong puffs and then sat it on a large ashtray near his drink. He rose from the table and asked a waiter a question. The waiter pointed to the lobby and more directly to the restrooms.

Jon stepped back, closer to the front doors and watched the man go into the restroom, but then come right back out and head for the exit. As he got near, Jon stepped directly in his path. As the stranger moved slightly to the right Jon again shifted in front of him and asked tersely, "Say, do I know you?"

The man stopped, looked hard at Jon and mumbled, "You don't want to know me, friend." He quickly attempted to step around Jon yet again.

Before Jon could move to block him, he heard another voice step in.

"What's your hurry, partner?" It was Murray. He had been watching the man as well and moved in behind Jon as the man walked up. Murray's hand was on the man's chest.

"Move that hand and get out of my way." The stranger demanded as he inhaled deeply, expanding his chest. He reached out and he pushed at Murray Bilstock. While doing that, Carl Holmes couldn't stop himself from taking a quick look back at his table.

Jon noticed this and looked with him. The briefcase now stood out as it sat under the table. Everything from that point seemed to be in slow motion to Jon. He turned to Murray while diving to the floor. "Get down," He screamed instinctively.

Murray had twisted Carl's arm and spun him around, inadvertently putting his body in front of his own. The stranger was held firmly in place, looking squarely at the package he had delivered. Jon hit the deck and covered his head with his arms.

A bright yellow light from the center of the room was followed by red. Heat pushed outward in every direction followed by the lethal contents of the case. The roar of the explosion did not cover the sounds of screams... cries and breaking glass. The package Carl delivered contained several blocks of C-4 and over three hundred half-inch steel ball bearings. Within the flashes and noise dozens died outright from the blast, the flying metal or both. One ball bearing caught Jon's arm, but the Kevlar fabric held. He looked up and Murray was still standing, holding the now dead body of Carl Holmes.

The bomber had been struck by more than twelve of the missiles. It was hard to be sure exactly how many. One hit him directly in the forehead. He was a mess.

The eruption and blast were over in seconds. Eerie, battery powered, emergency lights kicked in illuminating the site from odd angles. Objects and bodies near the epicenter were cut down or blown away; the clearing of that area was startling. At the perimeter of the kill zone lifeless victims were still in the act of falling. The dust cloud had been propelled beyond where Jon and Murray stood. It slowly swirled and came back into the blast area, covering everything with a fine coating.

It took Murray nearly a minute to let go of the bomber. The sound and concussion had stunned him. His hold on the killer's arm, twisted behind its back, supported the weight and kept the body upright. When he dropped the man he could see where four of the body blows had traveled through Holmes. They hit his Kevlar with enough force to have killed Murray as well. The shirt had done its job.

Murray said nothing, but he looked down at Jon in near shock and then back into the room as his mind attempted to make sense of what happened.

The club was devastated. The dead were uncountable at that point; bodies and pieces of bodies lay everywhere and the dust covering blended everything together. What initially had been missing began to seep up through the mess. Red pools of blood formed and soaked into the dust. With it came the reality of the event.

Jon slowly stood and took Murray by the arms and led him to a couch in the lobby. Sitting his friend down he looked back to what had been the main room for any signs of life. Carefully stepping around the obviously dead and checking those he wasn't sure about, Jon noticed other activity around him.

Survivors from the far sides of the room were helping each other. Injuries seemed to be either traumatic or mild, not much in between. All the glass had been blown out and sections of the ceiling hung down exposing holes through to the night sky.

Jon found several of the ball bearings imbedded into concrete columns and some with flattened sides lying on the floor. It was complete devastation near ground zero.

With little he could do for anyone else he went back to where Murray sat and they waited for the emergency team. Murray was exercising his jaw and rubbing his ears for several minutes. When he finally could speak he looked at Jon and simply said. "Here we go again, huh?"

Jon was staring at the body of the bomber. Murray noticed and looked back and forth between them and then said, "He won't tell us anything."

Jon sat upright at that comment and corrected his friend. "Not so fast." He bent over the body and searched the pockets. Car keys, rental car keys with the brand "Chevy" embossed on the main key. "Stay here, I'll be back," he nearly ordered Murray.

The uniforms were not there yet, Jon looked around in the closest lot for a Chevy. Surprisingly the lights were still on in the lot. Two rows back sat a blue one. Walking toward the vehicle he hit the "unlock" button on the keys. The car lit up, that was it.

He opened the door and sat on the driver's seat, pulling down the visor and checking the glove box. Nothing. As a last resort he looked down under the seats. One small piece of wadded up paper and a neatly folded set of rental papers were there. The name on the rental agreement was "Efrain Berrera" of Shreveport. He made a note of the name and address and then just took the papers with him. He could be held up for a while in the investigation and the authorities could get to Efrain first. That wouldn't do.

The small crumbled paper was the note about Igor's and the time 9PM. Jon put that note back under the seat and closed the door. As he got back to the front doors, a fire department ambulance pulled up. Jon stepped hurriedly around them and replaced the keys in the dead man's pocket.

"What was that?" Murray asked and then added sarcastically, "boss."

Jon realized what the cowboy meant and just ignored it. "I found his car. It was rented by a local." He looked around to see if anyone was watching them. "We need to get to this guy first."

Murray was impressed. He nodded and leaned back, "Are my ears bleeding?" He asked.

~

His pager went off at 9:10PM. Phil checked the text message from HQ and his heart jumped. "Huge explosion at Igor's Manor. All available respond." It was blunt and Phil knew what must have happened. He excused himself, telling Sara she could stay and have the car. He would call for a squad car to pick him up. Before he got off the row, Matt's cell went off and he too, was heading out.

Within twenty minutes Capt. Stone was walking into the lobby of the now former club, relieved to see his friends sitting on a couch. He reached out and grabbed them by the arms and his first reaction was, "What the hell are these shirts made of?"

266

"Are my ears bleeding?" Murray asked him in jest.

"No...you look fine... What happened...besides the obvious?"

Jon explained what they had witnessed and pointed to the body of the bomber. "If they have video surveillance it should be clear about the briefcase." He told him.

"Why didn't he get away?" The captain asked.

"We kinda got in his way," Murray offered. "He was acting hinkey and Jon stopped him to check him out."

"There was no time for that." Jon quickly added. "The timer or whatever was apparently for 9PM sharp."

Stone rolled the body over and grimaced. "Geez, you can tell me more about this later. What else you got?"

It was Jon's turn to be impressed. The old cop figured they hadn't just been sitting there, waiting. "I have a name of someone I need to talk to." He told the officer.

"Ok, how'd you get that," Stone pried and looked to Murray who just shrugged.

Jon told him about the keys and the note and the papers. He pulled them from his shirt and handed them to him.

"You monkeyed with evidence?" The cop challenged almost loudly. "What's wrong with you? I'm in pretty deep already backing you two."

"I have to find out who sent this guy," Jon answered while pointing at the body. "We know where one snake is, he's right here in Shreveport." Looking directly at Stone, Jon lowered his voice yet became extremely intense. "I have to find and do away with both snakes or this mess will never end."

The brutal bluntness of that stunned the officer. Captain Phil Stone stood straight up and took a breath. He slapped the papers in his hand and walked back outside. Standing there he thought of the pictures he remembered of the scene in New York back in 2001. What he stood in could easily resemble that on a smaller scale. He knew it could not be allowed to escalate any further. Turning back to Jon he spoke clearly and with conviction, "I'll get you an address verification and twenty-four hours. That's all I can do."

Jon's face bore a look Phil had not noticed before. He appeared older, grave and stern. The younger man raised his eyes directly into the older officer's gaze. Without blinking once, Jon nodded and continued his stare.

44

Charlene Bilstock had been trying to reach her brother for over an hour. She had gotten bad news from the authorities in Greenville, Caddo Mills' County seat. When the phone finally rang in Murray's pocket, Jon had to punch him and point it out.

Murray rubbed his still ringing ear and tried to answer.

"Murray," the sobbing voice started. "I thought something had..."

"What is it, Charlene? This ain't a good time, Sis." He interrupted.

He could hear her taking several sharp breaths, trying to control herself and then she finally spoke, "The traveling coroner for Hunt County won't be in Greenville till next week, late next week. So I've told them to bring Stephen to Dallas. They can do the autopsy late Friday sometime."

Murray made out enough to understand what was going on, "Ok, that's fine."

"Murray, how bad is Stephen?" She asked.

"What do you mean?"

"They told me I should not come to see the body. They asked for dental records from Brownwood to use for identification."

"Sis...he got burned pretty bad. You let them do their job, ok? You don't need to see him. Just remember him."

The sniffling began again, but just for a moment.

"That's what I thought, you just never said." She gathered herself and went on, "I will still try to have a memorial service Saturday afternoon. Can you make that?"

"Yeah, I think I should be done here by then." His voice was flat and detached from the subject she had called about. He had other things on his mind. "That'll work."

~

The investigation, as far as they were concerned, didn't take long that night. Jon worried a bit that the two incidents in two days might draw notice, but word from Texas had not reached Louisiana yet.

Their story made sense, two friends out on the town, bump into a guy in a hurry to leave. There were videos that clearly showed Holmes leave his table with the briefcase still there. The moment of detonation was also conclusive. The body carried ID, which was unusual for his profession. The name stated Carl Holmes and showed he was a salesman from Lubbock, Texas. The name later matched fingerprints, but the address was not legitimate.

Jon and Murray were at Stone's house by 12:30AM though Phil wasn't. Jon called Ben, asked about Marsha and then started with instructions. He wanted the two Barrett M-107 sniper rifles readied to be sent to him.

"Two?" Ben was confused, "Only one came in."

"That's the second. There's another in the First Street warehouse I hadn't had time to tell you about. Oh...and those remote firing units we ordered?"

"Got those downstairs."

"I need you to go through the instructions and do me a reader's digest version. Send those with the rifles."

"Jon," Ben injected. "I've got another one you want to look at."

"Another what?"

Ben told Jon about the T-Rex and how it had worked on the hit man across the way.

"Send it and three rounds for each...no more."

~

Vasily Torbof was once again awoken with bad news. This time an underling was forced to deliver it.

"Where is Lenoid?" Torbof demanded of him.

"We don't know, sir. There are many casualties...we don't know."

News reports were immediate and world wide. The numbers of dead were still being counted and identifications attempted. He watched the coverage for only a few minutes and turned the TV off in a huff.

Vasily went to his rooftop to think. It was cold that night; he had to retire to the downstairs, but only long enough to find his heavy coat. He couldn't think clear inside. He had been raised in the north country back home. They stayed outside most of the year back then. Living in the states had made him soft, he often complained.

He thought about the attack in Kentucky that was scheduled. Should he call it off? There were good reasons to delay it, but his anger and ego overrode them. *Perhaps they can even the score up there.* He told himself confidently. There was a long way to go to do that.

~

The news reached Santonio Lendono in Turbo, Colombia much the same as it had Torbof. A messenger awoke him to say the satellite TV was telling of the massacre.

Lendono wasn't surprised. He was pleased. It was about time he had some good news for a change. He had not heard from Holmes and wondered briefly about him. Carl was always efficient and careful. He would call soon and Lendono would shower praise upon him. He leaned back and watched the American TV coverage and smiled at the success. This would impress the MY-12 gang members he was recruiting. Money spoke to them first, but power and strength influenced them as well.

271

Through them he would regain the control of his territories in the states and money would again flow. He stepped to his bar and poured himself a drink. Sitting back down, he raised his glass high, "Holmes," he declared and turned the glass upward.

~

The name on the rental papers was Efrain Berrera. Such a person did exist, just not at the address shown. Stone was able to track him down quickly because the fake address was actually a bar he frequented. Other regulars were coaxed to give him up rather easily.

Efrain really lived in Keithville, La. some five miles south on I-49. He had told the guys at the bar he worked for an import company out of South America.

Phil Stone called Jon with the information and simply added, "be careful."

It was now 2AM. Jon was weary, but this was the time to act. By morning it would be too late. He put his arm unit on and drove to Keithville.

Efrain did not wish to talk at first. He even tried to get to some suicide pills he kept in a kitchen cabinet. Jon was able to convince him to talk.

The pain from the dislocated elbow made him hard to understand. But as Jon applied pressure to his knee, Efrain appeared to be saying, "Lendono, Lendono."

Jon grabbed his face and looked him right in the eyes. "Saul's Uncle?"

"Si."

Where is this Lendono?" Jon asked only once. "He's in prison isn't he?"

"No, No...Turbo...Turbo, Colombia," the man cried.

"What is Turbo?"

"Cabana, his beach house. Cabana." Efrain muttered. He was now resolved to his fate. Too much had been given up already, there was no need to endure any more pain over this.

"I will tell you what I know," he pleaded to the tormentor.

The conversation went smoother after that. Jon set the elbow back and waited a few minutes for Efrain to come to after that. The man explained in detail how Lendono operated and proclaimed, "you can't get to him anyway."

Jon asked about Dewey Hanson, who Efrain knew of, but claimed he was out of the picture. Out of favor with the family and marked for destruction.

Before Jon left Efrain's apartment, he knew about the prison cell in Sabanalarga, that the family was out of the country and that Lendono was working a deal to make his comeback.

Jon left the man alive, but that didn't last long. Knowing what he told would be his end anyway; Efrain got up and made his way to the kitchen cabinet.

~

Phil was waiting up when Jon returned from Keithville. He was very sullen and only wanted to share what he had learned and go to bed. As Jon came in he didn't even ask about the trip south.

"You can call your Captain in Kentucky and tell her it's tomorrow night for sure."

Jon looked a bit surprised, "You know for sure?"

Phil stood to say what he had on his mind. "They identified one of the bodies as one of my lieutenants'. One that was on the list of possibles."

"Damn, Phil I'm sorry."

"They found the body next to one of Torbof's aids, some guy named Lenoid."

"I'll call Swanson first thing in the morning."

273

"Good." Stone snapped.

"Man, I'm sorry about your lieutenant."

"Yeah...I was hoping it wasn't her." Phil said walking away.

"Her?"

"Huh..." the cop looked back at Jon. "Does that shock you? That a woman could be a traitor?"

Jon shook his head and watched his friend and ally walk to his own room and close the door. The question had to be rhetorical; Stone was clearly shaken by the turn.

What a mess this whole deal was, he thought and headed for bed himself.

~

Capt. Swanson had received a call from Jon around 7AM that Wednesday morning.

"I saw what happened in Shreveport last night," she paused to see what Jon would say about it. His quiet told her it was serious to him. "So, are these the guys we're expecting...the ones that did that?" She added.

"Actually," Jon hesitated for a second, "The ones you are expecting are from the group that were the victims last night."

The Kentucky State Police Captain was quiet this time.

"This has been going on...back and forth," Jon tried to explain, "for about a week now."

"They play rough." Swanson commented sternly.

"Yeah, and they don't care who gets hurt. That's why we've got to stop them and fast."

"Well," she started with no shortage of confidence, "consider these guys out of the picture after tonight. They're mine if they show up here."

"Thanks, Captain." He could tell she meant everything she said. "Please remember what we talked about and just be careful, ok?"

"We've got this...talk to you later." She responded and hung up.

Her plans for the stable ambush were already underway. The news simply gave her added incentive to make it right.

Cars were trucked into the area and placed around the stable to look like those of gang members. Some were older, but several were new, flashy models to give an appearance of leadership in attendance. They and the building were wired in the event they needed heavy repulsion of the attackers. Lights were rigged to make the building look occupied.

The fields surrounding the stable had high grass and trees. The trees were wired with high-powered lights and bullhorns. Military style bunkers and trenches were dug for the officers who would lay in wait for the attack.

By 4PM she had the site as she wanted it, cold sandwiches were ordered for the troops and everybody settled in to wait. It would be after dark when they came.

45

Charlie Conroy had been a Private Investigator for twelve years, retiring from the Floyd County Sheriff's Department after a thirty-seven year career. He looked his age, but didn't act it. Charlie was up on the latest gizmos and gadgets to help with his work, miniature cameras and microphones, long-range digital cameras, anything to even the score to his age handicap.

Ben knew of him through George. They had worked together many years ago and George used his services now and then. Jon knew of him by reputation.

Charlie had been to the Chrysler dealership early that Wednesday morning asking for a part that required research to identify. While the counterman was doing that research, Charlie hooked up the entire service department with both audio and video. The wireless connections made his job easier. He now sat in his car across the street and monitored the goings on.

Juan's taxi arriving was obvious enough for him to start paying close attention. The visitor would be disappointed this day with the service a small town can offer. The parts needed for Juan's repair would be delayed another day for transfer through the Atlanta hub of the parts distribution network.

Juan protested to no avail. The service writer offered to pay for another cab and Juan went back to his motel, Charlie followed. His report to Ben that afternoon was simple. After reporting in to Ben, Charlie went back to the dealership to adjust the frequency of his equipment to a longer range. The plan was to be able to listen from his apartment till something good happened.

While making those tuning adjustments, Charlie heard another man asking the service writer questions about Juan and the car. Charlie quickly set up a video monitor and dialed it in.

He saw a short, older man in fine clothes vividly animating his words with his arms as he spoke. He didn't look like anyone from the area and his accent was "a bit Yankee" as he would later describe it. He punched a button and made several pictures of this individual before again calling Ben.

"Sorry to bother you twice, young man. But there is something you might need to know." Charlie then sent the pictures to Ben who compared them with ones on file and thanked Charlie empathically.

Jon's phone rang many times before he answered. It was 4:20PM and he had slept most of the day away, catching up from the previous two.

"Yeah," he answered. "What is it Ben?" Rubbing his face to wake up.

"Dewey Hanson is in Rome." Ben told him. "He's in Rome right now."

Jon sat upright and shook his head. "Send the plane for me, Ben. Right away."

~

Juan didn't stay in his room long. He called for another cab to take him up to the Landmark Diner. He was there enjoying his dinner while a short man pounded on his motel room door. The man made enough commotion that the management threatened to call the police if the man didn't leave.

After his dinner, Juan walked across two parking lots to the shopping mall and spent a couple of hours there. He did not get back to the motel until late, but the manager was waiting for him. He told Juan of the short, angry man pounding on his door. This rattled Juan, who then checked out of that motel and took yet another taxi across town to a Holiday Inn near the Chrysler dealership. There he checked into a room facing the highway, a highway that separated his new motel from a Hampton Inn where Dewey Hanson rested from his long day.

~

"Wake up," Jon hollered through the door. "We're going to Georgia."

Like his new friend, Murray Bilstock had had a rough couple of days and nights. Sleeping till 4PM in the afternoon was different to both men, but in this case it was a necessity. They had been going none stop for almost two whole days.

Waking up at that time of day could be disorienting enough, but hearing about a trip to Georgia just didn't make any sense.

"What?" Murray rolled over and attempted to sit. "Georgia, what?"

"Just get moving. We've got a couple hours to get ready and I'll explain everything...when you're...awake."

The cowboy cleaned up and got dressed. The water from the shower brought his thinking into focus and he had several big questions. He stepped into the hall with his travel bag and saw Jon going into the Stone's living room.

"Hey, hang on a second, will ya?" he yelled.

Jon had a lot on his mind. He still responded calmly. "Yeah, what's up?"

"I'm all over helping with whatever's going on but...we're going to Georgia and we need to be in Whitewright on Friday night." He held his hands out to his sides, "how's that gonna work?"

"We'll be there, don't sweat it." Came the rather short reply.

Murray walked up and threw his bag down with a thump. That caught Jon's attention and the two men glared at each other momentarily. Jon spoke first.

278

"What's that all about?" he demanded.

"I'm gonna be in Whitewright...with or without."

"Look, I know this doesn't look like I have that as a priority, but I do." Jon's voice was more asking for patience than before. "There's a thing I had planned to deal with later. But the suspects...the principals have both come to me. I can't let this go."

Murray's intent was to be reasonable as long as he had assurances the problem in Whitewright, Texas would be handled. "Where in Georgia are we going?"

"Rome."

"You're kiddin' me?"

"No...why's that?" Jon was puzzled.

"They've got an Athens and a Rome in Georgia?"

Jon gave him a dirty look and took the bags out to the car.

"Hey, who knew?" Murray laughed.

~

Dewey Hanson had used up his experience in being a heavy. He was lost; this was stuff he normally paid for so he did what he knew. He called for an escort service to get a line on some enforcers or drug dealers he could buy. The girl who came to the door looked at Hanson like he had lost his mind.

"You want what, Mister?"

"I want somebody who can perform a service for me." He told her. She still didn't understand. Hanson pulled her into the room on the second floor of the Hampton and pushed the door closed. "Listen, if somebody roughs you up, who would you call?"

The girl's eyes became the size of dinner plates. "Don't you try anything weird," she warned him.

"Who's your pimp, darling?"

The girl pulled a cell phone from her purse and looked up to see if he was going to stop her. When he didn't she froze, not knowing what to do.

"Call whoever you were going to." Hanson ordered. "I want to talk to 'em."

Within the hour there was a knock on the motel room door. A large black man stood in the hall and demanded to know, "what the hell is going on here?"

Hanson explained his business proposition and what he was willing to pay for the service. The man was interested.

"Who is this guy?" he asked.

Dewey smiled. He had his employee. He was back in control and comfortable with that position. Laying out the plan and describing Juan took another hour. The man wanted a down payment. Not wanting him to see where his stash was kept, Hanson asked him and the girl to wait downstairs and he would bring it to them.

"You owe her for her time, too ya know." The big man said sternly.

"No problem."

When they had left, Dewey retrieved the amount needed and went downstairs. But he went down the back steps instead of the elevator and walked around to the front door from the outside. The appearances were that he had gone to his car for the money.

"I'll be round the corner in the morning watching for him." The man told Hanson.

Dewey nodded and they shook hands. An empty gesture from the congressman, but he did it anyway.

46

If Murray was impressed with the G-5 he didn't let on. Jon really didn't notice or think about it either, he had too much on his mind.

Darkness was falling on the east coast and the Kentucky hit would be starting any time now. The job they were heading to do had no plan at the moment. They would have to get there, meet with Charlie and figure it out. Then, always on his mind was Marsha and how she was.

He looked over at the cowboy who was leaning back in one of the huge leather seats, looking out the window. His hat took up the seat next to him and his boots were on the seat back of the chair in front of him.

At least he folded it down, Jon laughed inside. *This trip should take care of Argus in America for once and for all.* he dreamed. *Then there's the Colombia and Shreveport heads of the cartels.* It didn't get any easier, but there was a course to follow.

He looked out his window to the north, as though he could see it when it started and thought about Kentucky again. *So much going on.* he repeated in his head.

~

It had been dark for nearly an hour when the radio on Sharon Swanson's shoulder sounded.

"Traffic...north bound." It said and then there was a break in transmission. Everyone held still and waited. Within 20 seconds it crackled again, "Three vehicles, one car and two vans approaching the off road on I-75."

Captain Swanson keyed her mike, "Positions people, this sounds like them."

The radio cracked again, "All three turned off and coming your way, over."

"Hold your position till I call for you, could be a false alarm."

"Ten-four," came the reply.

The lights flickered inside the empty stable building and all appeared as though a large gathering was being held. Recorded talking noises were barely audible, but might come in handy. They were ready.

The headlights became visible as the vehicles drove through the grass and turned one last corner. Then one by one, the headlights went out and sight of the car and vans was lost for a few moments. When eyes adjusted they found the three vehicles still where they were, but the doors were open.

"They're on foot, radio silence." Swanson whispered into her mike.

The mobsters spread out through the grass and trees and approached the building from three sides. One group of four actually stepped over a bunker cover where twelve State Troopers hid and waited. As they moved closer to the building the Troopers could see the men spread out even further. Some gave the parked cars a quick look and then they all, twenty that could be counted, gathered at the three door openings for the stable.

"Now." Swanson ordered into her radio and the floodlights up in the trees lit the stable up as daylight. "Hands in the air, you are all under arrest." Came her next order, now through the bullhorns.

The Russian gang members reacted as one, spinning into crouched positions and firing wildly into the night. There were no Troopers exposed to be injured so they allowed the men to shoot for over a minute before the Captain issued her warning, "Drop your weapons, now."

The warning was not heeded and the Troopers next heard her, over the sound of the continuing gunfire, holler. "Fire."

Bunker doors popped open and rifles emerged from trenches and began peppering the stables. Several of the mobsters fell immediately. Others, three with backpacks, forced their way into the stable. Sharon Swanson knew from both her own experience and what Jon Crane had told her that going in after these guys would be foolish.

Her troops had not wasted time while preparing the area. The inside of the stable was set to burn in four places - the center, the back and both sides. She waited for the shooting to lull and again issued an order over the bullhorns. "You have one minute to come out, hands up. One minute."

The quiet that resonated for the next bit of time seemed out of place to everyone, it was eerie. Swanson gave them more than the time she had said. Then finally keyed her radio and commanded, "Hit one."

The rear of the building ignited and flames flickered across the windows and could be seen through the open front doors. She waited three full minutes more and ordered, "Hit two."

The center erupted and the flames came through the roof vents, still no movement from the men inside. Within another minute the stable looked like nothing could survive in there and she again hollered through the bullhorns for them to come out. The lack of response would normally call for a rescue surge, sending in troopers to bring the perpetrators out. But that order did not come.

A strange look came across Swanson's face. Instead of ordering an advance she keyed her mike and ordered her troops to fall back, "Quickly!" she screamed.

Time did not allow her fears to bother her long. The building came apart in pieces of fire and smoke. Sections of walls flew past her and hurled into the trees. Her troops who were in trenches fell back into them. That was the best thing. Whatever those men had in the backpacks, it was powerful. An officer beside her was hit by a piece of something and fell to the ground, silent. Blood oozed from his head.

The scene was devastation she hadn't expected. Even with the warning from Jon. The stable was gone, totally gone. The cars they had parked around it were flipped over, turned around or in some fashion, not as they were before. All were on fire. Half of her spotlights were blown out.

She looked around and called for a casualty report. Seven down, three seriously hurt.

"Get the ambulances in here." she screamed. They had staged the emergency crews just outside the fire zone; they were on scene within minutes and offering aid to the injured. Those numbers didn't include any of the men who had attacked. The bodies that fell outside the building had been claimed by the explosion and fire. Those inside were never accounted for. Some few "parts," as the medical examiner called them, were found. But little else.

Checking on her wounded, Captain Swanson heard a medic assistant ask her if he could take care of her wound.

"What?" She challenged him.

"You're hit, Captain." he said calmly.

Blood ran down her right pants legs and she grabbed at the thigh. Nothing. It was actually coming from her side. A hunk of metal had gone completely through, inches from vital organs on her right side.

Her knees weakened a bit and she reached for the table for support. The medics grabbed her and they placed her on a gurney.

"Damn." was all she said and they cleaned her wound and patched her up. Inside her mind she completed the thought quietly. *He was right about them. The kid from Georgia was right.*

~

Vasily Torbof sat up until after 2AM waiting for word on the hit in Kentucky. He drank as he waited, partly to stay warm since he started out the evening on the roof. Even vodka could not keep the chill off of him for long and by midnight he had moved indoors.

The news of the Kentucky raid would not make national attention until just before noon the following day. When Torbof awoke at 10AM with still no word from his people he began to get a bad feeling. Pacing was uncommon behavior to Vasily yet he became aware that's just what he was doing. Frustration boiled over and he pounded a small table near the stairs and cracked the top. Mrs. Torbof both saw and heard the damage to her furniture and stood glaring at her husband from the living room doorway.

Vasily's answer to her was to reach for a heavy coat and storm up to his rooftop. He wasn't in any mood to explain himself or apologize. The leader of the Russian CCCY in North America stood at the east wall of his rooftop for over half an hour, staring at the river in a near trance. *What could have gone wrong with this*? he wondered.

~

The Gulfstream G-5 eased into Richard B. Russell airport near Rome, Georgia just after 11PM that Wednesday. Ben had arranged for a rental car to be waiting and the Crown Victoria sat ready next to the hanger set up for the plane.

A map lay on the seat with directions to motels near the Chrysler dealership they would be going to. On top of the map was a note to Jon, "your package will be delivered tomorrow morning. Call with your location."

Good thinking, Jon nodded to himself as he handed the note to Murray and asked him to help remind him of it later. *Ben adapted well to change.* Jon thought as he smiled.

The drive across town was quick. Rome was not the size of Dalton and had less traffic except for rush hour. This was not rush hour.

They tried the Hampton Inn first, but it was full. The Holiday Inn had two rooms on different floors and they gladly took those. The plan was to sleep till around 6AM and meet in the restaurant at 6:30AM for breakfast. Jon took the closest room and settled in.

Murray threw down his stuff in his room and decided he wanted some ice for a drink. He walked down the exterior corridor and found the ice machine in an alcove at the opposite end of the building. On his way there he passed a neatly dressed Hispanic man who had just retrieved a Dr. Pepper from the vending machine.

They glanced at each other and Murray dipped his hat slightly, thinking nothing of it.

47

Warm breezes off the Atlantic drifted in through the lanai and to the bedroom of Lendono's beach house. The morning was quiet, Thursdays usually were. Santonio was up early, reading his newspaper while he awaited a call from the MY-12 gang's leader in Texas. The ocean front villa appeared like a normal vacation home unless you looked very closely. Guards were everywhere.

He loved the Turbo location, but being a cartel boss was very dangerous business. That was the main reason his jail cell office was normally preferred, but like anyone else he needed to get away sometimes. The bad luck of late had brought on one of those times.

The TV flickered in the corner and somehow a story with little volume caught Santonio's eye. He grabbed the remote and turned up the sound.

The report was from Kentucky where a big shootout had taken place overnight. The perpetrators were still unknown. None carried identification and the bodies were in bad shape. One thing that caught the drug kingpin's eye was the picture of the vehicles the attackers had arrived in.

Lendono leaned in closer as the screen showed a four-door sedan and two eight passenger vans left in the field near the disturbance. Police said they found nothing in them to help. Still Santonio smiled and leaned back in his chair. He recalled vividly the description of the three vehicles that had been noticed fleeing the icehouse in Georgia. *One car and two vans*, he remembered. *This was those guys, trying again.*

Verification would take time, but he was sure. No coincidence could be so close. He stood and clapped his hands in celebration. Then wondered, *Who is doing this? How did the police know about these guys*? He thought of the MY-12 gang, but they did nothing without upfront payment. It was Kentucky police that had confronted them and then the location came in focus in his mind. *This was only miles from where Dario had killed that girl*! That too was a coincidence way over the line.

~

The breakfast bar line was busy, but Jon got through it and found Murray at a table near the windows. He sat down without speaking and took an exaggerated deep breath.

"Yeah," Murray said, turning his coffee cup up, "I feel your pain."

They ate and then Jon reached for a notebook he had brought with him. Rubbing his fingers together he commented about the grease from, well, everything he had eaten and excused himself to the restroom.

Just as Jon entered that area Murray heard a commotion in the back of the dining room. A Hispanic man had dropped his tray and was standing, dumb struck, staring at the restroom doors. Before Murray could realize he had seen this guy before, the man hurriedly stepped out through a side door and was gone. Staff rushed over to clean the mess and Murray was watching that when Jon sat back down.

"What's going on?" he asked.

"Ugh...nothing," Murray responded. Jon had his book out and was ready to go so there was no need to clutter the talk with speculation. Organizing his papers, Jon began.

"There's two guys here we are after. One..." and he laid out several photos of Dewey Hanson. "Is this guy."

Murray picked up a photo and nodded, "Ok... Is this somebody I know? I feel like he's familiar."

"Congressman from Pennsylvania, he's been in the news some."

Murray leaned back and started to make a comment. But Jon continued.

"He's also the current head of Argus Imports in the states. Or...he was, don't know what his status is right now."

The cowboy studied the picture and handed it back to Jon.

"The other is a fellow I've seen, so I'll look out for him." Jon stated. "Don't have a picture. But I'll know him." He put the loose papers and pictures back in the notebook and looked over at Murray. "They should be armed and considered dangerous."

"I may have seen that other one too," Murray half mumbled under his breathe.

"What?"

"Never mind," The cowboy corrected himself. "I'll watch for old Dewey, here."

"Ok, I've talked with Charlie Conroy this morning. He's sitting across the street from the dealership already." Jon put his notebook away and drank the last of his coffee. "I'll go to the north side of the service building if you'll go south. Then we just watch and wait."

"Let's go." Murray challenged and they left.

~

Juan Castrono had called into the service department earlier and found out the car would be ready by 10AM. His legs could hardly carry him to the room, but there he hid and waited. When the time came he would slip in and get his car. He had to get away from this town.

Dewey Hanson had left the Hampton Inn and was sitting in his car parked about a block south of the service building. The road was packed this morning and all the parking spaces outside the service department were taken up by a load of new vans. They were parked nose to tail all up the road next to the building. Hanson wasn't pleased with his spot. But he could see. When his "pimp" took care of Juan, he didn't want to miss it.

A black Caddy rode around the block several times, but did not stop. The car's glass was tinted out and Hanson figured it was his newest employee keeping an eye on the area. A cowboy walked past him, tipped his hat without pausing and continued further south. Half way down the next block the man with the big hat took a seat on a bus bench. Hanson watched the stranger for a few minutes in his mirror and then quit worrying about him. Checking his wristwatch, it said 9:35.

It was about that time when Juan left the Holiday Inn. He had called a cab, which took him around and two blocks over from the Chrysler dealer. He carefully worked his way back through and between the buildings until he was directly across the street from the service room doors. He checked cautiously all around. The only movement was to his left, a homeless man wrapped in a blanket and wearing a baseball cap pushed his grocery buggy to the corner. There, he stopped and began mindlessly inventorying his belongings that were in the cart.

At 9:58AM, Juan made his break, dashing right in front of Charlie's parked car. Apparently not noticing Charlie, he crossed the street and went through a small gap between two of the vans parked on the street. He was in the building in a flash.

Dewey threw open his car door and stood up, looking for his hit man who was nowhere to be found. He pulled a revolver from his coat pocket and headed toward the service department. So intent was he that he did not notice either the cowboy, who quietly followed him, or the homeless man. The bum threw his blanket and cap to the ground and entered the dealership through a door on the showroom side.

Charlie Conroy got out of his car, thought better of it and sat back down to watch. Memories of younger days had pulled at him, but the reality of his seventy-two years won out. He did check his 9mm and held it in his lap at ready.

Hanson pulled the service entrance door open and lurched inside, but no one was there or at the counter. Nervously, he scanned the room, *where did he go?* his mind asked. An archway to his right led to another area. The service bays on the right were half full of cars. The sidewall to the left was a row of frosted glass windows and an overhead sign pointing the way to the "Cashier." There, at the opened cashier's window only forty feet away, stood Juan Castrono.

"You!" Hanson screamed. "Stand right there!"

Juan frantically looked around for an escape route before his eyes settled on his former boss. Instinctively, he raised his hands.

Dewey Hanson moved slowly towards him, glaring and brandishing his weapon.

Dealership employees stepped around corners and peeked from behind vehicles. One yelled, "What is this?" Then ducked away when Hanson waved the gun his way.

Dewey stopped some four feet from Juan and pulled back the hammer on the small revolver. Juan's face went white, but not because of the gun. It was clear that Juan's gaze went past Hanson and slightly to his left. Dewey could not help himself; he turned to see what was the matter.

It was Jon Crane, standing just inside the archway in complete silence. As Hanson started to turn that direction Jon moved toward him and to the right. The congressman raised the weapon and aimed at Jon. Murray Bilstock leaped from between two cars in the service bays as Jon instinctively nose-dived behind a large toolbox. Dewey Hanson tried to follow Jon's movements with his eyes and his gun. The cowboy grabbed a large wrench from an open drawer and crossed the

291

remaining eight or ten feet to Hanson. As the congressman extended his arm to fire at Jon, Murray leapt head first over a bench. In a blur, he came down across the congressman's wrist with the large wrench.

The gun fell to the floor as the sound of breaking bones echoed in the building. Hanson cried out in an odd, shrill scream and grabbed his wrist. He looked around and quickly fled back through the service area and out the door.

Jon pushed himself up from the floor and went after Hanson. The cowboy was on his feet and right behind. Juan Castrono remained frozen in place with a gun at his feet.

Dewey Hanson headed toward his car, looking down and holding his wrist. His attention was grabbed by the large frame of Terry "T-Bone" Slater. The black pimp was briskly walking down the sidewalk gun in hand. Slater had noticed Juan going in, but had to park up the street and he was just arriving.

The sight of the large man with a gun startled Hanson who turned back not recognizing Slater. But he immediately saw Jon and Murray coming from the other direction. Panicked, he saw a space between two of the parked vans. The congressman ran into the gap and darted through, into the street.

The 10:10AM bus would be late that morning. Its scheduled stop for that time, two blocks away would have to wait today. It impacted Dewey Hanson at over forty miles per hour, and then rolled over him some twenty feet down the road.

The sound and the condition of Hanson's body made Jon and the strong-stomached cowboy, wince. Turning away they saw Juan standing outside the service areas doors, with Hanson's gun in his hand. He was concentrated on Jon, still trance like and not speaking. Murray reached for his Glock, but Jon held out his arm and said, "No."

Stepping toward Juan, Jon opened his hand and extended it to Juan.

292

"Diablo," the man mumbled barely audibly. He was holding the weapon backwards and he held it out to Jon.

"I'm no devil, man." Jon told him as he took the revolver. "But, hell. What am I going to do with you?"

Murray grabbed Jon's shoulder and motioned up the street. Police and emergency vehicles were on the way. "Ditch the gun." He suggested and Jon tossed it under one of the vans not far from where Hanson ended up.

Charlie Conroy had gotten out of his car and crossed the street to Jon. "Mr. Crane, I presume?"

"Yeah," Jon reached to shake his hand. "You must be Mr. Conroy."

"Nice to meet you, but you guys need to leave...now. I'll deal with this from here." Charlie urged them. "Get out of here."

Jon put his hand on Juan's shoulder and led him away. Murray nodded at Charlie and was right behind them.

Slater, the pimp was gone. The witnesses inside the dealership wanted no part of being drawn into a mess like this, stating they saw nothing. Charlie's story of what happened outside set the tone for the other witnesses who were outside and in the area.

The congressman would be reported to have been fleeing a known pimp in Rome, Georgia. A student from Berry College had been on the bus and was interviewed by the school paper, The Campus Courier and The Rome News-Tribune. His account, from his right side seat on the bus, was similar to Charlie's. It would be the basis for the national story.

Daniel Seay would write his story for the hometown Pittsburgh Post Gazette from the mansion in Dalton, Georgia. Wire service reports were relayed to him by Ed White his editor, who added a note, "This is your story...I'm waiting."

He wrote the story of Dewey Hanson's death completely void of the facts of where he, Daniel and his wife were and why they were there. He did not mention the fear that had driven them to a friend's home for safety. Hanson connections to the drug world were eluded to, but only lightly.

Lori came in while Daniel was working, she looked happy for the first time in over a week.

"We can go home now." She beamed and hugged her husband's neck from behind. Daniel reached up from the keyboard, caressing her arms and leaning back against her. A huge sigh of relief escaped from him and then he responded to her.

"I think so." But then he paused and sat back toward the computer. "I just want to check with Jon first."

Lori knew what that meant. It may not be completely over.

48

Turnip Tyler leaned back in his barber chair trying to think. He had taken off from work early to pick up the latest message from the Sponsors. What he found disturbed him. They were wanting yet another hit less than a week after this next one. The Governor of Arkansas was to be taken out next Thursday and now they were ordering a dangerous move against a U.S. Senator.

Tyler wasn't an overly smart man, but he was self-aware. That knowledge alone placed him well ahead of his other gang members. By mutual consent he was their leader and in an odd way, he felt responsible for them. That minor feeling of obligation was pure narcissism and in no way interfered with his self-loving nature. But still, someone had to be the boss.

Too much, too fast, Turnip was thinking. He rubbed the brass tacks that lined the red leather of the chair. A thought crept in, but he lost it to a commotion behind him. The banging, knocking noise interrupted his chain of thought. "Damn it," he spun the chair and hollered. "Shut him up."

Several members of the gang were perpetually unemployed and would gather at the club's office to drink the afternoons away. It would often get rowdy.

Two members quickly acted to silence the troublemaker and Turnip returned to his contemplation. One of his men was to be sacrificed in the hit on the Governor, a fact that only a few of his people knew and that number did not include the selected one. That would cause a slump in morale. The group would recover from it, but not so quick that they could pull off another job in less than a week. Tyler stood and walked toward the door.

"Gincy," he called loudly. "Outside." The leader stepped out onto his building's porch. The streets of Whitewright were clear. They were that way much of the time these days. Tyler grabbed a support pole near the step and turned around to wait for Gincy. An idea had just run through his mind and he wanted to see how it played on someone else.

The underling came out and pulled the door closed.

"Yeah, Tommy?"

"When we take care of this cowboy Friday night... I have a prize for whoever puts him down."

"You sure he'll come?" Gincy asked.

Tommy Tyler flinched and looked at the door to his building, "Oh hell, yeah. He'll come." He stepped down off the porch and walked toward the van parked in front. "I want to know what this cowboy knows about us before we kill him," he raised his arm as if declaring an edict. "But after that, we play the hunter game. Winner gets the prize."

"What do you think he knows, Tommy?"

"Damn it...stop using my name!"

"Hell, man. There's nobody here. Just us." Gincy pled in frustration.

Tyler glared at his associate and finally shook his head in disgust, "Gincy, you...."

"Yeah, Tommy?" The other man still wanted an answer to his question. "What do you think he could know?"

"That's what I need to find out, fool..." The leader kicked at a stone in frustration. "How could I know till I find out?"

Gincy scratched his head and tried to appear satisfied with that answer. He understood pushing the subject any further would not be good for him.

"Tomorrow night," Turnip ordered. "Check on things here before you come to the bar. I'll be in Greenville by 9PM."

"Gotcha." Gincy answered and he went back inside the building for a beer.

He didn't even ask what the prize was. Tyler lamented to himself.

That prize would be the opportunity to go at the senator, willingly or not. After they had killed someone, Tyler would hold even more leverage over them. Shaking his head he walked back up on the porch. *Still don't like this,* he mumbled under his breath. Tyler stuck his head in the door and yelled, "Lock up before you guys leave."

~

Jon sat with Juan in the back of the Crown Victoria while Murray drove.

"Where's your stuff?" He asked his passenger.

"The Holiday Inn right around the corner."

"You're kiddin?" The urge to laugh was strong, but he held back.

"Naw..." Murray piped up slowly shaking his head. "No... he ain't kiddin."

Jon gave a confused look, but moved on. He had more questions for Juan.

"You were with Harley in Washington, right?"

Juan became uncomfortable and looked down at the car's floor. Jon reached out and took his arm to get his attention. He pulled the man towards him slightly.

"I'm not asking you...I know. I saw you there."

"Si, I saw you as well." Juan managed to get out. While Jon leaned back and absorbed that comment Juan came out with a statement of his own. "I saw you at the airport in Atlanta before that." He looked right at Jon, "You were in a Jeep."

Jon smiled in surprise. "Touché," he responded respectfully. Jon was not aware he had been "made" on that trip. Leaning back

297

to put the man at ease, he asked him, "So...what do you want to do now?"

Juan's eyes squinted as he looked slightly toward "Diablo" in quiet fear. "I always wanted out." The answer was sullen, yet firm. "I still do."

"Well... Hanson's gone. What's stopping you, other than me?"

"You don't understand, Sir." Juan looked back down.

Jon waited for the rest of that statement. He finally had to ask the man what he meant by that.

Juan again was blunt, "Hanson is not the end of it. DeMarcos is still out there." Then the Hispanic man laid his head against the headrest and rubbed his temples with both hands. "And Lendono..." he said softly. "Lendono above all."

Murray turned into the parking lot of the Holiday Inn and pulled to a spot near his room's door. Jon was weighing how to react to the name he had just heard. It was one he had heard before.

"Are you afraid of this Lendono?" He asked Juan. "Isn't he in Colombia?"

Juan was shaking his head rapidly. "His reach is long. He is the real leader."

Jon opened the car door, but didn't get out. He looked back at Juan and asked him, "Do you know just where this man is? Colombia is a big place."

"If not at the prison... he is in Turbo."

"Turbo? What is that? A town or what?"

"It is his beach villa near the coast. Very nice place."

"You've been there?"

"Si." Juan remembered a trip with Vaga, "once."

Murray turned around at that and looked at Jon. They were thinking the same thing.

Jon leaned into the man sitting next to him. "You want out, huh?" He asked Juan. "Will you help me find this Lendono if I promise you your freedom?"

The boldness of that struck Juan as almost silly. "You want to find him? Ha...he will find you, sir."

"Not if I find him first." Jon smiled in confidence.

"What would you do if we found him? Juan challenged.

"Answer my question first, can you and will you help me?" Jon repeated himself.

"Us." Murray corrected him.

"But the law will protect him, he is in his country." Juan protested.

"Let me worry about the law." Jon's stare was as firm as his statement and Murray simply nodded from the front seat.

Juan looked at them both. They didn't appear to be kidding. Normal people would not stand a chance. But these men...he quickly assessed what Jon had already done and made up his mind. He nodded "yes," but not with much enthusiasm. "I have no other choice."

"Go get your stuff and we'll meet back here in ten minutes." Jon slid out of the car. Murray climbed from the driver's seat and gestured to Jon about the need to keep an eye on Juan. Jon immediately shook his head "no."

They were all back at the car within seven minutes. Murray had planned to check Juan for a weapon but the man held it out for them as he approached.

"Is that it?" The cowboy asked taking the gun from him. Juan held his arms up inviting him to search and Murray did. "No offense, but I don't know you yet."

"Is fine." Juan told him.

Jon could feel himself thinking as Silas as he watched the scene before him. It might not make sense, but he believed Juan was sincere. Trust was hard for Silas. Still, he had a feeling about this.

"Let's go," Jon suggested. Then as they got in the car his phone rang before they could get under way. It was Ben.

"Where are you?" the voice asked.

"We're at the Holiday Inn, where are you?"

"Aw, sit tight, will ya?" Ben replied. "I'll be right there."

Within minutes Ben drove up with Albie Kurtz, one of Gil's men. They had driven down with Jon's package rather than risk shipping it.

"Good that you're here." Jon told them. He shook Ben's hand and then pulled him to a hug. "Nice work lately, my friend."

He then shook Albie's hand and thanked him. Jon pointed to the cowboy and introduced them both to Murray.

"Pleasure to meet you, Mr. Bilstock," Ben said as Albie tipped his hat at the man in the bigger hat.

"I hear you're quite a young man." Murray tried to be complimentary.

"Not bad yourself," Ben joked and then asked how things had gone in Rome. As Jon told him the events of the morning Ben pretended to wince and then noticed Juan sitting in the back of the Crown Vic.

"Is that him?"

"Yep, that's Juan." Jon motioned for Juan to step out and a thought came to him.

"Juan," he measured his words carefully, trying to not add to Juan's already heavy concerns. "These are very good friends of mine. I want you to go with these men back to my home. You'll be safe there till I get back and we can plan our other trip, okay?"

It didn't take Juan long to agree, he was neck deep already and couldn't see what difference this would make. "Si," he answered and grabbed his belongings.

Ben opened the trunk of his Ford 500 for Juan's bag and looked at Jon with a wry grin. "Any chance I can see where the guy got hit by the bus?" He inquired.

"I doubt it's still there, I mean, they were cleaning up." Jon wasn't good at lying. He just didn't want them anywhere near the area. "We really weren't there, so the story goes, okay?" he added, "Thanks to Charlie."

"What's he like?" Ben asked. "I've only talked to him over the phone."

"Keep his number." Jon pointed his finger at Ben. "Look... Murray has business in Texas so we need to go." Then almost as an after thought, Jon sheepishly asked about Marsha.

"George says she's getting better. But still needs a little time." Ben told him. "Maybe by the time you get back from Texas."

Jon couldn't express how he felt about needing to stay out of the way of her recovery. He knew it was necessary and accepted it, but he didn't like it.

The men all exchanged good-byes and loaded into their vehicles. Ben put the package in the back seat of the big Ford Crown Vic and went over the contents with Jon verbally.

"The remote firing units are cool and fairly easy to set up," he added.

"Fairly?" Jon twisted his head to an odd angle.

"You can handle it." Ben started to turn, but reached out to hold Jon up a second, "Say, you heard about Stubblefield's family in Maryland, right?"

Jon face dropped, "Yeah, I heard. Anything new on that?"

"I don't think so," Ben told him. "They're still looking for them and he's still in Washington. Some creep, huh?"

Jon felt bad enough about that situation, but he had made a decision not to act and now he could only live with it. There was way too much else going on right now anyway. Things he could do something about right now, so he needed to concentrate on them.

"You heard about Kentucky, right?" Ben added.

"Been kind of busy this morning, is everything alright?"

"I guess," Ben paused for a second. "That lady Captain you mentioned got hurt but not serious. The bad guys blew themselves up. It's a mess."

"Is Swanson ok?"

"I just heard the report on the way down here. It said she got hurt, but it wasn't bad. That's all I know."

Jon felt he had almost forgotten about the raid in Kentucky, *too much going on.* He said inside. He thanked Ben again as thoughts of the people, his friends held up at his home in hiding, came to him.

"Tell the others to hang in there, will ya?" He said climbing into the Crown Vic.

"Sure... you be careful." Ben threw at him.

The cars pulled away from the Holiday Inn and quickly went different directions. Jon and Murray would be in the air within thirty minutes.

49

Matt Turlock had coordinated with Daniel on the story of Dewey Hanson for the Shreveport paper. Daniel had also been in touch with Earl Johnstone of the Burlington Hawkeye in Iowa and Williams Gaines of the local Dalton Daily Citizen. The four men would reach out to others in their profession to "guide" the angle of the coverage away from Jon Crane as much as they could. But knowledge of Jon was growing and his name was becoming involved with the take down of major crime figures. No connections were alluded to as far as The Son was concerned, but Jon was a real life individual who just always seemed to be there.

Daniel began to think of a cover story Jon could use. He came up with the idea of a wealthy industrialist who financed the exposure of crime and the taking down of its leadership. He talked with Ben about a Crane Enterprises and what Jon would think of that.

"He can't just keep showing up. It's already wearing thin." Daniel explained to Ben. There was no argument from Ben. The fact that Jon wasn't noted as being at Dewey Hanson's death was a small miracle unto itself. Ben understood the concerns. They were legit.

The younger man knew of the bank accounts and the holdings that Jon had. He didn't share anything about those with Daniel. That would be Jon's prerogative. But he knew what was proposed was necessary and doable.

"I think he'll listen," Ben encouraged the reporter. "But not till he's done with all this."

Daniel was satisfied with that. He remembered what he had suggested to Jon last fall and his friend's reaction to it. Despite the reservations Jon had, the coalition with him at the center was becoming a reality.

~

Vasily Torbof was nearly catatonic. The news of Kentucky hit him like a ton of bricks. It was hours before he called for a count of what he had left in his arsenal. The final death count from the bombing at Igor's was seventy-four. Fifty-two of those were part of Vasily Torbof's force. Add the twenty lost in Kentucky and the facts were grim. His phone call to New York for more reinforcements had to be referred for a call back. The referral was to Pestrovo, a village in a northern province of Russia.

The head of the mob was there on vacation. He asked for a count of how many men were still in the New York area. He was told there were now only forty men left in New York and some twenty-seven in the rest of the country.

"Twenty-seven!" The boss screamed in Russian. "He has squandered an army, this man." There was consideration of simply having Torbof and his family taken out and doing away with the operations in the U.S. But an accountant brought up figures from last year. Cheap drugs were high profit in America.

The subject matter quickly changed to where they could spare enough men for him to get a handle on the situation there. Between Poland and the Czech Republic they found seventy-five. It would take three weeks to gather them up and prepare them for travel.

"Send him word," the mob boss said. "That will have to do."

Torbof understood his vulnerability by the way the response came. He thought of running, taking his wife and disappearing into the U.S. countryside. Reason and logic brought him out of that. *They would find us.* He lamented to himself.

Three weeks was a lifetime in the drug business. Product was backing up and would soon be sent elsewhere if he didn't distribute it and pay. He had to come up with a local alternative until the troops arrived.

Shreveport had local gangs like any major city in the U.S. The Latin Red Highlanders controlled their territory along Highland Avenue from Wine Street to King's Highway. They bought heroin from Torbof, black tar mostly and pounds of it weekly. He would reach out to see if they would like to be couriers as well as customers for a few weeks. The LRH were Hispanic, but no friends of the Colombians. Primarily Mexican with a few from Guatemala, their members would shoot a Colombian on sight. A meeting to set the deal was arranged for next week.

Unknown to Torbof, recordings of his plans were waiting for Jon to retrieve them.

~

The morning and early afternoon had been quiet at the Dalton hospital, particularly in Marsha's room. She had been into another period of sleeping heavily much of the day as well as through the night. This was worrisome to George, although the doctors assured him it was a good sign.

"Her mind is busy reorganizing itself." They told him. "We will need to do physical rehab for her later, but now she has to rest."

George could go home or to the office now, but he felt he owed it to her, actually more to Jon, to stay with her through this. While his morning update from the office was mundane for that Thursday, the supplemental to it he received by special courier was far from that. The word about Kentucky had to involve Jon, but he knew his friend was in Georgia. Getting details of that would need to wait till later. The news of Dewey Hanson's death in nearby Rome though, had his department on alert. There was a BOLO, or "be on the lookout," for a Terrance Slater of Rome who was witnessed running from the scene of Hanson's death by at least one observer.

George could get all the juicy details from Jon by simply asking, but his belief in his own ethics wouldn't allow it. Others would question the reasoning. But he believed, as long he did not know the circumstances or specifics, he could avoid his responsibility to the absolute law.

How Jon had pulled this off, to look as it did, would be the first story George would ask for at his retirement party. As he sat down and smiled from that thought, Marsha rolled over and made a soft sound. He listened and leaned toward her. But she settled down and back into her deep sleep.

~

Jon's mind was concerned with the fact that Hanson's death would be seen as an accident. He mentally thumbed through his catalog of quotes looking for one that fit this situation. Murray glanced at him and noticed an expression he had not seen before. It was Silas and Murray was not that familiar with Silas. The cowboy turned to stare out the window again. He had plenty on his mind as well. His cousin, the house in Caddo Mills and the men he would soon deal with in Whitewright. He tried not to think about Charlene and his mother. That was too hard. He would handle that when he had to, not now.

~

The G5 made good time back to Shreveport and Captain Phil Stone was waiting along with Matt Turlock. Dinner would be at The Club tonight. There was much to talk about and they wanted details.

The men went to Stone's house to clean up and rest a bit that afternoon. Jon spent his time going through the package Ben had prepared and Murray stared at the ceiling for a while.

Murray noticed the noise from Jon's room as he walked down the hall. Knocking gently, Jon pulled it open and told him to come in. Together, they read the instructions on the remote firing devices, but the cowboy was more amazed by the Barretts and the T-Rex.

"We need to take these tomorrow," he suggested.

Jon didn't look amused. He considered the statement for a minute and then picked up one of the Barrett rifles.

"There's ammo for this in the bag somewhere. We'll take this one and two rounds."

The specifics were weird to Murray, but he liked the idea. He had heard of the Barrett before. The T-Rex though, was unknown to him. So he didn't lobby to carry it as well. They stored the other rifles and ammo, along with the remotes in the closet and wrapped the Barrett Murray had selected in the bag. The other bag, with Jon's suit was not opened that day. Jon had tried it on once before. He wasn't comfortable in it, but would take it with him tomorrow night. If the situation called for it he would have it. If not, it would remain a secret.

At dinner the men discussed what had happened and the luck their preparation allowed them. Phil and Matt were captivated by the story of Juan Castrono and that he was now at Jon's home.

"He will be able to help us once we get into Colombia, but that will be the trick." Jon explained. "Getting there."

Matt leaned back in his chair and thought before he spoke, but he had something important to say. The others continued to go over Hanson getting smacked by the bus and then Matt finally rocked back into the conversation.

"I might be able to help." He started.

The others looked at him and Phil asked, "With what?"

"I can't promise anything. But I know several people over at Barksdale." Matt was referring to the large Air Force Base across the river. "They send stuff down to Panama every week," he continued. "Sometimes more often than that."

The newspaperman shared that these folks had lost friends or family to the drug trade and had often stated how they would help destroy the cartels if they had the chance. "Let me have a couple days to check with them, I don't know but…"

"Panama is mighty close to where we need to go." Jon interrupted. "That would be great."

Matt nodded and sipped on his beer and Jon asked him about another story.

"Do you know any details about Captain Swanson of the Kentucky State Police?" He asked.

"I know she is in a hospital in a small town. She's doing interviews so I assume she's ok."

"I'd like to get in touch with her if you can find out where she is."

"I'll do what I can." Matt smiled. He was pleased to be a functional part of this and not just a silent witness.

The discussions continued for another hour before the guys needed to get their rest. All they told Phil and Matt was that Murray needed to check on his house and Jon was going with him. That was true, the day would start exactly that way.

50

Breakfast that Friday at the Dalton mansion was considerably more animated than dinner the night before. Having a member of Argus's organization in their midst took some getting used to. Doris and Lori were the most standoffish while Daniel was the curious one. He held back on the questioning that preoccupied his thoughts just to be polite.

Juan tried to remain to himself. He understood the lack of welcoming and warmth to his visit. He answered questions asked him and did not volunteer much else.

Ben and Albie had left him alone on the trip to Dalton, not being rude just not prying too much. Gil recognized the difference in this man and the other Argus types he had come up against. Juan wasn't a thug. Whatever he was, it wasn't dangerous.

The excitement of the day before had almost caused Lori to forget a message she took.

"Ben," she explained. "A call for Jon came in yesterday from a Hingley's Autos in Gainesville, Florida."

"Yeah, I know them." he told her. "They tricked out the pick-up truck for Jon."

"Well, they say the others are nearly ready to ship."

"Others?" Ben squinted. He obviously didn't know about that.

"That's all the man said." Lori finished. "That was the message."

Ben smiled, but admitted to her, "I have no idea."

~

Captain Sharon Swanson awoke in the University Hospital in Cincinnati, Ohio. She and her injured troops were taken there as a precaution. The extreme violence displayed by the men they had stopped left multiple questions. Were there more of them, for one?

They appeared to be deathly vengeful so disclosure of the wounded police officer's location was kept secret. Captain Swanson's injury did require a bit of surgery. Mainly to seal the internal wounds before stitching her side, front and back.

"Hell yeah, it hurts." She told her major who had come to visit. He laughed, knowing that meant she was fine.

"Who's this guy you want me to get in touch with?" he asked.

"His name is Crane. Jonathan Crane. He's from Georgia somewhere, connected to Draper out of Iowa...you remember him, a friend of Col. Sawyer's?"

"Oh yes I do." The major nodded with his response. "Can I ask what this Crane has to do with anything?"

"He came to the girl's murder scene down in Pendleton County. Draper arranged clearance for him through some friends of his, anyway...the young man knew a lot about who had killed the girl and what they were up to."

The Major pulled up a chair and sat to listen.

"The guys that came up here Wednesday were looking for the ones that killed our girl... or part of their group." She added.

Shaking his head in disbelief the Major challenged what he was hearing, "You know this how?"

"How it played out, that's how." She was her forceful self. "That Crane guy knew where they were going to hit and that it had pissed off the Russians in Louisiana." She was becoming frustrated trying to explain. "Look, Warren," she stared a hole in his forehead. "If I had not listened to Crane I would have followed our procedures Wednesday night and gone in after those jerks."

The Major was very aware of the procedures she spoke of. When persons are in immediate danger, even persons suspected of crimes, it was policy to attempt to save them. That action would have been catastrophic in this case. He said nothing.

Sharon Swanson lay back against her pillow, in as near to emotional stress as the Major had ever seen her.

"I would have gotten my people killed..."she stammered. "If I hadn't listened to Crane."

Swanson's boss continued to stare and consider the facts. "How do I find him?" The major finally asked.

"I had his number in my phone, but it got destroyed in the confusion that night." She leaned forward regaining her stern composure. "Try calling the Shreveport PD. He mentioned a guy named Stone in the department there."

The major stood and smiled at his officer. "I'll do that." He waited a minute and then inquired, "What's the message besides that you're ok?"

"Tell him thanks. I owe him."

~

As Murray checked his gear, including the outfit Jon had supplied him with, Jon was fashioning a message to go to Daniel and one to Hanson's office in Washington, DC. The death of the congressman was accidental, but Jon did not wish that to be the total impression. He knew Daniel would both understand and go with it, spreading the word that the Son still lurked around evil congressional figures. The message went out to Daniel in Dalton with the request that he have Ben forward it through secured means. The message was a quote from John Adams in 1777. *Let justice be done though the heavens fall.*

Daniel smiled when he saw it. The response in Washington was closer to fear and panic. It had been months since Harley and all was quiet. Now, the mystery man was claiming ties to Hanson's "removal." The Son was back in the news.

311

~

The trip back to Caddo Mills was quiet. Lucy cruised at just over 1200 feet and both men were into their own thoughts. Murray scanned the horizon now and again, as any good pilot would, but stared ahead most of the time. Jon was thinking about how this would play out tonight. The motorcycle gang would not roll over easily, he was sure.

Jon became aware of commercial aircraft passing over them as the flights approached and left Dallas Fort Worth Airport. The jetliners were several thousand feet above them though they looked much closer. Murray seemed unaffected by it all, his hand steady on the controls and his jaw locked in a serious expression.

As they neared the burned out ranch, Murray pulled Lucy up slightly and rolled to the left. He slowed to a hover at only 500 feet above the highway and the drive leading to his house. They sat there, checking everything on the ground before creeping forward toward the charred structure. The yellow crime scene tape stood out against the rubble.

Slick's Jeep sat where it had been, also burned from being so close to the house. Murray's truck sat near the barn and as they got closer Jon could see bullet holes in the truck's body. The tires were all flat.

Still without a word, Murray landed on the circle of dirt that was to have been his pad within a few weeks. The concrete pour was already scheduled, *something else to cancel*, he reminded himself. The impact was quite soft this time. Jon figured there was no hurry so he sat with his friend until the blades had slowed. It was then that Murray spoke.

"Is that a note pinned to the Jeep?" he asked.

Jon saw it, but wasn't sure. It gave them a reason to exit the helicopter; so reluctantly, they did. Jon felt bad for Murray as they

312

walked toward what had been his house. He could only imagine what it must feel like and then the loss of a relative on top of it all. Murray was slower than usual, but he remained stoic.

"It's from the insurance man," he proclaimed as he tore the note from the side of the vehicle. "He wants me to call him."

Murray rubbed his mouth and chin with his bare hand and moved toward the front of the house. The porch area had collapsed completely, even before they had removed Slick's body. He stared at the hole and then the entirety of it all, saying nothing... but speaking wasn't necessary.

Jon had stayed near the Jeep to give Murray some time with his thoughts. He watched as the cowboy moved over to the truck and then Jon's phone rang. It was George.

"Hey, man. How's she doing?" he answered.

"Great news, Jon." George's voice was excited. "She's up and asking to see you."

Jon was struck dumb. It was what he had been waiting to hear for over a week and now he didn't know what to say.

"You there, Jon?" George piped in.

"Yeah, I'm here..." there was another pause and then he went on. "That's terrific. What do the doctors say?"

"She's ready to see you. Things seem to have lined up for her. She remembers everything except a couple of details about the night she got hurt."

"George..." Jon started.

"Yeah, when can you be here? She's really wanting to see you."

"Tomorrow afternoon...at the earliest."

"Tomorrow? It's only 3PM there. You could be here by tonight."

Jon felt pulled like he had never experienced before. He told George straight out. "I have a commitment here, I owe somebody. I owe them big and I can't leave right now."

George had never heard that tone from Jon. "Are you alright?" he questioned.

"Yeah, really. I'm fine. I just have to finish this...Can I talk to Marsha?"

"Sure, hang on a second. The doctors are still checking stem to stern, you know how that goes." George tried to lift the mood.

As Marsha got on the phone, Murray noticed him and began to walk back that way.

"Jon?" She started. "Hey, is that you?"

"It's so good to hear you speak my name."

"George says you can't come till tomorrow, is that right?"

Murray had stepped to within hearing distance.

"Yeah, tomorrow for sure. I'm on a job right now...for a good friend."

"Your girl friend... she's better?" Murray interjected. Jon covered the phone with his hand and shook his head, "yes."

"Then you need to go. I can handle this." Murray pulled his hat off as he spoke.

Back into the phone, Jon said to Marsha, "Tomorrow for sure, I missed you."

"I missed you, too." and he could hear her blowing kisses, which wasn't her norm. But it didn't hurt. She hung up with, "Be careful."

"I said...you need to go, man." Murray chided him and stepped almost into him.

Jon put his phone away and looked straight into Murray's eyes. "I told you we would do this together. That's it." Jon walked toward the house, basically to get away for a second. The timing was enough to drive a person nuts, but Jon was a patient man. He reminded himself of that and regained his ability to breathe as he walked.

Nothing more was said except Murray adding how glad he was Marsha was better. They looked around the ranch for a couple of hours and then flew into Plano, just outside of Dallas, to get some dinner.

"Insurance is fine. It just takes too much time," Jon offered during a discussion about rebuilding. "I'd like to help. I have resources and you can get your plans moving right away."

Murray put his fork down and leaned back, "My plans at the moment are to bury my cousin." His look was serious and not to be discussed. "All this talk about the new house...hell, I'll change my mind a dozen times before I get started." Glancing down, he realized his speech sounded ungrateful. "Look, I appreciate your offer and I know you mean it. Thanks...let's just deal with tonight now," he had an awkward pause, "then Saturday."

Jon had listened intently. He nodded and tried to change the subject.

"So, you going to set me down near the clubhouse in Whitewright?"

"Yeah...I'll put you on the roof if you like." The cowboy smiled and finally picked up his fork to resume eating.

51

Santonio Lendono was not disturbed by the news of Hanson's death. He had also learned that several of the icehouse victims were distributors of his, but he had put that news in perspective. The remaining Argus customers were quite anxious and expectant, but that could be handled.

The resurfacing of the Son rumor made him relocate back into his prison cell office in Sabanalarga. If that man did exist he was not limited to or by the laws of any country. The messages sent to Hanson's office and the press shook him to his core. And then there was what was missing from the messages. There was no word on Juan Castrono. He knew Castrono had been in Rome, Georgia. He was the one who had told Hanson about it. Why was there no mention of Castrono in the account? Those cryptic messages and the tales of the killer who leaves no trace, this must be the work of bad spirits.

From the security of his jail cell he checked the bank accounts in Colombia. He needed liquid funds for payment of National Guard troops to guard him back at Turbo. Scraping it all together he had 24.4 billion Pesos, or roughly 18 million US dollars. The cartel had over 65 billion pesos tied up in product that had not moved in three months. The bottleneck was Argus and it's American markets. Argus was killing the cartel.

The security at the prison was not as it had been before. Due to either fear or lack of payment the troops were not as plentiful as they had been. At this rate, the Turbo house would soon be safer and he already had a boat hidden there to escape into the Atlantic.

~

Matt Turlock had been busy that Friday morning. One of his contacts at Barksdale AFB was very interested in the question of access into Panama. Col. Winston Meyers was assigned to the 96th Bomb Squadron, B-52 flight training division. They flew over Panama, but did not land there. He knew that the 23rd Mission Support Group out of Moody AFB in Georgia had added flights to Panama with mechanical and medical support items.

"I know a C-130 pilot assigned there," he told Turlock. "Let me check with him."

"I don't want to get anybody burned." The newspaperman told him.

"Matt, you're talking about getting drug dealers. There's a bunch of us ready to help with that, cost be damned."

"I really appreciate what you're doing."

"No worry, some of us have to do it. Our government has long since stopped dealing with illegals and that has enlarged the drug problem. We're tired of sitting on our hands."

"You have my number?" Matt asked him.

"Roger that, my friend." The colonel answered. "You'll hear from me."

Matt sat back in his desk chair as the line went dead. He knew he was asking a lot. What amazed him was the immediate response he was receiving. There was no hesitation or reservation. The drug culture had become so vast that many simply tried to ignore it. Those who had been touched by it's toxic nature were completely different. They were ready to act, on their own if need be, to stop the epidemic.

~

The trip to Plano, Texas for dinner was a better tactic than Jon or Murray were aware of. Turnip Tyler knew all along that the body left on the porch was not Murray's. They had seen the cowboy at the bar.

He drew attention to himself that night so there was no mistaking him.

Tyler figured that Bilstock would stop by his burned out home on the way to Greenville that night. He sent the van with two of his boys down to Caddo Mills to see. They drove past the ranch several times between 6:30PM and sometime after 8PM. They saw nothing. As they left Caddo Mills heading for the Friday night gathering, they didn't know the small dot in the sky above them was Lucy. She carried her cargo and two men toward Whitewright, Texas.

The men finalized their plans through the radio as they rode.

"It should be dark time we get there," Murray noted. "You'll want to turn the lights on inside while you look around."

"Right?" Jon didn't quite understand where the cowboy was going with that.

"Well, you're gonna need to know when to cut those lights as they come up."

Jon nodded, he was now on the same page with Murray.

"I don't know if they have radios or not, but it ain't worth risking." Murray explained. Jon found himself lost again.

"What are you saying?" He asked.

"I'm not going to call you on the radio." Murray stated in near frustration. "I'll go and hang out over the bar, ok? When they head back to Whitewright I'll come ahead to let you know."

"How? If you're not going to talk to me...how?"

"When you hear Lucy buzz the building, kill the lights."

That made perfect sense to Jon. *Why didn't he just say so?* He wondered under his breath.

Murray's thoughts were along the lines of *How thick can a guy get?*

"What hardware did you bring?" Jon asked to break the silence.

"I've got my .308 and your Barrett."

"You ever fired a Barrett?" Jon laughed.

"Actually, I have. But it was tied down on a tripod."

"Think you can handle it?"

"Don't know...yet," the cowboy proclaimed with a grin.

~

Marsha had gotten up that afternoon and had dinner, in her room, with George and Doris. It was decided that George would go home and get a shower and some rest in his own bed and Doris would stay tonight with Marsha.

"Lori sends her wishes." Doris told her. "You're really going to like her."

"That's Daniel's wife, right?" Marsha asked.

George smiled at the positive sign of her recovery. "Yep."

"Well, I've met her before. But it was in an official capacity." She thought about it a second and continued, "when Daniel got hurt in Charlotte."

"Yes, you did." George beamed this time. "It is so good to have you back."

"Good to be back," she sighed. "I can't explain what the last few days have been like."

"Don't even try." Doris reached over and put her hand over Marsha's. "You have fought hard and we are all so proud of you."

Jon wasn't mentioned, but thoughts of him were in the room. George caught Marsha's eyes wandering around more than once. He didn't have to ask.

52

As Whitewright, Texas came into view it was obvious there were lights on in the building, that and the dim street lamps shone clear from miles away.

"Crap," Murray decried in anger as he swung Lucy around.

"Hold on," said Jon. "I only see one bike down there. Give it a minute."

Murray arced Lucy high and left to the northwest and hovered. Within five minutes the lights went out in the building and then the lamp from the bike lit up and tracked down the main road through town. They waited a bit longer to be sure.

Just before 9PM Murray sat Lucy down just north of the building and Jon grabbed his big bag, gave Murray a nod and ran to the porch. The door was locked. That didn't take but a few seconds. Jon was in, with his night vision glasses at first, and then he turned the lights on.

A quick walk through and Jon stepped onto the porch giving Murray the "ok" sign and the helicopter lifted off. He rocked the machine back and forth as he flew overhead and roared off toward the town of Greenville, Texas.

Pulling the special glasses off, Jon walked back inside to look more thoroughly. The walls were adorned with "Nazi" flags and several Venezuelan flags. Pictures of torture from WWII to Afghanistan dotted the spaces between the flags. The walls were lined with flat top tables and one desk at the far end. The most notable item was the barber chair, its red leather the cleanest thing in the room.

A sawed off shotgun lay on the table near the door. Other handguns and large knifes either hung on the walls or lay around loose on the tables. Papers, newspaper clippings, computer paper and all other types lay everywhere.

The clipping told of robberies, one at a Dallas Armory a few weeks ago and other small crimes. A big headline was about the Mississippi shooting.

He noticed a pile of still more papers on the desk and picked them up to go through. It was more of the same except for several typed out messages marked, The Sponsors." These pieces appeared to be instructions. Requests for the crimes recorded in the newspaper clippings. The Sponsors were not identified but one message was with an envelope marked Connecticut and another was from California.

What would people from that far away care about crimes in Texas? Jon thought. He left the items out, in plain view and then found some scribbled notes about "The Son." The info contained was mostly wrong, but that wasn't the point. It was clear these were the guys claiming to be him. He left those papers out in clear view as well.

He took a notebook from his bag and made notes for himself, notes about the Sponsors and what they said and how they said it. The language used was educated, not just backwoods lingo. These people were clearly using these guys or checking them out. As he cleared a spot to set his notebook down he uncovered a paper he had not noticed before. It was about the Arkansas Governor and the hit scheduled for the next week. Attached to that, was another message dated only two days earlier, it spoke of another hit they were demanding on Senator Cogburn of Oklahoma. Neither of these events had taken place. "Now they won't." Jon muttered softly.

A slow walk around told him the confrontation would be harsh, he didn't mind that, not at all. He sat the bag up on one table and pulled the suit from it. This was Ben's major achievement. No other suit like this existed and Jon would soon be betting his life it worked.

The entire outer layer was made up of small rectangles approximately 3/8" thick. The largest were one inch by two-inch across the torso and graduated down through his extremities. The smallest shapes measured only a half-inch by a quarter and extended down the first joint of his fingers. Those ten rectangles were also thinner, down to 3/16".

The rectangles consisted of gelled impact absorbent material, STF that was coated in Kevlar. The Shear Thickening Fluid rectangles butted up against each other in rows with enough spacing to allow free movement. These protective shapes offered twelve times the barrier of the original Kevlar fabric suit. Spaces between them, when exposed by movement were double the resistance of the prototype.

The hydraulic mechanisms lay just under the outer layer and ran through the right arm and hand, down both legs and across the back, up to and supporting his neck. The left arm, while not enhanced, would be covered in the protective shield of the suit. The leggings flared out over his boots and a skullcap of the same materials exposed only his eyes, nose and mouth. The Kevlar Helmet fit closely and could accommodate the self-adjusting, night vision glasses or the regular safety glasses. The suit was impenetrable and the strength increases to his legs, back and right arm were nearly two times the original arm gear. Total weight of the suit, seven pounds.

It fit loosely until he was ready to form fit it, and then a push of a button and the fabric conformed to his shape and the hydraulics were activated. Not restricting in any way. It actually made movement easier. The color was Seal Team black, which offered no reflective value and became virtually invisible in the dark.

As Jon pulled the skullcap on he heard a noise behind him, a muffled cry and a thud against the wall. He reached for one of the two full sized Glocks this suit carried and turned toward the sound. Another thump zeroed in on a closet he had missed because of the massive posters over it. He stepped up to it and jerked the door open. A man, wrapped in duct tape and rope, his mouth tied with a rag lay on his side in the closet.

~

While Jon was going through the clubhouse and Murray circled and hovered above the Flying Deuce Bar, the men inside the bar became more and more unsettled. There was no party atmosphere this night. Tommy "Turnip" Tyler was anxious. As the time grew past quarter to ten he lost faith in his idea that the cowboy would come that night. He threw a beer bottle across the main room to gather everyone's attention and announced, "We're outta here."

As the men poured from the bar, Murray rolled Lucy back and further out of vision from the ground. He watched as they saddled up and two climbed into a van. The gang then headed towards Whitewright.

Lucy went high and to the northeast, wide of the convoy and around them. As he approached the small town of Whitewright Murray saw the streetlights flickering and the lights from inside the clubhouse building. He lowered Lucy's altitude, but not her speed.

~

Jon pulled the man up into a sitting position and removed the gag. As the man's eyes focused on who or what was holding him, he nearly panicked. The face was framed in black and the eyes squinted into a stare that hurt to look at. While the bound man wanted to scream out, his fear wouldn't allow it.

"Who are you?" Jon demanded, pulling him face to face.

The man shook violently as he tried to speak, "I'm Stephen Bilstock," finally came out.

Jon pulled back and looked hard at the man. *Could this be?* he thought. Then an obvious clarification jumped into his mind. He pulled the man to him, face to face.

"What's the helicopters name?" Jon demanded firmly.

"Lucy?" the bound man answered without hesitation.

As if on cue, Lucy roared overhead at that moment and Jon knew what "buzz" meant. He knew he only had time to get himself ready.

"Look," he told the man. "I know you're uncomfortable, but I need you to lay back down, stay low and stay quiet." He helped the man lay down on his side, "Can you do that for me, for a few minutes?"

"I can." Slick answered. "Is that Murray out there?"

"You bet it is." Jon told him. He put a finger straight up in front of his nose, leaned in and whispered, "Stay quiet for us, ok?"

Jon closed the door and ran to the light switch. He pulled his night vision glasses into place and looked around for a place to wait. The red barber chair stood out and Jon climbed aboard and spun it around with it's back to the door, and waited.

~

Murray stayed airborne until he saw the lights go out. *Ok*, he thought as he swung the helicopter around and landed about three hundred yards to the north. From there he could still see the building and the now approaching headlights.

Turnip pulled up right in front of the door and kicked down his stand rod. Others pulled up on all sides and dismounted and stepped toward the door. As he twisted the knob, Turnip Tyler yelled at Gincy, "You left it unlocked, you moron."

Gincy thought about denying it, but it would not have mattered.

Tyler and three others stepped inside and flipped on the lights.

The place had obviously been gone through. Jon's empty bag lay on the floor and posters pulled from the walls were strewn about. As the phrase, "what the hell," passed Tyler's mouth, Jon spun the chair and looked straight at the leader and his sidekicks.

The sight of Jon in his suit, frankly scared the crap out of one of the men at the door, he fell against the table in a near faint. Tyler and the others froze for an instant then drew their weapons. Jon held one of his Glocks in his left hand, as they fired he took out Gincy, two others and shot the fainting man in the leg. Tyler fired twice with his 9mm, but having watched his rounds bounce off the man in his chair, he stepped back and screamed for help.

Five men pushed through the door and rushed at Jon. He pulled up his right leg and caught one of them flat in the chest. As the man pushed against him, everyone there could hear the ribs breaking. A guttural moan escaped from him as Jon extended his leg. The man and two others behind him were shoved across the room knocking over a table and crashing onto the floor. The three were out, the crushed chest was fatal, a second broke his neck against the table and the third was unconscious.

The other two men had grabbed Jon's left side and one took hold of the Glock. Jon reached across his body seizing that man by the neck. He heard it snap as he pulled him away. The added power of the hydraulics would take some getting used to.

The other gang member tried to back away at the sound of his friend's neck breaking and stepped into the firing line. Loud gunfire erupted from still more of Turnip's men and Jon fired back. He was hit several times by .45 caliber and 9mm rounds. Even a 30-06 slug from a deer rifle hit the suit in his chest, but he was only mildly aware of the strikes. Jon continued to return fire and the gang members fell, dead and dying.

As the shooting slowed, Jon saw that only the leader stood in the doorway glaring at him. Tyler grabbed the shotgun that had been on the table near the door and fired both barrels at Jon. The pellets rebounded in different directions from Jon's chest as Turnip turned and ran across the porch.

Hearing the motorcycle crank, Jon pulled himself up and stepped over bodies on his way to the door. On the porch, he raised his arm and aimed carefully at the fleeing motorcycle.

Before he could fire a large boom and flash went off to his right. Murray had cut loose with the Barrett, standing upright and holding it like a deer rifle.

The man on the escaping bike threw his hands upward an instant before the motorcycle exploded. The round from the .50 caliber rifle had tumbled through Tyler's back at wallet height and impacted the gas tank. Tommy Tyler would later be identified through his dental records.

The flash and explosion had taken Jon's attention for a moment. He looked back toward Murray. The cowboy was still holding the rifle, but just barely. Firing rather quickly, he had not pulled the weapon firmly to his shoulder. The recoil left what would be a blue mark.

Murray had not dropped the large rifle. It swung from his right hand, the arm hanging low as he held that shoulder with his left hand. The cowboy stared at Jon with a look of complete confusion. Not from the firing, but what he saw standing there.

"What the hell are you, man?" he called out. The suit was unexpected.

Jon pulled the skullcap off and ran to his friend. "You alright?"

Murray still stared at the suit. It showed signs of being struck, but not penetrated. He stood up straight and rubbed his shoulder some more, handing Jon the Barrett.

"I could have told you..." Jon started, but then remembered something more important. "Come with me," he told the cowboy while running toward the porch. "I found something. Come on... quick."

Murray Bilstock had been through rough conflicts in his time. He hadn't said anything about it to Jon or anyone else for that matter, but having flown Bell UH-1N Huey rescue helicopters in Afghanistan exposed him to a lot of chaos. Those experiences not withstanding, what he saw inside the gang's clubhouse stunned him.

Jon stepped over the bodies as though they were landmines. As he got to the closet door he looked back at the cowboy. Murray had ceased rubbing his shoulder. He was standing just inside the doorway, appearing immobile until Jon hollered for him. "You're going to want to see this," while opening the small door.

~

It was 10:45PM in Dallas. Charlene Bilstock had put her mother to bed and had been trying to read to clear her mind. She needed to sleep, but too many things were going on in her head.

Tomorrow would be her dear cousin's memorial service and at that very moment, the autopsy was on going at the medical examiner's office. What had been scheduled for 5:00PM had been pushed back until 10PM due to a conflict.

Charlene suddenly sat her book down and looked at the clock. She did not know why, but her mind was at peace. A great weight had been lifted from her yet she couldn't understand what that could be. She threw back the covers and placed her feet on the floor. Sitting there, looking at her feet, her cell phone began to ring. It was Murray.

"Sis, Sis are you sitting down?" he started. The cowboy was excited.

"What's wrong?" She could feel her mood going south again.

"It's Slick, Charlene." Murray's paused seemed like an eternity. "He's ok. I've got him."

There was celebration and crying and Mother had to be awoken for this. Joy and hollering nearly overpowered the house phone as it rang while they were all talking.

It was the coroner's office. They were confirming that there was no match between the dental records and the body they had. Charlene told the man about the call she was on and that they would get in touch with the officials in the morning.

"Congratulations," the man said to her. "It doesn't often work out like this. I'm so happy for you."

~

Murray and Slick had their reunion with Jon as a witness. It took them nearly half an hour to unwrap the duct tape from his frame. The cousin shared the details of his capture. Slick had learned to breath shallow during his five-day ordeal. The gang fed him once a day, usually a Whopper or the like and a coke from a Burger joint. He was kept in the closet the whole time. He tried to stretch as much as possible to keep the blood flowing in his legs and arms. The bruising was extensive all over.

"Why didn't they just kill you," Murray asked bluntly.

"Once they figured out who I was, they intended to use me to get you to talk."

Murray found the sawed off shotgun. "This is the one I took from the bar," he proclaimed.

"Yeah," Slick told. "When they came in the house I cut loose with that thing and put one of 'em down. He fell back out on the porch. They grabbed my ass and tied me up. Some big guy told 'em to throw me in the van they had and that's all I remember about that day."

Jon broke up the party saying, "We really need to leave here, or at least, I do." He had changed back into his normal clothes and packed the bag.

328

Slick looked Jon up and down. The current appearance was quite different than when they met. Glancing at Murray then staring a hole into Jon's head he asked. "Say, who are you, anyways?"

Jon and Murray looked toward each other and Jon answered, "I'll let him tell you...a bit later."

He then took Murray over to the main desk. He showed Murray the evidence piled on the desk and other tables. They tried to figure how to handle this because somebody needed to stay for the cops. Murray wrote out a note to the police, telling them he had found his cousin being held captive and was taking him to the hospital in Dallas.

Jon shrugged his shoulders, "Sounds good to me."

They loaded up all three of them into Lucy and took off. It would be two hours before authorities were on the scene in Whitewright. By then they were in Dallas.

Jon sat in the waiting room while Murray had his cousin looked over. He was a bit dehydrated, but overall in good condition.

53

Even before the news from the small Texas town had hit the major news outlets, Daniel Seay was at work. A call from Jon gave him the details he needed and his story was ready for release, as soon as wider knowledge of the shootout offered him cover.

A skilled cowboy had found and fought a vicious gang in their hideout. The gang that had burned his home and, as he believed at the time, killed a relative. That relative, who had been feared dead, was found to be a kidnap victim of the gang. He was rescued; reasonably unhurt, in the mêlée. The story played well in papers across the country.

The attempt by this gang to co-opt the identity of the Son was played heavily in Daniel's piece. Those in Daniel's circle carried that theme as well and the circle was getting larger. It now included Williams Gaines of the hometown Dalton Daily Citizen and Arthur Gomez of the Charlotte Observer.

The Sponsors were as yet unknown, but the heat was now on. Postal markings from California and Connecticut were mentioned prominently in the stories.

Leaders of the group were disappointed in the loss of their investment, but not completely deterred by the events. More gangs were being groomed in cities throughout the country. They would need to select a new operational team. Other than that they remained confident. The Sponsors were sure their efforts were well insulated from any possible identity. One member expressed concern about changing the name of the group.

"The folks we use are not the type to be aware or bothered by the news." He was told. "Possible exposure would be greater through attempts to notify everyone of such a change. We leave it alone for now."

The concerns had been delivered from somewhere in California. The response came from a ranch in Montana, via Connecticut.

~

Lucy slipped into the night sky from Dallas soon after Charlene arrived at the hospital. Jon needed to get back to Shreveport and commercial travel was out of the question with the baggage he carried. Murray was clearly thrilled with finding his cousin alive. Yet he remained quiet through most of the flight. Officially, Jon had not been there or involved. Murray knew different and he tried to state his appreciation.

"Without what you did," Jon answered. "I would still be looked at as the man who killed that guy in Mississippi."

Murray said nothing. Quiet once again reigned in the helicopter cabin. Jon finally added this; "You stuck your neck out for me. I don't plan to forget that."

"I'm proud you see it that way," Murray spoke in a low, humble tone. "What are you up to now?"

Jon was slow to respond even though what he was up to next was all that had been on his mind. He formulated an answer and looked over at Murray.

"Going to see Marsha, first and foremost. I'm so relieved about her." A deep breath was audible through the microphone. "Then I have unfinished business in Shreveport."

"You need my help there?"

"I think I've got that figured, but thanks." Jon smiled. "What you've done helped me get ready."

The cowboy nodded slowly in appreciation. "Promise me this," he asked. "I go to Colombia with you."

331

Jon wasn't surprised. He just didn't know just how to react. "I can probably handle that."

"Bull.... I'm going with you on that one. No argument, ok?" Neither said anything for a couple of minutes but Murray added, "You'll have that Juan fella with you, I can baby-sit him if nothing else."

Jon laughed. "You're a certified baby-sitter?"

"They get papers now?" The cowboy smiled back. "If I need to be, I'll get one."

"We'll get together and plan it out." The Son looked at him, "Thanks."

Phil was waiting as Lucy sat down.

"They're looking all over Texas for you, man." He told Murray.

"I know. Can I get a fill-up, and check the tires would ya?"

Captain Stone grinned as he waved for the service team to come over. They unloaded Jon's bags and within ten minutes Lucy was lifting and doing a 180 turn. The law was not "looking" for Murray as much as they wanted details. Murray Bilstock was a hero on several fronts. It was something he wasn't used to or prepared for, but as he told Jon later, "You get used to it."

~

Waking up early that Saturday morning at the Stone's home, Jon's mood and focus were on a quick turn around. He was anxious to get to Dalton to see Marsha. When he got in the night before he noticed the light blinking on the video recording. The cameras on the rooftop had picked up something.

The meeting Torbof planned for the leadership of the local gang, The Latin Red Highlanders, had been set for Tuesday, but then changed to Thursday due to rain predicted for earlier in the week. That assured Jon that his prey would be on that rooftop for the meeting.

That was Torbof's power zone and where he liked to conduct

332

business. The time for the meeting was unclear, but he could figure that out in one of many ways.

Packing and sorting everything he had with him, the gear he had brought from Rome didn't need to travel back and forth again. He stepped down the hall and asked Phil Stone if he could store the bag there and hopefully be welcome to come back.

"You're welcome here anytime, son." The captain smiled. Walking back to his room, Jon twisted to look strangely at him. The host realized what he had said. "You know what I mean."

It was Jon's turn to smile, "I do and I thank you for the offer and the sentiment. I really do." He dug back into his organizing of what to take and Phil stood in the doorway and did not leave. Jon finally stopped and stood to look at his friend.

Phil did not wait for him to ask, "I got a report this morning about a skin-head group over in northeast Texas." The pause was not for any particular purpose, but he did take a few seconds before continuing. "They got shot and broken up pretty bad."

"Really?"

"Yep, won't be too much time wasted on 'em either."

"Wasted? What does that mean?" Jon tried to look puzzled.

"Looks like they were the ones responsible for the shooting in Mississippi. You remember?"

Jon leaned back over his bags and answered, "Seems like I do, yeah."

"Some tough cowboy found them. They had kidnapped his cousin and burned down his house." The pause this time was for his enjoyment. "He's looking like a hero." Phil smiled and continued, "and probably saved a Governor's life in the process."

Trying to contain himself, Jon played along, "No kidding?"

"Yeah... you know? Would you put this one on the list of stuff I'd like details of after I retire?"

333

"I'll try."

Phil turned and stepped out of the room, even though he was still talking. "That's some bad-assed cowboy, you know? He'd make a good partner for somebody."

Within the hour Phil was driving Jon to the airport to meet the G5 jet.

As they walked to the jet, Phil put his arm around Jon's shoulder, "You give that gal a good hug from us, too. We've been pulling for her."

Jon smiled so wide he could feel it in his jaw. They shook hands and Phil turned to go back to his car. He stood there as the jet taxied and then roared east into the morning sky.

Lying on the leather sofa, he stared at the cabin ceiling. *How long had it been?* he thought. In reality it was just over a week since she had been hurt. That didn't seem possible, but time is a relative thing. So much had happened, so much had changed. *What was that she said to me about change? It truly was the only thing constant.*

He sat up as the plane leveled off. The pilot had the afterburners on, this would be a quick flight to Dalton, even if it didn't feel like it to Jon.

The phone rang. Ben relayed the message from the auto detailing company in Florida.

"Thanks," Jon responded.

"Is that it?" the younger man pried.

"Yep, that's it. See you when I get in."

Jon looked up the number for the Hingley's Autos and dialed.

~

Gainesville, Florida was known for many things. One that few knew about was Hingley's Autos. They were a very specialized service provider. They had first built the body for Jon's old pick-up and reworked it after the run in with Argus last fall. At the time he sent

334

the truck back down to them, Jon had also discussed two new vehicles he wanted customized. One was a four-year-old Dodge Charger and the other a 2014 model Jaguar XJ.

The bodies were removed and replaced by titanium replicas with reinforced joints and roll cages. The chassis were remolded from tungsten carbide with ceramic carbon pins and bolts.

The glass was replaced with the latest in polycarbonate materials offering total protection from up to a 7.62mm round with a thickness of less than 7/16".

The interiors were flame resistant and coated in Kevlar and carried two-way radios with direct satellite hook up.

The power plant in the Dodge was the 5.7-liter V-8 with 425 horsepower. The Jaguar was fitted with a Bugatti, Veyron. A sixteen cylinder, 8.0 liter beast that could achieve 60 miles per hour in 3 seconds, even with the added weight of the reinforced body. Suspension systems and braking were all custom designed for the two vehicles.

Since they were a surprise, Jon selected the colors. The Charger was painted a factory color in deep metallic bronze, which looked nearly dark brown. The interior was deep, dark brown leather.

The Jaguar would go beyond the standard colors available. The exterior was a black/green with deep reflective tones, which set off the "bone" tan leather interior. As a youth, Jon had often dreamed of a "bottle green and bone" Jag. He would now have it.

The price for these improvements topped over two million, not counting the cost of the vehicles. Jon saw pictures of the progress to date and okayed the price. After final bodywork the cars would be shipped carefully and delivery was expected in about three weeks.

54

The cowboy sat low, nearly slumping, in the chair. The interview process felt more like an interrogation. His hat brim pulled down made his answers seem to come from somewhere else.

"How did you find where they were, again?" The officer asked.

"Followed 'em from the bar." Murray answered.

"And you knew about the bar...how?"

"Slick had run into 'em by accident. Since my Daddy was said to be a victim of this...Son fella, I wanted to see what they were all about."

The officer looked to his superiors who motioned their satisfaction with the responses. One rolled his hand as to say, "move on."

"So," the young cop continued. "You got the drop on them in their clubhouse."

"Yep." Murray looked up for the first time. "That I did."

"How many weapons did you have?"

Murray had to think about that one. After stirring in the chair he remembered what Jon had with him. "Three."

"Three...what?"

"You asked about the guns, didn't you?"

"Yeah, but what were they?"

"Two Glocks...40 caliber 23's and a Barrett rifle."

The cop scratched his ear, "Where are they now?"

"I had borrowed 'em from a friend. He's got 'em back in Dallas."

With a perplexed look, the questioning officer looked again to his superiors. The same "move along" motion was offered again.

"How about all the broken bones...and necks?"

Murray finally sat straight up and pushed the hat brim high on his forehead. He took a breath as though weary of the whole ordeal and said, "I can't say about all of 'em. Hell, they were running around, banging into each other, falling down and stuff." He looked directly at the officer in charge and made eye contact. " It happens, you know?"

At that point one of the other men stood and asked a question. "What about the man on the bike that blew up?"

"That one knocked me down running out." The cowboy's eyes clearly showed the search through his mind for what else to say. After another round of twisting in his chair, Murray tried to explain. "Time I got up he was on the bike and gone." The slightest of smiles crossed his face as he went on. "The Barrett was all I had that could stop him."

"Stop him?" Laughed the younger cop who was quickly stared down.

The senior officer reached out to shake Murray's hand. "Sir, that's enough for now." He went to the desk and picked up a piece of paper. "This is a personal "thank you" from the Governor of Arkansas. You may just have saved his life with what you did."

Murray nodded in silence and took the paper. The older cop then waved for his underling to follow him and they left the room. He looked back at the cowboy from the doorway, "You're good to go. Just be careful out there, will ya?"

Again, Murray acknowledged with a nod and the least of a smile.

~

Stephen Bilstock had given his statement from his hospital room. Other than being taken at his cousin's home, he knew little until Murray found him in the closet.

"I kicked that wall till he heard me." He told them.

Charlene listened making no comment. She knew her brother was tough, but this seemed beyond human capability to her. *He'll tell me someday.* She thought. For now she would accept the partial story she had been told. Slick would be released from the hospital later that day so Charlene and her mother went home to prepare a room.

Murray flew back to Dallas after the interviews in Whitewright. He passed his mother and sister while walking into the hospital.

"How's he doing?" He asked them.

"Comin' home this afternoon." Charlene told him.

"I'll wait with him here, ok?"

"Sure." The sister smiled. "What would you like for dinner?"

"Anything you care to make, just make lots of it." Murray quipped. As he turned to go to the elevator he noticed a man sitting on a small couch in the lobby. The man was reading a newspaper, or so it was to seem. The newspaper was upside down.

Murray rode the elevator to a floor one short of Slick's ward. Stepping quickly to the stairs he opened the door and listened. The sound of footsteps echoed through the stairwell. He quietly closed the door behind him and moved to the next upward flight where he sat, just out of view.

The approaching footsteps got quicker as they rounded the corner. Murray braced himself against the step. A shadow appeared on the landing and the man was soon standing right in front of the cowboy. Murray pushed himself upright and grabbed the stranger, turning and pushing the man into the corner.

"Care to tell me who you are, friend?" Murray asked calmly.

"I'm a reporter... Dallas Morning News." The frightened man answered.

After checking him for any weapons, Murray turned the man back to face him and put his nose up against the reporter's.

"I do not enjoy being followed." The cowboy's glare intensified. "Why?" He shook the reporter for added effect. "Why are you here?"

"My...my editor didn't believe the story you told. He doesn't think you could handle those skinheads by yourself."

"So, you came for a demonstration?" Murray dropped his grip and stepped back.

"No, God no. I'm just supposed to check you out."

Murray leaned back in, even closer, "Anything else you need to know...right now?"

"No, sir. I'm good."

The cowboy stood back and straightened the reporter's coat for him, "Nice to meet you, then." He smiled with a glare and a grimace. "See you around, huh?"

The reporter went out the door and toward the elevators. Murray took the remaining steps to the right floor and then to Slick's room.

~

In Shreveport the clouds began to form that afternoon. Rain was coming and would continue through Wednesday, so said the weatherman. Capt. Phil Stone took the Saturday off as a chance to clean up the yard and clear his mind. It had been an exciting couple of weeks.

Sara came outside waving his cell phone in her hand. "It's somebody from the Kentucky State Police."

Phil took the phone and got official. "Yeah, you've got Stone." He spouted.

"Captain Stone, this is Major Warren Hillenbrand of the Kentucky S.P. I'm trying to reach a Jonathan Crane."

Stone took a few seconds to respond, thinking it through before he said anything.

"That might be a tall order, Major. Can I ask what it's about?"

"Sure...no problem with that at all. One of my Captains, Sharon Swanson wanted to get a message of thanks to him."

"Really?" Phil instinctively answered. He had heard the name and knew who she was and what she had done. "How is she?"

"She's fine...you know her?"

"Know of her. Brave cop."

"Oh, hell yes. She sure is...anyway, you must know this Crane then?"

"I can get a message to him. You want him to call you at this number?"

"Yeah, that'd be fine, thanks."

"Thank you, sir." Stone offered.

"Say...can I ask you a question?" The major suddenly sounded meek.

"Of course, shoot."

"This Crane. He's good people, huh? I mean all the mystery and stuff around him. Seems like he has insights to things that help. If that makes any sense at all."

"Major, it makes all the sense in the world." Stone stopped himself short, but then offered, "someday we'll get together over a beer and I'll try to explain it all."

The Kentucky officer hung up and Stone made a note of the number. He would call a bit later. It would be close to 2:30PM in Dalton now and he figured Jon was at the hospital with Marsha. *Not gonna bother them for a little bit anyway.*

He re-fired the lawn mower and continued with his chores, but with a bit lighter step now and a smile on his face.

55

The sight of Hamilton Medical Center sent a chill down Jon's back. It wasn't the hospital of the big shootout. That was a smaller satellite unit a few miles away. But this was where he had taken Doris after finding her in the cabin last year. His adrenalin was on high that day and the memories had strong physical effects.

Ben picked him up from the airport in his Ford 500. He had attempted to hint around for more information about the call from Florida, but Jon wasn't in the mood.

"How's Juan doing?" Jon asked.

"Fine, no trouble at all. He's hung out with Gil most of the time. Gil has shown him more attention than the others, so…"

"That's good. I'll need him later."

There wasn't much more to the conversation after that. Not till they pulled up at the hospital.

"You ok?" Ben asked carefully.

"Yeah, I'm good."

Realizing what was in his friend's thoughts, Ben didn't push it. He drove into the drop off area so Jon could go on in.

"Third floor…316 on the left," he told Jon.

With a nod and jump from the car, Jon was on his way. The ride up took forever or so it seemed. He didn't remember these halls being so long either, but soon enough there it was. Room 316. He knocked and pushed the door open slightly.

George was standing by the window smiling and Doris was sitting next to Marsha's bed. He entered in silence and slowly stepped to the foot of the bed.

Marsha looked straight at him and cocked her head to one side.

341

"Look, George. It's that cute doctor from Charlotte." She blurted out.

Jon's eyes became large and his brow wrinkled severely before George's laugh gave it all away. Marsha sat up and threw her arms open at Jon. "Come here, silly." She grinned. "George told me what I did to you in Charlotte...I was just teasing."

Jon Crane nearly fell into her hug and George patted his back as he motioned for Doris to leave with him for a while. There was much to discuss and catch up on.

George saved the less than great news for later. The doctors were pleased with the progress, but felt she needed to stay in a controlled environment for a few more days. Any sudden agitation or jarring of the brain could cause a relapse or worse. They described her condition to George as that of a severe concussion. The recommendation was another full week in the hospital and then two weeks bed rest at home.

I'll let them enjoy their reunion before I explain the details, he thought. *It's not that bad, but another week in the hospital won't be good news to either of them.*

~

The man sat on his deck overlooking the Pacific Ocean. That part of Malibu was beautiful year round and he tried to be there as much as possible. When the special cell phone rang he muttered a small curse and put down the Corona Light he'd been cradling. Wiping his hand dry on his shorts he saw the call was from Montana. He sat up quickly and answered, "Yes, sir."

"Notify Florida they're up."

"You sure?" he questioned. "Do you think they're ready?" he continued without thinking.

The quiet from the other end let him know that question had already been considered. He finally followed up with, "what direction do they go?"

"Something local. Pick one from the list." The boss spoke in firm short statements. "We're behind schedule as it is. I want to see their results before we go too big."

"Got it." He replied and then all he could hear was the beach again. The man went into his bedroom to search for the phone to be used to call the Florida contact manager. Stopping at a desk in the den area, he took out a notebook with cryptic notations on each page. Thumbing down to a caricature of an alligator with a number 221 on its back, he picked that congressman. Florida's 5th District Representative.

The code wasn't all that involved, but it would slow down anyone who came across the list. The gator was obvious, but the 221 number had taken a bit more planning. Florida has twenty-five congressional districts. Since the number was more than that it was to be added together, 221 equaled five. A regular double-digit number would simply be reversed. District twenty-five would be shown as 52.

The representative there was on the list for no other reason than as a test. The unknowing congressman didn't pose any threat to the group, so his removal would not be looked at as an identifiable sanction.

~

Ben's afternoon took on a mission Jon had requested on the drive from the airport to the hospital. He really didn't discuss it; he just gave Ben a folder with maps and topical information about Shreveport, Louisiana. The request was for locations with line of sight access to the Russian Consulate building.

One needed to be at a height of twenty-one stories, another approximately seventeen stories and the third at twenty stories.

There was no explanation of why these factors were important; there never was much in the way of explanations.

The locations also needed to have vacant space available, which could be leased for short terms. A list of real estate offices was in the package. The spaces could be minimal, but all must face the Consulate building's southwest corner.

Ben dug into some special mapping programs he had found and started inputting coordinates. The cross references would be vacant space for rent. This one took some doing, but he loved the challenge.

As the programs finally were left to do their business he turned his attention to the bag of gear Jon had brought back. The suit was there. Ben pulled it out and held it up in front of him. The battle scars were there. Scuffs and scratches, but no signs of penetration.

He didn't even mention a fight. Ben thought to himself, *and this must have been some deal.*

The marks and abrasions cleaned up with ease and he checked for any weakness that may have been caused. After about an hour of concentration on the suit, Ben heard the main computer accessing a printer.

He walked over as his program began to spit out possible locations fitting Jon's needs. There were eight in all, with the listing agent's phone numbers attached. Ben double-checked the information and it appeared to be good. Placing the maps into a folder, he sealed and marked it. He could let the boss know his project was completed.

~

There was finally a piece of good news for Santonio Lendono. He had heard from Tomas Vaga, the personal secretary of Sergio DeMarcos from the hospital in Panama. Sergio was not any better. But all the news was not gloomy. Their connections through the U.S. State Department were showing some promise.

344

The men held in Shreveport were now under the control of ICE, the Immigration and Customs Enforcement agency. Deportation had been being delayed by the local authorities in Louisiana. The purpose was to keep these folks out of circulation as long as possible. With ICE in control, their men would be on the way back to Colombia and Guatemala within days.

Lendono asked Vaga, "Who was in line to take over from Hanson?"

"Nobody," the secretary responded and his voice was quite frustrated. "Hanson was new himself. He spent most of his time at fancy parties and playing big shot. I asked several times about a successor list. But he never answered."

"The fool." Lendono muttered in English. "Perhaps my brother-in-law's biggest mistake." There was no comment from the other end of the phone. "So, there is no change with Sergio?" He repeated as an afterthought.

"No." Vaga paused to organize his response. His mind was on other problems. "The stroke was bad. They feed him now by tubes and he doesn't respond." Vaga took a moment and Lendono could hear him sigh before continuing. "Saul's death didn't seem to register so bad, or he did not let on other than to send the revenge squad. But the raid on our men in Louisiana rocked him badly." The secretary listened, but Lendono had no comment on the matter. Vaga then finished his thought. "Then the massacre at the ice house in Georgia was all he could take, I guess. He hasn't spoken since."

"I need a leader," Lendono changed the subject abruptly. "At least for the fighters." The men being released in Shreveport were not mules they were warriors. He would need to hit the Russians before distribution could begin. "I'm working on some people to move the product. I must clear the way first. Who can I use to lead that?"

"I can try to find Bertalli." Vaga thought out loud. "His contact said he was working for Hanson a week or so ago, but I haven't heard from him."

"Find him." Lendono ordered. "If he's alive."

"That's what I was thinking." The secretary sounded worried. "I'll get right on it and see what I can line up as another choice if needed."

"Good." The leader then hung up.

56

Captain Stone found out about the ICE involvement late Saturday afternoon. The extraditions would begin Monday morning. His friends in that department shared with him that the pressure to release these guys was strong. Pressure radiating from the U.S. State Department through Homeland Security and right down the ladder to Louisiana.

This would complicate things, perhaps dramatically. He put out a call for a meeting of his officers for Monday and also realized Jon needed to know. He walked passed Sara in the kitchen as though she wasn't there and stepped out on the back patio of his home dialing the cell phone.

"Hey, Phil," Jon answered. "What's up?" Jon knew his friend would not bother him without a good reason, and this was surely a good reason. Phil Stone explained what he had learned and how that would effect the situation.

"Ok." And that was followed by a long pause. That was all Jon could think to say. It wasn't ok, not at all. But none of this had been. "Are you beefing up security there?" he finally added.

"First thing Monday... I have to." Phil told him. "I've got citizens to protect."

"Right, I understand. I will be coming back to Shreveport Monday, if that's all right. I have some things to check on and set up." Before Phil could answer Jon threw in, "You won't need to entertain me. I know you're gonna be busy."

The police captain told him there was no problem at all and then asked about Marsha.

"She's so much better, thanks. I can't wait till you and Sara can meet her."

"We look forward to that." Then Phil suddenly changed direction as he remembered. "By the way, a major with the Kentucky State Police called to get a message to you. It's from Sharon Swanson."

"Really? How is she?" Jon perked up.

"This Major Warren Hillenbrand left a number for you," and Stone gave him the phone number.

"Thanks for this, too."

"See you Monday sometime." Phil said as he hung up and turned to go back into the house. Sara stood, leaning against the doorframe with a blank look on her face.

"What's going on?" She normally would not interfere with Phil's business dealings. Her intuition told her this was different.

Phil kissed her neck as he went by, "It's all good, sweetheart."

In Dalton, Georgia Jon closed his phone and sat quietly for a couple of minutes. Marsha finally asked what the problem was.

"Nothing," he told her with a smile. But that wasn't true, not even a little bit. He needed to move on Torbof next week. He could not afford to have him panic and go to another location or city. And now, Capt. Stone's people would be watching even more closely than before.

Jon stood and pretended to go look out the window. His mind was calling for Silas. *He could handle this*, he told himself. Then with a quiet yet deep breath his confidence swelled and he became calm.

"What do you want for dinner?" Marsha called to him.

He turned to her with a smile she had seen before, but didn't remember why. "I've ordered fried chicken, mashed potatoes. The whole works. How's that sound?"

"Wonderful."

~

While on his way to the mansion after dinner, Jon spoke with the Major in Kentucky and then Captain Swanson herself for a few minutes. Jon thanked her for what they had done, to which she was dismissive.

"That's our job." She stated defiantly.

"I still thank you," he insisted and then impulsively told her. "I hope to close them down completely next week."

The Kentucky officer thought that was a strange thing for a civilian to say, but she didn't question it. "I thank you for the good info you offered." She took a second to gather her composure, "Saved many a good life that night."

"I'm proud of that, believe me, but you did it." Jon assured her. "You get healed up and I'll come visit you soon, ok?"

"I look forward to it. You take care young man."

"Yes, Captain. I'll do that."

Rounding the corner on Highway 71 the house looked different to him. All lit up and occupied. He liked it. As he parked at the top of the drive Daniel came out to greet him. The handshake quickly became a hug and Daniel whispered, "Thanks, man."

"Thank me?" Jon laughed. "You guys have been pretty busy here."

They walked inside to where everyone seemed to be preoccupied by the news on the TV.

"Jon's here." Daniel announced and they all turned and came their way. "What's the big deal on the tube?" He asked.

"That creep congressman from Maryland, Stubblefield. They stopped him at Reagan Airport tonight trying to fly to Paris," Doris responded without looking.

Lori rose from her seat and gave Jon a big hug. She said nothing, but smiled and nodded and then hugged him again. Taking her husband's hand, they then sat on the sofa.

Jon stood in silence listening intently. Daniel asked the questions.

"Isn't he the one whose family is missing?"

"That's him, the jerk." Lori threw in. He claimed it was a fact finding trip to study Muslims in France."

"Huh?"

"Yeah, right?" Doris chimed in. "They found he was heading to Switzerland from there. You know... no extradition treaty, Switzerland?"

Jon finally spoke, "Any word on the family at all?"

"Naw, but he ain't leaving the country till they find 'em." Said Gil. "They've pulled his passport."

Jon looked over at Ben who was standing completely quiet as well. Ben's eyes showed he knew and understood. This was a congressman they had tracked a few weeks ago, but Jon didn't feel the evidence was strong enough. Ben could see the hurt in Jon's eyes as this story played again on the TV.

Jon spoke to everyone; hugs and handshakes all around and then he excused himself. He found Juan sitting alone in the kitchen.

"You being treated alright?" he asked the man.

"Si, never better in fact."

"Good." He patted the man on the back and crossed the room. Jon then motioned for Ben to follow him. As they neared the stairs Jon looked back at Juan, "We'll need to talk in detail later." The Hispanic man nodded. Ben had stepped ahead of Jon on the stairs. They went directly to the elevator and workshop on the second sublevel.

"You didn't tell me about the fight." Ben challenged him as they walked into the workshop.

Jon's mood changed and he answered with a look more than words. "No."

"I need to know about these things, if the equipment worked right and all."

350

Walking over to his bag, Jon turned and in a lecturing tone responded to Ben.

"Look, I don't want you getting too close to that side of this business. It's dangerous and you could be lured into it." He turned to the workbench in front of him, pretending to look for something. "The suit worked fine...more than fine, it was great. But don't you ever think of using it yourself."

"What?" Ben was playing dumb. He walked toward Jon and tried to add to his words with hand gestures. "I know my place in this arrangement. I know what it is I do... and what you do."

Jon sat down and looked right at his assistant. "Ben, your suit worked better than I ever dreamed it would. You're a genius. I just made an agreement with your Mom, you know."

"Yeah, no problem. I understand...say; you might better check the monitors you brought home in that bag. The red light came on earlier today."

Opening the bag, Jon pulled the monitors from the Shreveport rooftop and hit play. The audio was weak. Both men leaned in and strained to hear. They could tell it was human voices, but that was about it.

"They are too far from the mikes." Jon mumbled as he adjusted the volume. "They're on the roof, just not near the microphones." He rubbed his face and leaned back while Ben stood up and thought for a minute.

"Let me try something. I think I can boost the audio through this system." He hooked a Cat-9 cable up to the monitor and pulled it to one of the computers. A few fast fingers on the keyboard and sound began to pour from the speakers.

"Thursday, 4:30 in the afternoon. OK...I see them then." The voice was Torbof, the reference had to be the meeting with the street gang leadership. There was more. This was more audible; he wasn't on

351

a phone this time. "Have they found the girl?" He demanded. Ben looked at Jon. They both knew who "the girl" was. Torbof was still after Marsha.

"The son of a bitch," Ben muttered.

Jon held his finger up for quiet...the recording continued. It was another voice this time, "not yet. Our wounded have not shown up either. They know you are looking for them."

Sounds could be heard, like footsteps and then Torbof's voice was loud. He had walked to his chair. "Find them." He commanded. "Her first. We must make an example, then find our men."

Ben looked at Jon who was staring at the monitor and almost yelled, "You've got to get this guy." Ben thought he saw Jon nod slightly as he stood.

"Have you worked out the problem I left you?" He asked calmly.

Ben found the folder and gave it to him. Jon flipped through it and smiled,

"You are good, my friend." He then asked for another list, "the one of our companies. I need three that might be looking for space in Shreveport."

Together they picked out three companies and three cover names for Jon to use. Jon studied the buildings Ben had located and plotted out his plan. He picked three that would work and Ben e-mailed offers to lease the spaces chosen. Jon would call on them personally Monday as the representative of those companies.

~

Sunday felt different to everyone. It was the first totally relaxed day any of them could remember though in reality it had only been a couple of weeks.

Daniel and Lori packed and went by the hospital to meet Marsha and thank Jon once again. They were flying back to

Pittsburgh that afternoon. Everything wasn't done, but the immediate threat to them was over.

Gil and his guys also packed to go to their private lives again. Each carried a nice check for their trouble from Jon and his eternal thanks.

"Anytime." Each of them would tell him.

George and Doris also felt ok going home, though Doris would spend the days with Marsha, at least for the start of the next week. George needed to get back to the office.

Juan was the only one who could not "go home." He would stay with Ben at the mansion. Trust was no longer an issue. Juan would gain nothing by alienating his new "friends." His only chance for survival was Jon's success in defeating the two cartels.

In Dallas and Shreveport it was much the same. The Bilstock family, including Murray sat around Mom's house and rested with Slick. The Stones and Turlocks had dinner together after a quiet afternoon. Matt and Phil did step out onto the deck of the restaurant to talk for a minute, but just for a minute. It was a good day.

Jon spent the day with Marsha while Ben packed a new bag for him. The weapons were already in Shreveport, but Jon had asked for a few more rounds for each. The black suit would not go this trip. The regular outfit should be packed. Ben wired a special monitoring device with headphones and a viewer through the left side of a pair of goggles. This wireless device could choose between two separate inputs for the video and a different one for the audio.

Ben did not know exactly what Jon had in mind. *A clean shot from three different possible spots*? He wondered. All he could be sure of was that Jon had a plan.

Jon had called Phil back and asked about coming in Sunday night. The Gulfstream jet would be ready at 9PM. Getting into

Shreveport before midnight was a concession to the Stones. Jon knew that following Monday would be a busy day for everyone.

57

Antonio "Andy" Bertalli didn't want to be found. Not after his experience in Dalton, Georgia. But when the calls began to come from Colombia it scared him, more than the earth collapsing from beneath him and enough to make him respond to the messages.

Tomas Vaga tried to hide his relief in locating the hit man and maintain a directive tone in his voice. "Lendono needs you to head up a group for a mission."

The already skittish man recognized the name and had questions. "What's the deal? Where's Hanson and DeMarcos?"

"You haven't heard about Hanson?" Vaga was stunned.

"I haven't been around anything, ok? I've been hiding, man. I don't know who those people in Georgia are, but they have juice. A bunch of it."

"What are you talking about?"

Bertalli told Vaga the tale of his assignment from Hanson and how he never saw anyone come or go from that big house and then...

"Where is this house?" Vaga interrupted him.

"Somewhere north of a town called Dalton. The highway was...a...seventy-one, I think."

"Can Lendono count on you or do we consider you a threat to us?"

That question was heavily loaded and required little thought to answer. The large Italian hit man signed on verbally and agreed to meet with Vaga later that week. Where was not yet determined.

~

He had borrowed a briefcase from the overhead storage in the G-5. It's funny, the little things you forget. The case didn't belong to anyone, other than the jet's owner. Jon would have never thought about one being available. But while he was complaining to the pilot that he had forgotten a briefcase the man mentioned how well equipped the plane was.

He had awakened early that rainy morning. Phil was already gone and Sara offered breakfast. Jon thanked her with a "no" and got away before 9AM. He had rented a car, a Town Car this time. Phil teased him some the night before, but he had told him it was all they had left at the rental agency.

Changing shirts in the car he pulled the pre-tied tie over his head and snugged it up. The first stop this morning would be at Walker Hall Properties. Jon walked up to the first occupied desk he saw and reached out his hand.

"Charles Whitley, Donavon Press in Atlanta. I believe we wired a lease request over the weekend." He told the agent.

"Mr. Whitley, yes. Have a seat, please." The agent was pleased to see a customer, especially for that building. "You wanted a corner facing north, is that right?"

"Do you have one like that?"

"Oh, yes. Any floor you want."

"We'd like to be above the street noise if possible. Say, twenty or twenty-one."

The agent was thumbing through his paperwork and quickly apologized, "My mistake, I'm sorry. I see right here you picked a unit over the Internet."

"Is that one still available?"

"Oh sure...would you care to drive over and see it?"

Jon agreed that he, or Mr. Whitley would very much like to see it. The agent drove and they were standing in the small 1400 square foot office within thirty minutes.

"We can have the carpet cleaned later this week." The embarrassed agent assured him. The stains appeared to be caused by break-in vandals. Jon was interested in the windows. The ones in this office were all fixed glass that did not open.

"I like a breeze now and then," he commented. "Do all the windows stay closed like this?"

The agent appeared unruffled by the question. He flipped through his folder and found what he sought. "Could you stand to be a bit lower?" He asked.

"How much?"

"I have one on seventeen with top swing out, casement windows."

"Let's see it...please."

They went to the office on that floor and the window issue was solved. It cranked open enough space for the rifle barrel to clear or the fired round to travel.

Jon pretended to check a few other factors and then made his offer. "I know you have standard lease agreements, but I want to make an offer." The agent did not speak. He simply waited and listened. "We're not sure if the Shreveport location will be permanent or not. Still, we need a presence here, for a short while anyway." Jon explained. "I will offer three months rent, up front and non refundable, on the condition we can opt out with a thirty day notice, before the end of this month."

The agent had to let all that soak in, but basically it was agreeable. They returned to the real estate office to sign the papers. Jon had a check, which was pre-signed by Ben Shaw, Chief Operations Officer of the parent company, Liberty Funds.

Immediate occupancy was agreed to and Jon, as Mr. Whitley, shook hands with the agent, got the keys and moved on to the next real estate office.

Situations were similar at the other buildings except the Exposition House did not have opening windows at all. The eighteenth floor was the top floor, but the office had access to the roof. The sight line from there was perfect, so Jon signed an agreement much like the others. The total investment in leases amounted to just over $12,000. Jon had been willing to go a lot higher if he needed to.

The dealings took most of the day and the Stones were waiting for him when he returned. They did not pry as to where he had been.

It had stopped raining and the evening was cool, but tolerable.

"There you are," Phil laughed as he stood up from his recliner. "Come on out back, Sara has whipped up a pitcher of Cyclones for before dinner."

"Cyclones?" Jon asked.

"It's vodka and...hell...I'm not sure what all. But it's good."

Jon spoke to Sara and thanked her again for the hospitality as Phil rushed him out to the patio.

"The extraditions began early this morning. By 2PM they were all out and on their way."

"Why so quick?"

"Somebody's pulling strings," Phil complained in frustration. "I have no idea who, but they have pull."

Jon took a sip of his drink and winced, "Geez...that's strong." He looked at Phil while trying to untwist his face and grumbled, "Those guys can be back up here in less than a week."

"Yeah, damn it. We'll be watching for 'em. But you're right. It's a revolving door for sure." Phil thought a minute about that and then added, "but these guys can't fly back." He sat up and leaned toward

Jon to continue his thought, "They'll have to cross through Mexico and that takes more time."

Jon liked hearing that. He needed another week without something spooking Torbof. He couldn't tell Captain Stone, but he was pleased with that last assessment.

~

Andy Bertalli normally didn't mind flying. He had flown thousands of miles with his work for the cartel. This trip was anything but normal. He was going to Miami to meet with Tomas Vaga in person. This was highly unusual and extremely dangerous. Those guys never came out from Columbia themselves.

Vaga had arrived the night before and checked into the South Seas Hotel. He would meet Bertalli at the Florida Room on South Beach later that Monday night.

The "soldiers" released from Shreveport were arriving in their home countries all that day. Stone was correct about their return trips. The cartel had to arrange travel through the Central American peninsula and Mexico for each one. It would be nearly three weeks at best, before they could be ready to take any action in the states.

~

Vasily Torbof had his meeting scheduled for Thursday at 4:30 in the afternoon. The local street gang could possibly be used to move his products and that meant reenergizing his income stream. The "soldiers" he had asked for were being gathered in Eastern Europe, but would not be in the states for several weeks. The coincidence of the combined timing was unknown to either group. But it held the potential for a perfect storm in some unlucky city in the United States. Many lives could still be in danger besides those of the cartel's warriors themselves.

Jon was sure the Colombians would come back and soon. But he wasn't aware of Torbof's plans, other than the meeting with the Red Latin Highlanders on Thursday.

Jon spent Tuesday out in the fields away from town. He was zeroing in the three high-powered rifles he had. The range from the buildings he had rented space in, to the target area, varied from 700 to 1600 yards. He set each weapon up for a particular range and marked it for specific use at one location. The T-Rex would be hand held and used from the rooftop location. It's range from the Consulate building was approximately 1400 yards.

Jon used two rounds from each weapon to find his settings. After the first round from the larger weapon, he put on the hydraulic arm. The T-Rex tended to jump hard to the right and away from the shooter. The recoil was unlike anything he had ever fired. Dropping the weapon could not be risked, especially on Thursday.

He drove by the two offices that afternoon and checked what he would need to set up and tied down the Barretts. Heavy gauge, standing tripods were purchased at two separate local sporting goods stores using different credit cards. Mini scaffolds he found in two paint stores served to stand under the tripods and stabilize the weapons with tie down straps. Jon pre-sighted the scopes and transferred the images to the remote firing monitors. The systems appeared to work perfectly. At both offices he disassembled the units and stored them in closets that he locked with padlocks.

At the Exposition House the two closets had soft folding doors. He stored the T-Rex in the office bathroom shower stall and secured that door. A vagrant he noticed in the hallway forced him to change his mind. The T-Rex would stay with him. Carrying it Thursday might draw attention. He would have to work that out. Silas had dealt with bigger problems before.

58

Murray Bilstock had met with his insurance agent on Monday. He received some living expenses on the spot, but the news about the house wasn't as good. He knew the house was older and not very big. The value assessed to rebuild it was well below what he'd hoped for. Coverage for his personal items was tied to that value, but he had pictures, which mitigated some of that. Bottom line was, he couldn't afford to rebuild right now.

"Could I get a payout on the value and pursue this later?" He asked.

"Sure, in this case it's a total loss. There's no question." The agent pointed at the barn and suggested, " too bad it's not in any better shape. You could remodel it if it was." The other option the man offered was that Murray could put a trailer on the site until he could rebuild what he wanted.

These options weren't what Murray wanted to hear. His share of the inheritance was all in the ranch already. This wasn't expected.

When Charlene asked how it went the next morning, Murray told her, "fine." He couldn't see bothering her with it till he had a chance to think about it. Charlene knew her brother more than he realized. This entire mess was because of that "Son" investigation. Daniel Seay was the only person she could think of who was involved in it. She would contact Daniel first chance she had. Daniel could think of something, someway to help.

They took Slick out for a drive that afternoon. He was fine, but he enjoyed the attention so he milked it for all that he could.

~

Tomas Vaga had issued the orders from Lendono to their leader. But he also questioned the man extensively about the house he had told him about. Hanson had not shared what he knew about this house and the man who owned it. Bertalli only knew he was to take out the owner if he could find him. With the address supplied by his hit man, Vaga quickly uncovered the name of the owner of the house. The name had often been entangled with stories of Cartel members being killed.

This information was too hot to risk over the phone, so Vaga waited until he was back in Colombia to talk with Lendono.

"This guy could be that 'Son' they talk about." He declared to the boss. Lendono was already nervous about the phantom. This talk did not please him.

"Are you telling me this guy is real?"

"I...I don't... know." Vaga stuttered. He had not considered a reaction like this. He thought the boss would be proud of his work.

"Get someone to that house." The boss commanded.

"Who?"

"Why not Bertalli?"

"He won't go there again. He's spooked."

Lendono turned and walked to a cell window. He glared outside and spoke harshly as he did, "My leader is spooked?" His head turned and tilted back toward Vaga. "Find me a killer who doesn't spook."

"Si, Commander." Vaga tried ultimate respect to Lendono's authority in an effort to calm him down. "We have such a man just in from Louisiana. I will change his travel plans and fly him to Monterrey. From there he can be in Georgia in another week or so."

"Do it." Lendono ordered.

Vaga had made up all of that as he spoke. The reality of it all would take longer. He just needed to tell Lendono something better at the moment. He left the office cell and got on his phone looking for a hardened killer among the troops just sent home.

~

Daniel Seay's desk at the Pittsburgh Post Gazette was deep in memos and notes. No flowers or anything resembling that sentiment, just work. By Tuesday he could finally see his desk pad and he took a deep breath of relief. Bill White seized on that as clearance to move in with his questions. He knocked, but didn't wait for a response to enter.

"Oh, hey boss." Daniel pushed back in his chair to see what his mentor wanted.

"Alright, you've had nearly two days. What can you tell me?"

"We're ok, thanks for asking," he started with sarcasm. The boss wasn't impressed.

"Tell me about the bus, that sounded rough." White was almost gleeful.

"You really didn't care for Hanson, did you?" Daniel laughed.

Bill White pretended to wipe his face with his hand, "Does it show?"

"Boss, there's still a bunch in play and I can't talk about it because I don't really know much." Daniel put his elbows on the desktop and rested his chin in his palms. "The Russians are about out of guys and the Colombians have been released through some pressure from our State Department. The hate still runs strong and Jon believes there's more to come if they aren't stopped."

"Who's gonna do that?"

Daniel just looked at the man in silence.

His boss turned and headed for the office door, "I'd love to see that." He spouted as a parting shot.

Daniel was more worried for his friend's safety. He didn't know what or how Jon planned to stop the fighting, but he knew he would try.

~

Matt Turlock heard from Georgia on Tuesday. A Captain Willard Frye of the 23rd Mission Support Group was on the phone.

"Who do you know at Barksdale?" The Captain asked as a clearance question.

"Winston Meyers is an old friend." Matt told him.

"Yeah, he's a nice young man," the voice said.

"Young?" Matt challenged. "The Winston I know is in his late fifties."

There was quiet on the line and then the Captain spoke again. "I know. He was my C.O. in Afghanistan some years back. I just have to be sure who I'm talking to, especially with what I was told you're interested in."

"I understand." Matt took a minute and then told him. "I don't take the seriousness of this lightly. I can tell you I believe many lives in this country could be at stake."

"Drug Lords don't play nice, do they?" The Captain said. "I lost a good friend to drugs. He watched his son die of an overdose and went after the dealer himself." The voice sounded somewhat weaker, but it continued. "He got the bastard. But his men shot him down." The pilot gathered himself and added, "They were Columbians. I want to help if I can."

"If some people needed to get into Panama…" Matt asked.

"How many guys?"

"Three. With some gear I suppose."

"When?"

"Don't know… soon. The man in charge would need to tell you that."

"Mondays and Thursdays we go to Panama City. The old main airport."

"Can I have my friend call you?"

"Use this number and ask for Willie."

"Thanks Captain." Matt said to a dead line. The man had hung up.

Matt called Phil to tell him he had a message for Jon. "I think I got him a ride."

"Excellent!" Phil was pleased. "He's not here, but I'll reach out for him."

"Dinner?" Matt inquired.

"You buying?"

"Of course, you cheap bastard." The editor laughed. "See you at seven unless I hear otherwise."

~

Jon got the word about the guy's night out dinner and found Matt and Phil although he was a bit late.

"You're two beers behind, man." Phil chastised him with a grin.

"Sorry, got to talking with some people. Lost the time." He explained.

Matt shared his news about the possible ride to Panama and Jon was visibly impressed. *These guys can do things.* He told Silas in his mind. Silas was pleased with the news, but not as swayed.

The dinner was enjoyable. Jon caught Phil half staring a time or two, but nothing was said. The man was a professional. Keeping his distance from this had to be difficult.

~

Nicky Sledge sat at the bar in Melbourne, Florida picking at his new lip ring. It was his third, but this one didn't feel right.

Infection? He thought. He strained to see his reflection in the bar's back mirror, but wasn't close enough to really see anything.

As he stood to go to the men's room for a better look he was called from the doorway of the bar.

"Nick...whoa...I need to talk to ya, man." The voice hollered.

Sledge turned around, still rubbing his lip and waited for his gang member to come to him.

"Man, that don't look so good." The approaching man twisted his head to one side and grimaced.

"Is that all you got?" Nicky barked.

"Naw...we got news. You know...from them."

"Them?"

"Yeah. Those Sponsor guys...the ones with all the money."

"Excellent, we could use some funds for a party." Nicky perked up. Word from the Sponsors meant cash. *They were like fairy God Fathers or something*, in his mind.

"They got a job they want done." The messenger announced.

Nick Sledge's mood went down again, fast. "A job?" He half mumbled, "what kind of job?"

The other man looked around and though there were only four people in the bar besides himself and his leader, he took Sledge by the arm and firmly suggested they go outside.

They walked to a VW bus that was painted like something from the sixties and climbed in.

"What the hell, dude?" Sledge was now concerned and ticked off. The word the messenger delivered made Nicky forget his lip.

"They want a congress guy hit."

The look on the leader's face wrinkled and he looked down at the steering wheel of the microbus. "Hit?" He then stared back at the messenger. "You mean...kill somebody?"

"That's what it says, a congress type dude."

Nicky rocked back in the seat and rubbed his forehead with his hand. He knew there would be a price for all the money they'd been given the last few months, but this wasn't expected.

"Just how are we supposed to do this?" He asked the other man.

"The note didn't say any how...just what. And they want it done right away."

Nicky slammed the wheel with both hands and leaned into what had become his tormentor. "You ever killed anybody, Lou? Huh? I don't hear you!" The words came so quickly they ran together and barely made sense. The messenger's face took on a look of fear and he spoke not a word. His concentration was interrupted by the close up view of Nicky's red, swollen lip. He'd forgotten the question he'd been asked, but that didn't matter.

"Call a meeting for tonight and bring that note." Sledge ordered.

"Where...where you... want to meet?" Lou stammered.

"Joe's house." The leader asserted. "His folks are out of town."

59

Wednesday was another busy day for Jon. He could still feel Phil's awareness that something was happening, but the man did not interfere or ask any questions. Jon had appreciation for the man's confidence yet Silas keep reminding him. *This is why it is best to work alone.*

He spent several hours in one of his newly acquired offices, drilling out the projectiles of three high-powered rifle cartridges, one .577 and two 50-caliber Browning machine gun rounds. The solid metal slugs had tremendous impact potential, but could leave traceable residue for ballistics technicians to find.

The metal was drilled out leaving a thin skin, strong enough to handle the heat of the firing and the high-speed travel through the air, yet thin enough to break up and dissolve upon impact. Inside the cavity would be filled to two-thirds full with fine, high-density gravel dust. The weight would not equal the metal that had been removed, but it was close enough for ballistic accuracy. The impact though, would be even more severe than the original payload. The slugs would act as "dead blow" hammers and then virtually disintegrate. The velocity would be slightly affected by the lesser weight, taking the Barrett rounds to less than a second to travel a mile, the T-Rex slug a tenth of a second longer.

The void at the top of each bullet was filled with a light candle wax to hold the dust in place at the back of the slug and maintain the flight trajectory. The hole was sealed with a drop of molten lead and the rounds cleaned and polished. No prints on anything.

The day's work also included the installation of motorized window blinds that opened like draperies. They were set with only enough space for the slug to pass out the window and the control connected to the remote unit Jon would carry. Jon wore gloves on all the projects, being careful to leave no traceable signs of who had been there.

The one problem encountered was the obvious tampering of one of the padlocks on a closet door. Someone had been in the office, looking around. They had not gained access, but the chance could not be taken that they wouldn't come back.

Jon moved the equipment into another smaller closet leaving the lock on the same one as before. He set up a pepper spray bomb in that closet. It would blast toward any offending person who forced the door open. It was risky, but that would have to do. He could not afford to be seen carrying a bag into two buildings the next afternoon.

A quick trip to the hardware store for some duct tape, bug spray and two signs and he was back at the Stone's with time to call Marsha. He looked into a mirror in the hallway and Silas was smiling. He was ready for tomorrow.

~

Daniel had talked with Charlene Bilstock on Wednesday. She explained the predicament her brother was in over the rebuilding of his house.

"What does he want to do?" Daniel asked her.

"He told me he wanted to replicate the Brownwood house, but that would be some time later."

"He wants to do one like you guys had in Texas?" Daniel confirmed.

"Yeah," Charlene told him, "we all loved that house. Despite some of the memories."

The reporter knew Jon well enough that he spoke with confidence as the thought came over him. "Do you have pictures of that house?" He had seen the mansion last fall and knew it was of grand scale, but couldn't totally see it in his mind.

"Sure, plenty of them." She stated. "Inside and out...most every room actually."

"Can you e-mail me a couple dozen that show what it is, you know...size, number of rooms...that sort of thing."

"I can, but what for?"

"Give me some time, ok? I may have an idea."

He turned to talk of wishing to see them all again and that maybe that could happen in the near future. Charlene agreed and thanked Daniel.

"Good to talk to you, again." She told him.

"Same here."

The reporter started to call Jon right then, but decided he would wait to see the photos. He was sure Jon wouldn't bat an eye at helping. What he didn't know was that Murray had already rejected one offer.

~

The meeting at Joe's house in Indialantic, Florida was attended by every member of the gang, all eight of them. Nicky had fudged a little when he was first approached. He told the man on the phone he had a gang of twenty-four. He figured the money would be increased if he had more guys, *so...what the hell?* He thought. He now knew what hell was.

"How do we do this...any ideas?" He stood in the center of the group, all with stunned faces that were turning pale.

"What did this congress fella do to them?" Was asked from the floor.

"I don't know...they don't say." Nicky was as scared as the rest, but doing all he could to hide it. "They paid us a bunch of money, up front and now we're stuck."

Silence prevailed for several minutes until one small guy, with less tattoos than the others spoke up. "We have to study his

370

schedule." The others just looked at him with blank stares, so he continued. "We find out where he goes everyday and when. If there's a pattern we use it."

Nicky pointed at the guy, "That's good. I like that. Then what?"

The small kid suggested they set an ambush based on what they learned. "It's the only thing we could even try."

"So...we go to Washington? Who can afford that?" The host challenged. Nicky nodded his head in agreement.

"No, no...Congress is out for Spring Break next week. He'll be back down here."

"You know where he lives?" The leader pressed.

"I can find out."

There was quiet in the room until Nicky rose and pointed to the smallest gang member. "That's good." He declared. "I like it. You're in charge, but report to me every damned day. You got that?"

"Sure." The smaller man said with the slightest self-satisfied smile.

The boss sat down and groaned holding his jaw.

"You really should see about that thing, Nick. It's bad," said the guy next to him.

~

Jon got back to his room at the Stone's house and looked at the note Matt had given him. He dialed the number, even though it was late. It rang several times with no answer and Jon hung up. Before he put his phone down, it rang. Caller ID showed a different number than what he had called, but one he still did not recognize.

"Hello?" He answered. The other end was silence. Again, Jon offered his greeting, "Hello."

"I'm waiting." A voice came back.

Jon remembered his instructions from Matt. "Is Willie there?" He asked.

"This is Willie...who is this?"

Jon understood the caution and felt it should work both ways. "Call me Silas." He responded.

"Ok, Silas. So you need to take a trip?"

"I like the Isthmus this time of year."

"Ok." The voice was calm and steady. "Three going?"

"Please."

"What weight of baggage, total?"

"No more than 200 pounds, I would guess."

"Needs to be a good, damn guess."

"Ok," Jon paused. "Yeah. 200 pounds is plenty."

"Both ways?"

"Yes, both ways."

"Go Monday, back on Thursday. Miss Thursday you wait till Monday, got it?"

"Yeah... Departure time, what is that?" Jon inquired.

"Zero four twenty, sharp."

"Roger, that."

"So, you served?" The voice asked with interest.

"Yes, sir. A few years back."

There was a short pause again and then the voice finished what he had to say. "Make your plans and call that same number you used tonight."

"How long do I have?" Jon asked quickly.

"Past four weeks, you start over. Deal's gone."

"Understood. Thanks." And he heard the line go blank. The entire call took less than two minutes.

Jon lay back on his bed and looked at the ceiling. *One snake on Thursday and the other within a few weeks.* He promised himself. *Then it should be over.*

60

He slept in till nearly 9AM. He could hear Phil and Sara talking earlier, but Phil was gone now. Jon's feet hit the floor and he breathed deeply. Then stood and went to the mirror to see if he was alone. He was not.

A quick nod to Silas and he began to clean up and dress for the day. The regular uniform and a couple of costumes he had packed would go with him today.

Sara was reading her paper as he walked into the kitchen. She rose to get him coffee and told him of a message Phil had left with her.

"The security will be extra tight today all around the Russian Consulate building."

Jon took a large sip of coffee and thanked her, for the coffee and the message.

He seemed a bit different to Sara that morning, still kind and considerate, just different. He was quieter than usual for one thing. They had coffee, he ate some toast and then he excused himself.

Jon grabbed his bag, loaded it in the Town Car and drove away. Sara stood at the front door and wondered. *Phil would sometimes act like that.* She remembered.

~

Vasily Torbof stood on his rooftop and called to an aid.

"What is all this police traffic down there?"

"I do not know, sir. I had not noticed."

"That's five cars gone by in the thirty minutes I've been here." He turned from the edge and looked at the aid. "Are they still coming today?"

"Yes, sir. So much as I know."

The Russian gang leader walked to the opposite side of his building and looked toward the ground again. The top of the wall was less than belt high so he did not lean too far. Reaching with both hands, Vasily grabbed the top row of bricks for support as he checked up and down the street.

"Send two men to find out what is happening. I see police everywhere."

"Yes, sir."

"Damned cops," he mumbled to himself. *If they scare away the Highlanders it would set back the plans.*

He looked to the sky and finally smiled a bit. *At least the rain has stopped,* he thought. *This is a good sign.*

Strolling to his favorite corner, checking his plants along the way, Torbof picked up a duster and carried it to his lawn chair. He gently swished it with the duster, seat, back and arms. *Important meeting today,* his thoughts told him, *even if they are just punks.*

~

Murray Bilstock had spent a great deal of his time this week going over Lucy. The machine had performed well and he liked keeping her that way. Besides, he could think much better when he was working on the helicopter. It relaxed him.

What to do about the house was his main concern. *Don't cry over spilled milk and Water under the Dam,* thoughts came to mind. That's what his dad always said. He slapped a rag against the side of the machine, angry at himself for even thinking of that man.

He wondered when Jon would be ready to make plans to go to Colombia. He wondered if he would double cross him and go alone. *Naw,* he assured himself. *He wouldn't stiff me like that.*

Murray remembered he had some gear of his own. A black leather holster and a chromed Colt 45 revolver were among the stuff. It was a bit flashy, but he could shoot the hell out of it. *Six shots is a*

374

might limiting today though. He decided he'd get it out and clean it up anyway.

He thought about Jon's girlfriend and that she was doing better. Murray was happy for them and glad they were back together. He had a girlfriend once; he shook his head as he thought about it. Charlene warned him about her, but he hadn't listened.

They'd nearly grown up around each other. She was the pretty, popular one and Murray worked the cows after school. They hung out with a group of friends for years and tried dating a little in the tenth grade. *What a disaster that was,* he remembered.

It got serious for a while after graduation, or at least he thought it had. Turns out he was just the only game left in town. Most of the guys went off to college and Murray stayed with the land. His daddy was a freshman in congress back then, somebody had to work the ranch. They were doing good together, saw each other every Saturday night and talked on the phone every other day. And then she ran off with guy from Dallas, didn't even say "bye" or nothing.

He didn't understand why it hurt so badly and he hated that it showed when he talked to folks. He had to get away and learn to deal with it.

Murray turned the ranch duties over to Slick and Charlene and joined the Army. They taught him to fly helicopters and he was damn good at it.

They sent him to Afghanistan once, twice...three times. He had one bird shot out from under him. Autorotation saved his life and the three others on the copter with him. But he broke his leg and they sent him home, that time for good.

His daddy was Senator Bilstock by then so it was little trouble talking him into a helicopter for the ranch. Murray named her Lucy.

People who hear this story ask if that was the girl's name...the one who left him.

"Naw..." he always replies. "That was Sue." Then he smiles and adds, "Lucy won't leave me."

Murray had dated other ladies now and then, just nothing serious. He got past that weird feeling he had over Sue, but he didn't forget it. It would take something really special for him to chance that again. *Really special*, he confirmed.

~

Jon got to the Winchester Suites building just before noon. The police car out front was not a welcome sight.

The economy was still sluggish nationwide so most businesses were withering rather than expanding. The buildings he chose, for location and angle to his target, were not in the best neighborhoods of downtown Shreveport. Those two factors added up to one main fact that could not be controlled. Occupancy of the office spaces in his buildings was low.

That was both good and bad. Fewer business people meant fewer curious eyes and drop by visitors. He didn't need someone from the "welcome wagon" popping in as he set up the Barrett rifle. The other side of the coin was where the negatives lived.

Near empty buildings, especially those with enough tenants to require lights and air be left on, drew unwanted guests. Homeless street people, gangs and variations of those worlds would invade these buildings to plunder and find comfort from the elements. Jon had hoped his short-term stay would not bring awareness that he was there. None-the-less, it was a chance that needed to be taken. The presence of the police car was not a welcome sight. There wasn't time for this.

He only had a small bag to carry in here and all it would contain was the tape, bug spray and a sign. More than a little nervous, he walked in and waited for the elevator.

The doors opened and a young officer stepped out with a very dirty and smelly man in handcuffs.

"Excuse us, sir." The officer said as they went around Jon.

"What going on?" Jon could not help but ask.

"Captain has a crackdown on homeless breaking into vacant offices. We just started working it today."

Jon watched the two men walking for the doors and his mind spun wildly around what he had just heard. *Naw, it couldn't be*, he thought as he sought verification.

"Captain?" Jon took a step with them and asked loudly, "Captain who?"

"Captain Stone, the man I work for." The officer barked back at him.

Jon watched the officer load the smelly man into his patrol car and drive away. He went upstairs and found nothing disturbed with his office. "Captain Stone." He repeated out loud as he unlocked the closet and began his set up. "I'll be damned."

He was finished with the rifle mounting and sighting it in by 1:20PM. He opened the bag he had brought with him, took a last look around and went to the wooden office door.

Jon sprayed the doorframe heavily with the bug spray and then soaked a small rag in the foul bug deterrent. Stepping into the hall, he pulled the door closed. He then stuffed the rag under the door and taped the edges with the duct tape. The sign he brought read, "No Entrance – Heavy Fumigation – Dangerous Exposures Within."

He mounted the sign with more tape and was on his way to the next building.

~

Nicky Sledge finally sought help. His lip was approaching ping-pong ball size and oozing something that smelled bad.

As he walked out of the free clinic in Melbourne, just across the causeway from home, a familiar face was leaning against his car.

"What are you doing here?" He managed through his bandaged lip.

"Your dad said you'd be here. I've got information on that dude."

Sledge realized who it was. The geeky kid who was new to the gang. "What's your name again?"

"Max." The kid told him.

The leader was in more pain than he thought speaking would cause so he gestured for the kid to continue.

"The dude is from across the state, he lives in Dade City. That's where his district is."

Max could tell Sledge didn't like that news. Dade City was a good ways from the coast where they lived. But the boss said nothing other than shake his head so the younger man went on.

"The newspaper said he plans to take his family to Disney World on the congressional break...that's closer. Maybe we can get to him there."

Nicky's eyes indicated he was thinking. When he finally blinked he looked straight at Max and suffered through the pain of speaking.

"That's good," he nodded approval. "Work on that some more."

Max smiled that his proposal had been accepted. He thought about saying something concerning Nicky's lip, but let it go. Dipping his head, Max walked away toward where he had parked. Nicky Sledge just wanted to get home to sleep. The pain pills were starting to kick in.

61

Murray Bilstock's phone rang as he was finishing up with waxing Lucy's nose. It was Jon.

"Hey," Murray answered. "How's it going?"

"Busy, I've just got a minute and need to ask you a question."

"Yeah...go ahead."

"Can you be ready to go this weekend?"

Murray didn't need to ask "where?" "Absolutely. Just say when."

"I'll give you a call Friday sometime."

"Hey..." Murray caught him before he hung up. "Be careful man."

"Thanks. I'll try." Jon smiled as he hung up. He was nearing the second building.

~

Santonio Lendono was not a patient man. He had already given Vaga more time than he felt necessary. He wanted action and he wanted it now.

"Who did you find?" He shouted into the phone. "You should have called me by now."

"Sorry, sir." Vaga searched his mind for an excuse. "Sergio needed to go to the hospital. He had a seizure of some kind."

The news set Lendono back. After all Sergio was family, his sister's husband. The anger he felt had caused him to forget what she was going through.

"Have you had a chance to find someone for that job?" He rephrased the question.

"Yes, he's to get back to me tomorrow with a schedule." Vaga bluffed.

Lendono was suspicious. To verify his concerns he would have to talk to his sister. He didn't want to do that. She was difficult enough to talk to after Saul was killed. Now she was intolerable.

"Ok then, I will hear tomorrow. Correct?"

"Si...tomorrow for sure." Vaga wasn't sure what he would do, but he had bought himself another twenty-four hours.

~

Jon stood at the window of the second rented office. There had been no obvious police presence as he came in so he was checking the area from the seventeenth floor.

Maybe Phil doesn't know about this location, he thought. It would be a topic they would never discuss.

The set-up was nearly the same inside the second office. Most all the settings on the rifle and scope were pre-established so all they required was confirmation. The set up was complete by 3:15PM. He was right on time.

Jon did have an extra bag at this site, one he had left in the closet a day earlier. The door was sprayed and taped with the same story as before. The smell from the rag and the door edges gave realism to the charade. This building had a hallway restroom a few steps from his office. He went in and made sure it was empty.

The extra bag held a uniform he would change into. It was really for the third building, but he wanted to change before he got there. Driving into a mostly abandoned parking garage, he left the Town Car on level two. Jon took his bag from the car and went to the stairwell where he changed into the uniform and proceeded up to level four.

A van he had rented the day before sat waiting. Jon applied some labels he'd had printed to the van so now the vehicle and his uniform said "Watson's Heat and Air."

The T-Rex broke down into sections about three feet in length. His bag, looking like tools would not attract undue attention.

Getting to the roof at 4:20PM he first checked the monitors. The Consulate building was quiet, but he chose not to worry about that yet. The visuals from the other gun sights were spot on. He blocked the access door with a pipe to prevent being bothered and began to assemble the huge rifle. Finally, he took the hydraulic arm from the bag and placed it over the uniform.

~

Vasily waited in the parlor of the residence level for his guests. The gang wasn't concerned with timeliness and it showed. They were to meet at 4:30PM. At 4:45PM a shiny red, classic 1964 Ford Galaxy pulled up to the building. They were just late enough to be assertive.

There were five of them in the entourage. Three stayed outside with their car while the two leaders went up to the penthouse with Torbof's aid.

As if the tardiness wasn't enough, their Hispanic appearance was a further put off to the Russian mob leader. He tried to conceal his feelings. The initial greeting was short. These guys cared little about formalities so Torbof led them to the stairs and his rooftop. The gang members took a few minutes to admire the view of the Red River before Vasily could direct them to the opposite corner and the chairs he had set up. The Red Latin Highlanders sat facing the corner and glanced at each other about the strange arrangement. Vasily briefly looked around, the cops were gone, so he turned and took his usual seat. It was 5:05PM.

~

If the view had not been as good, Jon would have gotten worried. The car drove up at quarter to five and he could tell they must be the gang. He sat down below the roof's knee wall and checked the other weapons again. He set the firing order for the Hunt Building to go first, the Winchester second and his location would be last. A small button was attached to the stock of the T-Rex that would allow him to start the firing without looking away from his sights.

Vasily's head was barely visible above the brick line. Jon checked the monitor to assure himself it was in fact Torbof in the lawn chair.

A quick look around the area and all was quiet. Traffic began to build up as people were heading home after their workday, but that was all normal. He settled in and took a comfortable position. He activated the hydraulic arm for added strength. When he was steady and sure on his aim, Jon pushed the button on the rifle's stock.

The first Barrett discharged a bare tenth of a second ahead of the second. Traveling at just over 2900 feet per second the impacts were actually six-tenths of a second apart. At the sight of the first impact, Jon gently squeezed the T-Rex's trigger. The larger projectile was moving at closer to 2600 feet per second from almost a mile away. Travel time, three quarters of a second.

Through the scope he had a complete view of the result. The first .50 caliber round struck the brick veneer a foot inside the corner on the south side. It hit three feet below the top of the parapet wall with the impact of a sledgehammer blow.

The second round smashed into the west face, striking higher and some three feet back from the corner. It shook loose the outer layer of bricks and they began to fall away exposing the edge of the roof's deck. The parapet wall in that corner was gone. Concrete blocks supporting the decking cracked and crumbled.

Based on Murray's calculations, Jon was already zeroed in on the spot where that concrete edge now laid bare. Softly squeezing the trigger, Jon had put the .577 projectile in flight and it slammed into that edge a half second later. The concrete blocks under the deck shattered causing a large corner of decking to break and fall away.

Within a microsecond of the first two strikes, Torbof's arms flew out and skyward in a reaction to the impacts behind him. He had unconsciously shifted his center of gravity to his backside and as the last round slammed into the concrete decking, his chair began to fall backwards with the concrete, blocks and bricks.

On the street, the first falling bricks landed on the Red Ford Galaxy and the three men inside reached for the door handles.

Vasily Torbof tried desperately to lean forward, grabbing at the jagged bricks surrounding the ever-widening hole. The Russian's feet left the rooftop and flayed about in his panic. The Hispanics had jumped from their seats, instinctively reaching out for the falling man. But his weight against the seat and the back of the aluminum chair carried him out and down.

The occupants of the Ford climbed out and jumped away, unable to understand what was happening.

As the two Hispanic gang members standing on the roof watched the man go over, the first distant sound of a rifle retort reached them. It was quickly followed by the others. Most people on the ground or in surrounding buildings mistook the sounds as that from jet aircraft out of Barksdale. The three booms in rapid succession sounded like a sonic boom echoing high above the clouds.

The Highlanders on the roof caught a glimpse of Torbof's face before they turned and ran to the stairs. His eyes were wide in wonder as he reached for anything with both hands, finding only air.

There was a slight pause in the falling debris and the men on the sidewalk heard the rush of air and the man's screams. But they did not see him until he hit.

The sound of Torbof's body landing on top of the gang's car was more like a truck accident than anything else. The impact shattered the windshield as it crushed the car's top into the seating area. The side windows blew out and bits of glass struck the three gang members who were now lying on the sidewalk. The back glass of the Galaxy popped out in one piece and oddly fell over on the trunk's rear deck.

Pieces of the aluminum chair, which were not still with the body, flew in all direction like the glass, one section impaling itself into a telephone pole nearby.

When the dust cleared, Torbof was laying with his head on the rear seat decking, mouth and eyes still open in the panicked scream he died with. At that moment, the CCCY was no more.

~

A block and a half away, Phil Stone had sat in a coffee shop where he'd been watching the Consulate building for over an hour. When the bricks first began to fall he ran outside. Stone had hardly gotten five feet down the sidewalk before Torbof landed on the red Ford.

"10-87 at Russian Consulate Building," he hollered into his radio. "Code 20...code 8 at my location, all units available code 2."

Captain Stone got to the men on the sidewalk as the other two came out the front door, pale as ghosts. One foot patrolman ran up and then a car with two more officers arrived. At Phil's direction, he and the other officers secured the scene.

~

The three high caliber projectiles all disintegrated on impact. The metal housings melted or rolled into unrecognizable pieces that would be lost in the other rumble. The wax was gone and the granite dust mixed with the mortar and was gone forever.

Jon sat down and began to disassemble the rifle. After waiting ten minutes he unlocked the roof's door and made his way down the back steps. He drove the van back to the parking garage and removed the labels. He changed back into his regular clothes in the stairwell before exiting on the level where the Town Car was parked.

~

As much as he wanted to, Captain Stone and his first responders could not question the Red Latin Highlanders or the remaining occupants of the building. They could only hold them and take any volunteered statements. No charges had been established so there was no need to Mirandize anyone yet.

"Do you need medical care?" Phil asked one of the bleeding men. His question was met with a defiant glare. The young hoodlum held his hand over a cut on his arm and blood seeped through his fingers, but he refused to speak.

"Fine," Phil shrugged. "You get blood on my sidewalk and you'll clean it up." He turned immediately to the arriving patrol car. "Somebody grab a blanket and cover that body." He ordered.

People were beginning to gather and stare at the grizzly scene. They shielded Vasily Torbof from the spectators as two unmarked cars squealed up to the curb. The detectives were there. The investigation could begin.

~

Driving to the Hunt Building Jon saw three emergency vehicles headed toward the consulate building, but no one bothered

385

him. He parked on the street in front of the main doors and went up to the office with caution. The door was as he had left it.

He pulled on his gloves and went inside, nothing appeared to have been disturbed. First thing he pulled the window closed and checked the blinds. The rifle had not protruded through the window so he checked the surrounding casement for flash burns or residue. None were visible, but he wiped the area with the nearly dry bug spray rag anyway.

There was a mark on the wood floor. The recoil of the weapon had jerked the scaffold just a bit. One of the hard rubber wheels left a scuffmark that was about a half inch in length. Jon dug into his pocket and found a small piece of 150 grit sandpaper. A few quick buffing strokes and the black mark was gone. The dull spot left looked too new so he rubbed that with the rag until it blended in with other blemishes.

Then he began quickly disassembling the Barrett rifle and tripod. He put them into the carry bag and set it beside the door. Looking out into the empty hallway Jon then went down to another office just around the corner. He listened at the door and when satisfied no one was there, he picked the lock.

The scaffold unit was pushed into that office where he had noticed painting work going on the day before. It was after hours and the workers were gone, he left the scaffold there after wiping it down completely.

Back in his office, a quick yet thorough look around satisfied him that he was done. Jon grabbed the bag and stepped back into the hall. After peeling the remaining duct tape from the door and removing the rag, he closed the door and rode the elevator to the lobby. As the elevator doors opened, he carefully looked out, not knowing what to expect. All was clear and the Town Car sat where he had left it.

Two down...one to go, he thought to himself.

386

~

It was now more than forty minutes since Torbof had made his big impression on the red Ford Galaxy. There were six patrol cars, three detective's units, two fire trucks, an ambulance and three local TV stations on the scene.

Phil turned the crime scene over to the lead detective and called for a car to come get him. There wasn't much he could do there anymore and he wanted to be home. That feeling was strange to him. *Thirty-three years on the job and I've never felt like this*, ran through his mind as he called Sara.

"Hey!" She answered. "I saw you on TV."

"You ok?"

"Sure..." She paused. The tone of his voice suddenly bothered her. "What's wrong?"

"Nothing, nothing at all." He wanted to ask if Jon was there, but that would only cause her to wonder. "I'm on my way home. I'm done here. The detectives and the cleanup are all that's left."

"Ok," Sara told him. "I'll get dinner going. Have you heard from Jon?"

There was his answer. "Naw, not all day." He climbed into the cruiser and pulled the door closed. "He had a busy day planned, I think. See you in a few minutes."

Phil hung up and looked ahead, there was a dark colored Town Car about a block in front of them.

"Pick it up a bit," he told the driver.

As they closed the distance between them and the Town Car, Phil could see it was blue, not black like Jon's rental. The waning light of the late hour had fooled him for a minute.

"You in a hurry to get home, sir?" The driver asked.

"Yeah, I'm hungry." Phil responded as he slumped back, finally relaxing.

~

Driving up to the Winchester Building Jon noticed another police vehicle sitting at the corner. Jon gave the cop a good, long look as he went by and then parked.

He exited the Town Car and went into the building. From the office's seventeenth floor window, he looked down and watched the police vehicle slowly drive away. He didn't know for sure what to make of it.

As he closed the window he could just hear emergency vehicles in the distance. He set about his work, much the same as in the other office.

Within the hour he was packed and ready to go. The scaffold in this case was folded and left in the closet with the padlock. He would deal with it later as well as the van in the parking garage.

Jon was back at the Stone residence just before 8PM. He walked in as they were sitting at the kitchen table watching the live TV coverage of the roof collapse downtown.

"Anybody get hurt?" Jon pretended to ask.

"I think so." Phil commented as he half winked at Jon. "What a way to go, huh?"

Sara stood and went to the stove, "You hungry?" She asked. "I've got your plate in the oven."

"Please," Jon smiled. "Just let me clean up a bit. It's been a long day."

62

Breakfast that Friday morning was hardly different. Sara made eggs and bacon; Phil stared at his paper and kept one eye on the TV. Jon still had work to do. The main task was accomplished, but important details remained. He wondered just what all Phil knew or thought he knew. Didn't really matter. They weren't about to discuss it, not now anyway.

Sara excused herself from the table and left the room. Phil's paper hit the table and he leaned toward Jon, "This one goes to number one."

Jon sat up with his best look of surprise. He squinted and asked, "What?"

"On the list."

"The list?"

Now Phil was clearly getting frustrated. "The list for after I retire, dummy."

Jon took a deep breath. The humor his friend was attempting to use partly answered his question. Phil knew Jon had pulled it off, but was at a loss as to how. Those facts had to remain secrets for Jon and Silas. Phil was a good man, but the less he knew the less threat he could be in divulging anything.

"Number one." Jon smiled, "Right after we cut the cake."

~

Sharon Swanson watched the news from her hospital room. She was scheduled to be released that morning and was paying more attention to the paperwork involved with that. The mention of the dead man being tied to the Russian mob stopped her cold.

"Turn that up," she yelled.

The officer assigned to help her froze at first, then picked up the remote and began to fumble with it. Captain Swanson leaned over and grabbed it from her, hitting the volume button all in one motion.

"Vasily Torbof, General Console of the Russian Republic was killed in a fall from his consulate building roof in downtown Shreveport yesterday afternoon." the report repeated.

"I'll be damned...he did it." Swanson muttered.

"Did what, madam?" the young officer asked.

The captain looked at her assistant and grinned. "Nothing, child," she told her and stood up to smooth out her uniform. Standing tall and proud, she then asked the girl.

"Ever feel like you were in on the start of something big?"

The officer didn't know what she meant and simply gave a blank stare.

"Let's get out of here." Swanson directed. "I need to check on my men."

~

Juan Castrono sat in the den of the mansion in Dalton. The big screen TV was on the cable news channel and Juan was glued to it.

Ben walked up behind him from downstairs and Juan reached out, "Did you see this?"

"Yep, had it on in the workshop." Ben told him matter of fact like. "We'll be hearing from Jon any time now."

~

The investigators in Shreveport were at a complete loss. They knew this wasn't an accident. But what could have caused it. Witnesses on the roof saw the corner collapse and fall away. People on the street couldn't agree on the boom sounds they heard. They were from different directions and different times, yet all together.

Barksdale, AFB acknowledged aircraft were flying over the city around that time, but none were authorized to go super sonic.

"That doesn't mean it didn't happen." One experienced detective offered to the others.

The rubble presented no help. Each tiny piece was shifted and gone over. The bricks were broken and some ground into dust. Much of that dust had blown away in the wind. Physical evidence of anything causing the collapse just did not exist.

There were tiny pieces of what appeared to be a small microphone found under the front seat of the Ford Galaxy. They were bagged and tagged, but not seen as significant to the incident.

Questions turned to the people present at the time.

"What were the Hispanic Red Latin Highlanders doing there?" was asked. "Wasn't there a war between the Russians and the Hispanics?"

"Get your cultures straight, man." The senior officer responded. "It ain't all the same. Those Reds were there to sign on for something. The Russians were low on manpower, everybody on the street knew it."

His argument was insightful and accurate. The street gang members had spent the night as guests of the Shreveport Police Department, but were released about mid-day. There was nothing to hold them on.

~

Jon, aka Charles Whitley stopped by the Walker Hall Properties main office around 10:00Am that Friday. He spoke with a different agent this time. Explaining that he needed to go back to Atlanta for the week, perhaps more and asked would they keep on eye on the office till he got back.

"I have the phone company scheduled to be there Wednesday to put in a new line and would appreciate it if someone would let them in."

The agent was more then happy to help, "Certainly, Mr. Whitley. We have people who can handle that for you. What time on Wednesday did you say?"

"Between 10AM and 2PM I'm told." Jon responded. "Nasty business uptown yesterday, huh?"

"You can say that three times," the agent quipped. "That'll put a long needed hole in the drug market around here." Then he looked down just a bit, "One part of it anyway."

"A start's a start, right?" Jon asked as he headed out the door.

"That's for sure," was called out after him. "You have a good trip."

~

Daniel Seay didn't take long to understand the point of what happened in Louisiana. It did not qualify for a local story in Pittsburgh. But he did get on the phone, talking to those who shared connections through their new network.

Some immediately wanted to do stories offering acknowledgement and praise for "The Son." Daniel was quick to discourage that notion.

"If you ever want this man to offer his talents to an issue in your area, you will honor his desire for a low profile."

There was no denial on Daniel's part, but a lesson to them that knowledge is power and that power can be used or stored for a better day. The wisdom of his ideas won out. There was local and some southeastern regional coverage of the death of Torbof, but the mention of it on a national scale was left to the big networks and cable.

~

Murray Bilstock had to be told about what had happened. When Charlene called him he laughed out loud.

"Something I should know," she asked at his outburst.

"Nope..." Her brother recovered to say. "That Russian fella just wasn't a nice guy. Got what he had coming in my book."

"I thought you must have heard about him while you over there." Charlene added.

"Oh, yeah," Murray about lost it again. "That we did."

~

Word of the Russian Console's demise reached Colombia late on Friday. Lendono didn't know whether to be delighted or frightened.

He checked all the news outlets for any comment about the mysterious killer, but there was none. The evidence was actually pointing towards an unusual, but tragic accident. Storylines spoke of infrastructure decline and lack of upkeep. One mentioned the recent rains might have damaged the building foundation. Speculation ran wild. But even the Colombian gang leader noticed the lack of any compassion for the victim.

"Get Vaga on the phone," he shouted at one of his guards.

~

Jon Crane's alter identities visited both of the other real estate offices before the day was through. The courtesy calls let the leasers' know he would be away for a while and further deepened his cover from any suspicion. At around 4:45PM he called Murray.

"Can you be here in the morning?"

"Sure," the cowboy answered.

"Call as you're getting close." Jon added. "I'll come meet you."

He didn't even close the phone, just held the "hang-up" button for a few seconds and then dialed Ben.

393

"I'll be coming in tomorrow. Could you send the G5?"

"Sure, you bet." Ben was tempted to say something about the news, but he didn't. "Got notice from the school this morning," he said instead.

"Yeah?"

"I graduate at the end of the month."

"That's earlier than you thought, ain't it?"

"Yeah, a little bit," Ben said with pride. "Took a couple of exams early."

"Don't you let me forget that." Jon warned him.

"Ok, see ya tomorrow, then."

"Oh...Ben?"

"Yeah?"

"I'll be working at the warehouse a good bit while I'm there. Send some stuff over for me, will ya?"

"Will do." Ben assured him, and then asked. "Setting up some chemicals, huh?"

Jon didn't respond to that. "Congrats on the graduation, Ben. See you tomorrow." Then as an afterthought he added, "I'll be bringing Murray with me this time, set him up in my room at the house."

"Cool...I've been wanting to meet him."

Jon hung up and headed to the parking garage. It was time to turn in the van he had rented.

A quick cab ride back to the garage and he took the Town Car for a look-see at the consulate building. The car, body and rubble were all gone. Yellow tape wrapped around blue tarps that covered the corner of the roofline. There was no activity visible from the street.

63

Sebastian Cordoba had been the protégé of Carlos Morales who died in the hotel room in Shreveport. Morales had tried to set off the bomb in his backpack as Captain Stone's people rushed into his room. He didn't make it.

Sebastian spent the full time in jail with the others before ICE intervention sent them home. Tomas Vaga had a message waiting for Sebastian when he got in.

They had only talked about the job Lendono wanted done for a few minutes when Vaga's phone beeped with call waiting.

"Santonio wants to talk to you, now...please hold." The voice said.

Vaga quickly clicked over to Cordoba and told to the hold on. He was back just as the boss chimed in. "You hear about Torbof?"

He had not. He had been busy trying to find a hit man. "What? Nada, no sir."

"He's dead! Dead, I tell you. Son of Bitch falls from his roof."

Vaga was stunned. He didn't know what to say in response, so he just listened.

"There is no Russian drug gang in Louisiana. The bastard is dead."

"What do I do about the house in Georgia? I have our man to do the job."

"Yes...yes, take out that house and everyone in it. This is when we must act. Get everyone back up there, quickly." The excited leader was near rambling, "Clear the passages and get the powder moving."

"Si, yes Commander." *The respect angle had worked before,* he thought. *Why not try it again?*

Vaga heard Lendono laughing as he hung up and he clicked his phone back to Cordoba. The young man was thrilled with the chance to make good. He was similar to Dario in attitude, but not as experienced. He was all Vaga had.

"Do I report to Juan when I get there." Cordoba asked. Vaga then realized how much had happened while Sebastian and the others were out of the loop.

"No," he told him. "This you do on your own." He decided not to clutter things with all that about Castrono...or even Hanson.

"I will have a ticket for you to Monterrey by in the morning. From there you are on your own."

The young killer apprentice did not ask any particulars, but Vaga told him. "Money will be with the ticket. Buy what you need from that, including a cell phone."

Now he needed to organize the rest of the warriors and get them going. The boss was right about one thing; this was the chance they needed.

~

Lucy landed in Shreveport about an hour ahead of G5's arrival.

"Can we run by the Consulate Building," Murray asked. "I'd love to see it."

Jon appreciated his friend's interest, but even with the lighter Saturday morning traffic it would delay the schedule.

"How about we go there when we get back?" he suggested.

They did have coffee with Captain Stone in the hanger's lounge. It was Murray who broached the subject of the incident with Phil.

"Any ideas as to what happened?" he asked him.

Stone grinned around the Styrofoam cup he held in front of his face. "Not yet. Looks like the corner just fell off." He was having more trouble containing himself so he tilted his head, looking at the floor. "Weirdest thing I ever saw."

The cowboy cut his eyes over to Jon who offered no reaction. Phil coughed a couple of times and changed the subject.

"So, you guys are planning a Caribbean vacation, huh?"

Jon perked up at that. "Matt really came through for us."

"Well," Phil raised his cup as in a toast. "Be careful, both of ya and watch out for sharks."

It was Murray's turn to laugh a little. "Never rode one of them things," he cracked.

The distinctive sound of the G5 coming in stirred them into motion. They grabbed the bags, shook hands with Phil and Jon looked the officer in the eyes, "Thank Sara for me again, please. I owe you guys a bunch and I won't forget it."

"Anytime, son. You come back anytime."

They were loaded and in the air in ten minutes. No need to refuel till they got back to Dalton. The guys looked out the starboard windows to see Phil Stone standing beside the hanger with his hands on his hips. He didn't wave, but he didn't take his eyes off the jet until it was out of sight.

~

George Vincent tried to sleep in that Saturday. The full week back at work, catching up and still keeping up with Jon's exploits had taken its toll. Doris called from the hospital a little before 11:00AM.

"Marsha just heard from Jon. He's on his way here."

"Ok," George rubbed his eyes, trying to wake up. "Have the doctors been by yet?"

"Nope," she told him. "But that's a good thing. I still think she's ready to go home."

George yawned audibly and then asked. "Home here or home in Charlotte?"

"I expect she'll stay around here for a while, don't you?"

His questions unanswered, George stood and told Doris he would start getting cleaned up. "I'll be there in about an hour, ok?"

George was anxious to see Jon himself. He didn't know if he would get any answers from him either, but the news from Texas and Shreveport had the legend growing. The national police intranet was buzzing about rumors of the Son's involvement in both cases.

He realized he had lain back down across the bed. Rolling to his side and sitting back up with yet another yawn, "that was close..." he thought out loud. "Better get moving."

~

Jon talked about Shreveport with Murray on the flight. "Your input was super," he told him. "That ledge was right where you said it would be. I just had to chip away the outer layer of brick."

"That was your plan all along?" The cowboy pressed him.

Jon looked somewhat hurt by the question and didn't respond.

"I thought you were just gonna shoot the bastard." Murray proclaimed.

Still Jon remained silent.

Murray thought for a few minutes and then stretched back against the big leather seat. "You're never there...are you?"

Jon cut his eyes toward his friend, but still said nothing.

"That's it," now sitting forward with his forearms on his knees. Murray laughed, "There's always the big question...what really happened?"

Jon smiled.

The pilot broke up the one sided conversation through the intercom. "Hey, Jon. Can I ask you something...up here?"

"Sure," he hollered and then remembered he needed to push a button. "Sure, I'm on my way."

As he stepped into the flight deck area the pilot spoke up, "can I ask if you thought anymore about what we discussed?"

Jon realized he hadn't mentioned the purchase idea since that night. "Man, I'm sorry. I've been kinda busy...but that's just an excuse. I'm sorry I left you hanging."

"Yeah," the pilot commiserated. "I could tell that."

"Fact is...I had no idea how much these things cost."

"Oh yeah, they're pricy."

"I haven't justified the expense completely, but I have noticed your service."

The pilot looked straight ahead and said nothing. Jon continued, "There's a nice bonus waiting for you through Gordon's pay service."

"That wasn't necessary, sir."

"That's why I did it. I appreciate the service, your willingness to help and your attitude."

The pilot nodded.

"I still may buy one of these, or something like it one day. When I do...I hope you're available to fly it for me."

"Me, too."

64

Ben and Juan met them at the airport. They loaded most of the bags into Ben's car and then Jon reminded them his Mercury was parked there.

"I'm going straight over to the warehouse. I need to see what I have and if I might need to order some stuff."

Murray protested slightly, wanting to accompany Jon. "I don't like anybody in the area when I work with this stuff," Jon told him. "I'll explain it later. Ben will get you settled in at the house." Then he remembered the schedule, "don't get too comfortable. We go Monday...zero early thirty."

While they drove toward the mansion Ben commented, "it's a shame Daniel couldn't stay longer. He was looking forward to seeing you again."

"Daniel Seay?"

"Yeah."

"He was at Jon's house?"

"Well...yeah," Ben responded. "About the last three weeks."

Murray shook his head and mumbled under his breath, "Why am I surprised?"

As the Ford 500 turned the curve on Highway 71 the cowboy noticed a big house built into the mountain. When Ben turned up the driveway, Murray sat up with a startled look, "you're kiddin' me?"

"Nope," Ben assured him. "This is home. Wait till you see the inside."

~

Jon inventoried his chemical stocks and convinced himself he had what he would need. The delivery systems were thoughts in his

400

head at the moment and he may well need Ben's help in fabrication. He wasn't sure how helpful Juan could be with details about the residence and the jail cell office, but he planned to talk with him tonight over dinner. *Marsha would understand*, he hoped. He would stop by to see her this afternoon. But tonight must be about answering questions and securing the plan.

Matt Turlock had found them a ride into Panama and that was a good start. Getting into Colombia from Panama was another challenge altogether. He hoped Juan's knowledge and experience with the area could help.

The little he'd been able to look up about the border was not good news. Even though Panama had once been a part of Colombia, travel between the two countries was anything but simple.

The Pan American highway, which connects Alaska to Chile has one short section that is incomplete. It's known as the Darian Gap and it sits right on the border of Panama and Colombia. The area is a mass of heavy jungle with humid swamps and stories of paramilitary groups occupying the region. Crossing the area is a challenge both physically and mentally.

Challenges never cease. He thought.

~

Max Sneal was working on a plan. He stared out at the Atlantic from his room in his parent's home, a two-story beauty on the beach in Indiatlantic, Florida. Max's dad had been an investment banker prior to the government take over of the banking system. He retired five days before the new rules took effect with a tidy sum stuck aside.

Max remembered a college friend, from that one semester he attended, who worked at Disney in Orlando. It took calls to four other contacts to finally get his number.

"Jerry?" he started the call. "It's Max...Sneal. Max Sneal from Coastal."

401

"Oh, yeah," the slightly at a loss former friend replied.

"How's it going, man?"

"You know...working." Jerry told him.

The conversation went into where and what he did at the park. It seems Jerry worked in the "It's a Small World" ride as a lighting technician. He changed light bulbs that burned out. Small World was one attraction no one missed so everything had to be just so.

"Do you think you could get me on?" Max asked bluntly.

"I don't know, man." Jerry hedged and then thought of something. "We've got vacation time coming up. Different guys want time off so we need a replacement for 'em."

"That would be great."

"Don't jump the gun, man. I mean...I got to check it out with my super."

"I've got a couple of friends who could use the work too." Max added.

"Give me your number, man." Jerry told him. "I'll get back to you."

Jerry wasn't comfortable at all with the phone call. He reopened his cell phone and pushed the button for his older brother.

"Hey, you're awake on a Saturday?" the voice answered.

"Listen..." Jerry started slowly. "I don't know how to explain this, but something is weird about a call I just got."

The older brother gave his sibling a chance to gather his thoughts before asking any questions. "Just what was weird about it?"

"Some guy I hardly knew in school just called."

"School...high school or what?"

"Coastal College. We were in, maybe one class once." Jerry remembered. "We might have gone out for a beer or two with some other guys, I don't remember."

Feeling his brother getting anxious over the situation, the elder brother again let him calm down. Then asked the serious questions. "What did he want, Jerry?"

"He wanted to know about a job at Wally World...and not just for him, for several guys it sounded like."

"He thinks you can get him a job at Disney?"

"Yeah, I guess. I kinda told him we had some openings at times for fill in work."

Jerry could hear a desk phone ring and his brother asked him to hang on a second. He could hear over the cell phone as big brother did his job. "Major Crimes Unit, Detective Nelson speaking."

The Orlando police officer took some information from the caller and was back with Jerry in a few minutes.

"Look," he told his younger brother. "It could be just a guy trying to find work or it could be something else. Let me check on a couple things that might have bearing on this and I'll call you back." He was making notes as he spoke. "I may want you to go through with this deal for him and his friends."

"Really?" Jerry didn't understand. "I can't do that myself."

"I know...if it goes that far we'll pull some strings to make it happen. Might be more to it than just a job. Like I said...let me look into a few things."

Detective Nelson had just been alerted to the fact that a high profile guest was planning a trip to Disney World next week. The police had the task of preparing for the worst in visits like this. Getting caught flat-footed was not an option.

~

The K-Lind was out of Hampton, Virginia. She was a shrimper, but had been refitted to drag crab nets. Late that Saturday the men pulled the nets up and they found more than blue crab. A severed hand in one net and a piece of a thighbone with some tissue intact was stuck to another.

They called the Coast Guard who took the remains in with them. Any identification would have to be through DNA. One coroner who met the Coast Guard cutter wondered if there was even enough tissue left to sample.

"Been in the water a little over a week," he declared to the news media. "It's gonna take some time to figure out who we got here." Then for effect, he turned back to the camera with a smirk and added, "or maybe whom all."

The hand had been detached in a rough, tearing manner yet the palm had a smooth cut running crosswise. The appearance indicated a potential defensive wound.

Large ships were brought in below where the parts were located to drag the bottom and the shoreline. The friends of the Stubblefields were notified, as was the congressman.

He didn't react with any emotion.

65

Doris Shaw gave him a big hug as he entered the room. "You've been busy, I hear?" She teased him.

"I sure hope you haven't overdone everything." Jon said with a wry smile. "How's my girl?"

"I'm fine." Marsha answered as she threw off the sheet and stood up from the hospital bed.

"Whoa...are you supposed to be doing that?" Jon reacted.

"She's going home Monday, they say." Doris piped in. "Question is...where's home?"

"She can go to my house," he volunteered.

Marsha tilted her head to one side, "you going to be there?"

Jon looked a bit sheepish and rubbed his forehead before speaking. "I'll be back by the end of the week."

Sitting back down, Marsha nodded that she understood. Her body language said otherwise.

Doris broke the new silence, "How about I go home and fix up a guest room for her? She can stay with us till you get back."

Before Jon could respond Marsha agreed. "Thank you." She said to Doris. "That will be nice."

Doris hugged Jon again and picked up her purse. "You two have a nice afternoon." And she headed out.

"It's great to see her walk without that cane." Jon tried.

Marsha lay down and gave him her best, disgusted look.

"Where to now, that's so all fired important?"

"It's almost over. There are still a couple of loose ends that can't be let go." He remained in the same spot he had stood since he got there.

Her female side wanted to argue with him. But her training and experience, which were coming back to her fast, convinced her that he was right. She patted the edge of the bed, "Come here."

He stayed with her until just before 7:30PM. He was to meet the guys at Longhorns out by the interstate around 8PM.

"I'll come by tomorrow before we leave."

Marsha blinked and nodded without answering. Her look was of concern, but she said nothing.

~

Silvia Torbof was packed and nearly ready to leave. Her husband's body had been autopsied and released to her earlier in the day. It and the exhumed body of her son would be shipped home to Rostov next week.

She was not directly in touch with the group in Pestrovo, but they had made a decision. The gathering troops would have no one to report to, no mission to achieve and therefore no purpose. They hated losing the revenue from that area. But for now, there was little they could do.

"Send Mrs. Torbof whatever funds she requires to get home." The leader in Pestrovo commanded. "Shut down the operations there and close the consulate until the government picks it up."

The Russian government never sanctioned the additional consulate building for legitimate means so that would be that.

"What about the product that is there?" one underling asked.

"Do you want to go retrieve it?"

"No, sir."

The boss glared at first and then nodded his head. "We write it off and remember what happened there."

"And the Colombians?"

"They have their own problems as I hear it." The leader then stood to leave the room. He looked back at the men there. "With this myth running around creating havoc on them...the DeMarcos clan." He looked serious and thoughtful as he considered his words. "I give them two weeks...tops." He stepped back towards his men in a warning posture, "There will be a void for sure...but I want no part of it." As he again turned to leave he muttered under his breath, "I do not know of fighting ghosts."

~

The Longhorn was winding down by the time Jon arrived. This restaurant catered to early diners and 8PM was late for their crowd.

Ben's car was there and he checked his watch to see if he was late. He wasn't.

They were in a large booth near the rear. Ben knew what to ask for so they could have some privacy and talk. Murray was controlling the conversation as he walked up, no surprise.

"Hey, how's the girlfriend doing?" He asked with all sincerity.

"She's good, thanks. Have you guys ordered?"

"Just drinks," the cowboy told him. "What are you having?"

Jon asked for an iced tea, no sugar and sat down. "Did you bring the folder?" he asked Ben who reached down and handed it to him in one motion.

Ben spoke up, "I couldn't find any better way to get in there." He opened his hands at the table level in a gesture. "There's not much information about that "gap" area."

Juan looked over at Ben, but said nothing. Jon nodded acceptance of what Ben had to say and changed the topic slightly. "Ok, Juan...what can you offer about inside the country. The prison area and his beach house?"

Juan had been thinking about that question being asked for a day or two. He pulled a wrinkled piece of paper from his coat and unfolded it. He handed the notes to Jon and began a recap of what he had written.

407

The insights were very good and Jon was impressed. Juan explained how he had worked on the staff of Sergio DeMarcos. He was an accountant and reported directly to Tomas Vaga in Bogotá. He knew of Lendono and knew the real orders came through him.

Several years ago he accompanied Vaga to the Prison cell in Sabanalarga. They were there for two weeks and then traveled with Lendono to Turbo. The Cartel was preparing to send mules to the U.S. through Panama.

"You know the routes they took?" Jon asked him.

"Si, some went by boat across the Gulf of Uraba, others used the tunnels along the coast."

The table got quiet and everyone looked at Jon. He leaned across to Juan and nearly whispered, "They have tunnels across the gap?"

"Si." Juan nodded. "The main one is on the coast. There are two others." He revealed. " But they were rumored to flood in the fall."

They talked and drew maps and pictures of the prison compound, the Turbo beach house and access to both. Travel time between Sabanalarga and Turbo was estimated at six to seven hours because of the terrain.

The Turbo house was near an airport and a National Guard post. Another set of facts to consider. "The LaGuardia do not come when Lendono is there. It is an agreement the government has with the family." Juan told them.

"Who is at the beach house when he is in Sabanalarga?" Jon asked.

"No one. It sits empty until he needs it."

"No guards to keep it safe from robbery?"

Juan laughed, "To steal from the family is suicide. It is not done."

Jon asked why Lendono was now out in the open.

"Sergio must be ill." Juan was certain. "I haven't been in a position to hear anything, but for Santonio to be out running things directly, DeMarcos is sick...or dead."

There was more discussion and planning. Jon asked Ben if he could adapt the first black suit to fit Murray?

"Sure, you guys are close to the same size...no problem." Ben smiled.

Jon kept many of his ideas to himself; he needed time to think them through. He announced that he would spend the night back at the warehouse getting "things" ready. "Things" meant chemicals and Ben knew Jon allowed no one around while he worked with those. He had been outside a containment barrier on the floor once, but only because of the work he needed to do for the delivery devise.

"Be packed, ready to go at 7PM tomorrow evening. I will pick you two up at the house. We drive the first leg."

Jon went back to the warehouse and applied his new information to the plan. He contacted Daniel at home in Pennsylvania.

"Can you create a fake story for me that will get picked up in South America?"

"Sure," Daniel laughed. "No problem. I'll just figure a soccer angle for it."

"Seriously," Jon realized how ridiculous his request was; yet he had to try. "I need a bad guy in Colombia to think I'm there now, in his country."

Daniel thought and told him, "I know an editor in Miami who could run a rumor about that. The Cuban community would be good fodder for it. The story should spread to Latin America at least."

"Try it, please. We won't leave until Monday early. But I need him to believe I'm already there."

"I'll do all I can. Who's 'we'?"

"Murray and Juan are going."

"You've never led a team on one of these deals, have you?"

"What kind of deal is that, Daniel?" Jon shot back.

"Ok, be careful."

"Always, Daniel my friend...always."

If the story got to Colombia, that would help. But he still had to be ready for anything. Without being able to scout the victim's territory first, he would have to have options before he left. All with the same basic task, but flexible to contingencies they might run into. He studied the maps Juan had given him, over and over.

He fell asleep on the old couch in the warehouse at around 2:15AM.

~

Jon was packed in one bag. The lethal chemicals were compacted and sealed in silicon tubes that would not breach. He left the warehouse at 9AM and went straight to the hospital.

"Knock, knock..."he said as he pushed the door. "I've got muffins."

Marsha was up, sitting in the big chair a blanket wrapped around her. "Hi." She said meekly.

"Something wrong?"

"No. I just worry." She looked out the window away from him, "is this how it's going to be from now on?"

"I can't say." There was no delay in his answer. "You know what I do." He thought of telling her about Representative Stubblefield and his mistake on him. But that wouldn't help anything. He didn't even like to think about it.

"Can we have a nice day or would you rather I leave?"

She turned back to him and forced a smile. "Muffins, you say?"

66

Detective Charles Nelson was bothered by his younger brother's call. His sixth sense, or whatever you want to call it was already kicking him. Then, when the posting for volunteers to guard a U.S. Congressman's trip to Disney World came across his computer screen, he stood up behind his desk and called for his partner.

"Steve," he barked. "Let me run something by you."

After sharing what he knew about the call Jerry had received, Charles had Steve agreeing the coincidence was too strong to be ignored. They went to their Lieutenant.

"There's an alert for things like this nationwide." The Lieutenant told them. "Can your brother get back to this guy?"

"Yeah, he's more or less expecting to hear from him."

Flipping through his business card folder, he found the one he sought. Human Resources, Walt Disney Corporation it read, and a phone number.

"What area does your brother work in?"

"It's a Small World."

The Lieutenant's face wrinkled up, "Geez...I hate that song."

"Tell me about it." Nelson answered.

"I'll get Disney to work with us. You have your brother tell these guys it's on. I'd rather try another day, but the congressman's schedule is already out there."

"So we get one try, if we're right." Steve threw in.

"Better than none at all, right?" Charles reminded him.

~

Mid-way through Sunday afternoon, Marsha had gotten into stories about her Dad. Jon didn't mind. The exercise was good for

Marsha's memory rebuilding and besides, he didn't have to pay that close of attention. He tried to hide it, but he was preoccupied with his planning, mentally.

The ideas he had were all workable. Even though they depended on events he could not be sure would happen. Normally he would be more convinced of direction by now. As he listened, he replayed scenarios and results over and over.

"I remember this time," Marsha continued her reminiscing. "When I got so mad at Daddy. He let my best friend 'borrow' my diary."

He wasn't sure why, but Jon looked at her and started to pay better attention.

"She got into my secrets and the lists I had of all my friends... in the order of how I liked them..." she complained loudly.

"What?" Jon sat up straight and asked her to repeat that last part.

"She found my secrets."

"And what else?" Jon was excited and grabbing at his cell phone.

"My list of friends?" Marsha didn't quite understand what she had said.

Jon pushed the button to call Ben and looked at Marsha, "Where do we keep our lists of friends today?"

Marsha thought for a second and then smiled, "In our cell phones."

"Bingo!" Jon reached out and shook her leg as Ben answered the line.

"Ben," Jon tried to rein himself in. "How is that satellite link up program of yours working?"

"Fine." There was a question in his voice.

"Can you track a cell phone with it?"

"If I have the number, sure."

"Can you hijack the info on the sim card?"

Ben now thought he knew where Jon was headed with this. "I should be able to download everything on it."

"Excellent. Get three or four international phones and add them to the bag for me."

"Got it."

"Oh...is Juan nearby?" Jon asked.

Ben didn't respond in words...he just handed Juan the phone.

"Si...I mean, yes, sir."

"Juan... who was your contact again?"

"Tomas Vaga."

"Can you call him?"

"He was trying to have me killed, I threw away the phone with his number."

"But can you remember the number?" Jon was prodding him.

Juan was quiet as he thought. He finally answered, "Si, I mean...yes, I remember."

"Write it down. I may want you to use it for me while we're on our trip."

~

The story in the Miami Herald caught Lendono's eye. "The Son" the story said, was rumored to be on his way to Colombia. No one was credited as a source for this tale; it was more a human-interest piece. The idea was, this patriotic killer wanted to close out business with a drug cartel. The story all but named Argus and the DeMarcos family with its innuendo and the gang leader was livid.

"Where would he go?" Lendono asked Vaga over the phone.

"I do not know. This was not in the Panamanian paper and the Miami paper was sold out this morning. I was late getting to the store, Sergio had another bad night."

413

"Is it known that Sergio is in Panama?" Lendono asked him.

"No...it should not be. We took all the precautions."

"Then this man will go to Bogotá to find DeMarcos, no?"

"One would believe, yes...I think so." Vaga agreed.

"Ok," the boss felt better somehow. "Do all that can be done for my brother-in-law."

"Si, commander." Tomas was getting good at kissing up. "Are you still in Sabanalarga?"

"And...I shall stay here till I can arrange proper guards for the beach house. Say, tell me our hit man has made it to the U.S."

"He has, sir." Tomas left out the part about the delay. "He should be in Georgia, soon."

"Keep me informed." Lendono ordered and hung up.

~

Jon drove up in the Mercury and they loaded the gear. Ben showed him the cleaned up black suit and the one altered slightly for Murray.

"I made a chest protector for Juan, just in case," he told Jon who nodded in approval.

Jon gathered them around and told the men what to expect. "We have about a seven hour drive to the pick-up spot. Our flight leaves at 04:30 military time so we have time." He looked to see if they had any questions. "We should be in Panama by noon tomorrow."

Ben handed him an extra bag, "Cell phones for that deal we talked about."

Jon acknowledged him with a smile and a handshake. "Stay near your cell phone tonight, ok?"

"Understood." The younger man smiled back and then quickly offered good wishes to the other two.

"That funny suit ain't like no cheap hotel is it?" Murray chided him.

414

Ben looked confused and didn't answer so Murray paid off the joke, "A cheap hotel ain't got no ball room." And he laughed by himself.

Ben smirked and threw back, "Depends on the size of the party, I suppose." Which drew a good laugh from everyone.

The Mercury turned its lights on as they got to the highway and quickly disappeared out highway 71 and into the night.

~

"We'll have guests this morning," Captain Willingham announced. "Anyone with a problem, speak up now."

Everett Willingham flew Air Force C-130J – Super Hercules cargo planes for a living. His five-person crew had flown together for six years. They knew what he meant by "guest". With no one stating a concern with the plan they set about the pre-flight ready check. Willingham pulled his executive officer to one side.

"They're driving down right now. Is there room for a car in the back hanger? It will need to be there most of the week."

Liz Murdock answered right away. "We just had a AFIA inspection last week so nothing is due for a while. There's plenty of room and we'll cover it. Bring 'em on." She told him. Liz was a First Lieutenant and first officer on Willingham's Hercules. They had carried DEA agents and NCIS specialists many times on clandestine trips. The drug war sometimes needed a little "help." Willingham was more than willing to do that.

He drove out to Interstate 75 near a spot called Morven, about a mile from the town of Hahira, Georgia. Around 03:00 headlights approached his Suburban at a slow speed. He blinked his lights twice and the Mercury sedan blinked three times.

As the men exited their car, Willingham stepped toward them. "Silas among you?" he asked.

"That would be me," Jon responded. "You must be Willie."

They shook hands and Jon introduced Murray and Juan to the Captain. Willingham explained where they could leave the car. "Stay close and follow me back to the base." The pilot climbed back into his vehicle. They were on their way.

The suburban slowed at the one-man guard shed and issued instructions to the lone attendant. The uniformed airman then waved the Mercury through and they followed Willie to the hanger.

As Willie parked the suburban and walked back to them again, another airman also came up to the car.

"He'll take it from here," Willie told Jon. "We'll take good care of her while you're away."

Jon and the others took their bags and walked with the Captain toward the large aircraft. It was lit-up and all engines running. The rear cargo slide was open and Willingham led them up into the airship.

"We don't have leather seats, I'm afraid." He half laughed as he pointed to the side mounted jump seats. "Just pull those down and strap in when we get ready to go." Huge crates and a large T-20 Communications Van were tied down along the mid-section of the cargo bay.

"That stuff will float a bit while we're in the air...don't let that bother you."

Juan looked at Murray and held his hand out straight. Then lifting the palm up and down in a floating motion until Murray slapped him on the back.

"It'll be ok, little buddy." he told him. "It'll be ok."

Jon paid little attention to Juan's concerns as he moved forward in the cargo area to a spot where the jump seats were replaced by heavy rope netting. Unhooking one edge, Jon placed his main bag into the net and wrapped it against the sidewall of the plane. Murray and Juan soon did the same.

416

They went back outside and followed the Captain in his walk around inspection and before they knew it, it was time to go.

The Hercules rolled out the taxiway to a southbound runway. Engines running at a pace that made a Nascar race sound tame, Captain Willingham released the brakes at exactly 04:20 and they were airborne shortly after.

The trip was uneventful, with the exception of Juan losing some of his dinner while watching the large green van lift off the deck in front of him.

They landed at the old Howard Air Force Base at 11:40AM. It was hot, it was sticky humid and they were in Panama.

The huge rear door laid down and the air became thick. It was as though they had forgotten how to breathe. The shock of the heavy, humid air was soon overcome by the heat, which seemed to radiate like a convection oven.

The concrete stretched in every direction. Some was cracked and worn. Obviously it had been let go since the bulk of the military left. Larger gaps even had grass growing up to a foot tall through those crevices.

The sections that were currently used as runways were in much better shape, kept clear and clean. They were maintained and patched where needed. But the expansive concrete meant heat, unrelenting heat.

The sun reflected up from the thick, flat surface with a vengeance. Murray seemed to fare the best with the change in climate.

Though Juan was from the area, he appeared to wilt as fast as Jon. "It's been some time since I was down here," came out through labored breathing. "You adjust pretty quick, really." Juan added for reassurance.

Jon smiled and cut his eyes towards Murray. The cowboy was already standing just off the ramp, looking around.

The buildings in sight were like the concrete. Some kept up and some not, since the main Air Force Battalion left over twenty-five years ago. The base was a supply-receiving depot now. Guarded by a few old F-16s scattered about and some helicopter gun ships sitting over close to one hanger.

With perspiration running down his sides, not even touching his shirt Jon thanked Captain Willingham. Then the pilot and his C-130 crew rolled to their unloading point. They would be back in the air within the hour and home just after dinner.

The three visitors and their gear headed to a covered table just outside a small building. "Willie" had pointed it out as a place they could figure out what to do next.

Acclamation would take a bit longer, but they were able to converse after a few minutes under the shade.

With a huge exhale; Jon tried to jest, "Whose idea was this, anyway?"

~

The city of Monterrey was familiar to Sebastian Cordoba. On the last trip up to the U.S. only a few weeks ago, they were allowed free time in Monterrey. Sebastian had met a girl then. His orders, this trip, were to get to Georgia. But he figured there was time for a short side trip.

The bus to Reynosa ran everyday so he exchanged his pre-purchased ticket for Monday morning's trek. Crossing the Rio Grande wasn't the problem it once had been. The executive ordered amnesty of 2012 all but killed the desire for enforcement along the border. Ferrys operated openly, twenty-four hours a day and transportation to McAllen, Texas was also available.

From there he must get to San Antonio where a package awaited him in a locker at a UPS store. The package would contain clothes, papers, and cash. What he did not understand was that he was expected in San Antonio a full day prior to when he got there. The package had been removed.

He used his last bit of cash to purchase a pre-paid cell phone and desperately called for Tomas Vaga.

"Que pasa?" he pleaded. "Dónde está mi dinero...where's my money?"

"You're late." Vaga challenged him.

"Missed the bus, sorry sir."

"Come back to the store tomorrow. It will be there in the name Fernando Jones."

"Si."

"Don't be late, again."

"No, lamento...I'm sorry."

67

Ben had been half awake most of the night, waiting to see if he was needed. A short while past noon his phone rang and the incoming number was one of the international cell phones.

"Ok," Jon said. "You ready?"

"I take it you made it?"

"Oh...yeah." Jon stumbled. "Sorry, I'm just focused right now. It's been a long night."

Ben let it pass, "Ok. I've got your number. Which phone is Juan going to use?"

Jon called out both the serial and phone number assigned to the unit and turned it on. "Can you find this one?"

Ben tuned in and gave the system a minute to lock in. "Damn!" He said. "This is cool. There you are...in Panama."

"Good, stay on that signal. I'm having Juan call his contact now."

It took Tomas several rings to respond. He didn't recognize the calling number, yet no one was supposed to have his number. He finally gave in to curiosity.

He answered in Spanish, first saying simply... "Hello?"

Juan also spoke in their native tongue, "Tomas? This is Juan Castrono."

There was long silence before Tomas Vaga spoke again. "Juan, where are you?"

Jon had rehearsed the dialog with Juan before the call. "I'm in Miami." Success made him smile, but he maintained his composure, "I need to get to you, Tomas." He continued and he nodded to Jon who was several feet away.

Jon spoke to Ben... "He's on, you got him?"

Within a minute Ben answered. "Yeah I got him. But something ain't right."

"What?"

"That signal is coming from Panama too."

Jon looked at Juan and circled his forefinger in a loop. Juan understood what it meant. *Keep asking questions... find out what you can.*

"Are you in Bogotá with Sergio?" Juan asked.

The question caught Vaga off guard and honesty broke through. "No, Sergio is ill." He caught himself as he said it, but what was done was done.

"So, you are in Panama, then?" Juan guessed as he stared at Jon. The family did not trust the Colombian hospitals under normal conditions. Serious illness would send them to Panama where left over American technology was available.

"Si, the Ancon Hospital. He is very sick." Vaga told him.

Juan started pointing at the ground furiously.

'Ben," Jon whispered. "Tap that phone and get everything you can. It is in Panama."

Ben started typing in commands and within thirty seconds a page began to print across the room.

"Got it, Jon." He half yelled into the phone. "The whole sim card. There's eight numbers on here."

"Anything labeled Lendono?" Jon asked.

"There's a S.L."

"That's got to be it...give me that number."

Juan continued to talk to Vaga who was trying to manipulate the call for his benefit. "Why did you run, Juan?"

"Hanson sent a man to kill me, Tomas. Why would he do that?"

"You know Hanson did that?"

"Si, I know. I was with him when the dark agent killed him."

"The what?" Vaga didn't believe what he was hearing. "Dark agent?"

Juan had to cover the mouthpiece and get a grip on himself. It was working. Vaga was taking the bait. "Si, Tomas." He said with exaggerated excitement. "The one they call The Son got him. He's coming after Sergio and Lendono, too."

Vaga froze. This sounded too much like the rumors that were in the paper. "How did you get away from him?" He asked Juan.

"I am not important. He only kills the important ones."

"He told you he was going to Colombia?"

"Yes." Juan paused a second. "That was four days ago."

"I must go," Tomas told Juan. "Can I call you at this number?"

Jon whispered to Ben again, "Stay on that new number...he's gonna make a call that can confirm what we have."

"Si," Juan responded to Vaga and hung up.

Ben monitored the other number originating from Panama. It indeed called the number listed for S.L. and when Ben traced its location it came up Northern Colombia.

"The north coastal part of Colombia," he told Jon. "And it sounds like he's talking to his boss."

Jon looked at Juan, who had been conversing in a mix of English and Spanish with his old co-worker. "I hope I can trust everything you told him."

"You can," Murray spoke up.

Jon turned to Murray with a questioning stare. The cowboy went on. "I know a bit of Spanish. I grew up around it... He said what you wanted him to."

Juan smiled at Murray and Jon simply shook his head up and down.

"Thanks." He said to Juan.

~

With Ben listening in, and recording because he didn't understand Spanish, Lendono and Vaga discussed the call from Juan.

"He says the man is coming for you...and Sergio."

"Where will he go first?"

"I do not know. Are you still in Sabanalarga?"

"Yes. I can't get any men to guard the beach house. They want money I don't have."

"What about Juan?" Vaga asked.

"Take him out, quickly," the boss said without emotion. "Can you divert your man to Miami? Have Juan wait for you somewhere there and ... problem solved."

"I'll set it up today." Tomas assured him."

~

Max Sneal was ecstatic. He turned into the Sledge driveway in Indiatlantic, Florida and almost hit the car parked there.

Nicky heard the commotion and opened the door. His lip was doing much better.

"What the hell?" he screamed at the visitor.

"I got us in, Nicky." Max bobbed up and down. "I thought of this guy I know... and I got us in."

"In where, dude?"

"Disney, man. I got us into Disney when the mark is gonna be there."

Nicky looked around and pulled his over-exuberant guest inside the house. "Keep it down, man." His face was completely serious at this point. "What are you telling me?"

"The congress dude you want will be at Disney this Thursday, right?"

Nicky nodded, but still looked confused.

"I got us jobs at the 'Small World' ride starting tomorrow morning." He waited for that to soak in and then went on, "all we do is sit around waiting for lights to go out."

Sledge couldn't believe it. It had to be providence. Part of him said it was too easy, but the "sponsors" didn't exactly give him much time to plan. The phrase with "gift horse and mouth" in it ran through his mind.

"This is for sure, the jobs I mean?" he asked seriously.

"Yes." Max reiterated yet again.

"Where do we stay?" Sledge thought of a problem.

"They have a guest house for new guys...and get this...it's free for two weeks!"

A knot formed in the leader's stomach. *"This was wrong,"* he told himself again. *"It's too easy."* He feared this plan. But when he considered the alternative, he feared the "sponsors" more.

"Get Jo-Jo. We leave this afternoon," he ordered Max. "Tell him to bring the guns."

68

Jon knew where his prey was. Now he had to get to him. The distance from where they were to where they wanted to be was not that far...but it was tough territory to cross. He asked around about a boat and was not getting anywhere. The idea of the tunnels didn't appeal to him, at all. It would take too long, plus he knew the released men from Shreveport would be on their way back to the U.S. He didn't want to walk into six or fifteen guys in a tunnel heading the other way.

He noticed a small bi-plane and headed toward the man standing with it.

"I was told you take passengers." Jon started.

The old man spit on the ground and slowly looked up at him. "Maybe."

"I need to get into Colombia."

The man looked him over with distain. "Drug runner, huh?"

"Not really." Jon smiled.

The old man turned away, pretending to check on a strut from a wing. "It used to be easy." He said where Jon could hear him. "These days they come out to check you as you land."

"Can you land somewhere unconventional?" Jon suggested.

"Now you're talking about how to get shot," the man spun back around and stepped up to Jon, nose to nose. "Right on the spot."

The elderly pilot glared at Jon, his hot, chili pepper breath cutting through the humid air. Jon held his ground. The old man grunted, turned away and began to leave.

"What do you suggest, then?" Jon called after him.

The disgruntled pilot stopped and appeared to be giving the question some consideration before he turned back to Jon. "I know a man with a fishing boat." He stood still as Jon again approached him and then continued. "He went out this morning and goes out again Wednesday." Spitting again, the old man finished, "Best I can do."

"I'll think about it...thanks for your time." Jon tried to hide his disappointment. This was the weakest part of his plan. It's why he normally made advance trips to check things out. *Wednesday would be too late*, he thought. As he excused himself and walked back to the covered area off the tarmac, he noticed Murray coming toward him. He had another man in uniform with him.

~

Murray had found some fling wing birds. A squadron of Black Hawk Helicopters sat on the runway with rotors in gear. He approached the aircraft in a wide circle, staying clear of the tail rotors.

You a rotor head?" the voice called out. "I see you clearing the tourist killer." That was slang for the tail rotor. "Rotor head" meant someone familiar with helicopters or a pilot at best.

As he turned to face the challenger, the man sounded off again, "Dusty? ... Are you kidding me? Is that the Dusty Bilstock?" An ambulance pilot was known as a "dust off" or a "duster." The term was respectful.

Murray stared at the Chief Warrant Officer coming to him and finally recognized a soldier he had evacuated from under enemy fire in Afghanistan over nine years ago.

"I know you." Murray stumbled. "But forgive me, sir. Your name escapes me." He admitted.

"That's fine. You are excused." The officer wasn't at all insulted. "You pulled a bunch of us outta there that day." The Chief Warrant Officer introduced himself as Luke Diaz. The name still meant nothing. "You flew that little machine in with Taliban all around us. You saved my life, man." He stuck out his hand and Murray took it. "You were a legend over there. I asked who you were and they said

426

Bilstock. The Huey jocks were known as "dusters" so everybody called you "Dusty."

"Guess I heard about that a little." Murray smiled. "Good to see you're still flying."

"Oh...I wasn't flying then. I was a grunt. What you did made me want to fly."

"So, you work on the Black Hawks now?"

"You could say that." Diaz said, nodding profusely. "I'm Commander of that wing you see before you. Twelve birds." He smiled with a great deal of pride. "Want to go for a spin?"

Murray's face lit up. "I just might take you up on that." He smiled and blurted straight out, "Could you take me and a couple other fellas to Colombia?"

"Colombia?" The CWO stepped back. "Whoa...you haven't gone druggie on us, have you?"

"Hell, no." Murray's expression suddenly went to very serious. "Quite the opposite, but that's all I can say."

"That's still a tall order." Diaz said as he rubbed the bridge of his nose and looked across the flight line. His hand then climbed to his forehead as he thought. With his face turned away, looking at his birds he finally asked, "When do you want to go?"

"You can do that?" Murray was almost stunned.

"I've got some training hours left this month." Looking back at the man who had saved him so long ago. "Hurry before I change my mind, though." He laughed.

"Come with me," Murray coaxed. "I want you to meet my friend."

"Is that the Captain Midnight character you came in with?"

Murray remembered that slang term. "Captain Midnight" meant a bad assed, highly skilled, nighttime commando. "You could say that." Murray answered. "You sure could."

It was then that they walked over toward Jon who was returning from his discussion at the bi-plane.

"Jon," Murray called out. "Meet Warrant Officer Luke Diaz. He's offered us a ride into country."

Jon looked surprised and pleased with caution also mixed in. He shook the man's hand, "What have you got?" he asked.

"Twelve Black Hawks." Diaz grinned.

~

The autopsy in Maryland identified the hand found by the shrimp boat. The hand belonged to Henry Wilcox, the boyfriend of Stubblefield's daughter. The cut on the palm was made by a large blade knife and was pre-mortem. It was what the coroner called a "defensive wound". Investigators opted to wait for the other results due to the sensitivity of the case. You didn't charge a sitting congressman without proper evidence. The news was kept in house, other than limited police notification. Heavy pressure was put on the DNA analysis team who were working on the thighbone.

~

Juan's phone rang. The one he had called Vaga with. He and Jon walked away from the others so Juan could answer.

"I am coming to bring you home." Tomas told him. "Wait for me at the South Beach Towers, in Miami. I'll be there in the morning."

Juan knew what that meant. He agreed verbally though he had no intention of going. It struck him to add something to the fear Lendono must already feel. "The killer only knows about the prison. He asked me questions about it. I'm sure he's going there first."

Tomas didn't comment, but it was confirmed through Ben that he immediately called Lendono.

"This fills in the spaces." Jon smiled. "Now...he will come to me." He looked at the maps of the Turbo area and asked Diaz for an opinion. The officer leaned over the map and spread it out further, opening it more to the south.

"This is Turbo," he said. Moving his hand down he continued, "this is the airport and below that the National Guard post."

He stood and smiled for a minute. "We've done this gig before. We go in hugging the coast over the Gulf of Uraba. Staying low, say 100 feet or so. We follow the coastline as it curves back up toward Turbo."

He flipped through the maps on the table looking for something specific. "Here we go," he said putting the close up view of Turbo on top. "Turbo sits just north of a peninsula that hangs into the Gulf, kinda like a limp...."

"Yeah, I see." Jon interrupted.

"Anyway," the Black Hawk Commander continued. "The bottom of that peninsula is where the National Guard base is." He stood up and added, "Just above that is the airport. There's hardly any traffic there at all."

"Where is Lendono's house?" Murray asked.

Juan leaned over the map and pointed to a spot right on the coast, just north of the town.

The Army Officer nodded and picked up again, "We fly in from below the Guard base, right at them, all twelve, spread out wide and low...they won't know whether to shit or go blind."

No one said a word, *this was so nuts it makes sense.* Jon thought quietly.

"Then," Diaz continued, "we spread out all over the southern area of the peninsula, cris-crossing and giving them plenty to look at." He placed his hand over the area near the water that Juan had pointed out. "This is Lendono's house. We set you right on the roof...touch and go, you have to be quick. Then we weave our way back out." The copter commander leaned back. "When the Colombians call to complain, we don't know what they're talking about."

Murray looked at Jon who was expressionless. Juan sat with his eyes as big as silver dollars.

"Lendono should be on the move within the hour, I would think. They say it's a six to seven hour drive to Turbo. I bet he makes it in five." The cowboy said.

Jon stood and asked the warrant officer, "Can we go pretty soon?"

Diaz turned toward his pilots and whistled. The men all turned in unison and headed toward a small building. "Give me thirty minutes to explain the flight plan to my guys."

As Diaz walked away Jon's phone rang. It was Ben. He played the recording of the last call Vaga had just made to Lendono for Juan to translate.

"He not leaving Sabanalarga till in the morning. Something about his car not being ready."

Murray jumped and ran toward Diaz, "Hey." He hollered out. "Can we do this in the morning?"

The commander didn't take long at all to agree, "Sure," he answered. "That's really good cause now we can go into Balboa for dinner tonight."

"Balboa?" Murray asked.

"Yeah...it used to be a Canal Company town before Carter gave it all away. Got a couple of good restaurants there."

"Ok, we got to eat."

Jon had sat quiet for several minutes, looking at the maps. He finally raised his gaze up to Diaz with a question. "How do we get back here?"

The copter commander paused for effect before his answer.

"You plan to survive this then?"

Nobody thought that was funny other than him. He quickly tried to recover with, "See that sliver just off the coast?" while pointing to the map and a small thin peninsula dropping down toward Turbo. Diaz took a blank card from his vest pocket and wrote a number on it.

Handing the card to Jon, he said. "Call me on this number as you leave the mainland toward that spot." And he pointed out an area on the peninsula. "I can be there in thirty minutes." He looked at them with the most serious expression they had yet seen from him. "I can make one pass in. If you're there I'll set down...if you're not...I'll have to go."

"You'll be in your Hawk?" Murray asked.

"Nope." Diaz pointed to a small Robinson R-22 personal helicopter sitting at the end of the tarmac. "They will be on alert by then." He grinned while explaining. "I can get in under their radar in that."

The Robinson R-22 is small aircraft, barely rated above personal status. The bubble style cockpit sat on a light tubular frame with landing skids that resembled Santa's sleigh. The engine compartment held an oversized Lycoming engine, tweaked to 155 hp. Diaz had also reinforced the struts and motor mounts as well as the frame itself. This was intended to enable the craft to withstand the added torque he would put it through with his aerobatics. Those reinforcements and the additional power from the engine increased the takeoff weight capacity from 1400 lbs. to just over 1700 lbs.

Murray jumped to his feet, "That's a two seater."

"Yeah...but I have twin medivac gurneys for the skids." He looked at Jon and Murray, "you two look about the same size. You can ride the outriggers."

Those gurneys were very familiar to Murray. Wire framed baskets that attached to the landing skids. A wounded soldier could be strapped in for an emergency evacuation.

"Can that egg-beater carry all of us?" Murray asked.

"Sure, no sweat." Diaz did his best to sound convincing. "You guys go about, what...190 or so each? The little guy there can't be much over 140, right?" There was no objection to the estimates. "Just don't bring too many souvenirs with ya."

69

Marsha was checked out of Hamilton Medical Center in Dalton at around 2PM that Monday afternoon. She and Doris went immediately to the Depot for lunch.

"This is where Jon and Daniel met before they knew they would work together." Doris explained. "Ben told me all about it."

Marsha wondered if Jon would describe it quite that way, but did not argue the point. "I hope things are going well for them...whatever they are up to." She commented.

"They're fine." Doris assured her. "If ever there was someone who could take care of himself, it's Jon."

They enjoyed lunch and Doris tried to avoid further talk of Jon. She could tell Marsha was concerned and she didn't need that. She needed to relax and rest.

"We'll go shopping tomorrow..." She teased Marsha." Remember that?"

After lunch they went to George's home where Doris had a very nice room set up for Marsha.

"You really went to a bunch of trouble." Marsha faked a complaint.

"Yeah...I did, didn't I?" Doris laughed.

George Vincent was in his office at the time. An internal bulletin came out about the identities of body parts found in the Chesapeake Bay. "Not for release" the memo stated. That meant police agencies were to be aware while keeping the news quiet.

Jon had never mentioned this Stubblefield guy, yet George had a feeling about it. The background story told of the congressman's son who had died mysteriously last year.

That wouldn't slip past Jon, he thought. *Was this guy on the list?* He considered calling Ben, but remembered Ben wouldn't tell him anyway and the memo was not for release. Then he noticed the small story about the mysterious killer who was rumored to be headed for Colombia.

Nice work, Daniel. He said under his breath. *That should put a scare into the cartel.*

~

The small time Florida gang got to Orlando that afternoon and the people at Disney were expecting them. As set up by the Orlando Police, they were welcomed into the guesthouse and started their "training" for light bulb replacement technician positions.

Nicky was nervous at first, but soon began to swallow the staged proceedings.

"You done good, Max." He told his assistant. "You done good."

Charles Nelson monitored the gang from a command post set up near the front entrance. Jerry would be allowed to work today through Wednesday, but not on Thursday.

"Make up some excuse," his detective brother told him. "I don't care what it is. You are not going to be near those clowns on Thursday."

~

The message Cordoba saw on his phone was clear, but it didn't make sense at first. He was to return to McAllen, Texas and fly non-stop to Miami. One good thing was he hadn't gotten too far from the south Texas border town. He u-turned on US 281 and headed back south. The message said a ticket in his name; his new name of Fernando Jones would be waiting at the counter.

Cordoba was to call Vaga when he reached Miami for his instructions.

434

Somebody should make up their mind, he thought in Spanish. He would never say such a thing out loud, not even when alone.

~

The surf in Malibu was rough that Monday afternoon. Rain fell on the beach and the wind brought sand up to his deck. The man who lived there didn't care about that or anything else. He had received a message from his team in Florida, the new and as yet untested team. They reported things were going smoothly. The leader simply bragged to him that he should keep an eye on the news Thursday.

Trying to feel confident, he stood looking out at the Pacific as he waited for the phone to be answered in Montana.

"Yeah? What is it?" Came the reply.

"They're doing good," he told the leader. "It should happen this week."

"It better." The voice declared and then hung up.

"Well, kiss my shiny, white..." The man in California screamed as he threw the phone across the room. "Arrogant SOB." This was not the first time he had felt less than respected by the voice in Montana. Since the Texas gang was taken out by that lone cowboy, his stature was being diminished.

The man walked to his desk and opened a drawer. He pulled a file with newspaper clippings. They were the stories about The Son character, the mystery man his group tried to deflect blame upon in Mississippi.

The stories were written mostly by one man, a reporter named Daniel Seay in Pittsburgh.

The man stood and walked back to his large patio doors and looked out at the now raging ocean. A thought entered his mind and brought physical chills with it. These people he worked with were void of ethics. They were ruthless and vicious.

Glancing to the phone he had thrown earlier, he took a deep breath and returned to the desk. This time he pulled fresh paper and a pen from the center drawer and began to write,

To Whom it May Concern. I am a member of a large and powerful organization. We never act ourselves; we accomplish our goals through others. We seek to regain the power and control we enjoyed for a short time as we drove our country towards the ideals we hold for it. The struggle for that power is not understood by the public who, despite our efforts, was not ready for our system at that time.

He went on to describe how they sought to regain power by removing opposition to their cause and casting blame on the other side. Then he explained the reason for his letter.

Should you receive this message it will be because of my untimely death. I believe that may be caused by those I have worked so hard to support.

He then listed places and phone numbers of members of the organization. Names were not included, but were easily determined. When he was finished he sealed the letter in a large envelope and addressed it to the reporter in Pittsburgh.

In the now driving rain, the man walked four houses down along the Malibu coast to a neighbor he had only met a few times.

"I know this sounds strange, but I hope you'll do me this favor. Should you hear of my death in the near future, would you mail this right away?"

The neighbor looked at him as though he had lost his mind.

"I know this sounds a bit crazy, but I made some investments that haven't panned out. This person," he pointed at the address, "will be able to find my nephew should I go missing or die."

"You're afraid someone may kill you?" The neighbor asked bluntly. "You should go to the police."

"Yes I know," he told the near stranger. "All that is taken care of in here as well. Can you promise you'll do this for me?"

Hesitation was strong in the neighbor's eyes. He finally took the envelope and nodded in agreement.

"Thank you...thank you so much. I really appreciate this. Oh, and I sincerely hope you never have to mail that thing."

The neighbor watched as the man walked back toward his own home in the rain.

70

A Black Hawk helicopter landed at the far end of what used to be Albrook Air Base of the Panama Canal Territory. It sat at the base of Ancon Hill, a most famous landmark in the region. Four men climbed from the ominous aircraft.

Juan pointed to the top of the hill and said to Jon, "I'll bet he's in there."

"What's that?" Jon asked.

"Gorgas Hospital." He gestured again. "That's the building on top of the hill."

They were going to dinner early, way early as a matter of fact, because of their day and their schedule. It was 1500 hours or 3PM. Jon put an arm around Juan and spoke low, "It's early yet. After we eat, you and I will visit that hospital and see what we can find out, Ok?"

They climbed into the jeep CWO Diaz had waiting for them and drove off to The Commissary in Balboa. The Commissary had been just that, a military chow hall until the Canal was turned over to Panama. In recent years, civilians had complained of the lack of restaurants in the area so The Commissary was reopened, as a steak house.

The meal was not memorable, but at least there was air conditioning.

Would that only make it worse when we go back out? Jon thought in silence. The others at the table seemed to share that sentiment. No one was in any hurry to leave. Murray asked for more water, three times.

As the hour approached 4:30PM, or 1630 military time, Juan began to get antsy. Jon leaned back against his chair and looked at their host. "Luke," he began. "Could we stop at that hospital for a few minutes on the way back?"

The CWO sat up and looked concerned, "The steak wasn't that bad, was it?"

"No." Jon laughed. "We just want to see if someone we know is in there. Shouldn't take long."

"Sure," Diaz said almost dismissively. "We got all night, really."

As they rode up the long, steep driveway from Panama City's main central street Jon leaned toward Juan and asked, "What name will he be using?"

"Good question." Was the reply. "I doubt it will be DeMarcos. There are several aliases the family uses. I wasn't close enough to the leadership to really know any of them."

"Ok, so we don't ask for a room number at information."

"What's wrong with him?" Murray asked.

"His heart hasn't been strong for some time. He's been on blood pressure meds, I paid bills for those." Juan explained.

"We check for a cardiac care unit or ICU." Jon was thinking out loud. He looked right at Juan again, "You might recognize somebody hanging around outside in the hall."

Diaz parked the jeep and they climbed out. "I don't want you in any trouble over this," Jon said to the CWO, who was in uniform. "Why don't you stay with the jeep?" Their host looked disappointed, but agreed. "I'll be right here," he said and leaned against the vehicle.

The signs within the hospital were in Spanish and English. Jon pointed to a large graphic showing the Intensive Care Unit was located on the fourth floor, "See anything about a Cardiac Unit?" He asked the others.

Heads shook in the negative so they went to the elevators.

"Which end of the floor is the ICU on?" Murray questioned.

"Good point," Jon added. "We don't want to get off the elevator right in front of them."

A hospital staff member came by and informed them the ICU was indeed at the opposite end of the hall, so they headed up.

The fourth floor hallway was straight, but littered with obstructions. There were few people, but many carts, wall hung equipment and even chairs blocking the view. They proceeded slowly, giving Juan time to see if he recognized anyone ahead of them. As they neared the Intensive Care area Juan stopped and turned 180 degrees.

"That's one of Sergio's bodyguards sitting up there."

Jon didn't respond. He quietly stepped ahead a few feet to get a better look. He found a chair that was behind a large cabinet and signaled for Juan to advance. With Murray in front of him, he walked to the chair and sat down. From there, he could glance further down the hall without being noticed.

When a slightly built man stepped from a door on the left, Juan pushed his body and head against the wall and stared at Jon. Nervously twitching his head in the man's direction, he let Jon know who it was without speaking.

"Tomas Vaga," Jon muttered softly and nodded at Juan to calm him down.

Murray, sensing the need for a diversion, stood up and walked down the hall toward the room Vaga had emerged from. While Tomas and the guards watched Murray, Jon pulled Juan up and they slid back down the hall toward the elevators.

"That's him," Juan stuttered. "What are you going to do?"

"Nothing today." He hit the elevator button and the doors opened.

"The cowboy?" Juan now asked. "You're not waiting for him?"

"He's a big boy, he'll figure it out." Jon assured him.

Juan did not quite understand...they found Vaga, but did nothing about it. He asked Jon, "why?"

"He may still call his boss tonight or in the morning. I don't want to spook Lendono before he gets to Turbo, ok?"

"Si, Yes I mean."

"We know where your boy Tomas is and DeMarcos is there with him. We deal with that later."

They stepped off the elevator and could see Murray coming down the hall. He had used the lift near DeMarcos' room. "Get what you need?" He asked.

"Yep. That was quick thinking, thanks." Jon smiled.

"Just needed to stretch my legs." The cowboy winked at them and headed for the main doors.

~

The flight from McAllen to Miami touched down at 7:30PM that Monday. The new contract killer grabbed his bag from the overhead and made his way to the rental car counter. As he asked for a car being held for him, the counter agent held a finger in the air, "There's a package for you here, sir."

The package held his instructions and Tomas' phone number. *Call me when you get in,* the note said.

As he drove out of the parking area, Sebastian set the GPS for the South Beach Club and dialed the number for Tomas Vaga.

~

Within twenty minutes, Ben was calling Jon. "He's had an incoming call from Miami. It's in Spanish so I'll just forward the tape to you."

Jon played it over the speaker so Juan and Murray could hear. Juan's eyes squinted and Murray took on a smug grin as they heard the phone call.

"He's telling this kid how to kill me." Juan explained to Jon.

Murray confirmed that with a nod and then shook his head, saying "Son of a Bitch."

"When do they expect you there?" Jon asked.

"At 10:00AM tomorrow. He's supposed to knife me in a tent by the pool."

"You should be getting a call soon." Murray piped in. The others looked at him with questions in their faces. "He'll need to tell you where that tent is, right?"

Jon smiled at his friend again, "You're hot tonight, aren't you?'"

"Can I get a raise?"

71

The Capitol Police were put on alert at 8:00PM. The results from the identification process were pointing more and more to homicide. They were not yet cleared to arrest the congressman, but they were to closely monitor his movements.

Oddly, Congressman Stubblefield was still in his fifth floor office at the Eisenhower Building. His door was locked and he had no one in there with him. Red flags were everywhere as far as the police were concerned. Still, their policy held them back. It would be another hour and a half before they could approach the legislator.

Inside the office, Stubblefield sat behind his desk in a full stupor, eyes looking straight ahead without blinking. He had cleared the desktop completely. No papers, no phone, computer or even a desk pad. Those items were now on the floor where he had pushed them. One side window's draperies were pulled back, but the opening was still closed.

A police sniper watched his every move from the roof of the White House. The officer reported what he saw. The congressman sat in silence, staring at the locked door of his office.

~

Santonio Lendono had moved from the prison cell office to a one-floor motel across the street. The Escalade would be ready for the trip to Turbo by morning, but he didn't want to risk another night in the prison.

His plan was to leave Sabanalarga by 6AM and be in Turbo before 11AM. He would take two guards with him, plus his driver and that would have to do for a while. He was nervous and shaky. He couldn't remember ever feeling this bad before.

Sleep would not come easy that night, if at all. Lendono could feel his heart jumping up and down. The normally sedate organ pounded severely in his chest. It wanted out.

~

Tuesday morning was busy. Just before 7:40AM Miami time, Murray was on the phone to the Miami Police Department. The call was being routed off a couple of satellites by Ben. It appeared to be coming from a room at the South Beach Hotel and Casino.

"Yeah, officers...there's a guy down by the tents...I mean the cabanas, you know, around the pool? Anyway...he's got a big ole' knife in his belt. I don't know what he's up to. It just makes me nervous."

Murray listened to the cop on the other end for a minute. "My name? Pete Ferguson. I'm here from Utah...yeah I'm in sales." Then he started clicking the phone..."Hello...hello. Oh heck I'll have to call back."

The disconnected line left the police with an incomplete description of a man with a knife at the South Beach pool area. After a brief check with the desk sergeant, two cars were dispatched at 8:05AM to see about it.

~

Jon went to see WCO Diaz about an hour before they were to leave. "Say, do you have a couple of those camouflage jump suits in extra large?"

"I'm sure we do. I'll get one of the guys to bring 'em over to you."

Jon thanked him and then found Murray. "We need to go ahead and get suited up before we go in. We don't know what we'll run into there."

"Suited up?" The cowboy tilted his head, "You mean one of those Seal suits like you had on?"

Jon tossed it at him and he caught it, opened it up and held it out in front of himself.

"Where's all the little bumps... like yours has?" Murray peeked around the suit and teased him.

"You get the prototype." Jon smiled.

"Hand me down, huh?"

"Yep." Jon was laughing now. "Just don't get scared and piss in it."

Murray half laughed with him and then went to try it on. As he came back Jon was decked out and stepping into a jump suit. "Why the camo?" He asked.

"Don't want to advertise too much. We'll pull these off on the roof in town."

Murray stepped into his jump suit and offered one last complaint, "This thing itches."

~

Earlier that day they heard from Ben. He had intercepted another call between Vaga and Lendono. Juan translated the recording. "I'm on the road now." Lendono said. "I'll call you when I get to the house. Is the man in Miami yet?" Then Juan speaks what Vaga said in response, "Yes, he's there and ready. When Juan calls in this morning I'll send him to the tent. That's it."

Then Lendono spoke again, "Good. I should be at the house by 10:30AM, no later. I want it over by then."

Vaga assured him it would be and the call ended.

"Somebody's gonna be real disappointed you're not there, amigo." Murray slapped Juan on the back. "Damn. What are you wearing?"

It was the bulletproof vest Ben had rigged for him.

"Me James Bond...no?" Juan teased in an overdone accent.

The guys headed to the flight line and climbed aboard CWO Diaz's Black Hawk. At 0800 hours the squadron lifted off and plowed ahead toward the Atlantic Ocean. They rode in four rows of three with Diaz front and center for the first part of the trip. At forty-seven minutes into it, they spread out making a straight line.

The twelve gun ships lowered altitude as they approached the coast. Horns sounded at the National Guard base as they flew over at barely seventy-five feet. Within a minute they were over the airport and began the ballet dance Diaz had told them about. Some went up, some went further down. Three peeled off to starboard and four turned to port.

The helicopters mixed in and out, up and down with two touching down on the airport runway for a second. Another touched a house to the south of their flight plan while Luke Diaz yelled into his microphone, "Get ready!"

The Black Hawk dropped toward a house near the beach. Jon looked at Juan for confirmation and the Hispanic man nodded. The helicopter barely touched the flat roof of the main house and Jon rolled out the right side pulling Juan with him. Murray rolled out the left and all three of them lay flat as the black bird roared back into the sky and banked hard to port.

They stayed still for more than five minutes, waiting and listening. Nothing happened. As Jon rose to his knees he asked Juan softly, "Could it be there's no one here?" The Hispanic man shrugged and shook his head.

They heard a whistle and it was Murray. He found a way off the roof near the back of the lanai. They were soon on the marble floor of that spacious, open back room. Still cautious, Jon pointed for Murray to go right while he surveyed to the left. All the rooms were checked. The place was open, but unoccupied.

They met at the front door, convinced they were alone. Jon turned the doorknob and it opened. "No alarm?" He asked.

"Who's going to steal from this man?" Juan asked sarcastically.

Jon sent Juan with Murray to check the surrounding yard and look for a boat. As Murray looked out over the gulf waters to the tip of the peninsula they were to travel to later, he said. "Yeah...a boat would be nice."

Jon pulled the small fanny pack he carried around to his front and set about looking for placement and arming locations. The bathroom had floss and toothpaste that didn't appear to have been used in a while. *What if he brings new?* He thought.

He placed a small pressure release pouch under the pillow on the bed and another under the rug in the bathroom. Jon spent time connecting a miniature "bouncing Betty" release device that would jump up as he lifted a bottle of Scotch from his wet bar. Each device would use the Saxitotoxin with the quick dispersing powder.

He walked out back at 10:00AM and found Murray and Juan pulling a trailer mounted, twenty-four foot ski boat from a dry dock shed. They turned it and shoved the back half into the water. Murray asked where the gas might be, so Juan went back into the shed. Then all three heard the Escalade drive up out front. It was early.

~

The Speaker of the House of Representatives signed off on the arrest of Congressman Stubblefield. He was to be held for questioning at 9:50AM that morning. The sniper reported that the congressman had sat at his desk all night, hardly moving.

When the knock came at his door things changed.

The sniper reported through his radio that the congressman almost jumped up and ran to check the door. He did not open it. Rather, he pushed a cabinet against the door from the inside. As

447

the police officers began to attempt to force the door, Congressman Stubblefield calmly walked back past his desk to the window. The one with the drapes pulled back.

The sniper reported that the congressman tried to open the lower sash, but couldn't get it to budge. The pounding on the office door was getting louder and the wood showed signs of cracking.

The congressman stepped back several feet from the window, took one last look at the door and ran...head first into the glass.

"He's jumping!" The sniper cried out.

Stubblefield's body broke glass and bent the sash frame. But he got caught up in it for a second. He hung by his belt, unconscious from the impact.

"Hurry," the sniper yelled. "Get in there.

The heavy wooden door finally gave way and three officers rushed to the window just as the belt gave way and the limp body fell.

The sniper watched as Stubblefield fell two stories and hit face first on a concrete ledge that stuck out about a foot. The impact caused the body's legs to go over and Stubblefield flipped the remaining three stories, hitting the walkway with the back of his head.

Paramedics were on the scene and got to him within seconds. The man was still breathing.

TV stations were hustling to edit their footage into something they could show. What they had was far too gruesome for daytime television. The paramedics took about 40 minutes to get the body on a backboard for transport. As they carried Stubblefield to an ambulance, one of the medics was seen making a cut motion across his neck to a supervisor. The disgraced congressman would not stand questioning or trial.

72

Jon pointed to the lanai and Murray took up a position there behind a wall. Jon went on to the front room and stood by a doorframe. The first two to enter were the guards. They walked casually, expecting nothing.

Jon watched them pass him and head to the lanai. As the two stepped out on the marble tile Murray grabbed one and Jon leapt onto the other. With their mechanical arms they made short work of it. Murray then dragged both of them out back, unconscious. He left them behind thick bushes at the rear of the bedroom.

The front door opened again and Lendono walked in. The cartel leader's eyes were looking down as he stepped in through the door. Obviously preoccupied, his thoughts were of Miami, Juan Castrono and the crews of soldiers regaining Argus' cocaine routes. Suddenly he stopped. An odd shadow lay ahead of him and cautiously turned his head to the left.

In the middle of the den loomed an unfamiliar figure. As Lendono eyes focused on the figure his heart leapt into his throat. His face contorted as though pain had struck him. What he saw made no sense, or he didn't want it to. It had to be a spirit, a bad spirit.

Jon Crane stood quietly in his black suit with headgear and goggles in place. He raised his right arm slowly and deliberately, pointing at the drug lord. Lendono dropped his bag and ran to his right for the bedroom.

Murray had stepped into the bedroom through the open back of the lanai. He stood in his black suit and goggles near the bathroom door. Lendono stopped again. For all appearances to him, it was the same spirit, the same man in black in both places.

Sweat broke out on the Lendono's forehead and his color was draining fast. The "spirit" now blocked his path to the nightstand and his gun. He turned and ran again. This time for the safety of the front door and escape. Within four steps from the bedroom door he froze once again. The black spirit was already there. Jon, standing with both arms to his sides and his palms outstretched toward Lendono, blocked the front door.

His color now completely drained from his face, Lendono whirled and made one last dash for the lanai. As he stepped onto the marble floor there was Murray again, twenty feet in front of him at the edge of the back opening. This time the drug lord quit running.

Santonio Lendono locked up perfectly still. He said nothing. No sound came from him at all. With a blank look on his face, his arms dropped to his sides and the fingers on his hands unfolded. His legs twitched slightly and suddenly he dropped, straight to his knees. His upper torso waved back and forth in small movements.

Jon moved closer from behind and Murray took two steps toward the man. Before they could get to him his upper body fell backwards folding over his legs. Lendono's head impacted the marble floor with the sound of a coconut landing on a rock. The thud was sickening. Lendono's eyes were open and fixed, staring upward, but not seeing.

Jon rushed the final feet to him and pulled off a glove to check for any pulse. "Damn," he said looking to Murray as though he had been cheated.

Lendono was dead. That scared heart had finally made that one last jump. Murray pulled his goggles off and stood over him in silence.

Juan Castrono slowly came in from the back yard. Jon looked at him and then Lendono, asking in silence if this was indeed the man. Juan nodded verifying the identity.

Jon got to his feet and the three then stood and just looked at each other for a moment. None thought of anything to say. The mission was done. Not as they had thought it would be, but completed none-the-less.

The sound of the front door opening got their attention. The Escalade driver walked into the scene and screamed as he saw the body and the three men standing over it. As he turned to run, Murray slid to a small table, grabbing the first thing he could. He threw a softball-sized paperweight that struck the driver in the back. With the added strength from the hydraulic arm, the impact left the driver unconscious. He was dragged out back to be left with the guards while Jon still stood over Lendono. His hand made a fist and then relaxed.

It's almost over, he thought.

They left the body as it lay and Jon went about removing what chemical traps he could. The bottle of Scotch took the longest. It had to be encased in a heavy plastic bag before disturbing it. The release "poof" made Murray jump though he was over thirty feet away when it went off. They finished the clean up and dusting for any prints they might have left, then put on the coveralls once more.

Juan had found a small amount of gasoline for the boat. It was half in the water and half still on the trailer. They shoved the craft off its trailer into the water and climbed aboard. Jon and Murray paddled while Juan wrestled with the engine. The tip of the peninsula looked to be about a mile away.

"Can you get that motor to work?" Jon asked.

Juan said nothing. He pulled the starter rope and the inboard / outboard motor fired into life. He dropped the blades into the water and took the controls, they were moving. As they neared the expanse of land, Jon called Diaz.

"What took you so long?" The CWO asked him. "I'm in the air...be there in twenty."

The three climbed to shore and pointed the boat back out to sea. With the engine running full speed, Murray threw it into gear and jumped clear. The ski boat raced out to sea. In a straight line at first, then veering off to the right and open water. The men walked toward a flat spot some hundred yards inland. It was clear of brush and debris and looked like a good place for Diaz to land.

~

Sabastian Cordoba was confused. Juan was to have been there by 8AM. Cordoba had checked all the tents surrounding the pool deck and found only one passed out young lady, obviously left from the night before. As he stepped back outside that last tent he walked right into four Miami Metro Dade Police officers. The shock of their sudden appearance caused Cordoba to flinch. That slight gesture was all the officers needed to jump and take him down to the pavement.

A quick search revealed the ten-inch knife and one officer announced, "You're under arrest."

Cordoba carried no identification and he refused to speak. Shackled both hands and legs, he was carried away and placed in a police van for transport. His day was over by 8:20AM that Tuesday.

~

It was an hour past the time Tomas was to hear from Lendono. Sergio DeMarcos was near death. His wife, Lendono's sister and other family members had been called to his bedside. Tomas wanted to call Lendono himself, but feared doing so. His boss said clearly that he would call, so Tomas opted to wait a while longer. His mind sought other things and he realized he had not heard from Cordoba either.

Dialing that number he received a "not in service" message. The phone was turned off or not working for some reason. Tomas did not know that as the Miami police wrestled with Cordoba and threw him to the pool deck, the cell phone slipped from his coat pocket and fell into the pool. It went unnoticed by everyone, including the officers.

~

Luke Diaz and his miniature helicopter were hardly visible until he was there. The slight craft sat down on the flat spot and Diaz gestured emphatically to hurry.

Jon and Murray climbed into the wire baskets on either side and pulled the safety straps tight. Juan stepped over Jon and climbed into the passenger seat. Diaz picked up one end of the seat belt and handed it to Juan. The frightened man snapped into reason and connected the belt.

As they strained to lift off, Jon could see spots circling the beach house. One of the guards or perhaps the driver had come to and called for help. The spots Jon saw were Colombian National Police helicopters looking all around the neighborhood of Lendono's house.

Diaz did a 360-degree pivot and headed out over the Gulf waters at only feet above the waves. The spray blown up by the propellers showered the baskets.

Now it was Murray who could see back to the beach house. "Get moving," he hollered as the Colombian copters changed course and came their direction.

The Robinson aircraft gained a few more feet in altitude and seemed to be traveling faster, but not fast enough. The Colombians started from over a mile behind, but were gaining on them. Murray could see the targeting lights of the weapons being turned on. He reached for his gun, but it was under the layer of the coveralls.

Diaz calmly picked up his radio microphone and pressed the talk key. "Baby Papa Echo, boogies two coming hard. I say Mayday."

With that he simply released the key and put the microphone back on its cradle. Juan was now aware of the helicopters chasing them. He turned and saw the two Colombians nearing to almost 500 yards. Diaz stared straight ahead and pushed on.

Murray had unzipped the coverall, still trying to reach to his pant's leg for the Glock handgun. There wasn't room within the basket to maneuver his hand to the pocket. He glared at the approaching aircraft while continuing to strain for the weapon. Suddenly, the two approaching machines peeled off course and turned back.

A huge shadow flashed over the little Robinson aircraft as eleven Black Hawks screamed above them toward the Colombians. Diaz picked up the microphone again, "Baby Papa Echo, roger that and thanks guys. Now get the hell home." He again replaced the microphone, looking over at Juan as he did so. The Hispanic man grinned widely and nodded.

The Black Hawks splayed out in another impressive air dance and swung back toward home. Ten roared past the Robinson mini-copter and disappeared quickly into the horizon. One lagged back, rocking back and forth behind the smaller aircraft until Diaz could see land. At that point, the CWO reached out with his left hand and gave the thumbs up signal. A deep throated roar spread from its engine as the remaining Black Hawk pitched forward and raced by. The pilot saluted, rocking gently as he went out of sight ahead of them.

73

News spread quickly of the suicide in Washington, D.C. The nation had been monitoring the situation closely, especially since the attempt to leave the country. Stubblefield would have only been questioned about the mounting evidence. No proof yet existed and now that was even less likely. His actions sealed the case. While proof may have been denied, to many the questions were now answered.

Daniel Seay stared at the story as it flashed across his monitor. He had a funny feeling about it. Jon had never said a word. There were older rumors about the congressman's son who had died last year.

Surely this deal had not gotten past him. Daniel thought.

There was hardly time for him to ponder the thought before the phone started ringing. First was Earl Johnstone of Burlington, Iowa. The Stubblefield story hit him the same way it did Daniel. Awkwardly, Johnstone asked the obvious, "Was The Son aware of this man?"

Daniel could only answer what he knew. The discussion went on and without either verbalizing it. They both understood the connection they felt, to stories of unscrupulous men in high positions of power and the cure for their disease, the mystery man known as the Son.

The call from Johnstone was quickly followed by a similar call from Matt Turlock in Louisiana, then several others from all over the southeast. Daniel's boss even stepped in to inquire. Bill White knew Daniel would come to him if there was any connection, yet he just had to ask.

It was past time to go home when Daniel realized he had been sitting, in more or less a stupor, trying to place a value on the network he had just heard from. Those influential people in the media could counteract much of the current disdain the public held for their profession. It would be simple. Act for the greater good and dislodge the mask of secrecy the corrupt hid behind. They could even go so far as to enlist the efforts of Jon Crane in these cases. *It's time to go. Dinner will be waiting.* He finally scolded himself.

But the thoughts would not leave him entirely alone.

~

Police officers reached out to fellow trusted members of their profession as well. Many of those also wondered the same thing, only through their own tilted prism.

Captain Sharon Swanson had heard from Col. Sawyer. The colonel had heard from Lt. Dan Draper of Iowa, each trying to find the appropriate way to ask what the other might know. The question was always the same. *What about this Son character? What did he know about Stubblefield?*

That network stretched through the Carolinas and down to Louisiana. It touched New Orleans and the NCIS office there and back to Dalton and Atlanta, Georgia.

Captain Phillip Stone had the epiphany moment like Daniel's, *what good could we accomplish if we worked together...behind and under the scenes?* He thought.

He sat down and began a list. He made plans to contact each officer on that list and gain their contacts who shared similar ideas.

The politics that tarnished the efforts of the police, in many jurisdictions, could be overcome by their cooperation. *It's worth the try.* Phil convinced himself.

~

The four men and the tiny-framed helicopter landed at Howard air base without any fanfare. None was anticipated or wanted. After a brief account of what had happened for Luke's benefit, Jon,

456

Murray and Juan headed to their barracks to clean up and plan what to do next.

"It won't be long till Tomas Vaga tries to call Lendono and figures something is wrong." Jon stated.

"Yeah, how do we handle him?" The cowboy pulled off the coveralls and sat on his bunk.

Jon lay back on his wire framed bed to think. "Ben knows the cell numbers. At least he can monitor them and let us know when Vaga does try."

Juan had stayed quiet, but walked toward the other two grinning. "He already has tried to call him."

Jon stared up at him without speaking.

Juan pulled a cell phone from one of his pockets and held it up. "He called this phone just a hour ago."

"What is that?" Jon sat upright

"It's Lendono's phone." Juan beamed with pride. "I took it off his body while you were cleaning up."

"Nice." Murray piped in.

"Ok...that brings us to our next question." Jon looked right at Juan. "What do we do with Vaga?"

Murray said nothing and Juan looked at the phone in silence. Jon laid back down and spoke again, "We can't just leave things as they are, can we?"

Juan stepped a bit closer, "I want to confront him, myself." He looked as though he expected the others to disagree. "I need to talk to him."

Murray reached to the top of his bunk and pulled his chrome Colt .45 from under the pillow. He handed it butt first towards Juan. "Great...you handle it then." He laughed.

Juan only looked at the gun. He didn't take it. "I just want to speak to him."

Jon studied the Hispanic man for several minutes. He understood what the man was hoping he could make happen. "I'll see if Luke can get us to the Ancon Hill hospital in the morning, Ok?"

Juan nodded and spoke very softly, "Gracias."

"How many times has he tried to call?"

"Three...so far."

Jon checked his watch; it was 3:45PM civilian time. "Should we go tonight?"

The anxious Hispanic man nodded. Jon looked to Murray who simply shrugged and said, "Let me go talk to Diaz."

~

Nicky Sledge called a meeting right after training that day. He wanted to go over the plan for Thursday. They met at a Burger King on the Bronson Highway just outside the park.

"What time does the guy get there?" He asked Max.

The younger member looked confused by the question, "I don't have any schedule...he's just coming that morning, I think."

Nicky looked down at his burger and fries spread out on the wrapper in disgust. *How can I lead this job with no info*, he thought quietly. Turning his head to the other member there with him, he spoke in low tones. "Jo-Jo, you're position is the closest to the ride, right?"

"Yeah... I guess." The young man swallowed and answered.

"You take the shot." Nicky declared.

"Whoa...dude. Why me?" Joe Reyes nearly stood up in protest. "I never done anything like that, man." He swung his head back and forth and his shoulders slumped. "I'm a thief...Ok? I don't kill."

Max looked away and added nothing to the conversation. His boss didn't appear happy.

"Fine," Nicky said under his breath. "I have to do everything myself."

The other two did not argue that point with him. They ate, somewhat, and left their table a mess.

As they climbed into the car, a longhaired man in a tee shirt and jeans who had sat down near them in the restaurant pulled a phone from his pocket. "The big kid will be the shooter." He said into it. He listened for a second and then hung up.

~

A phone rang that afternoon at the home of Congressman Lewis Nall in Dade City, Florida. A staff person answered and soon walked to the congressman with the phone extended towards him. "It's the police in Orlando, sir."

Detective Nelson explained the situation to the congressman and the plan they had to prevent any harm to him.

"We will have an officer pretend to be you who will actually go on the ride. You and your family will stay at the gate surrounded by guards."

"What if we just don't go?" The congressman asked point blank.

"You can do that too, but the problem is...these people we know about are not the brains behind it. If we don't make a splash against them here, they'll just try somewhere else."

"A splash?"

"Sorry...I mean we stop them and get some information from these clowns about who they work for."

"You don't know if they are 'clowns' or not." The congressman was concerned about the whole deal.

"Look, sir...if you really don't wish to come at all. Would you please... just not tell the media about the change?"

Lewis Nall was quiet on his end of the phone. He looked at his wife who had come into the room. That made his decision for him. "I'll come and do what you need me to, but my family stays here, under guard."

"Yes, sir." Nelson agreed. "Can we use officers to look like your family as you enter the park?"

"Whatever you need to do...just be careful, please."

"You got it." Nelson assured him.

74

CWO Diaz landed his Black Hawk behind Ancon Hill and the four of them walked to the Jeep.

"What do you plan to do with this guy?" Diaz asked. "Do I need to keep the motor running?" He hoped he was kidding.

Jon rubbed his chin and answered, "We want to just talk to him. Let him know the new score and see what goes from there." He looked at their new army friend and added, "If we come running out of there...you just leave. We won't drag you in any deeper."

"We'll see." Diaz responded.

Jon, Murray and Juan climbed the stairs to the rear entrance to the hospital. The elevator to the ICU floor was just down the hallway.

Murray stepped out first and looked up and down the hall. Two guards sat outside DeMarcos' room. Jon came out of the elevator and walked to the room.

The door was open enough to see inside. The man lying in the bed was surrounded by sobbing women. There was a small man standing in one corner of the room. Jon turned to Juan and nodded.

Juan Castrono pushed a button on Lendono's cell phone and a ringing sound could be heard coming from DeMarcos' room.

In Spanish, Tomas Vaga answered, "Si, hello."

Juan responded also in Spanish. "Come into the hallway, Tomas."

"Juan?" Vaga's eyes grew large and glanced around the room as if for assistance.

"Come into the hallway, Tomas." Juan repeated himself.

Vaga remembered his guards and stepped out into the hall. His guards were busy. Jon and Murray each had one against the

461

wall at gunpoint. Before he could go back into the room, Juan walked up. "Come with me if you wish to live." He told the other man.

They walked to the area near the elevators and stopped.

"Where is Santonio?" Vaga asked.

"He is dead."

"Dead? You killed him?"

"Nada, his heart gave away on him. He is dead none the less."

Vaga looked at the floor and leaned, almost falling against the wall. With his hand to his forehead he spoke in broken words, "What do I do now? It is over."

"DeMarcos?" Juan asked him.

"He died an hour ago."

Juan took the man's arm and led him to a chair. "Sit, I have things to say." The slight man sat and looked at Juan with eyes that didn't focus.

"This is all over now," Juan told him. "Look at me, I'm serious." He shook the seated man by his shoulder. "Argus is gone...the DeMarcos Cartel is gone...all gone."

"What do we do?" Vaga trembled.

"I am going back to the states with my friends. I applied for citizenship while working for Harley. There are only a few months more till I take my test."

"I do not wish to go there." Vaga told him.

"Have you any family?"

Tomas thought a moment, "Si...in Guatemala."

"Go to them. If you stay here you will die. If you try to do anything with the Cartel, you will die."

"How do you know this?" Vaga challenged him.

"My friend over there," he pointed to Jon. "Does not like drug lords."

"Is he...?"

462

"Si." Juan smiled. "The spirit...in the flesh."

Tomas called for the two guards. Jon and Murray let them pass. Tomas told them what had happened. "You are free," he told them. "You may go on your own."

The two looked stunned at first, then smiles broke out on their faces. One hugged Tomas, the two shook hands, laid their guns on the chair and left.

Juan sat next to Tomas and leaned closer to him. "What of the men from Shreveport?" He asked. "Where are they now?"

Vaga had forgotten about them for the moment. He appeared dazed by the question.

"I know they were sent back to Colombia, Tomas." Juan lectured. "Where are they now?"

"The first group is on the way to Louisiana. They are to meet Bertalli in Texas..." he thought for a minute and looked at Juan, "tomorrow. They meet tomorrow."

"Who is Bertalli?"

"A European hit man, Hanson had him working on some project of his own. It didn't work out."

Juan lit up like a Christmas tree, "Project? Like a house in Dalton, Georgia?"

"How do you know of that?" Vaga asked.

"Call the bastard...call him now." Juan ordered.

Vaga dialed a number and the man answered.

"What? I'm busy right now. They don't get here till tomorrow, right?"

"There's a change of plans, Antonio." Tomas told him.

"What do you mean a change?"

"It is over...go home or wherever. It is over."

The Italian did not understand. "Over? What over? I've got expenses in this thing."

"Lendono is dead...DeMarcos is dead...it's over I tell you."

The silence on the other end was deafening as the hit man tried to think. "You owe me. You people owe me money and I want it."

Juan could hear the conversation and at that point he grabbed the phone from Tomas. "I will see you get paid, friend." He spoke sharply. "Everything you have coming."

"Who is this now?" Bertalli was confused.

"This is Juan Castrono."

"Castrono?" Bertalli then became quiet again.

"My friends from the big house will find you and pay you." Juan screamed into the phone.

The line went dead.

Juan stood up and looked to Jon and the cowboy. He turned as though he were now the leader and pushed the button for the elevator. The three left, with Tomas Vaga sitting by himself in the hallway. Before the elevator doors closed, Juan stuck his head out and called to Vaga one last time. "Cordoba," he yelled. "Sabastian Cordoba is in jail in Miami."

Vaga had no comment or come back.

Diaz thought they looked pretty sedate for what they had gone in to handle. His attempts to get details went unacknowledged.

As they flew back to Howard AFB, Juan spoke again to his friends. "It is truly over."

Jon nodded and smiled slightly. The copter pilot looked to his cowboy hero for an answer. Murray was stretched out in his seat with the big hat pulled down over his eyes. Answers would have to wait.

75

Her phone rang at quarter past ten that night. She didn't grab it right away. Instead Marsha Hurst stared at it through a few rings, then got up to walk across the room. She opened the folding unit and waited for his voice.

"Marsha?" His voice inquired.

"Hey." She said. The voice was very monotone, especially for her. It caught Jon off guard.

"You ok?"

"Me?" She still sounded unattached and unemotional. "Where have you been?"

"It's over."

Marsha had to let that soak in. The events of the last three weeks seemed like a lifetime, particularly to her. For him to say it was over didn't compute. *How could it be over?* She thought. *It had become a way of life.* She finally heard herself say, "What's over, Jon?"

"Argus...all of it. It's done." He began to wonder if there was some relapse or something. "You don't have to worry about them, ever again. Neither will Daniel and Lori."

"Are you hurt?"

"No...no, no. It went smoothly, really." He assured her the best he could over the phone. "We're all fine."

"Good," she responded. Then still with little passion in her words, she threw him completely with, "I need to get back to work soon."

An impulse to argue ran through him. It rode down his spine and landed in the new empty spot that developed near his stomach. Something was wrong, but the near 1800 miles between them didn't allow for a discussion. His mind searched for the right thing to say.

"I'll be home Thursday night. Could we talk about it then?" came out.

"Oh," she seemed surprised. "Thursday? Good. I'll see you Thursday."

"I love you." Came out before he could measure it.

She hesitated, responding coolly, "Love you, too."

As he hung up, Murray stepped into the room and immediately sensed the tension. "Trouble in paradise?" He tried to quip. The comment was greeted by a glare, but little else. "Hmm," he recovered. "I'm going to have a beer with Diaz. Want to come?"

"Maybe in a minute." Jon managed. "Keep one cold, will ya?"

The cowboy nodded and went on his way. Wednesday was to be a rest day, but it was looking like a long one. They all were ready to get home.

~

The plan to get the gun into the Small World ride was probably the best of all their plans. Realizing that security would be tight on Thursday, they had started bringing pieces of it in on Tuesday. The cylinder was hidden under a section of foam, the barrel in a fake tree trunk and a side plate under loose tile. Smaller pieces like the hammer spring and thumb piece assembly were brought in inside sandwiches and stashed in the break room.

The two cartridges were brought in on Wednesday. They were inside a thermos of chocolate milk. Any strict additional security search on Thursday would come up empty.

Nicky planned for Jo-Jo to ring his cell phone as the congressman came into the ride area and then Max would unscrew a bulb across from Nicky's position when the ride car carrying the target was in range for a shot.

By late Wednesday, the Orlando police had located all the parts except a firing pin. The cartridges were replaced with blanks and the rest left as they were found. The fellow maintenance workers Nicky and his pals had worked with all week were actually police and FBI.

The escape plan was the weakest part, but Nicky suspected the screaming, yelling and running about would cover their departure. They ate separately that last night, so as not to draw suspicion.

~

While the rest of the country studied the Stubblefield case, George Vincent was more interested in the list Jon had obtained from the biker gang's headquarters. The intended victims list, which included the Florida congressman who would soon be in the news, had a definite pattern to it.

Some years ago, the country had gone through a period of unrest. The electorate had given power to a group that planned much deeper changes to the fabric of our country than the people originally understood. The actions of the group in power so shocked the public that the outcome of the mid-term elections was staggering. Members of the party associated with the group were removed from office in large numbers. Their power was diminished and the leadership attempted to further push their agenda through a lame duck session of the congress. It did not work.

The next election also went back to the former party through new members. They promised to guide the party away from past inequities.

The losing party and their supporters, mainly in the media and celebrity classes, could not believe the reaction of the uneducated masses at the polls. Their shot at utopia was gone.

George noticed that the victims' list was made up of congressmen and governors who had replaced the losing members in many of those races. To him, these "sponsors" were trying to eliminate those who had usurped their power.

The evidence was flimsy at best, but it was disconcerting. Whoever these people were, they were using others to do the dirty work, with no connection to themselves apparent. *Was this even enough to warn those on the list about?* he thought. *Or would it be seen as overreaching by a local district attorney.*

~

Ben had not heard from Jon since Tuesday evening. The calls between the cartel leaders had ceased and it didn't take his genius to figure out why. The computers had been busy, spitting out info about the cartel's demise and who would fill the void. No high-ranking officials were being named yet, so that was good.

The Stubblefield case would not be taken well by Jon, Ben knew. His boss and friend was a perfectionist. Making the error in judgment had cost the lives of innocents. Ben had not told Jon the outcome of that standoff in Washington. He would hear about it soon enough.

Bills were starting to come in. The last several weeks had been expensive. Fortunately, the computers set to track the earnings of the investments showed those earnings had somehow not only kept up with the expenses, they had exceeded them.

He did hear from Jon late on Wednesday. Both Murray and Juan would ride with him back as far as the Atlanta airport. Murray wanted to get back to Dallas, by way of Shreveport and Lucy and Juan would need a car to pick up some belongings he had stashed in north Georgia.

"I can get him a car here or down in the Kennesaw area." Ben suggested. "Nope," Jon relayed on. "Juan wants a little time to sort out what he's going to do. The airport will be fine."

"Ok." Ben answered. "You've heard about Stubblefield?"

"Yeah," there was a pause and then Jon finished with, "we'll discuss that when I get in."

"Care to tell me what's coming from Gainesville yet?" Ben tried. "They called again. It'll be here next week."

"Good," Jon said wryly. "Next week is good I think."

Ben gave up, "One ticket for Shreveport around 7 or 8PM and one car for Juan."

"Thanks, Ben. See you tomorrow evening about 9:30 or so."

~

UH-60 Helicopters were designed to carry a crew of four. CWO Diaz's squadron of twelve had three crewmembers each. The Black Hawks sat on the tarmac that Wednesday evening as their crews held a celebration. Celebrations were fairly easily contrived, most any excuse was good enough for pilots to drink and get crazy. Tonight, it was the departure of new friends, warriors, as it were, who came and made a difference. Their contribution would not and could not be shouted from the rooftops, but it could be celebrated by the men and women who had helped.

Thirty-nine people drank beer and talked and told stories, most of them anyway. A couple of them were quiet by any standard, but that was ok. Jon Crane wasn't much for bragging and Juan just wanted to get away, but the party was well intentioned and they obliged their hosts.

Murray Bilstock, Dusty to his new friends, had a wonderful time. These were his kind of people.

The next morning was a bit quieter, but Jon and Juan were up, getting ready and Murray tried to sleep it off.

The C-130J landed right on time, 11:41 hours and coasted directly to the unloading and loading area. Jon, Murray and Juan offered their final thank you to Luke Diaz and his crews and then walked across the concrete toward Everett Willingham's aircraft.

Liz Murdock came down the rear-loading gangway and welcomed the men. "I trust your mission went well," she offered.

"Very well." Jon smiled. "Is Everett here?"

"He stayed back in Georgia today, but he didn't forget you guys. Say...you don't mind a woman driver do you?" She laughed.

Jon and Murray chuckled, but Juan didn't understand. "Driver?" He asked.

"Heavy equipment driver," Murray explained. But when that didn't appear to clear it up for Juan, the cowboy flapped his arms and pointed at the First Officer. "She's gonna fly us home."

"Oh, ok."

They loaded their bags and got into the jump seats. At 12:29 they rolled down the runway and arched into the air. Next stop...Georgia.

76

Lewis Nall had been in the congress for three years. The man he replaced had died in a plane crash a few years after the purge. That's what they called it, both sides. The purge was the largest swing in congressional seats the country had ever seen. The losing side carped and complained that the people simply weren't sophisticated enough to understand what they were doing.

Nall's predecessor was influential in that purge. He had been very outspoken about the direction the other party was taking the country. His voice resonated with the people. So much so, that he had been asked to speak on behalf of other contenders of his party.

The plane crash was suspicious, but nothing ever came of the investigation.

Nall relived those events many times since hearing about the plot against him. The trip to Orlando that morning was not pleasant for him, but he went. The police had asked him to wear something distinguishing. His wife picked out a bright yellow polo shirt and a multi-colored sport coat. *It would make him stand out for sure.* He told himself.

Detective Nelson waited outside the main gates to Disney. He had with him a female officer and two undercover narcotics officers, who happened to be "little people." There should not be any danger to those involved in the takedown, but you could never be too sure. No children would be allowed, in or around the ride at that particular moment. The perpetrators might notice, but that was a chance they would take.

The congressman's car arrived at 10:25AM. The team went over the plan one more time and then Nall, accompanied by his fake family and police pretending to be members of the press corps, headed through the main gate.

~

Marsha Hurst was up early that morning. She had been doing a great deal of thinking, both the day before and through the night. Her memory was back, or she believed it was. The feelings she had for Jon were very real to her. She understood all too well the concerns she had for what he was doing. The problem was, she understood the reverse of that as well.

Lt. Marsha Hurst was a cop. That's what she had always wanted to be. She would put her life on the line every day when she went back to work. He would worry as much as she did. *I could cause him to not think clearly.* Her mind repeated over and over. *I could get him killed.* The situation had no solution, not really. The relationship was there, but she could try to pretend it wasn't as serious as it was. *It was the only way.* She told herself.

A knock on her door startled her... it was Doris.

"Come in."

"Morning," her hostess started. "You're up before breakfast I see." As the words left her, Doris could tell Marsha was upset. "Can we talk?" She asked her instinctively.

"About what?" The attempt to cover up was weak.

Doris walked across the room and sat on the edge of the bed. "You know...I was in love with George for years before we ever said a word to each other about it."

Marsha could not help herself from showing interest. She looked up and turned to Doris, not saying anything... but asking her to continue with her eyes.

"He wasn't a cop, neither of us are...yet the dangers were there. Ha." She laughed impulsively. "That's pretty obvious now, huh?"

Marsha's face broke into a slight smile.

472

"I realized, as time went by, that I worried about him anyway. But I wouldn't change what he did...because then, he wouldn't be him." Doris turned with a serious expression and paused for a moment. "Does that make any sense at all?"

"I'm concerned about him...worrying about me." Marsha finally shared. She didn't speak the rest of it, but that wasn't necessary. Doris understood that as well.

"Do you think he would want you to change who you are?"

Marsha did not respond to that, but Doris took it as a good sign. It meant she had gotten through to her. Doris stood and walked to the door, "Breakfast in thirty minutes," she announced. Marsha's eyes lifted enough to acknowledge her.

~

Nicky Sledge had assembled the gun right after his morning break. The firing pin the authorities could not find had been with him the whole time. He carefully loaded the weapon and stuffed it into his belt. A few nervous minutes later he checked his cell phone... all was ok with it.

At somewhere around 10:50AM he noticed a commotion that he could not see. The cell phone rang shortly after that. It was Jo-Jo's signal.

"Loud coat, yellow shirt." The voice said.

Splitting the curtain with his pocketknife enough to see the ride area, Nicky watched the lights directly across from him. When the single bulb suddenly went out, he froze. His mind locked up and his limbs would not work. *Come on, jerk!* he screamed inside his mind. After what felt like minutes, Nicky Sledge finally drew the weapon and stuck it through the curtain.

~

George called the house right before they sat down to eat.

473

"There's news coming over the wire about a drug lord in Colombia." He told Doris. "Seems he had a heart attack in his beach villa, no other details."

"There won't be any either." Doris said smugly.

"Probably not. Just thought you'd like to know."

"Any word on them?" She asked.

"Everything seems fine. They're coming home today far as I know."

"Do you think it's really over, George?"

"Far as Argus is concerned...yeah." There was a pause... "Beyond that, I can't say."

"The others won't care about us and Daniel, will they?"

"Don't see why they would be." He lied. He really had no way to know.

~

Simultaneously, agents and officers grabbed Nicky and Max. The gun went off into the air with its blank discharge. Jo-Jo jumped as he was approached and fell through the curtain. The fall wasn't that far, maybe ten feet, but he landed poorly. It was clear to the officers that got to him that his neck was broken.

Hopes to keep the whole thing quiet were now gone. The death would require reports and exposure. The police needed to act quickly now.

Nicky and Max were transported to headquarters in separate cars. They were interrogated for about an hour before Nicky broke down. He gave the phone number of his contact and what he knew, which wasn't much.

Congressman Nall returned home to his family. They would visit the magic kingdom some other time. The beach would have to do for this week.

~

It was barely after 8:30AM in Malibu. The man waited anxiously with his coffee. He should have heard something by now. The phone he expected to ring was turned on.

The authorities were tracing the signal to that number through towers in the area. The number Nicky had given them was unlisted, but that wasn't unusual. It would be only a few more minutes until they had him.

The man noticed a helicopter passing by out over the ocean. It had made several passes already, like they do when there's a swimmer in trouble. The copter slowed and hovered over one spot directly out from his deck. Through the curtains he thought it was only a couple hundred yards out.

Curiosity took over and the man opened his glass door and stepped to the deck railing. He picked up his binoculars and focused in on the copter.

The muzzle flash may well have been the last thing he saw. The .308 projectile struck just above the binoculars on his forehead. The body launched backwards and fell into the glass door, breaking through it and laying half inside and half out.

The helicopter eased away slowly and was gone. It would be forty minutes before officers looking for the cell phone broke down the front door and found him.

77

The C-130 leveled off at 28,000 feet and the red lights went out. Jon and Murray unbuckled themselves and both started toward the flight deck. After four silent steps they each stopped and turned to look at the other.

"Where are you going?" Jon asked.

"Thought I'd check on the Lieutenant...see if she needed anything."

Jon laughed and rubbed his chin, "You like that, huh?"

"What?" Murray faked being offended. "I don't know... what's the big deal?"

"Nothing cowboy," Jon chided him. "I don't see any ring on her finger." But he reached out and took the man's arm as Murray started back towards the front. "Do me a favor while you're up there?"

"I know," Murray glanced back and smiled. "Find out about Willingham." He shook his head and added, "It's weird... I know. I'll see what I can find out."

Jon nodded and turned his grip into a pat on the back, "Good luck...you'll need it."

Murray gave him a phony glare and knocked on the cabin door. A red light turned green and he pulled it open. "Mind some company?" he asked.

"No...not at all." Lt. Murdock smiled. "I hear you fly, is that right?"

"Yeah...not fixed wing. I fly fling wing."

"Oh, whirly birds, huh?" She teased.

Murray tilted his head and smiled wide, "I prefer eggbeaters, if you please."

"Flying's flying, right?" She countered.

476

He nodded in agreement as he looked around. "You got a few more instruments than we use."

"Bunch of hydraulic stuff we have to watch. The thing is so heavy that the avionics are what power flight control systems. We just push buttons and monitor gauges."

"I get it." He settled into the right seat and continued. "So, where's home?"

"Home, home? Arkansas." She answered. "Near Magnolia in the south."

"Well, heck...we're neighbors."

"How so?"

"I'm out of Texas, northeast Texas."

"I see." She offered with no further comment.

This wasn't going so good, he thought as his right hand reached up, quite on its own, to touch a row of switches overhead.

"Don't do that." She cautioned sharply.

Murray became aware of what he was doing and looked at the hand in disbelief. He pulled it down without any excuse, but heard himself ask her. "Who's waiting at home?"

"Excuse me?"

That was subtle! He knew he was blushing now and tried to recover. "I guess I meant, are you married?"

"Oh..."she laughed and turned to look at him. "No... and no boy friend either."

"Good." He said...and then realized he was smiling. "I mean...Oh."

"I figured that was what you meant." She had returned her attention to the skies.

"Maybe we could have dinner and talk about flying sometime?" He asked.

She let him wait a minute or two, then smiled with, "I'd like that."

~

The report of the death in Malibu came out ahead of anything from Florida. Daniel noticed the name and it rang a bell and sent chills through him. He grabbed the file he had been working on and thumbed through it.

The name Mason Steele was there, he had looked him up by the numbers and other cryptic information found in Texas. Steele had been a child star on T.V. and a few movies before becoming a producer about twenty years ago. He was outspoken in his political views and could always be counted on for a lively comment.

Steele had at first made his personal disgust with the "purge" election known, but soon quieted down and said little else. His associates were more assumed than known. They all said similar things, yet nothing that could be connected to each other.

"Bill," he spoke into the intercom. "Have you got a minute?"

"Sure, Daniel." The boss answered. "Come on over."

Folder in hand, Daniel entered the office of Bill White, his editor.

"Boss," he held out the folder. "Did you see the story about Steele getting shot?"

"Mason Steele?"

"Yeah." Daniel laid his folder on the man's desk.

"Huh? Who would want to kill that SOB?" White said with severe sarcasm.

Daniel pointed to the folder. "He was on the list."

White looked down at the folder then back to Daniel. "The list from Texas?" he asked cautiously.

Daniel nodded.

"Damn." The boss stood. "Who else knows about this?"

"I don't know... Jon gave me this list and I uncovered the names."

"You got enough to write about it?"

"I don't want to write about it...yet."

"What?" White almost screamed. "You've got a national exclusive here."

"It might be bigger than just this, boss." Daniel held his ground.

The editor rubbed his head with both hands. "If there's any whiff of this getting out, I want a story ready to go...you got it?"

"Yes, sir."

Daniel went back to his office to call Jon. He would be told he was in the air and not available until much later.

"Have him call me will you Ben?" He asked.

"Yeah, sure Daniel."

Ben had gotten the word and done the math himself. Mason Steele was definitely on the list. The reporter hadn't said anything, but Ben knew. He was impressed at how quickly Daniel had pulled it together.

~

Detective Nelson was interviewing Sledge when the knock came on the door of the room. An officer opened it and called the detective outside.

"What is it? I'm getting details from this kid," he demanded.

"The guy linked to the phone number he gave you..." the officer said.

"Yeah, did you find him?" Nelson asked.

"He's dead." The officer stated. "Shot about an hour ago on his damned deck in California."

"How the hell?"

"We got a leak somewhere. A big one with direct access."

Nelson leaned against the wall. He thought for a minute and then told the subordinate, "Call the Captain. We wanted to keep the FBI out of this. But we can't now."

"Yes, Detective." The man responded while turning and was gone.

Nelson gathered himself and reentered the interview room. He leaned over the table in a threatening posture. "Who's phone number was that?"

"My contact, man. That's all I know." Nicky trembled as he looked up at Nelson.

"What's his name?" the detective demanded.

"It's just a voice...a voice I'm telling you. I never had his name, man."

Nelson slammed his fist on the table, but said nothing else.

The damned fool is probably telling the truth. He thought. *I wouldn't tell this idiot anything either.*

78

The police and emergency vehicles scared the hell out of the neighbor four doors down the beach. He had walked to the street to try to see what was happening, but to no avail. The distance between the homes along that part of the shore was about seventy-five feet each. The neighbors between them were not home so his was the closest occupied residence.

It took an hour, but the knock on the door came. The two detectives asked if he had heard anything. He didn't mention the helicopter. He'd heard it, but there were copters along the beach all the time.

"What's happened?" He asked them.

"Your neighbor has been shot." One officer said. "I'm afraid he's dead."

"Shot?" The man asked as his complexion went from flushed to pale. "Did he kill himself?"

"Do you think he might have?" Was thrown back at him by an officer.

"No...no, I just don't understand, that's all."

"It came from out on the beach it looks like." The detective closed his notebook. "I'd stay back away from your deck and windows till we check everything out."

"Sure...my God, I just don't believe this." The neighbor exclaimed.

"It happens," the cop said bluntly. "We just have to figure out why...and who."

He watched them walk back down toward the home of the now deceased man who had visited so recently. Closing his front door, the neighbor almost ran to his desk in the den. The letter in the oversized envelope was there. He looked at it as though it might explode, then he calmed down. With a rag from his kitchen, he gently wiped the envelope to remove any prints he might have left on it. Then opening a side bottom drawer, he stuck it in and closed the drawer.

What do I do? He thought as he shook. *What do I do?*

~

Nearly four hours into the flight and the conversation on the flight deck of the C-130 had improved greatly, from Murray's prospective anyway. She was still talking to him.

He had not brought up the subject of Everett Willingham. Nothing had left that door, where the pilot was, open for discussion yet. Then when Liz reached for a switch overhead and mumbled a soft curse about the seat being too low, he saw his chance.

"Damn it, Willie" she said quietly while adjusting the height.

"Where is Willingham?" Murray jumped in.

"He had a meeting to go to." She said and then cocked her neck to look at him a bit funny.

Murray didn't want to chance a screw up so he left it there. Liz Murdock was thinking though, he could tell.

"You guys did something to screw with the cartel, didn't you?" She suddenly asked.

Murray leaned back and looked straight ahead in silence. *Damn*, he thought.

"The Captain doesn't offer rides to just anybody," she continued. "You have to come recommended."

Still looking to the sky, the cowboy responded. "Oh. How's that?"

"He talks very little about it. Now and then he'll share something. There's a group that communicates with each other against the drugs and the cartels. They found out about this guy last year..."

The plane hit a patch of turbulence and her concentration went to her work. The cabin bounced around and Murray looked for something to hold on to. He kept his eyes on the pilot, who calmly pulled on the controls until the excitement was over.

After the air smoothed she picked up her story and went on. "The rumor was he hunted politicians." She looked over at Murray who still stared straight ahead. "Then he went after this group called Argus or something."

Murray nodded ever so slightly, "I think I heard of him."

"Really?" She smirked. "Well, the command got wind that Willie might be talking to or helping this guy. I don't know how or from where, but they called him in about it." She paused and took a quick look to see Murray's reaction. There was none. "So...anyway, just to be sure, Willie set up this fake meeting today down in Florida. You know, to draw attention."

Murray leaned forward and turned toward her. "Attention from what?"

"From you, silly." She answered frankly as the plane hit more rough air. "I bet that trailer is jumping back there."

Murray didn't take his eyes off her that time either. She looked over and smiled. "One of you two is that Son fellow, right?"

The cabin got quiet as the cowboy smiled in silence. She looked back at her gauges and Murray slumped into the seat looking out into the bright sky ahead of them. He took his hat off and rolled the brim. "I don't know what to say to you." He muttered.

"Don't say anything." Her voice was confident and cool. "It's worth the risk and the gamble." That seemed like an odd statement, but Murray let her finish. "Willie lost a daughter to drugs. A really good kid ...I knew her." Lt. Murdock adjusted a few more switches and then looked back at the cowboy. "Whether you are or you aren't...

you've got something to do with it." Liz smiled and turned to him again. "So 'you're welcome' if you were going to say 'thank you.'"

The plane plowed through a cloudbank obscuring vision for a few seconds. As it emerged into the blue sky with the sun slightly to their left Murray's mind cleared with the view. "Is that dinner thing still on sometime?" He asked.

"Of course," Lt. Murdock smiled. "Why wouldn't it be?"

~

Even with the FBI's help, it didn't take long for the authorities in Orlando to understand what they were dealing with. Paid idiots. Not enough common sense among them to burn a nightlight. That one phone number was all they had.

The funds sent to them were not traceable. Electronic transfers to their leader through Western Union from different locales under fake names. They sent agents to start attempting to trace back by any means possible , starting with the banks and other transfer offices. Little would come of it.

Nelson had spoken with the lead detective in Malibu. They shared what they knew. But the new leads looked like they would need to come from California, if there were any. The Malibu house was being stripped and taken apart, looking for anything. Names, numbers anything to go on.

Nelson had sent word to Indiatlantic to have the other gang members picked up. They knew less than the ones they held in Orlando, but they needed to be off the street.

~

Dusk was settling down on Georgia as the C-130 glided its way into Moody AFB. Everything appeared normal with the exception of one extra vehicle on the tarmac.

"You guys sit tight for a minute after we roll up." Lt. Murdock basically ordered.

Murray got up and went to the cargo bay to tell Jon and Juan of the concern. "I'll have to explain it all later," he hurried. "Just get our stuff and try to look small."

Ground crews gathered around the airship as she stopped. The procedures were all as expected. Liz ordered the loading door to be lowered and stood at its entrance with her hands on her hips. Two Air Police officers came up the ramp and asked Liz if the flight went well.

"No problems," she responded. "Did Willie get back from Florida yet?"

"No ma-am, but he asked us to give you this for his friends." The AP held out a note. She noticed a slight wink as she took it.

"I'll do that when I see them," she nodded and smiled while taking the paper.

The Air Police went back out and got into their car. As they left, Liz turned and hollered, "Ok, get your butts off my airplane." She handed Jon the note as they passed by.

Murray got halfway down the ramp before stopping. He sat down his bag and walked back to the first officer. "You got a phone number...someway to reach you?"

She stuck out her hand with a card. "Home phone, cell number and flight ready room number here on base." She grinned. "Will that do?"

"Yes ma-am. That'll do fine." The cowboy tipped his hat and slowly turned to join his friends. Jon was reading his note and Juan just stared at Murray.

"What...?" The cowboy demanded. At which Juan grinned and let out a rare laugh.

"News travels fast." Jon said looking up from the note. "It seems these good people think they know who we are."

"I was going to mention that..." Murray started.

"It's alright." Jon grabbed his bag and walked toward the hanger. "I'm getting used to it."

"They're not going to say anything," Murray offered. "They appreciate what you do."

"Just what we need...a fan club."

"Not a fan club." Murray's voice became louder. "There are people out here who want to help clean the mess up." He took several steps with Jon and Juan before he added, "Trust needs courage sometimes."

They found the Mercury. Washed, gassed up and ready to go. The cowboy waved his hat at the big airplane as they drove away. He wasn't sure if Liz was watching or not.

She was.

79

Marsha Hurst had been to the doctor that afternoon. After a brief lecture on what not to do, he released her to go home. Home meant Charlotte and the return to work. She could begin with light duty next week, at her own discretion. The news brought a smile to her face.

A quick call to her captain in North Carolina was well received.

"Take your time, Lieutenant." He assured her. "We're under control here. It will be good to have you back, though. But no rush."

They agreed on Monday and mornings to start with. Light duty wasn't on the overnight schedule. Marsha looked at her phone and thought about calling Jon, but he was in the air on his way back. She'd talk to him later tonight. *There was no hurry.*

She jumped when the phone rang a second later. It was George.

"Doris told me you were going to the doctor today," he started. "I hadn't heard anything, what time is your appointment?"

"I just got out, George. Everything's fine."

"Great. What did he say?"

"I can go home and start back to work."

"Really?" George sounded concerned at that and took a pause before he went on. "You ready for that?"

She responded instantly and with conviction, "Yeah...I sure am."

George tried to think of what next to say. He went with humor. "Ok then. If you're checking out I'll have your bill ready in the morning."

"I do owe you more than I could ever pay," she said sincerely. "How do I thank you and Doris?"

"You already did." The D.A. told her in a low tone. Then he joked again, "You know though? I would like to come to Charlotte and see more than the hospital. Maybe you could show us around sometime?"

"I'll hold you to that." Marsha jumped on that idea in a verbal sense. "And dinner is on me."

"Oh...hell yeah."

They had a good laugh and then George needed to go.

"So glad you're ok, really. You had us worried there for a while."

~

Gil Gartner walked into George's office as he got off the phone. His look was half smile and half puzzled. "Have you heard about this?" he handed George a printed out story from the police intranet. The story was from Orlando, about the attempt on the life of Congressman Nall. "Does that guy fit the pattern?"

"Not really much of a pattern, yet." George passed it off, but continued to look at the name on the paper.

Gil didn't leave nor did he speak. He just stood there in deep thought.

George looked up at him, "This one is in the wide range... yeah. But he's new and not as important a figure, the others were higher ranked in the party."

"Something about this fits...to me anyway." Gil stated. His unspoken stare was asking if George would check with Jon about it.

"I'll call Ben," George relented. "See what he knows."

Gil nodded and gave a "thumbs up" sign as he turned to go.

The D.A. dialed Ben while trying to think of some excuse for the call. He didn't need one.

"Well," Ben answered. "You too, huh?"

"What's that supposed to mean?"

"I've got printers spitting out reports on this Orlando deal with input from all over the place. Our watch teams seem to feel it's part of the organized group that used The Son label in Mississippi."

George listened rather than answer him. He could hear machines still whirling electronically. *More than Gil are thinking the same way.* He thought.

Ben finally spoke again. "That is what you called about, isn't it?"

"Actually, it is."

"I don't have enough to say either way. I'll get Jon to look at this stuff with me when he gets back. I don't think the evidence is enough for him to get excited though."

"What all are you getting?"

"Rumors from Florida, Montana and a so far unrelated story in California."

"Unrelated? Why would somebody throw it in then?"

"Conspiracy theories. Most of it is that, to start with anyway."

"Tell me more." George was getting interested.

"You heard about Mason Steele, right?"

"The movie guy? I saw something about a shooting."

"Well...one of our people is convinced he was part of this group called the Sponsors."

"Do you think a group like that could be real?" George had heard about the rumors, but was very skeptical.

"Today?" Ben paused a second. "Why not?"

"Then what would that have to do with Orlando?"

"Well...our guy believes Steele was a handler for the group. It looks like the gang in Orlando wasn't exactly what they pretended to be." He let George think about that for a second. "What if Steele was in charge of those morons...and got whacked because of it?"

"Interesting...but almost too silly to be real."

"Well..." Ben didn't finish the thought. He went to another, "you asked."

"You say people in your watch groups are all over this?"

"Oh yeah, big time."

"Where is all over?"

"Like I said, Montana, New York, Washington DC, Florida...California. There's something from everyone we hear from."

"Ok, I'll make a few calls." Then a thought came to him. "How about Daniel? Have you heard from him?"

"Not yet. No."

"Ok, talk to you later...good job."

~

Forensic Teams poured over the Malibu beach house finding little more of interest than a cell phone and a new theory. The theory was about the shot. It was first considered to have come from the beach. That was soon disproved by the location of the slug and the trajectory of its flight through Mason Steele's skull.

The shooter would have had to be thirty-four feet tall to pull off the shot from the beach. Not likely, even in Southern California. But where did it come from? Even a shot off a boat at sea would have an incline of measurable degree. This shot, if anything came in at a slight downward angle.

More time and further study would conclude the shot had to be taken from an aircraft some 400 yards from the beach. Those efforts would take time. The aircraft they would eventually seek was already long gone.

Of more immediate use was the cell phone found near the body. In fact, it appeared the phone had actually been in a side sweater pocket that was torn open as the body flew through the glass doors. The phone was a pre-paid model with no registration listed to it, a burn phone, as they were known in the criminal world. All numbers stored in the call records were no longer in service and had been to similar type phones.

"We can trace where the calls went by transmission towers and signal repeaters." One technician offered. The last number called went through a high altitude repeater station in northern Wyoming, near the town of Dayton. That signal boaster serviced the areas of the Bighorn National Forest as well as the Crow Indian Reservation in Montana. Both areas were heavy users of non-listed, pre-paid cell phones.

"Steele was up to something," the lead investigator would say. "Whatever it was has been well camouflaged."

If they had access to the envelope Mason Steele gave his neighbor to mail for him, many of their questions would have been answered, but with more mystery and conjecture. The envelope was on its way to Pennsylvania by that Saturday. The neighbor considered giving it to the police, but then...those who killed Steele might trace that act to him.

From his car window, he pulled the mail drop door open and carefully dropped the envelope in. His hands covered with a new cloth, work gloves from Ace Hardware.

80

The drive to Atlanta airport took just over three hours. The Macon bypass was more cooperative at night and slowed them down less.

"I'll call you in a few days," the cowboy said with his hand outstretched to Jon. "I need to take care of a few things at home and spend some time with mom and sis."

"And Slick?" Jon inquired.

"He'll be in the middle of it all." Murray smiled. The cowboy didn't let go right away from the handshake. He held on searching for what he wanted to add. "This has been an experience." The words rattled around and finally fell from his thoughts. "I think I like working with you. If I can help again...say the word."

Jon squeezed the handshake before letting go. "You haven't seen the last of me."

As Murray stepped to the trunk to get his bag, Jon climbed from the Mercury and walked back with him. "When you get back to Caddo Mills, there's a builder who will have left a card for you."

Murray looked at Jon like he was lost.

"Charlene called...she got me through Daniel. I know what kind of house you wanted for the ranch and I've made arrangements with this builder to take care of you."

"Take care of me?"

"Look, I'm not stepping on your pride...or at least I don't mean to be. But I might just be needing your help quicker than you think. I don't want you worried about the house when I call."

"Use English, man." The cowboy still didn't get it. "What have you done?"

"I'm replacing your house. The builder knows the basics. You tell him the specifics." Jon squinted his eyes. "I want to do this, Murray. Let me thank you for getting involved, risking your life and probably saving mine a few times."

Murray shook his head, "You don't have to..."

"I know." Jon looked at him sternly. "Neither did you." Jon walked back to the driver's door. He looked again at his friend. "If you don't like the plan Charlene picked out...just work it out with the builder. You call the shots, I don't care...just long as it's big and includes the new pad for Lucy I designed."

Murray stood speechless for a minute then smiled, tipped his big hat and grabbed the bag. He headed for the terminal as Jon pulled away from the curb. Standing at the terminal door, he looked back and watched the Mercury slip into traffic. "Just damn," he muttered and smiled again before continuing on his way.

It was quiet in the Mercury until Juan spoke up. Jon had nearly forgotten he was there. "I'm fine... thanks." The Hispanic man teased. "But a house would be nice."

Jon laughed and turned to look at him, "What are you going to do?"

"Charles Harley had left some money at his office, I have that. Then Hanson...well, I took some from him before I left."

"Where is it?"

"A storage unit in that town with the delightful bus service."

Jon had to think about that for a second. "Oh...you mean in Rome?"

"I will be going by there to pick it up, then who knows? No more cartels. I thank you for that, sir." Juan became very serious.

" You could have just killed me, I know." He added.

"No. You don't know." Jon told him. "That's not what I do. Just make me one promise?"

"Absolutely...I owe you my life." Juan leaned forward from the back seat.

"Don't tell anyone, I mean anyone about me or Murray...ever. Understood?"

"Si. Can I get hold of you should I need you?"

"Call Daniel. He can get to me through Ben."

"Si." Juan said as the car pulled again to the curb. They were outside the rental car office. Jon leaned over to shake Juan's hand and offered some money for the rental.

"No...thank you. But I was not kidding about the money. I have a bunch of cash from those two guys I worked for."

"How much is a bunch?" Jon asked.

"$493,000 is left in the storage unit. I have about $12,000 on me."

"That should stake you to a new start." Jon laughed. They shook hands and Juan headed off to the office door.

Two hours to home, Jon thought. He pulled away from the curb again and headed for Dalton.

~

It was past midnight when he picked up a cell phone and called George Vincent.

"I know it's late, George. I'm about ten minutes out. Can I come by?"

"Hey, we're all waiting up."

The Mercury pulled into the Vincent driveway and a door opened on his four-car garage. Jon pulled into the slot and was greeted by the three of them.

"I don't sponsor sinful behavior," George grinned. "But you're welcome to stay here tonight."

"George!" Doris slapped his shoulder and then hugged Jon. "I haven't seen you since this all started."

494

"Thanks for everything you've done." He whispered back to her.

Marsha stepped up and they hugged in silence for several minutes. George and Doris went inside and George hit close on the garage door.

"You smell good." Jon said, it was all he could think of at the moment.

"You don't." She laughed though she wasn't kidding. "Let's get you inside and cleaned up."

He took a shower and decided to take George up on his offer. He and Marsha talked about little things and just got used to looking at each other for a while. They fell asleep and he slept in until nearly 10AM the next morning. Her voice calling him to breakfast woke him.

"Is that all you're going to do, just sleep?" She challenged as she pulled on the covers.

Conversation and breakfast were recharging for all of them. *It was over*, he thought as he looked at George, Doris and Marsha all within his reach again.

After breakfast, George asked him in private about Stubblefield. Jon's reaction belied his words. He claimed no real involvement or interest in the tragedy. George could read his eyes and left it alone.

Then George brought up the Orlando and Malibu cases that were all the news. Jon listened with great interest about those, but made no statements that let George think he was concerned about either.

With the dishes taken care of by all, Jon and Marsha walked out back to the sun porch. That was where she told him. "I'm going home tomorrow."

At first Jon didn't respond.

She added. "I have my flight booked and I start back to work Monday."

"You don't want to stay here?" He finally let out in a weak voice.

"'Want... isn't a fair question." She scolded. "I'm a cop. I do what I do...just like you." Then she realized that came off a bit stronger than she wanted to. "I need to get back into my routine for a while. Make sure I'm really ok...you know?"

He looked at her and nodded. "I'll take you in the G-5."

"No...I already have my flight scheduled." She was firm and didn't leave room for any discussion. "Charlotte PD has chartered a flight for me from right here, so I don't have to go to Atlanta or anything. Let me do this...please." That was the first sound that she made that wasn't strong and deliberate.

Jon took a deep breath. Looking right at her he answered solemnly, "I understand...really I do."

"Don't worry about me." She stepped into his range and he took her in his arms.

"Ha, same to you."

"No...I know you worry. That's what we need to learn to deal with. Both of us."

They stood in a quiet embrace for a few minutes and then she spoke again. "Will you come see me next weekend?"

He answered as if a calendar was in his brain, "Ben graduates next Friday night."

"Oh..." She pulled back and declared, "Then I'll be here for that. How about the next weekend?"

"Wild horses couldn't keep me away." He pulled her close again. Whispering this time, he added, "We're going to be ok, you know. This was a lot and all too fast. Remember what you told me about change?"

496

"The only thing constant." She answered.

"That's right. It got me through all this." He paused for a minute... "It's good to have you back."

The remainder of that day and night they spent together. It was hard to watch her get into that plane at the Dalton airport on Sunday. But not as bad as he first thought it would be.

81

Ben was happy to see his mentor and Jon was glad to be home. The house was still new to Jon. A month had passed without him being there, but it had proved a good sanctuary for his friends and his secrets.

He asked Ben for details about the Stubblefield case. Ben was the only person he would discuss it with.

"I checked him out the best I could," Jon told the younger man. "I missed something somewhere."

"You did what you could with what you had, Jon." Ben assured him. "It wasn't your fault."

But Jon didn't feel that way. The deaths of the family would ride his shoulders for some time. *What was it he could have looked at differently to see that man's guilt.* He thought to himself. "That can't happen again, ever. I have to get back to the basics...back to the rules and the discipline. People lost their lives because I missed something."

Ben argued, "Stubblefield was a classic psychopath. You can't read one of them because they don't have feelings like we do."

Jon appreciated Ben's effort, but still asked for all the details from start to finish. He would study the case to look for what he had missed. This should not, and in his mind, could not happen again.

They also discussed what Ben knew about the California and Florida links to the sponsors. That interested Jon, but not like the obsession he had over Stubblefield.

"Keep a close eye on that, it may well be something we need to act on. I have this other to resolve for myself." Jon sat down and looked through other notes and correspondence he had missed while away. Inside he really enjoyed being back, going over cases and potential cases with Ben.

The cars would be here next week, in time for Ben's graduation. He thought. *He hoped Doris wouldn't mind the muscle car, but Ben had earned a trophy.*

The afternoon went by quickly. Marsha called when she got home, that took a while. But it was back to the paperwork soon after.

~

The information in the letter from Malibu would reach Daniel Seay's desk the following Monday. It would begin a search and confirmation of wrong doing by many high-ranking figures in the country. The list included current and former political icons, several well-known media personalities, independent billionaires and Hollywood moguls. The most shocking would be a current Justice of the Supreme Court.

Also in the letter would be a list of prospective victims and the reasoning for these acts could be construed without too much effort. Political vendettas that could be waged against members of the opposing party, demonstrated the desire to regain power.

Daniel's group would consider notifying the authorities. But they determined the disclosure would only result in ridicule for lack of proof. Daniel would share his information with Phillip Stone and the other law enforcement network. That network would shortly include Lt. Marsha Hurst of the Charlotte Police. If and when they could gather enough evidence against one of these "sponsors" they would pass it on to Jon. The problem was, without evidence that was confirmable, the Son would not touch it. Daniel knew this so he didn't even try.

~

Ben had gone upstairs to get a soft drink. He noticed it was dark outside and an idea came to him. Hurrying back to the workshop, he urged Jon to come with him to the third sub-level, where the cars are kept.

"You've never even seen the tunnel." He grinned as the tubular elevator dropped to the lowest level. The lights came on as they stepped into the space.

The old reliables were there, the Jeep, the pick-up and several others.

"The doors work down to the gas station?" Jon asked.

"Oh, man." Ben smiled wide. "They work great. How about a ride?"

"I guess we can." Jon headed for the Jeep.

"Hey...let me drive." Ben offered as he eased Jon away from the driver's door with his elbow. "I've done this before you know."

"Ok, smart guy, you drive." Jon stepped around to the passenger door while Ben started the electronics.

Climbing in Jon saw a video screen light up with the picture of the tunnel. Ben pushed a button and the wall door pulled back. The rocks over the metal access door were now a mere illusion.

Lights lit up in succession down the tunnel like landing beacons at the airport. The small video panel came to life on the dashboard. It now also had a row of LED lights across the top that glowed red. Jon's smile grew wider as he could see the tunnel lighting up through both the windshield and the video screen. His eyes could hardly keep up with all that was going on around him.

"Alright!" Jon proclaimed loudly as the last lights of the tunnel exposed the curve at the far end. The shadows just beyond that curve offered one last surprise he still wondered about, the secret exit through the old gas station on to the highway. He turned to Ben, snapping his seat belt tight. "It really works, huh?"

"Better than you drew it up," Ben grinned back at him. Then the young assistant hit another button and green lights replaced the

500

red ones across the top of the video control box on the dashboard. He turned the key and fired the engine. Slowly at first he rolled the Jeep into the tunnel. Green lights along the sidewalls lit up every few feet indicating clearance to proceed. Then Ben reached up firmly and grabbed the wheel with both hands. Looking briefly at Jon, Ben hit the gas.

"Hang on...." He hollered. "You're gonna love this."

"Every kind of service, necessary to the public good, becomes honorable by being necessary."

Nathan Hale

Also By

Doug Dahlgren

It Was Thursday

and

The SON *Silas Rising*

Coming......

The Basics of Fundamentals

The Jonathan Crane Saga continues...

Made in the USA
Lexington, KY
13 October 2014